India And The Clash of Civilizations

Rajendra Kumar Mishra

Pt. Nehru And MA Jinnah Icons And Enemies

PARTRIDGE
A Penguin Random House Company

To order additional copies of this book, contact
Partridge India
000 800 10062 62
www.partridgepublishing.com/india
orders.india@partridgepublishing.com

Foreword

The movement for the demolition of the politically infamous Babri Mosque in the Hindu holy city, Ayodhya, is at its height. Its professed aim is to rebuild the Ram Temple at the same site where it supposedly stood before it was destroyed by the Muslim invader, Babar, in the 16th century to build the mosque as a permanent sadistic reminder of the humiliation of a conquered people. However, the movement's real aim, a blend of political expediency and gnawing apprehensions of the Hindu nationalists, is to use Ram as a tool to prevent the possible disintegration of the Hindu society by the combined effect of two recent events: First, an amendment of the Constitution by the Rajiv Gandhi Government to put the medieval Muslim personal laws out of its purview. It had been forced by the Mullah-led diehard Muslims through violent country-wide demonstrations, whose unequivocal message was that Indian Muslims' loyalty is anchored in Islam and transcends the laws and Constitution of the country in which they live. In other words, theirs is a separate civilization composed of the universal Muslim ummah. The amendment among other things reconfirmed an Indian Muslim's legal right not only to simultaneously have four wives but also to divorce any or all of them on the phone by simply repeating his decision thrice, and do so without incurring any liabilities of a civilized people. However, the criticism of a patrician Prime Minister's politically convenient and evidently disdainful compliance with the Muslims' demand, which the enlightened members of their own community opposed and felt ashamed of, did not mean that Hindus were disappointed in their wish for the Muslims' assimilation into the Indian society or the development of a synthetic Indian culture, which they neither desired nor thought possible. It was an expression of their anger at the Muslims' presumption that they could coerce the government of a predominantly Hindu India into acquiescence with any wish by taking to the streets. The second event was the opportunistic timing of the adoption of the Mandal Commission Report by Rajiv's successor, Prime Minister VP Singh. It threatened, or seemed to do so then, the development of a nexus, which the devious Singh had calculated would enable him to retain power, between the Hindu backward classes and Muslims against the Hindu upper castes. It recalled the fear of an equally ominous nexus between Muslims, who enjoyed separate electorates under the British rule, and the Hindu Scheduled Castes, whom the British had offered a similar advantage. To prevent it, the politically astute Mahatma Gandhi, no less wary of Muslims than he wished them well, had gone on his most famous fast unto death, which had resulted in the historic Poona Pact with the revolutionary Dalit Messiah, Dr. B.R. Ambedkar.

While outwardly criticizing the constitutional amendment, most educated Hindus, especially the leftists, who loathe the atavistic mentality of Indian Muslims, at the same time secretly think it sagacious and preventive of further worsening of the historically antagonistic relations between the two communities. For the same reason they think it realistic to placate the worst reactionaries among Muslims, who also happen to be the most influential members of the community, by simultaneously bamboozling and appeasing them and entering into political alliances with them for achieving power. These same Hindu leftists and self-styled secularists never fail to castigate their co-religionists for any regressive act which would retard their modernization!

Even greater exploiters of the innate Muslim fundamentalism are the politically and economically strong but supposedly backward Hindu middle castes represented by the likes of Mulayam Singh Yadav and Laloo Yadav. They rival and even outclass the upper caste Hindu pseudo-secularists in deluding Muslims by falsely promising them, ostensibly at their own cost, favors and advantages like reservations in government jobs, which they know are constitutionally impossible! Like those of the largely upper caste Hindu leftists, their governments' policies are also influenced by the shrewd conviction that the history and nature of Islam in India being what they are, economic and educational development of Muslims will instead of lessening further increase their separatism and bargaining power! Despite feeling mortified by the moral snobbery and egoism of the largely insincere Hindu secularists in power, depressed by their community's gullibility to their false promises and the religious-cum-legal stranglehold of both the antediluvian and anglicized Mullahs over their poor and illiterate co-religionists, the progressive Muslims remain helpless onlookers, too weak to take on the alliance between their reactionary co-religionists and the patronizing and venal Hindu politicians.

Main Characters

Chandrmukhi: She is a member of Delhi's affluent bourgeoisie belonging to a Hindu upper caste. Despite her luxurious standard of living she is a violent critic of the exploitation of the poor Dalits and Muslims and a hater of Hindu fundamentalism and the Bharatiya Janata Party. She is famous for her good looks and lavish evening parties, which attract both genuine intellectuals and dilettantes. Her close friendship with one of the visitors, Somdutt, who shares her convictions and like her also belongs to Delhi's affluent bourgeoisie, makes her husband, Vishnu, jealous despite his belief that she is an honest and honorable person. If on the one hand she feels humiliated by Vishnu's jealousy and refuses to comply with his wish to give up her friendship with Somdutt, on the other, despite her fascination for Somdutt she resists his advances because he despises Vishnu, whom she never ceases to love, as a philistine. After a violent quarrel on the day of Babri Mosque's demolition, when she takes the part of Somdutt, wife and husband begin to sleep apart. One day she unexpectedly becomes the mistress of a man whom her husband trusts and who in turn never ceases to be his well-wisher and even after becoming her lover sincerely continues to persuade her to give up her friendship with Somdutt in order to achieve reconciliation with him. He continues to remind her, even when holding her in his arms, that their affair is transient and can never replace her married life. Eventually he succeeds in reconciling them by persuading her to stop Somdutt's visits to her evening parties. However, to keep up appearances she with the tacit consent of her husband continues to meet Somdutt away from home and maintain her social relations with him. The reconciliation does not end her passion for her lover, partly due to his transparent wish for her happy married life, which paradoxically makes him the more irresistible to her. The lover's identity remains a matter of conjecture. One day she discovers that she has become pregnant twelve years after her marriage. Despite her fear that most probably it is the lover's child and that her husband might think that she had been secretly carrying on with Somdutt even after the reconciliation she doesn't dare undergo abortion because it can't be concealed. Pregnancy after such a long time arouses Vishnu's suspicions. Unable to bear the thought that not only might the child be Somdutt's but was conceived after the reconciliation, he undergoes tests which to his dismay reveal that he is incapable of fathering a child. He naturally suspects Somdutt, blames his jealousy for the fall of a loving wife and an honest woman and loses interest in life. One day unable to resist her pathetic insistence on knowing the cause of his despondency he tells her the truth, blames his jealousy and expresses the hope that her lover will not betray her. She is relieved of her great tension and anxiety, when he doesn't ask the name of the lover. Unable to bear his grief she commits suicide. Even in her last moments she hopes that the identity of the lover will remain a matter of conjecture.

Jawaharlal: Vishnu's Gandhian uncle and a wealthy Supreme Court lawyer. While adoring Gandhi and Nehru and like them preaching secularism and advocating a composite Indian culture, he is convinced that given the exclusivity of Islam and the centuries old antagonism between Hindus and Muslims it is a daydream. Considers buying a kidney to save his daughter's life immoral, especially as he has two sons.

Govind Mehta: A social activist working for the victims of Bhopal gas tragedy. While loving his wife, has a mistress.

Harimohini: Govind's wife and Chandrmukhi's sister. She detests the hedonistic bourgeois lifestyle of Delhi's intellectual and political elites to which her sister and Somdutt belong. Marries Mehta and works with him for the welfare of the gas victims in Bhopal's squalid environment. Doesn't disclose to her husband her knowledge of his sexual infidelity in order to prevent distraction from their social work.

Part One

Chapter 1

1/1

Sipping his sweet milky tea, Jaiprakash was reading in a local Hindi newspaper the news and comments on the latest Hindu-Muslim riot at Shantinagar, a prosperous town of half a million. It was the latest riot since the demolition of the Babri Mosque. Thanks to the graphic and frenzied coverage of its gory details by the media, in less than six months the demolition had become one of the three or four most publicized and momentous events in the history of India after the end of the British Raj. The weeklong violence had already taken 157 lives and resulted in injuries to 306, according to a government press note, which was dismissed by everybody as a well-intentioned lie concealing higher casualties.

This particular outbreak in a riot-prone State of the country ruled by the professedly secular Congress Party, Jaiprakash like most Hindus almost unconsciously believed, would have been provoked by Muslims and escalated by Hindus with the help of the Hindu police. Exasperated at being called out now and again to disperse rioting communal mobs by tear-gassing and then firing and afterwards being routinely accused by the media and the politicians out of power of having used excessive force, the Provincial Armed Constabulary would have given way to their deep-rooted prejudice against Muslims, particularly the bearded and skull-capped ones. Not only the almost exclusively Hindu police but even many secular Hindus found this garb outlandish and teasingly reminiscent of the invaders who periodically descended from Arabia, Afghanistan and Iran to rob and destroy Hindu temples and shed Hindu blood. It distracted attention from the fact that the majority of Indian Muslims were converts from the Hindu low castes and now suffered from discrimination and degradation not only from Hindus but also from their no less feudal and caste-ridden co-religionists.

The immediate provocation for the riot was the verdict of a Tribunal headed by a sitting Hindu High Court judge that neither of the two militant Hindu outfits, Rashtriya Swayam Sewak Sangh and Bajrang Dal was guilty of any act to justify the ban imposed on them by the Central Government for allegedly having instigated the karsevaks to pull down the "decrepit structure", as a Hindi newspaper had contemptuously described the historic monument. According to the police sources, a shower of stones from a mosque on a victory procession by the Bajrang Dal on a Friday, after the Imam had delivered a fiery speech to his congregation against Hindu communalism in general and the Hindu judge's verdict in particular, had led to the riot.

The verdict had predictably outraged the Hindu leftist politicians, intellectuals and media persons, driving them to pour out conscience-stricken speeches, articles and broadcasts, urging the Muslims to frustrate the evil designs of Hindu communalists by exercising restraint. The Muslims, regularly exhorted by their fundamentally bearded and dressed Imams at the post-Namaz Friday sermons to be particularly wary of these ineffectual and bogus sympathizers, and to counter the *kafir* menace and establish the supremacy of Islam produce as many children as they could, depending on Allah to provide for them, had responded by staging violent demonstrations, stone-throwing and street-fighting in different parts of the country. According to the unofficial briefing of pressmen by the State Government's official spokesman, the Hindu-Muslim clashes over the demolition of the Babri Mosque, which were likely to spread again to the other parts of the state and the country, mightn't have taken place but for the unnecessarily extended focus on the Judge's verdict in the media. The journalists had retorted that it was their duty to elicit the opinions of the different political parties about the verdict for the enlightenment of the people and it was the responsibility of the government to maintain law and order, in which it had failed miserably.

All of a sudden, he was stunned to read a news item on the third page which it occurred to him with a pang he might have missed! With bated breath he read it again. Yes, it was she! It said that even after more than a month the police had failed to discover any clue to the mystery of the suicide by Mrs. Chandrmukhi Narayan, a wealthy and famous socialite-intellectual of Delhi.

He wondered why neither his uncle, Dr Awasthi, nor her husband, Vishnu, to whom he had been very close, had informed him about her death. Then he remembered his friend Charles Smith. He had also failed to do so.

To learn about the circumstances of her death, Jaiprakash quickly ate his breakfast, put on his safari suit, a gift from Chandrmukhi on his last birthday, and left for the Patna University library. He had been her and her husband's personal assistant for more than two years until three months ago. He felt sure that the Delhi press would have covered the sensational event in circumstantial detail.

He first went through those newspapers whose editors, correspondents and columnists were her friends. He was not disappointed. Something or other about her life, character, circumstances, health and activities indicative of her state of mind prior to her death, had been reported every day for a week in all of them. And once or twice a week on the following days. Particular stress had been laid on the fact that for weeks together until her last day she had been regularly seen at the Gymkhana Club, India International, Sriram Kala Kendra and other elite centers of the Capital. She was invariably accompanied by her equally popular husband, Mr. Vishnu Narayan. On these occasions both had been observed as usual discussing with their friends the current affairs, the merits of an artist, a classical musician or the latest best seller while lunching or dining.

According to her husband as well as those who claimed to know her closely, she had no financial, emotional or health problems except high blood pressure due to pregnancy. Handwriting experts had authenticated her suicide note and her friends had minutely analyzed it. Its unambiguousness was baffling. It said: I have entirely of my own accord and in full possession of my senses decided to end my life and nobody else is directly or indirectly responsible for it. I have no complaint against any person. Chandrmukhi.

But why?

1/2

'It's a real pleasure to see you after such a long time! It was two days after Chandrmukhi's suicide, when you were still not to be seen, that I enquired about you and came to know that your father's illness had caused you to go home. I hope that now he's all right,' said Somdutt, looking amiably surprised to see him, which caused Jaiprakash even greater surprise.

It was obvious that Somdutt, normally so frank and truthful, was fibbing out of politeness or for some mysterious reason that he had remained unaware for such a long time of the fact that he had gone back to Patna three months ago; he should have come to know about it within a week of his departure as well as of his continued absence for two months before Chandrmukhi's death. However, Somdutt's manner confused Jaiprakash's surmise that he might in some way be involved in her suicide or had secret knowledge of its circumstances.

He replied, 'Yes, I had to return home due to father's illness. Then what with one thing and another, I couldn't come back. I learnt about her death from a newspaper report by sheer chance only a few days ago.'

Jaiprakash had just come from Patna and after putting his luggage in his old room prepared against his arrival entered Chandrmukhi's large and still immaculately kept drawing room after nearly three months.

He was still talking to Somdutt when a uniformed police officer walked in. He looked around him with blithe nonchalance, like a man who has done his job well. In his wake entered Chandrmukhi's sister, Harimohini, who lived in Bhopal with her husband. From the way they looked at each other, Jaiprakash guessed that perhaps the officer had been talking to Harimohini in the adjacent room in connection with the suicide and was satisfied with their conversation.

The officer was about to leave when one of Jaiprakash's old friends said to him, 'Sir, meet Mr. Jaiprakash, who arrived from Patna today. He was personal assistant to Chandrmukhi until a few months ago.'

The officer shook hands with him and said, 'I was told about you. How are you, sir?'

'I am all right. Thank you.'

Their attention was diverted by the entry of Vishnu. He looked wanly at Jaiprakash, who was shocked at his appearance; he had lost weight and seemed to have grown ten years older. But Jaiprakash noticed with some relief and a little surprise that he was as well-groomed as ever, the epitome of a genteel grief-stricken aristocrat.

Jaiprakash was momentarily tempted to watch how Vishnu and Somdutt would behave with each other, though the occasion was too somber for either of them to think of their past relations, however unpleasant they might have been. He was right in thinking so; Somdutt immediately went over to him and with evident sincerity requested him to take the greatest care of his health. Vishnu thanked him for his kindness.

Remembering the newspaper reports that he had rejoiced in his wife's pregnancy, Jaiprakash wondered whether he unexpectedly came upon some dreadful secret and confronted her with it, causing her to kill herself. If so, what could it be? Or had he no clue and his condition was due to grief further intensified by mystery?

He recalled how solicitous wife and husband were of each other's happiness, when he left them three months ago. This fact had been particularly reported in the newspapers, as much from the journalistic wish to make the story more interesting by deepening the mystery of the suicide, as from personal loyalty to her by the pressmen who had been regular visitors to her evening parties.

Vishnu said to Jaiprakash, 'Dr Awasthi told me that you came to know about her death only a few days ago. I was not in a condition to inform anybody. It was done by her sister, Harimohini, who had flown in from Bhopal the same day.

Jaiprakash pressed his hand.

'Would you be so kind as to give me a few minutes?' said the police officer to Jaiprakash. He had been waiting a trifle impatiently to take advantage of this unexpected meeting to dispose of him also by asking him a few routine questions before submitting the report on Chandrmukhi's suicide, which was almost ready. They went into the same room from which he and Harimohini had emerged a few minutes ago.

Jaiprakash faced the officer with confidence. His assurance was due to the fact that during his journey from Patna to Delhi he had made up his mind to be as truthful and precise as possible in his answers to any questions that might be asked by anybody in Delhi, the police in particular. He had realized that discreet truthfulness, particularly the separation of doubts and suppositions, however strong and no matter whose, from verifiable facts, was essential to protect Chandrmukhi's reputation. It needed special protection from such friends-cum-beneficiaries as can't help speculating despite their admiration and gratitude towards their late benefactors. After praising them for their qualities, they proceed to confidentially share their conjectures and surmises about them with other like-minded friends-cum-beneficiaries; and then, without expressing their own opinions but by quoting each other coupled with their own dissent, do greater damage than detractors.

The officer said, 'I was told that you're one of the very few persons who knew her and her circumstances particularly well. What do you think may have led her to kill herself in such a shocking manner? Here everybody who knew her appears to be at sea. Even her husband seems completely astounded.'

'I'm no less shocked and bewildered,' Jaiprakash replied. 'It's as great a mystery to me as to anybody else.'

'According to our investigations, it's a not so complicated a case as it appears. Her journalist friends have professionally sensationalized it. From her suicide note as well as her behavior only a few hours before she killed herself, it is reasonably certain that she acted in a fit of depression. If something had intervened at the critical moment she might be alive today. We avoid injecting conjectures into such clear cases and unnecessarily bothering people with questions. That's why we didn't trouble you to come from so far away, though some of her friends suggested your name. However, since you have come, is it possible do you think that her pregnancy may have had something to do with it? You were close to both her and her husband as their personal assistant,' said the officer with a sudden change of expression.

'I don't think so,' Jaiprakash replied. 'Both husband and wife were perfectly happy with each other and had openly rejoiced over her pregnancy, a fact which has been reported in the papers.'

'Thank you very much!' said the officer, getting up. He effusively shook hands with Jaiprakash and left. Jaiprakash was surprised and disappointed by the brevity of the meeting. He had expected him to ask a few more questions, some of them obvious. He'd have liked to answer them now in order as far as possible to obviate the possibility of being called back from Patna by the police for further questioning. He was afraid that if the report did not satisfy the media persons and politicians who were her friends the enquiry might be reopened under pressure.

1/3

Left alone, Jaiprakash again remembered Charles Smith, his only confidant in Delhi. He hoped to hear from him some guess about the probable cause and circumstances of her suicide.

'Where is he?' he wondered. Charles had been Jaiprakash's predecessor as personal assistant to Chandrmukhi and her husband, Vishnu, before he became the junior of a Supreme

Court lawyer, Mr. Jawaharlal, who was Vishnu's uncle. He was about to resign the latter position before Jaiprakash left for Patna and to rejoin them in his former capacity. His decision to leave Jawaharlal reminded him that Jawaharlal's daughter had been on dialysis for a long time due to the differences between him and his strong-minded daughters-in-law over the ethics of procuring a kidney. He felt curious to know about her condition.

At lunch Jaiprakash was prevented by the presence of Chandrmukhi's sister, Harimohini, from talking to Vishnu. After seeing his condition he had begun to wish not to talk to him at all about his wife's death for fear of embarrassing him. He had been a witness to his see-saw relations with her, though when he left them they had become reconciled and were as happy with each other as when he had joined them as their personal assistant two years before. But in view of his close personal relations with him before he left Delhi, he felt obliged to ask at least a few formal questions while condoling with him. He hadn't been able so far to conceive them as clearly as he wished, because, though formal, at least some of them would still be determined by the extent of the confidence Vishnu would've liked to share with him in such a sensitive personal matter.

After lunch, contrary to his expectation, Vishnu did not send for him. Perhaps, he was too tired and wanted to take a nap. At the evening tea, he was scheduled to have consultations with his company's lawyers. Jaiprakash decided to take advantage of it to visit some friends.

He returned at the usual dinner time, but again missed him because he was not feeling well and had retired early. Jaiprakash was informed that Charles would be dining with him. Vishnu had left a message for Jaiprakash and Charles. They were to have breakfast with him tomorrow.

Jaiprakash was glad to have missed the dinner with Vishnu. It would be good to hear something from Charles about the circumstances of his wife's suicide before meeting him.

Charles, a late diner, arrived at nine o' clock. He was coming straight from his former boss and Vishnu's uncle and lawyer, Mr.

Jawaharlal, who was currently handling a case of his company. They retired to Jaiprakash's room. Charles had always been very close to both Chandrmukhi and her husband and, Jaiprakash suspected, knew many things about them that perhaps even he did not know.

'I read the news of her suicide in a newspaper at Patna. You didn't inform me,' said Jaiprakash, after Charles had taken a glass from the table, poured himself a large whiskey from a bottle he took out of his briefcase, filled the rest of the glass with ice which a servant had brought and comfortably settled down.

Charles replied, 'I kept meaning to but was too busy after her death. She had left so many things unfinished. I also thought that her sister Harimohini would have written to you. Vishnu had asked her to inform their friends and relations outside Delhi. In fact, I was beginning to wonder why you hadn't come, and I'd have called you in a day or two. It was terribly shocking. What's your guess? You were very close to them.'

'I have no guesses,' said Jaiprakash. 'By the way, is it true that she and her husband had been seen together as usual chatting with Somdutt, Syed Murtza Ali and other friends at the India International Centre a day before her death? '

'Yes, it's a fact,' replied Charles. 'And it was particularly reported by her journalist friends in order to quell stories that her unhappy married life was the cause of her suicide. It was a normal reaction; when one of the partners dies in that way, domestic discord is the first suspect. Thankfully, the stories have not been published, not even in the evening papers which thrive on tittle-tattle. In fact, on that day I happened to be with them at the Centre. She was in unusually high spirits. She had received compliments for a letter she had published in an English daily in which she had criticized the High Court judgment allowing the darshan of the idol of Lord Ram installed in the makeshift temple illegally constructed by the destroyers of the Babri Mosque at the same place where the mosque had stood. She had criticized the court's order for virtually legitimizing the mosque's demolition and making it impossible to rebuild it. Prime Minister Narsimha Rao had officially announced that the mosque would be rebuilt at the same spot. I particularly remember Syed Murtza Ali and Somdutt singling out for special praise her description of Rao's promise to Muslims as "consciously dishonest". She had mentioned in the letter reports that Rao, who had been performing puja of Lord Ram while the mosque was under attack, had ended it and smiled when he was informed that it had been demolished. She was particularly critical of the Court's description of Lord Ram as a Constitutional entity and a reality of our national culture and fabric on the ground that a sketch of Ram was depicted in one of the copies of the Constitution signed by the members of the Constituent Assembly in 1949. Somdutt praised the letter for courageously upholding the principle of secularism and also for its elegant language. Actually, she had risked imprisonment for committing contempt of court. I don't believe that she gave way to a transient impulse, as her sister Harimohini thinks. Having known her for so many years, I have no doubt that she was capable of the most stubborn resolution. Actually, she may already have decided to end her life when she was laughing and joking and receiving compliments for the letter. She also attended a cultural program and both she and Vishnu were in a happy mood. Nobody could have imagined in his wildest dream that only a few hours later she'd kill herself.'

'Press reports apart, what's in circulation in the drawing rooms about the most probable cause?'

Charles replied, 'Nobody can claim to know the truth for sure. When she died, according to her doctor, she was over five months pregnant. Both she and her husband had rejoiced and received their friends' congratulations. Whatever people thought nobody openly doubted, so far as I know, that Vishnu really believed or had chosen to believe that she was carrying his child; such late pregnancies are quite normal. But her suicide changed the general opinion and the same people began to think that maybe she had become pregnant by Somdutt, to whom she had been linked by rumors for a long time, and Vishnu accidentally came to know it. This conjecture has been buttressed by the fact that Somdutt, who had been a regular visitor to her evening parties despite her husband's less than enthusiastic approval of him, suddenly ceased to attend them. Probably something seriously objectionable came to Vishnu's notice, although for the sake of the world he and Somdutt remained mutually polite.'

'What do you think?' asked Jaiprakash.

'Like others I too can only guess and my guess is also that probably she became pregnant by Somdutt and her husband accidentally came upon the evidence on their return home from the Centre. However, knowing their mutual relations as well as I do, I should think that for the sake of his family's prestige he should still have preferred abortion, which could have been passed off as a miscarriage. Maybe when he came to know, her pregnancy was far too advanced and abortion seemed unacceptably risky. Or perhaps his doctor friends refused. Unable to endure the prospect of being saddled with the child of his antagonist, possibly he couldn't refrain from expressing his shock and reviling her.'

He added, 'If her husband and not Somdutt was the father of the child, a wise and strong-willed woman like her wouldn't have killed herself and thereby lent credibility to a baseless suspicion and untrue allegations. She'd much rather have left him if she was unable to convince him that the so-called evidence against her was false and misleading. However, at best it's a guess.'

Just then a servant came in and announced that the dinner was ready.

'Okay, we're coming in ten minutes,' replied Charles, refilling his glass.'

Jaiprakash said, 'Abortion even after five months is not too dangerous nowadays.'

'But it's also not completely safe. However, it's not impossible that Vishnu proposed it. The only reason I can think of for her preferring suicide to abortion, if he proposed it and found a doctor friend willing to take the risk, would be that she felt too humiliated by the discovery of her misconduct. Or, if she was innocent, she acted precipitately from humiliation and despair of being believed and in doing so acted out of character. I must say again that all this is no more than a guess.'

Jaiprakash said, 'I wonder what sort of evidence Vishnu came upon. Surely, he didn't catch her in the arms of her lover, whoever he was. I still find it hard to believe that a woman so full of zest for life should have decided to go in such a horrible manner. Whether she was guilty or innocent, abortion with or without her husband's knowledge would have been the wiser thing to do. And I have little doubt that eventually he'd have become reconciled in view of his own culpability. It'd also have been the kinder thing to do. Kinder to Vishnu. I was shocked to see him today. It seemed to me that he would have preferred anything to suicide and the consequent grief and scandal. She could have told him afterwards for his peace of mind that she had done it not because she was guilty but for the sake of the child, whom he'd have condemned as illegitimate.'

'That's true,' said Charles. He added, 'In such matters even true friends are often misled by the wish to reach some conclusion, and they interpret the circumstances accordingly.'

They continued to speculate but remained unconvinced of the various theories, especially as all of them despite being more or less exclusive of each other also seemed more or less equally probable. Before they parted, Charles asked, 'Did you meet any of their friends and what do they think?'

'Yes. I met several. While some said that probably she killed herself from remorse because she knew she was carrying Somdutt's child, others thought that her husband's accusation or suspicion humiliated her beyond endurance irrespective of whether she was innocent or guilty.'

After Charles had left, Jaiprakash remembered that he hadn't asked him about the condition of Jawaharlal's daughter. Had she received somebody's kidney or was still on dialysis? He began to wonder at the suffering she had already endured before he left. It seemed no less terrible than Chandrmukhi's, but would be forgotten much sooner if she died.

Chapter 2

2/1

Chandrmukhi was sitting at a large table in a revolving chair and arguing in a contentious voice bordering on arrogance with someone on the phone in English.

'Could I ever have imagined that this woman would one day commit suicide?' Jaiprakash thought.

Chandrmukhi was holding an open book in her left hand and looking at a plate containing salted cashew nuts and almonds. Jaiprakash guessed that she had been eating them and reading the book when the telephone rang. He noted the book's title: Dalits of India.

He remembered the letter of introduction, which had been addressed to this woman's husband by his uncle and their family physician and friend, Dr. Awasthi, who had described him as more easygoing than her. Looking at her and hearing her voice, he would've liked to have his interview with him. But he had flown to Calcutta in the morning.

She looked up and motioned him to a chair.

He guessed that she was meeting with strong opposition from the other end. He was struck by her magisterial temper. Although he had come by appointment, in the state of mind she seemed to be he thought it discreet to make his presence as unobtrusive as possible. He pretended to look at the cover pages of the newspapers and magazines placed on a low table in front of him, as if he wasn't listening in to her conversation. But as she was talking about the contemporary Indian politics and from her language seemed to hold her views strongly he couldn't help listening to them attentively. Mrs. Awasthi had told him with an ironic smile that she and her husband had the reputation of being highbrows and aesthetes. But it hadn't occurred to him to ask her about their political views.

On several important social and political issues her views were different from his. He felt lucky to have come to know them.

As from her way of speaking she also struck him as intellectually vain, it occurred to him that noticeable lack of interest in her conversation wouldn't be judicious; she might think him a philistine who wasn't interested in serious subjects! On the other hand, following her conversation too attentively might not be polite!

At last, he decided to relax and behave naturally, without bothering about the impression he was making. His eye wandered to the open bookshelves packed with hardbound volumes neatly arranged subject-wise.

She seems a well-read woman,' looking at some of the titles he thought hopefully and decided to try to impress her with his own reading.

All of a sudden, he was startled to hear: 'Why should there be a Ram temple at that very site at Ayodhya? A temple can be built anywhere, though we need schools and hospitals for people living in villages rather than temples. And where is the evidence that Ram was born at Ayodhya or that he's a historical person like Buddha or Christ? The so-called Ramjanmabhoomi Trust has already made a laughing stock of the country of Gandhi and Nehru by piling up at Ayodhya two hundred thousand Ram Shilas or Ram's bricks inscribed with the name of Lord Ram. The collection of these bricks from all over the country and even from abroad by fundamentalist travelers during their brazen Ram Shila Pujan Yatras has already caused dozens of Hindu-Muslim riots and the death of hundreds of people. With these blood-soaked bricks they propose to build the world's biggest temple at the site of Babri Mosque after demolishing it! And if I am correctly informed they have the nerve to ask the government to transfer by a fiat the legally disputed rights on this site to the Trust. As a Hindu I feel ashamed that the ultimate aim of this whole exercise is to humiliate Muslims by destroying one of their most important religious monuments, which is regarded by all sane Hindus as a monument to secularism and multiculturalism.'

'Contemptible hypocrite!' looking at her, he said to himself. Like an average educated Hindu, secular-minded or otherwise, he thought that the main raison d'être for a Muslim invader or ruler for building mosques in the Hindu holy cities like Ayodhya, Varanasi and Mathura, was to sadistically humiliate Hindus by first desecrating and destroying their most sacred religious shrines and then building them on their ruins as a permanent reminder of their disgrace. It's good sense to forget what happened in the past but to describe such buildings as symbols of secularism and multiculturalism! No wonder Muslims had felt insecure among such hypocritical Hindus and their leaders and voted for Pakistan, even those who had absolutely no intention of immigrating to their new Fatherland!'

Suddenly noticing the pictures of Gandhi and Nehru on the wall behind her he wondered whether even sensible and honest Indian Muslims believed in their assurances that after the partition of the country on rigidly communal lines in the Constitutionally, or nominally, secular India, as a community they would enjoy the same rights and opportunities as Hindus or that any sensible Hindu thought Muslims capable of such self-delusion. He personally knew or had heard of middle-class Muslims in Patna who despite being as comfortable in their spheres as Hindus and having Hindu friends and colleagues, complaining of discrimination against them on grounds of religion. Some of them openly regarded Jinnah as a wise statesman who candidly said that Hindus and Muslims were two separate nations and civilizations and in an undivided Hindu-majority India Muslims couldn't expect fair and equal treatment from Hindus, whose attitude to them would be influenced by deliberately or unwittingly false belief of their alleged persecution by the Muslim conquerors and rulers. He recalled the great opportunistic farce of the Khilafat movement Gandhi had launched in a desperate attempt to unite the socially and politically incompatible Hindus and Muslims against the British Raj. He did not doubt that even during this movement and the entire freedom struggle both Hindus and Muslims had more confidence in and respect for their British rulers than for each other and would have preferred to be ruled by them no matter how long than by each other. Even the uneasy peace which existed between the two communities was of post-British origin and owed itself to the British bayonet. How quickly had it been followed by hatred and violence after their departure, causing them to go for each other's throats.

'Please don't interrupt! You can't deny that the Ram Shila Pujan Yatras are a political gimmick. What's the use of talking to you, if you won't listen?'

Her interlocutor wouldn't stop and continued to speak in a loud voice, which Jaiprakash could hear without being able to make out what he was saying. Although irritated by the interruption, she took advantage of it to lay aside the book and pop in an almond. Silently chewing it, she began to listen with a frown.

Listening to her, his dormant but invincible inbred bias of an average educated Hindu against Islam, in particular against its Indian variety, even if he believed in secularism and had Muslim friends whom he admired, surged. It was strange but true, he reflected, that the criticism of Hindu nationalism by real or sham Hindu secularists, far fewer Muslims were guilty of it, further increased the Hindus' prejudice against Muslims! For political purposes, they never allowed the relations between the two communities to stabilize at a human level. Being an avid reader of Indian history, he recalled the anglicized Prime Minister Pandit Nehru frowning upon the renovation of the Somnath temple, which had been looted and sadistically desecrated by the Afghan invader, Mahmud of Ghazni, a thousand years ago, and a few centuries later again destroyed by the last Mughal Emperor, Aurangzeb. He couldn't remember a single Muslim politician or intellectual of note criticizing the renovation. Or, he sometimes wondered, did Nehru, who was after all a Hindu and an astute politician, suddenly turn against the renovation after the death of Sardar Patel and against his own Cabinet's resolution, because he did not want history to be tampered with and secretly wished the temple to stand in its present condition as a balancing factor against the Muslims' grievance against the Hindus' deep-rooted prejudice against them by reminding the former of the malignity of the Afghan, Iranian and other Muslim invaders whom not only Pakistani but even many Indian Muslims still regarded as their heroes? And whose acts Indian leftist historians continued their generally well-intentioned efforts to whitewash in order to promote secularism and tolerance among Hindus of Muslim insularity and religious bigotry. But only succeeded in making the Hindus more cynical.

Having finished the last cashew nut and almond, she pushed away the empty plate and said, 'Please listen to me. Please! Please!!'

He continued to speak.

She stopped listening and turning to Jaiprakash bestowed on him a smile in which were mingled a kindly welcome and the semblance of a courteous apology for forcing him, who had come by appointment, to listen to a long, contentious telephonic conversation.

He said to himself that he must try to learn as much as possible the kind of person he'd be talking to in a few minutes. He specially noted that she was dressed in expensive silk. Everything about her: her handsome features, lustrous skin, stately neck and ample bosom characterized a self-complacent, well-nourished and vain though perhaps still agreeable person. So early in the day she was as well-groomed as if she were going to a party. Looking at the empty plate of almonds and cashew nuts, and the book on the Dalits she had been reading, he couldn't help comparing the smoothness and roundness of her person to the severely ill-nourished and prematurely old Dalits living in a slum near his house in Patna.

Having finished the last cashew nut and almond, she interrupted the person at the other end, 'Please listen to me. Please! Please!! I do agree with you that the implementation of the Mandal Commission Report will dilute the educational and professional standards and to that extent impede progress. But as for your worry that it would promote caste divisions in the Hindu society, I believe the contrary would happen. The beneficiaries of the Mandal Commission, the so-called other backward castes, would on becoming educated and affluent begin to think and behave like the upper castes towards their unfortunate brethren. And in case your fear should prove true, the upper-caste Hindus, who now constitute the main vote bank of the reactionary Bharatiya

Janata Party—please let me finish—would be responsible for it by refusing to assimilate them. They have divided their own society by exploiting and degrading the Dalits, who can't enter a temple and go without even one square meal a day. And they have divided the nation and brought it into disrepute by persecuting Muslims. You're again interrupting me. In the 1969 riots in Ahmedabad 2700 people, an overwhelming majority of them Muslims, were killed. Even the official figure, obviously an understatement, was as high as 1200. According to the BBC correspondent, Mark Tully, who visited the city soon after the riots. Read his No Full Stops In India. And what provoked the riots? A violent campaign by the Rashtriya Swayamsewak Sangh to "Indianize" Muslims! Please read some history instead of arguing baselessly.'

Jaiprakash felt a sudden revulsion against this "priggish" and "snobbish" woman, who was smugly insensible of her own wealth, inevitably accumulated he felt sure through malpractice and exploitation, and who indulged in phony denigration of the upper-castes to which she herself belonged, a circumstance in which he had no doubt she like so many people he knew actually took a sneaking pride. He particularly detested the affluent upper-caste leftist Hindus, of whom she seemed to him a model, who enjoyed self-denigration to flaunt their progressiveness, while tenaciously retaining, by fair means and foul, all the benefits that accrued to them gratis from their higher social status, which owed itself to a significant extent to their high caste. He vividly remembered the fact that he partly owed his own metamorphosis during his university days into a Hindu nationalist, which he now didn't feel ashamed to acknowledge, to some students of wealthy upper-caste families, feudal landlords' sons, who domineered over their fellow students and offensively asserted, by the use of money and muscle power, their allegiance to one or another of the numerous fashionable leftist groups, and provoking people like him to join the groups opposed to them.

Jaiprakash would later come to know that the person she had been talking to was her business partner and a financier of Bajrang Dal and Vishwa Hindu Parishad.

Her adversary, no less determined to deliver himself and like her neither interested in hearing what she was saying because he thought he already knew it, nor caring whether or not she was listening to him, because he knew she was already aware of what he'd say, had continued to speak simultaneously with her.

Looking quietly at her, he thought, 'Living in physical comfort is not enough for these people. They also must have the pleasure of sympathizing with the poor to further enhance the quality of their life.'

At last, she cut off.

He had made up his mind to try his best to get into her service. The urgent need to alleviate his family's poverty, his uncle's assurance that both she and her husband were good-natured, and the luxurious ambience of her home, which would be the place of his work, had decided him.

However, in view of her vanity he had also decided to give her no hint that he particularly needed the job. He felt grateful to his uncle Dr Awasthi for his astuteness in telling her that he wished to come to Delhi because he felt suffocated in a backward state.

She said,' You're Dr. Awasthi's nephew?'

'Yes.'

To his surprise, she proceeded to talk to him with such sympathetic gentleness, tinged with sincere respect for his wealth of information, for nearly an hour that only his increasing admiration for her kept him from regretting his uncharitable reflections about her. She asked him about the subjects that interested him, the books he read, his views on contemporary social and political issues and why he thought what he thought and so on and so forth. Not once did he regret his answers, which were more often politic than frank. He was time and again surprised at his capacity for improvisation. He'd later explain it as due not only to his decision to enter into her service for the sake of his family but also because he considered the differences in their views irrelevant to the work he'd be doing as her personal assistant.

When the interview ended, he couldn't help wondering why she hadn't asked him as to what he thought about the Babri Mosque controversy. Despite having been a BJP activist and feeling repelled by her contemptuous cynicism about Ram's historicity, like her he also deplored the movement for the demolition of the historic mosque as vulgar and against the Hindu ethos. Did she deliberately refrain from asking his views about it because urgently needing a personal assistant and feeling satisfied with his qualifications, she had shrewdly decided not to risk hearing views that didn't coincide with hers, which might have put her in a quandary? He was somewhat deflated to think that another possible reason for her avoiding the subject might have been that, after all, she thought of him as a servant, whose views on it, even if different from hers, were immaterial. Or was it because she was one of those who professed views which were fashionable and respectable among the affluent elite and which they had consciously or unconsciously adopted as their views. And which they modified or even changed in accordance with the change in fashion and professed them as strongly as the preceding ones? He knew many such people.

Anyway, it didn't matter.

'Dr Awasthi may have given you some idea of the kind of work you'll be doing here. Your predecessor Mr. Charles Smith, whom you'll be meeting often, is his close friend,' she said at the end of the interview.

'He hasn't told me anything except that you need a personal assistant,' he replied. He would later come to know that Dr Awasthi had refrained from telling him about Charles and his superior qualifications lest he should feel even more diffident than he already seemed to do.

'I'll ask Charles to brief you. He was an able assistant, but too qualified for the work he was doing here, and some time ago we helped him to join the office of a Supreme Court lawyer, who is our counsel and relative. When can you take charge? In fact, we urgently need the services of a person like you!'

'I can join now.'

'Your office will be in a part of the bungalow proper. I'll have it tidied up by tomorrow. I understand that you're a newcomer to Delhi and at present staying with Dr Awasthi. I don't know what will suit you, but if it'll be convenient to you, we can accommodate you on our bungalow's premises.'

'I'll let you know in a few days. When may I join?'

'Come tomorrow afternoon.'

When he left her, it was with ineffable gratitude for her candor in virtually telling him that she was thankful for getting the services of a capable person like him. And he had thought that she would behave as if she were obliging him! He still felt no regret, however, because, as he said to himself, until she talked to him he did not know the kind of person she was. Regret also seemed rather a mismatch with the excellent impression he had made on her.

2/2

The next day Jaiprakash went to join his duties. To his surprise, he found Chandrmukhi's husband, who had returned from Calcutta, personally supervising the work of equipping his office with the necessary facilities. He introduced himself and shook hands with Jaiprakash so affably that he felt considerably reassured that they wouldn't inflict on him the indignity of living in a servant's quarter. After Vishnu had briefed him about his work and offered to put him up in a part of one of his bungalow's locked suites, as Dr Awasthi had guessed, the remnants of his misgivings about the kind of treatment he might receive from them also disappeared.

Vishnu took him to his own study, where a greater surprise than any he had experienced in this house so far awaited him. The study was hung with pictures of some of the most prominent Hindu icons: Mahatma Gandhi, Shri Aurobindo, Swami Vivekanand, Chhatrapati Shivaji and Veer Savarkar. The books on the shelves harmonized with the political ideology the pictures proclaimed. His interview with Vishnu was a simpler affair. However, as he had decided to betray no reaction to any discoveries he might make in this house, he concealed his pleasure and looked at the pictures impassively. Without showing the least curiosity about his intellectual interests, Vishnu explained his work to him in detail and then proposed a salary that exceeded his most optimistic expectations.

'Maybe, he's indifferent because he has already learnt from his wife that I am a "progressive",' he thought. 'And why should he bother with my views when his own wife is, or professes to be, a leftist fundamentalist.'

'It would be interesting to see how wife and husband get along,' he thought.

Chapter 3

3/1

The wealthy Supreme Court lawyer and famous Gandhian, Mr. Jawaharlal, who was even better known as an intellectual activist and columnist on social and political affairs, and his two sons, Vishwanath and Srinath, sat in the drawing-room of their luxurious bungalow in a posh colony of Delhi. They read the morning papers at breakfast, when they also discussed family matters and exchanged views about the current affairs. But today no one in the house had eaten anything because of the crisis created by Jawaharlal's daughters-in-law, Subhadra and Jayanti, about what had come to be known among their relatives and friends as the family's kidney problem. The women were trying to extort a pledge from him which was contrary to his principles.

In front of them on a low table were placed half a dozen newspapers, which they were reading while reflecting on their predicament and vaguely hoping that an unexpected solution might present itself! They told themselves that seemingly more insoluble problems are eventually solved than is generally thought. The papers' cover pages were splashed with the news and pictures of the "holocaust" at Ayodhya, where, according to the Hindi press, hundreds of karsevaks, or devotees of Lord Ram, had been gunned down by reluctant policemen, who sympathized with them, while they were climbing up the five-centuries old Babri Mosque with pickaxes, hammers and kulhadis to hack away in religious ecstasy at its dilapidated domes. These "martyrs", as the Hindi press in general described them, were among the over 50,000 anti-Muslim devotees of Lord Ram, who had converged on the town from different parts of the country, defying official ban allegedly with the connivance of the security forces. According to the BBC, All India Radio and the press, as soon as the news of the karsevaks at Ayodhya having been shot down by the police reached the people violent Hindu-Muslim clashes had taken place in many cities and towns. A special correspondent's story on the front page of an English daily gave the names of the worst affected towns and pictures of the dead bodies, burnt houses, shops, private and public vehicles, etc. Jawaharlal and his sons had already seen these on TV last night.

Jawaharlal had in the last few weeks received but due to his family's problem turned down several invitations from the print and electronic media to state his views on the impact of the anti-Babri Mosque movement on the Hindu-Muslim unity. Another reason why he had refused the requests was that he privately thought that it was the other way about and the anti-Babri Mosque movement was a belated but inevitable consequence of the almost total lack of Hindu-Muslim unity and the centuries-old antagonism between the two peoples which had resulted in the division of British India into the Islamic Pakistan and the so-called secular but in reality Hindu India. But in the prevailing political culture made fashionable by India's first Prime Minister, Pandit Nehru, it was not only politically incorrect but uncivilized to say so. Even those who secretly thought like him, that is, almost every 'progressive" Hindu, would slur him as a communalist, if he frankly expressed his views.

Jawaharlal like Hindus in general whether fundamentalists or communists did not doubt that the discordant Hindu-Muslim relations, epitomized by the Kashmir problem between India and Pakistan, which was at least in part a creation of Nehru, were at the core of the country's politics and significantly influenced its election results in the States where Muslims, who wanted Jammu & Kashmir to become independent or a part of Pakistan, were in a substantial minority. However, both the secular and pseudo-secular Hindu politicians who made consciously false promises to conciliate the innately fundamentalist and shrewd Muslim leaders as well as the latter, despite their awareness of being lied to and exploited, were obliged to stick together against their common adversary, the Hindu nationalist Bharatiya Janata Party. It was currently leading the anti-Babri Mosque movement to arouse and gain popularity among the phlegmatically but congenitally anti-Muslim Hindus, who far outnumbered those who believed in the loyalty of Muslims.

Presently Jawaharlal stopped thinking about the country's affairs and forced himself to think of his family's problem created by his sons' wives, Subhadra and Jayanti. His daughter Sarika was suffering from kidney failure and had been on dialysis for over four months. These women had been pushing for purchasing a kidney for her from the very first day. In answer to Jawaharlal's objection that the buying and selling of human organs was unethical and a violation of human dignity, they emphasized the humanitarian aspect of accepting the kidney of an honest man in severe pecuniary distress and paying him liberally. They argued that one who was prepared to sell his kidney had generally nothing else to sell and if denied this only means of alleviating his unbearable hardship, he might commit suicide, be forced into crime or become a victim of the crooks engaged in commerce in human organs. For the credibility of their stand, because they were against their husbands donating their kidneys, they were also against accepting the organ of a man killed in an accident who had posthumously donated it or whose relatives were prepared to donate it. In this respect their view coincided with Jawaharlal's, whose opposition was due to the fact that he had two healthy sons. Acceptance of the kidney of such a person could also involve the family in a scandal. There was no lack of criminal doctors in collusion with racketeers who procured kidneys of real or supposed volunteers or cadavers through corrupt means.

However, in spite of himself, Jawaharlal's eyes once again fell on the same news and pictures and from there rose to look at the expensive oil painting of Mahatma Gandhi in his loin cloth hanging on the wall in front of him.

Although worshipping the apostle of non-violence, like most Gandhians with their vegetarianism, glorification of sexual self-denial, in theory if not in practice, and idealization of non-violence, he was repelled by the Muslim culture with its deification of sex and violence in defense of their religion. However, he considered Gandhi's desire for Hindu-Muslim brotherhood sincere because its opposite meant aversion and hate which were abhorrent to his saintly nature. True saints even more fervently loved those whose customs and traditions were repugnant to them and who despised and hated them.

However, a glance at the pictures of the murdered humans, most of them Muslims, recalled to him one of the speeches of the Mahatma at his prayer meetings at which he had happened to be present as a young man only a few months before his assassination. Some portions of it had struck him as strange without however lessening his reverence for the great soul. Later, he had read the speech in a newspaper, which claimed that the report contained the exact words spoken by him almost in a trance, as if while speaking them he was in communication with God. He had exhorted the Hindus never to be angry against the Muslims even if the latter should make up their minds to put all of them to the sword. Instead they should court death bravely not only without ill will against their killers but with good will and love for them and with smile on their lips, which will give birth to a new India.

Jawaharlal looked at the dead bodies again and found himself thinking that if only the saintly but astute Mahatma, who could not but have been aware of the clash between the Hindu and Muslim civilizations and who seemed to think Muslims capable of murdering non-Muslims in cold blood, as his speech implied, had acted realistically. If only he had made the division of India conditional, as was pleaded by Ambedkar, on the exchange of Hindu and Muslim populations, in the interest of both the communities, which he did not doubt the increasingly frail and ambitious Jinnah, eager to become the Governor General of Pakistan and frightened of the imminent departure of the British, would have been forced to agree to, the Hindu-Muslim violence would have been largely eliminated from the sub-continent. And the politically opportunistic anti-Muslim anti-Babri Mosque movement wouldn't have started. On the contrary, at the height of the Hindu-Muslim violence after the departure of the British when millions were being slaughtered on both sides of the divided India, he had shocked the Deputy Prime Minister Sardar Patel by asking him to send back the Hindus and Sikhs, who had fled from Pakistan to escape being murdered or forcibly converted to Islam, and prevent Indian Muslims from migrating to Pakistan even at the risk of being butchered by the Sikhs and Hindus. Because his own faith in non-violence imposed the moral obligation on every human being to gladly take the risk of being killed with feelings of forgiveness and love towards the killer. Or, he couldn't help thinking, did he make that speech and ask the Sardar what he knew was evidently impossible for the sake of his conscience and left the matter in the hands of God? The question arose whether one's conscience was more important than the suffering and death of millions of human beings?

Jawaharlal stopped thinking. Gandhi like Buddha and Christ was a great soul and his morality deserved worship despite being beyond the comprehension of and impossible to follow by ordinary mortals.

Wishing not to hear the voice of his daughters-in-law, who were talking loudly for his sake in an adjacent room, he again looked at the pictures in the newspapers and began to think of the country's problems.

If only Nehru hadn't under the influence of Lord Mountbatten and even more his sweetheart, Lady Mountbatten, stopped the Indian army from capturing the part of the State of Jammu & Kashmir now under Pakistan's illegal occupation, and not committed the country in the United Nations to hold a plebiscite in the state to let the people decide whether to join India or Pakistan! There was no need to make the commitment for plebiscite even if he had made it with the shrewd conviction that a militarily nervous and weak Pakistan's decision to keep what they had illegally grabbed thanks to the cease-fire would give India legal and moral grounds for not carrying it out. Like the Hindus in general Jawaharlal hadn't the least doubt that the Kashmiri Pandit Prime Minister, who hated Jinnah and while wishing Muslims well considered them hopelessly insular and bigoted, had decided to hold on to Jammu and Kashmir because he had no doubt that if a plebiscite were held the State's Muslim majority would vote for accession to Pakistan. And they would either forcibly convert or throw the more than a million Kashmiri Pandits out of the State. And, worst of all, Indian Muslims would have rejoiced over these events! Nehru would also have been influenced by the fact, which as a professing secularist he could never express openly even to his most intimate confidants, that after having overwhelmingly voted for the creation of Pakistan, the vast majority of Indian Muslims had stayed back in India by taking advantage of the phony appeal of the Congress Party under the influence of Gandhi. Jawaharlal remembered his grandfather telling him that in 1947 when India was being divided, the Hindus who roared "Mahatma Gandhi ki jai" also abused and killed Muslims and told them to go to Pakistan or to hell.

He again forced himself to think of his family's problem. As he considered buying and selling of human organs unethical and his sons agreed with him, the solution of the problem apparently lay in the latter's hands. They were expected by him to try to persuade their wives and failing to do so disregard their opposition and offer to save their sister's life. What neither the wives nor the father knew was that both Vishwanath and Srinath, though affectionate brothers and upright men, suffered from a secret dread of what they considered a major surgery not entirely free of risk and the loss of a vital organ. Sarika's doctor was aware of the crisis in the family and sympathized with Jawaharlal's view. One day he had advised him that though her general condition was such that she could survive on dialysis for a long time, yet there was no point in postponing the kidney transplant and prolonging her suffering. As the advice, though natural in the circumstances, was yet tendered in her brothers' presence in the hospital without any warning and elicited an ambiguous nod from their father, it not only seemed to have been aimed at them but smacked of a tacit understanding between him and the doctor. Taken by surprise, Vishwanath and Srinath, who had planned to join a march of the city's secular elite next week against the Ramjanmabhoomi movement, a fact of which their father was not only aware but heartily approved, had looked at each other and sympathetically perceived each other's fear. However, jealous of their reputation as honorable men and loving brothers, with rapid heartbeats but composed miens they had offered to undergo the necessary blood and other tests. Their offer was promptly accepted by the doctor with the silent assent of the father, which confirmed their doubt that there was at least an unspoken understanding between them.

After the tests both were declared equally fit as donors. A date, which followed the march, another possible proof of an understanding between them, was fixed. And as both brothers were equally willing they were asked by the doctor to present themselves on that day, when he would decide after the check-ups prior to the transplant operation as to whose kidney should be grafted into his sister. He had noted their fast heartbeats but looking at their calm expressions regarded it as a normal reaction.

From the moment they learned of the circumstances in which the doctor had tendered his advice and their husbands had undergone the tests, the daughters-in-law had been furious that Jawaharlal should have scornfully ignored their view and their husbands should have gone along with him.

Acting in conjunction, Subhadra and Jayanti had instigated each other to prevent their husbands from going to the hospital where the doctors had made preparations to carry out the transplant. Finally, in view of their hostile attitude, the operation had been postponed indefinitely.

Subhadra's father, a doctor, had told her that getting the kidney of a "legitimate donor" was no great problem, if one was prepared to pay more than the current price. As the donation of human organs by non-relatives had not yet been explicitly illegalized and was subject only to the donor declaring his offer as voluntary and gratis, and since as a life-saving act he didn't consider it unethical in certain circumstances, he was prepared to arrange a kidney and pay for it himself. However, in view of the opposition of her daughter's husband and his father and brother to such a deal, he wouldn't go so far as to lie to them, if they asked him whether he had paid the donor and thus in defiance of their stand committed an unethical act. In other words, he couldn't help his daughter. He had assured her, 'if the worst comes to the worst and your husband has to donate his kidney, you shouldn't worry, as one can lead a normal life with only one kidney.'

Subhadra had replied, 'The operation may be a minor one for the surgeon but is not so for the man who is left with only one kidney and has nothing to fall back upon in case the lone kidney fails. Nor is it entirely free of risk. It also lowers the quality of life. However, if the loss and the risks are the same for every donor, I see nothing objectionable in letting the one who is tragically needy benefit. I have told Papaji that Jayanti and I also love Sarika and neither of us would have objected to her husband's donating his kidney, if no "legitimate donors" were available.'

Her father had assured her, 'Nowadays the risk is not significant. Nor does having only one kidney significantly lower the quality of life, considering that the donation would save the life of one's own sister.'

Subhadra had countered her father's assurance by repeating her by now familiar argument: 'If the loss and the risks are the same for every donor why not let the one who is needy benefit?'

3/2

After waiting for another couple of months in the hope that either Vishwanath or Srinath might disregard his wife's opposition Jawaharlal at last expressed his willingness to accept an altruistic donation, which to the dismay of his sons and daughters-in-law he described as not unethical in the circumstances!

Subhadra and Jayanti scoffed at his notion of ethicality. They said, 'How can a man who is so wealthy and has two sons solicit an altruistic donation for his own daughter and describe it as ethical? It's obvious that either his obsession with his notions has disabled him from thinking sensibly, or he is indirectly accusing his sons of being uxorious and selfish.'

Jayanti's uncle, a retired High Court judge and an old friend of both Jawaharlal and Subhadra's doctor father, was worried that as donation of an organ by a non-relative might soon become a legal problem, it would be better if Sarika received a kidney before it happened. Therefore, at the doctor's suggestion he had arranged with an indigent lawyer of Aligarh to "altruistically" donate his kidney. His blood and tissue groups matched Sarika's and as regards his antecedents, the judge had been assured by the doctor that they were unimpeachable; he was an honest man in need of money for the treatment of his wife, who was suffering from cancer. The judge believed that Jawaharlal was not so naïve as to think that any well off person living comfortably would altruistically or otherwise donate his kidney, let alone to a rich man's daughter who had two healthy brothers. Thus the donor would almost certainly be a pathetically needy person presenting himself as an altruist. The judge also knew Jawaharlal too well to think that a proud and munificent person like him, who regularly donated to charities, would accept such a man's kidney without generously paying him after the transplant as an expression of his gratitude. The doctor and Jawaharlal's increasingly nervous sons thought likewise, the latter regarding it as a happy reconciliation between the respective ethics of their father and the judge, which had the additional merit of saving not one but possibly two lives! The judge had explained to the lawyer the family's problem and that the patient's father and brothers rightly objected to the buying and selling of human organs as a violation of human dignity; yet they might accept a kidney, if the donor does not demand a price for it. He had told the lawyer that if his offer was accepted, he'd get plenty of cash not as the price of his organ but in appreciation of his spirit of sacrifice and as an expression of the family's gratitude. But he'd get it after the grafting operation in order for Mr. Jawaharlal to feel sure that the donation was altruistic. He had warned the lawyer that Mr. Jawaharlal was as astute as he was a man of principle. Therefore, while talking to him he should be extremely careful lest he should become suspicious that he expected to be paid afterwards and was virtually selling his kidney.

Jayanti's uncle, who first as a lawyer and then as a judge, had become accustomed to regard a plausible pretense as unimpeachable and ethical as truth, had told him, 'Although it should satisfy Jawaharlal's conscience, if the man doesn't demand money or recompense in any other form, yet it would be ideal if you can manage to leave the impression that although I have sent you, your offer to donate your kidney is really altruistic and I have luckily found an unselfish person. Such persons do exist and Jawaharlal is one of those rare men who believe that the world is not devoid of such people.'

'Is it necessary for him to know that it's you who have sent me?' the lawyer had asked.

'I've thought of it and come to the conclusion that on the whole it would be better. Since you don't live in Delhi, he might ask as to how you came to know that his daughter needed a kidney. Your reply that you learnt it by chance from somebody might not satisfy him. It might give rise to more questions. Therefore, maybe it's better to start by telling the truth that I have sent you. As I said, he's one of those rare men who even nowadays, when values have sadly declined and venality and corruption are rife, believe in the existence of virtue. And if he doesn't feel satisfied, which is not impossible, you can come back. It's up to you. If you think you can manage it better the other way, you can do that. Finally, I've told you what I believe, but you must decide for yourself. What I mean is that though I am fairly confident, yet I can't absolutely guarantee, that after accepting your kidney he will present you with a purse as a token of his gratitude. However, if I were you, I'd take the risk.'

Even after such clear briefing, the lawyer, who had met the father and sons two days ago, had spoilt his case. He had told Jawaharlal, though he had done so reluctantly and in answer to his unexpected questions asked with a benign expression, that his wife was ill with cancer, his two sons were studying in a public school and the maintenance of a widowed sister had lately increased his financial responsibilities. He had denied any connection between his hardship and his desire to donate his kidney, but his tale of privation had made Jawaharlal doubtful and raised his scruples.

In spite of his high opinion of the judge who had sent the lawyer, Jawaharlal said, 'We're infinitely grateful for your selfless offer. Just the same, would you mind accepting something, if I offer it as a token of my family's gratitude?'

Vishwanath and Srinath looked at each other with surprise. This question seemed to them as gratuitous and indiscreet as those about the lawyer's circumstances after he had said that his offer was altruistic. They were satisfied with his statement that his sole wish was to save a life. If father had agreed to meet him, like them he also ought to have believed what he said, instead of treating him as a person in the witness box and probing and embarrassing him with unnecessary questions.

The lawyer remembered the judge's warning that he must not say anything that might make Jawaharlal doubtful. However, the question, which was unexpected after he had said that his offer was altruistic, had perplexed the poor man. It had momentarily made him nervous lest a categorical reaffirmation by him that he won't accept anything should be taken literally by this man of principle and he should actually get nothing! He had enough experience to know that a principled man, even if he was by nature generous, could be as ruthless to others as to himself. Yet he was cautious and had replied, 'I am not sure whether I should accept anything at all. It's up to you. As I told you, my sole motive is to save a life.'

No sooner had he spoken, however, than he realized from the change of expressions on Jawaharlal's and his sons' faces that he had bungled.

Jawaharlal turned down his offer, politely telling him that he could not take advantage of his poverty and be guilty of an unethical act. This statement again surprised his sons. They couldn't appreciate its propriety or relevance after the lawyer's reaffirmation of his altruistic motive.

The lawyer had quickly recovered and said spiritedly, 'If you have any doubts or scruples about giving me anything there's absolutely no need to do so! It was your own suggestion. I never asked for it!'

Apart from his reluctance to accept a stranger's kidney, when he had two healthy sons, Jawaharlal had never been able to entirely get over his misgivings about accepting that of a poor man. First, in view of his wealth and well known generosity, because of the probability of such a donor's being pathetically motivated by a secret hope of gain and debasing himself by lying that his offer was altruistic; and, secondly, from his acute scruples about taking anything, let alone a part of his body, from one who was already poor, if his offer was really altruistic and he was a man of character who would refuse to accept anything even as an expression of the recipient's gratitude.

Looking at his sons to guess their reactions and feeling apprehensive lest the lawyer, who seemed to have been hurt by his doubts and had reacted passionately, should refuse his post-transplant gift, Jawaharlal had thanked him for his offer and repeated his inability to accept his kidney. However, his heart melted by his plight, he had offered to help him. It had awakened the lawyer's pride.

'I am not a beggar!' he had replied.

Within an hour, the lawyer had reported on the meeting to the judge. Although as surprised and disappointed as Vishwanath and Srinath that Jawaharlal should have asked those questions in spite of his assurance that the offer was altruistic, the judge had nevertheless lost his temper.

'Why did you have to tell him your tale of woe? Did you think him such a dunce as not to understand from your pathetic confession of penury that you were expecting to be paid for your kidney? In other words, you had gone to sell it. You have also compromised my position.'

Controlling his temper, the lawyer had replied, 'He should have had the decency not to ask any questions about my circumstances after I had told him that my offer was altruistic. Did he expect me to go on lying to him for his satisfaction? It was obvious that his questions were motivated by distrust of a poor man's word.'

The judge couldn't believe his ears when the lawyer, as he got up to leave, told him how he had spurned Jawaharlal's charity.

The same day the judge informed his niece of the outcome of the lawyer's meeting with her father-in-law and his sons and about his own decision to have nothing more to do with them in the matter.

Jayanti was furious at the treatment meted out to the lawyer. He had behaved with dignity, she had told her husband, by refusing to accept Papaji's charity and before that by honestly answering his tendentious questions.

'Papaji had no right to deprive him of his autonomy to give his kidney for a price in order to save his wife's life, which is not less precious than Sarika's life. In fact, Papaji should have appreciated his courage in taking the risk of getting nothing afterwards,' she had said. 'It's obvious that he had already made up his mind not to accept his offer and had met him only to mollify his daughter. You can tell him that if that was his intention, he has failed miserably and Sarika is angrier with him than ever.'

Srinath, though disapproving of his father's treatment of the lawyer, had been obliged to defend him, particularly because he and his brother had let him down after undergoing the tests. He had replied that since much before Sarika's kidneys failed, he had been a prominent activist against the commerce in human organs. It was obvious from the lawyer's replies to his questions that he was a good man in great distress and had come with the secret expectation of being paid. It would have been sheer cruelty, if Papaji had taken him at his word and paid him nothing after the operation. Or if at the last moment the lawyer's self-respect had prevented him from accepting anything even as a token of the family's gratitude. He and Vishwanath, though disappointed, could appreciate Papaji's moral dilemma.

Jayanti had smiled with pity.

Today Jayanti, who was in an advanced stage of pregnancy, was to have left for her father's home soon after breakfast to bear her first child there in accordance with the custom of both the families. Although not doubting Subhadra's honesty, she had been unable to sleep all night for fear that in her absence her husband might become more vulnerable. As for Subhadra, the elder brother Vishwanath's wife, she was no less afraid that Jayanti's absence might actually save Srinath and expose her husband to greater risk. Finally, at the morning tea, when preparations were being made for her departure, both women had aggressively raised the kidney question again. They had insisted that the matter be unequivocally settled before she left.

In the end, a solution, which was described by both women as wholly unsatisfactory and only ad hoc, was arrived at before a delayed evening tea, when Jayanti at last left for her father's home after taking only her second cup since the morning. To emphasize her grievance she had not eaten any solid food for almost twenty-four hours despite her condition. Subhadra had expressed her solidarity with her by eating only an apple.

The solution, which had been offered by the sons to the surprise and disappointment of their father, consisted of the promise that neither of them would donate his kidney without the concurrence of his wife! The wives, though secretly delighted and relieved for the time being, were no less surprised in view of their husbands' great love for their sister. They explained it by the thought that the promise was expedient and liable to be repudiated at a pinch, as neither of them would let his sister die; or that they depended on them to release them from it, if an emergency arose. However, it didn't contain the assurance that steps would be taken to get the kidney of a needy person by paying him. The wives also had another cause for anxiety: they and their husbands would be blamed everlastingly in the event of the sudden and unexpected death of Sarika from some other cause. Besides, both were fond of their sister-in-law and wanted her to get well as soon as possible.

Before entering the car that was taking her to her father's home, Jayanti had, with a bulging abdomen and flashing eyes in a face haggard from 24 hours' fasting and indignation, served her father-in-law and his sons with a stern warning, which Subhadra had endorsed: The household shouldn't hope for peace until their real demand was met.

Thus, the so-called resolution of the crisis had without appeasing the daughters-in-law left Jawaharlal and his sons with two equally grim options: Either they should be prepared to sacrifice Sarika's life or wait for the appearance of an altruistic donor who would also magnanimously overlook the brothers' failure to do what they expected of a stranger. As regards the first course, it was no longer a secret that the suffering girl had been won over to their point of view by her sisters-in-law and had openly said that she did not lose her right to life for the sake of a morality to which she did not subscribe. In fact, she was deeply aggrieved with her father for his refusal to buy a kidney to end her suffering. The second course was no less objectionable. If Jawaharlal, though wavering precariously sometimes, was secretly loath because of his sons to accept the kidney of a stranger, his sons felt that they had no right to expect such sacrifice from a stranger; in fact, they found it abhorrent.

Meanwhile, the sons thought that as according to the doctors there was no danger to their sister's life for a long time yet, the transplant could be safely postponed. And they could wait for the appearance of another person like the unfortunate lawyer who would have the wits to get around their father's gratuitous scruples.

They reminded themselves that they had not lured the lawyer by stealthily offering him money or by any other dishonorable means. Jayanti's uncle had honestly told him all the facts and circumstances, including the risk that he might get nothing, leaving him to decide for himself. He had considered them and finally come of his own accord. They hoped that in view of his love for his daughter their father would deal more reasonably and humanely with a newcomer. They had several poor cousins, who had been profuse in their sympathy for Sarika. Their hopes mainly rested on them. The cousins had heard from Subhadra and Jayanti about Jawaharlal's meeting with the lawyer and expressed their surprise at their uncle's treatment of him. Some one of them, Vishwanath and Srinath secretly hoped, might voluntarily offer his kidney in the expectation of being rewarded handsomely afterwards by his uncle, and their father might accept his offer because it was made by a near relative. But the cousins, though poor, had after discussing the matter among themselves decided that primarily it was the responsibility of Sarika's brothers and father to save her life, in which they had failed for reasons that were not convincing. They also thought that for them to offer their organs to their own cousin in the hope that they'd be rewarded by their uncle was not honorable.

While Subhadra and Jayanti thought the difference between their and their husbands' points of view insignificant, the latter considered it important: They were prepared to present a donor with a handsome purse representing the family's gratitude after the transplant in the unlikely event of their father failing to do so, but found it repugnant to surreptitiously lure a poor and helpless man through an agent, who was bound to be unscrupulous.

However, despite honestly believing that the difference between an ethical and unethical act was sometimes even slighter, they were uncomfortably conscious that their belief that helping a proud man in great distress like the lawyer was not the same thing as buying a kidney was also influenced by their fear.

Chapter 4

4/1

Chandrmukhi and her husband jointly owned four establishments in four different commercial areas of Delhi. Three or four days a week they traveled from one to another and met people in connection with their business. The remaining two or three days they operated from home. Without the benefit of any professional training, they managed their business profitably. After a busy day, they yearned for intellectual and aesthetic enjoyment. They visited art exhibitions, plays, music concerts, seminars and symposia at India International Centre, Sriram Kala Kendra, Triveni Kala Sangam and other elite centers, or discussed political affairs and cultural events at home with their friends. Without feeling any less grateful to them for their kindness to him, Jaiprakash attributed these activities also to their hedonistic disposition and culture, which urged them to earn as much money and enjoy as many decorous pleasures as were within their reach. They had a wide circle of friends and acquaintances and kept open house. Few were formally invited but any friend could drop in and have a drink or dinner or both. The people present at these evening parties, described flatteringly by some as Chandrmukhi's "intellectual evenings", generally discussed current affairs. If an important event took place, the number of visitors could be as large as a dozen.

So extreme was Chandrmukhi's intolerance of Hindu nationalism, which she contemptuously described as Hindutva, that only her husband, besides such of their business associates as were too important to be displeased and whom she dismissed as provincials and illiterates, had the privilege of frankly espousing it in her presence. Vishnu owed this privilege to Chandrmukhi's deep emotional attachment to him dating from their childhood and the close relationship between their families from before their marriage. They had grown up together and studied in the same classes in the same school, college and university. Besides, he was by nature genial and kind and as handsome, elegant and sophisticated as anybody she had ever known. His gentleness exerted on her ardent temperament a soothing influence, which she craved. Even then, as Jaiprakash would learn from Dr. Awasthi more than two years after he had joined her service and when she had already committed suicide, with an adoring smile she used sometimes to say to her intimate friends, that she would never have married him if she had known him to be a latent Hindu nationalist. But before their marriage Vishnu had never evinced any interest in politics. He was only interested in the novels and short-stories of Maupassant, Graham Greene and Somerset Maugham and in cricket and tennis. After their marriage, when Chandrmukhi began to hold her evening parties where Hindutva-bashing was fashionable, he, although a rationalist, gradually emerged as a champion of Hindutva or at least a critic of its sweeping condemnation. But Chandrmukhi had already begun to dote on him. Secondly, what was as effective as their deep emotional attachment to each other and their unflagging libido in preventing any friction between them, was the fact that both, having been born and brought up in mutually related rich merchant families, shared an inherent desire to augment their wealth. This fact Jaiprakash thought would by itself have sufficed to take care of their allegiance to antagonistic political ideologies. And in spite of his sincere gratitude towards both wife and husband, he used to observe with distaste and lack of charity typical of a poor man's naiveté and ignorance of the culture of affluent intellectuals, whether leftist or rightist, how they often held prolonged closed-door conferences with income-tax officers and financial experts, from which they emerged with smiles on every face. He did not doubt that at these meetings they discussed far from ethical means of earning money and evading taxes. Quite often, these consultations were followed the same evening by animated discussions on such momentous subjects as whether the disintegration of the Soviet Union was the greatest tragedy in history; how far were the progressive elements in the country themselves responsible through their complacency and vain mutual dissensions born of personal likes and dislikes for the increase in economic disparities and the number of people living below the poverty line, particularly among the Dalits; what should now be done to retrieve the lost ground and defeat the forces of reaction, etcetera. These discussions would sometimes go on till after midnight, sustained by innumerable rounds of drinks, delicious snacks and sumptuous meals financed by the money unethically saved through the ingenuity of chartered accountants and suborning of Government officers. By the time the dinner was over and most of what had been discussed under the influence of liquor blissfully forgotten, few persons seemed fit to drive their cars without causing an accident. Taxis used to be called for the people who had no vehicles and lived out of the way and their drivers given the addresses of their occupants.

4/2

Within a few months of joining their service, Jaiprakash had begun to feel and behave as though he were a member of the family. Apart from discreetly conforming to Chandrmukhi's views, in order to enjoy her respect as a knowledgeable person, and diligently performing his tasks to her and her husband's satisfaction, he made no conscious effort to ingratiate himself with them. Without realizing it, he impressed them with his natural and unstudied demeanor. Now he not only ate breakfast, lunch and dinner with them, he didn't feel constrained to leave their presence even when wife and husband got into an argument. Their differences of opinion were generally pleasant to listen to because of Vishnu's indulgent willingness to change the subject with a smile if they seemed irreconcilable and her tacitly affectionate acknowledgement of this fact.

After a hard day's work, Jaiprakash also needed relaxation and intellectual entertainment. With Chandrmukhi's and her husband's encouragement and a little adroitness, he had soon established himself as one of the better-informed and more articulate members of her intellectual set. As much from policy as out of respect and gratitude to her for her kindness, however interesting the subject, he carefully avoided expressing his views on it if they would disappoint her or force him to dissimulate. On the whole, however, there were enough grey areas and it was easier than he had thought to honestly express views that pleased her. Instinctively aware that benevolent and intellectually sensitive wealthy leftists like her and some of her friends sometimes suffered qualms about enjoying the plethora of pleasures available to them as heartily as they would have liked to in the midst of so much poverty and inequity (how heartily they still enjoyed them!), he let go of no opportunity to severely criticize the existing social and economic inequalities, which they personified. Generous acceptance of their own oblique criticism by him soothed their conscience and they applauded him for his candor and eloquence.

From the discussions at the evening parties which Jaiprakash heard attentively, it soon became clear to him that although Chandrmukhi was not sure of the real political views of many of her friends, or even whether they had any definite views at all, yet she gladly chose to believe what they said and welcomed them no less warmly, valuing friendship above all! This pleased him, as it confirmed his belief that much of the anti-Hindutva, anti-American and anti-liberalization rhetoric was basically devoid of malice and was aired fashionably, yet without any uncomfortable consciousness of hypocrisy, in order to enjoy an evening. That even the sincerely dedicated leftists, who had suffered for their convictions, and who still desperately hoped for the resuscitation of the nearly lost revolution, felt grateful for the sympathetic opinions expressed by people who they could divine didn't care this way or that. He had further observed that some of her Muslim friends who occasionally attended the parties had also noted the fact that like conscientious parents the Hindu leftists epitomized by Chandrmukhi and Somdutt scathingly attacked the slightest deviation from modernization, liberalism and the right to freedom of expression by their co-religionists and even encouraged Muslims to censure it. But they were chary of criticizing the Muslims' regression into the madarsa culture and their inflexible adherence to their antediluvian personal laws. They were content to treat Muslims as victims in perpetual need of their "secular" sympathy and support against Hindus who suggested that they were insular or doubted their patriotism. They were like a psychiatrist who said to himself that his patient might eventually be cured if not aggravated. However, unlike a psychiatrist they thought that meanwhile they could exploit him to their maximum advantage. This they did to the extent of forgetting their patient's interest. What they did not realize was that their so-called patient was perfectly healthy in his own way, was aware of their hypocrisy and selfishness and distrusted and despised them all the more because he had no alternative to keeping their company against the Hindu fundamentalist Bharatiya Janata Party.

4/3

In such a richly furnished bungalow with well-kept flowered lawns where Jaiprakash sometimes visualized gay, irrepressible children who were doted upon and often lovingly reprimanded, Chandrmukhi and her husband, childless even after nearly a decade of marriage, seemed to feel no longing for them. Both were young and full of zest. Chandrmukhi was in her early thirties and her husband looked even younger. She made regular visits to the beauty parlor and Vishnu was always well-groomed. Despite Chandrmukhi's decorous conduct and genuine modesty about her handsome figure, Jaiprakash felt that she was too human not to be pleasantly conscious of her sexual attraction to some of her intellectual companions. In fact, if she hadn't been as much interested in the social and political questions of the day as she was, and which lent a certain dignity to her sex appeal, her attractions would have been grosser and more irresistible to the same friends. Jaiprakash keenly watched her relations with a flamboyant journalist, Somdutt, who worked in an English newspaper. In his articles he particularly attacked his own class, the affluent urban elite. This man, who lived with his father, a retired Major General, in a posh colony of Delhi, had many other qualities that attracted or repelled an almost equal number of Chandrmukhi's and her husband's friends. He dressed smartly, some thought too smartly, spoke excellent English and Hindi, which like others Jaiprakash also envied, owned a second-hand but new-looking imported car, to which Jaiprakash enviously likened his opinions. Like Chandrmukhi and her husband he was also a member of Delhi's elite clubs. What surprised Jaiprakash was what he regarded as Somdutt's double life. Despite his frankly, not to say snobbishly, expensive and epicurean lifestyle, he not only deplored the plight of the people living at the destitution level, but did so with such transparent sincerity as though he personally experienced their hardships! After dictating his write-up vividly describing their pathetic condition and denouncing the Government policies for being responsible for it, he drove to the Gymkhana Club, India International or the Press Club of India for drinks and his favorite meal of butter chicken, paranthas, orange juice and ice cream, or whatever he took a fancy to. If anybody accompanied him, as Jaiprakash had done more than once at his cordial invitation, he continued to deplore the gross economic inequalities while attacking the sumptuous meal with a lusty appetite. Although with an indigent intellectual's mentality, Jaiprakash dismissed such sympathy as self-satisfied and worthless, he couldn't help acknowledging that his criticism of the system was at least intellectually honest. And he couldn't but recognize the difference between him and the people who were equally affluent but who incessantly complained of the rising prices of luxury items because of the Government's flawed taxation policies. They seldom thought of the poor, and when they did, mostly talked about their own servants, whom they described as not only no less contented with their lot than them but luckier and happier in the absence of the hassles which plagued the rich.

Jaiprakash had observed another fact. The leftist intellectuals like Somdutt, who were mostly well off, used the power of the media to encourage the Hindu low-castes and poor Muslims to keep their banner of victimhood flying. And the Hindu communalists and affluent rightists, despised by the former as reactionaries or political philistines, scorned them for their hypocrisy and accused them of disturbing public peace in order to remain in the limelight and gain power. Yet, because of their congenial life-styles as well as their fervent belief in the freedom of expression, these two sets of people also heartily socialized with each other and gladly intermarried. The obligation of keeping their irreconcilable political and ideological differences alive was discharged by their respective followers, most of whom were chronically poor, uneducated and "uncultured"; who often came to blows on the streets, were lathi-charged, tear-gassed or fired upon by the police and thrust into jail, thus giving their leaders an opportunity to engage in a war of words in the legislatures and through the media.

Jaiprakash had noticed that though Somdutt's and Chandrmukhi's views were more or less similar on almost every subject, particularly the "exploitation and persecution" of the Dalits and the poorer sections of the backward castes and the threat to the country's pluralism and multi-culturalism, yet it was with her that he had more animated and extended discussions than with those whose opinions differed from his. More often than anyone else he stayed for dinner to round off his unfinished talk with her over a couple of more drinks. Though Chandrmukhi's husband was almost invariably present during what he later contemptuously described to Jaiprakash as 'unloading of piffle', it was mostly as a polite listener.

4/4

Notwithstanding his dislike of Somdutt, Vishnu was blissfully happy with his wife, who reciprocated his passion with a frank sensuality which delighted him. But lately it sometimes made him anxious when he thought of the mutual attraction between her and Somdutt. They had taken to each other from the very first day of his introduction to them about a year ago by their common friend, Syed Murtza Ali. Although Vishnu could see that his wife's and Somdutt's liking and respect for each other were sincere and disinterested, yet, he also realized that such relations were the more likely to lead to an affair than ulterior motives, which might repel one or both parties. And he had been unable to forbear jealously observing their mutual behavior from the very beginning. His misgivings, which he earnestly tried to discount, were also based on the fact that in a matter of only a few weeks Somdutt, with his frank appetite for free liquor and good food, had become a frequent visitor. He seldom departed without eating and drinking his fill. He was also encouraged by Vishnu's formally polite requests to him for the pleasure of his company, which he also owed to his frequently renewed determination not to give way to jealousy!

Somdutt praised their whisky and food heartily, which, seeming like prompt repayment, instead of pleasing Vishnu, further irritated him. He deplored such insensitive lack of inhibition on his part. In a few months he had cooled towards him. Mistaking Somdutt's self-importance for self-respect, partly because Somdutt himself was incapable of distinguishing between them, he had begun to hope that he would detect the lack of warmth beneath his host's polite veneer and stop coming or at least come less often.

But soon he had realized that he would have to adjust himself as best as he could to his visits. Somdutt was too vain to perceive mere hints of being unwelcome and wouldn't stop coming as often as he liked in the absence of more overt signs of his visits being disagreeable. Such candor was beyond Vishnu, what with his fear of displeasing his wife and his inability to transgress etiquette. While thinking of some way of getting rid of him, Vishnu meanwhile found himself obliged to welcome him with uncomfortably phony smiles.

Sometimes, Somdutt, who used to attend the evening parties about twice a week, didn't come for several weeks. One day, on Jaiprakash's mentioning one such long absence to his predecessor, Charles Smith, with whom he had become close friends, he learnt that he was chasing after Chandrmukhi's younger sister, Harimohini, who was also a journalist. She had been transferred to Bombay some months ago by her editor.

Charles further told him, 'When Harimohini was posted in Delhi, she was a frequent visitor to her sister's evening parties and in the beginning Somdutt used to come more due to his interest in her than in Chandrmukhi. She's even more beautiful and graceful than her sister. However, according to Mr. Jawaharlal's daughter-in-law and her intimate friend, Subhadra, she seems to have rejected him in favor of a social activist, Govind Kumar Mehta, whom she came to know when she interviewed him for her newspaper a few months ago. He is reported to be a famous man and at present working for the welfare of the gas victims of Bhopal. He was an IPS officer before he resigned or was dismissed from service for serious dereliction of duty.

'This is surprising,' said Jaiprakash. 'He's friendly with Chandrmukhi to the extent of making her husband uncomfortable. At the same time he was also chasing after her sister! He's not a very discreet person. That's why Harimohini may have turned him down.'

'But his interest in Harimohini was of a different kind. He desired her as a wife, and as a lover only if she wasn't interested in marriage, as sometimes appeared to the despair of her father and sister. She's only a couple of years younger than Chandrmukhi, who has been married for over ten years. According to Subhadra and other common friends, in the beginning he was encouraged by her attitude. Or maybe he misunderstood her. Then she came to know Mehta and became indifferent to him.'

'What was the attitude of Chandrmukhi and her husband?'

'Chandrmukhi advised her to marry Somdutt. However, Vishnu is reported to have told her to be wary of the man.'

'It's surprising. Anybody else in his place would have endorsed Chandrmukhi's advice. Their marriage would have relieved him of his jealousy, especially as you think that she is even more beautiful and graceful than Chandrmukhi. I have no doubt that Chandrmukhi is an honest woman and a devoted wife despite her open admiration for Somdutt.'

Charles replied with a smile, 'Vishnu doesn't want to see Somdutt's face, let alone accepting him as a near relative. If at present he makes him jealous by admiring his wife because her political views happen to be similar to his, after marriage to her sister, he would have become his brother-in-law and much more difficult to get rid of.'

The next day Jaiprakash informed Charles, 'I've just come to know that Harimohini has decided to marry her boyfriend Govind Mehta and her father is greatly upset. He asked Chandrmukhi to dissuade her from "committing suicide" and when she refused to interfere, he shouted at her that he won't give his hard-earned money to a penniless man from a backward caste.'

Chapter 5

5/1

Vishnu's relations with his wife for the first time began to be seriously complicated following the announcement by Prime Minister V.P. Singh of the acceptance of the Mandal Commission Report, which had been put in the cold storage by his predecessors, Indira Gandhi and Rajiv Gandhi. If he denounced Singh's adoption of it as cynical opportunism and divisive of Hindu society, she defended it as calculated to remedy social injustice. Actually, Vishnu was not much interested in social and political issues and he wouldn't have minded her opinion, which he knew to be sincere, hadn't it been expressed in endorsement of Somdutt's view. The decision of the BJP President, L K Advani, as a riposte to Singh's Mandalization of the Hindu society, to proceed on a 6000-mile rathyatra from the Somnath Temple in Gujarat to Ayodhya to mobilize Hindu support in his party's favor further aggravated their relations for the same reason.

These developments provoked a media war between Hindu nationalists and Hindu leftists-casteists. The latter were aware but did not much bother that most educated and even uneducated politically conscious Muslims believed that they were primarily interested in their votes and not in their development. They did not bother because they felt assured that Muslims had no alternative but to politically align themselves with them against the Bharatiya Janata Party.

This contention made Chandrmukhi as aggressively anti-Hindutva as Somdutt, and her husband more jealous and resentful of him. Instead of treating the concurrence between their views as normal, Vishnu's jealousy made him contest them more strongly than he would otherwise have cared to do. As if at the same time he also wished to reassure himself that his wife loved him too much to feel concerned about her ideological compulsion to side with Somdutt against him! He had never been jealous before; at least she had never perceived it. Nor had he held his political views so strongly. She was therefore puzzled by the intensity of his reactions to her and Somdutt's views. Finally, one day after months of doubt, she understood its real cause, or her doubts were confirmed. However, to her delightful surprise, the same night as soon as they were in bed, he was especially tender. As if he had divined her anxiety and wished to reassure her that though she had guessed aright, there was no need to worry or that as the husband of an adorable woman like her, he deserved to be excused if sometimes he couldn't help feeling jealous!

One day when the situation in the country was particularly tense with the media full of the usually exaggerated and commercially sensationalized reports of clashes between Hindus and Muslims in various parts of the country, Somdutt was in a pensive mood. His ideological fervor had as usual caused him to consume more whiskeys than he otherwise did, a coincidence which had not escaped Vishnu's jealous watchfulness. While denouncing the Congress Party for not stopping Advani's rathyatra when it passed through Maharashtra and Karnataka, where it was in power, he downed another peg. He asserted that the majority of Congressmen, including MLAs, MPs and Ministers secretly sympathized with the anti-Babri Mosque movement as much as the supporters of the BJP. All of a sudden, to everyone's surprise, he began to attack Prime Minister VP Singh, whom he used to admire. He blamed him for being chiefly responsible for the present atrocious situation in the country by not arresting the BJP President L. K. Advani before the beginning of his rathyatra. He hadn't arrested him, he said, because he wanted to remain Prime Minister with the support of the anti-Muslim Bharatiya Janata Party. He looked at the bottle, but checking himself with an effort began to blame the media for having exaggeratedly publicized the rathyatra instead of killing it by not particularly noticing it. After delivering himself, he looked at the bottle again and this time was unable to restrain himself. Downing a large peg neat, he brushed away what looked like a tear. Vishnu had never seen his wife so moved. When he entered his car to go home around midnight, she anxiously asked him to drive carefully. Vishnu was shocked.

During Somdutt's declamation, Vishnu had as usual contested his views not so much because he differed from them or cared what he thought as because he couldn't bear to see his wife so deeply affected by them. To his dismay, it was not Somdutt but she who had rebutted him.

That night she was too excited by the discussion to respond to Vishnu's caresses.

Before he fell asleep, however, with the ingenuity of a jealous husband needing respite from his anxiety when it became unbearable, he managed to calm himself. He imagined himself to be a leftist like Somdutt and the latter a Hindu fundamentalist! There was little doubt that she would have been immune to his dangerous charm and violently clashed with him. With her magisterial temper, she might even have forbidden him her house! Within twenty-four hours they were reconciled.

Soon, however, he could not help observing that Somdutt had been becoming less and less circumspect in disguising his admiration for her, of which he believed she was aware, and was hopefully watching for an opportunity to become her lover. He did not doubt that if possible Somdutt would seduce her with a clear conscience, considering it no betrayal of his host's hospitality to seduce his wife if she was also willing, because the ethos of their society entitled him to this right. It imposed on the wives and husbands the responsibility to prevent their spouses from being enjoyed by a friend, who, exposed to the same risk, was merely exercising his or her right to have as much pleasure as possible. Somdutt had another advantage which the self-centered affluent philistines in his society lacked: His sense of moral and spiritual fulfillment due to his sincere devotion to the ideology of freedom and equality for all, for which he would have gladly endured any adversity, though there was near zero possibility of any such misfortune, left no room for guilt or remorse in any other sphere.

Although Vishnu thought it extremely unlikely that a sensible and dignified woman like Chandrmukhi would go so far as to succumb to him, yet he could not forgive her for encouraging his hopes by taking his side against him openly, when she might have been discreetly a little less categorical.

5/2

Chandrmukhi's and her husband's mutual fondness and shared interest in accumulating wealth failed to bear the strain of the slaughter of the would-be demolishers of the Babri Mosque from October 30 to November 2, 1990 at Ayodhya. On these days, when heavily armed policemen specially deputed by Chief Minister Mulayam Singh Yadav allegedly murdered hundreds of devotees of Lord Ram, causing the narrow lanes of Ayodhya to flow with Hindu blood, Somdutt vied with Syed Murtza Ali in describing these so-called devotees as anti-Muslim ruffians, who deserved to be mowed down for trying to pull down a historic monument and a symbol of co-existence and multi-culturalism.

While like any "reasonable and fair-minded Hindu", as Vishnu considered himself, he could forgive Syed or for that matter any Muslim for venting his spleen against the so-called secular but, in reality, a Hindu India, where Muslims were contemptuously left free to choose to be governed by the antediluvian All India Muslim Personal Law Board with the scornfully tacit approval of the government and treat themselves as a separate nation and civilization, and consequently distrusted and discriminated against, he could not excuse his wife for enthusiastically endorsing similar views expressed by Somdutt.

The next day at breakfast, as Chandrmukhi was consulting with him about the purchase of some shares and they were having a minor difference of opinion, such as they often had, Jaiprakash was stunned by Vishnu all of a sudden losing his temper and walking out without finishing his coffee. He looked at Chandrmukhi. Her face was devoid of astonishment, as if she had been apprehending some such behavior from him. She also did not look perturbed. Jaiprakash had no difficulty in guessing the cause of his outburst. He had more than once glimpsed it last evening itself. Having been a keen observer of their conflicting feelings towards Somdutt, he felt worried. His position in the household could not remain unaffected by the strained relations between wife and husband. He might be one of its first casualties by embarrassing them with his presence; after all, he was a servant.

What Jaiprakash did not know was that last night, feeling remorseful for the distress her support to Somdutt had caused her husband, Chandrmukhi had tried to induce him to make love, knowing from experience that her tenderness would assuage his resentment. Although he hadn't responded, she had felt assured that he was too loving a husband not to feel appeased by her desire to conciliate him. She was right. Two days later, Jaiprakash found them behaving with each other with their usual good humor. He was relieved. A couple of more such incidents finally reassured him that his position was safe!

At night Jaiprakash would often reflect with pleasure on the unlooked-for change in his status in this household, which was due to the kindness and generosity of both wife and husband. One of the reasons for this change, which he did not consider an unmixed blessing, was that the family, consisting of only two persons, could easily accommodate a third, provided he was agreeably compatible with both of them. He had never found any difficulty in getting along with Vishnu due to his easygoing nature. As regards Chandrmukhi, it meant, first, that his intellectual level should be at par with hers; secondly, and this was very important in view of her opinionatedness, his views on important social and political issues should not vary much from hers; and, thirdly, that he sincerely esteemed her as a person. The first and third conditions he fulfilled easily. Especially the third; he found her not only big-heartedly benevolent but also possessed of feminine charm. As regards the second condition, his understanding of her hadn't changed a bit, nor had his decision from the first day he met her to consider it essential in his position as her personal assistant to express views that pleased her. Yet he couldn't help occasionally regretting the fact that he was not perfectly frank with one whom he deeply respected and who highly regarded and trusted him.

Chapter 6

6/1

One day three months after her departure for her father's home, Jayanti, who had been delivered of a son, telephoned Subhadra from her room in the hospital to enquire if their father-in-law and husbands were still determined against buying a kidney and as impervious as before to Sarika's suffering and indignation at her father's attitude. She received the answer she feared.

'What else has happened?' Jayanti asked.

'I have come to know that Papaji is thinking of publishing an appeal in a couple of national dailies for altruistic donation. Right now they're in the drawing room and perhaps discussing the content of the appeal. I am not supposed to know it, but I have confidentially learnt about it from Charles Smith. As you know, he keeps me informed about their thinking because he sympathizes with our view that there is nothing wrong in paying for a kidney, if the donor is a genuinely needy and responsible man like the lawyer. The suggestion for issuing such an appeal was made yesterday by CP Ramnath in Charles's presence, and after some hesitation Papaji accepted it. He had not yet mentioned it to our husbands when Charles confidentially told me about it.'

'I know about the appeal and if I knew that Papaji had been persuaded to issue it I would've told you,' said Jayanti, surprising Subhadra. 'In fact, it's the idea of my judge uncle. At my request to him to think of something else after the fiasco with the lawyer, he asked C P Ramnath, when the latter came to dinner last week, to suggest to Papaji to issue such an appeal. CP said he had already learnt about the crisis in our family from Papaji and the appeal was not a bad idea. I was upset to hear the uncle's suggestion, but kept quiet during their talk for fear of vexing them. Such an appeal seemed to me so embarrassing that I thought that CP would laugh it off. It also occurred to me that perhaps my uncle had secretly begun to think that chiefly it was the duty of the brothers to save the life of their sister instead of expecting an outsider to do so. Perhaps uncle expected that our husbands would reject the idea of the appeal for shame and offer to donate their kidneys. Had I known that uncle was going to make such a suggestion and CP would agree to pass it on to Papaji as his own idea, I would've dissuaded him. It's hardly decent to issue such an appeal; it has already begun to be talked about that neither of the patient's two brothers is willing to part with his kidney to save the life of his own sister. Although I have no doubt of the integrity of our stand, the fact remains that it's we who're mainly responsible for their inability to help their sister.'

Jayanti added, 'So CP has convinced Papaji of the propriety of issuing such an appeal?'

Subhadra said, 'Yes. And, according to Charles, Papaji probably thinks, though you can never be sure about him, that apart from the question of ethics, it is also a better way to get a donor than by paying clandestinely, which wouldn't remain a secret for long. Neither Papaji nor our husbands would ever do such a thing. And from the way Papaji asked the unfortunate lawyer if he'd accept something as a token of his gratitude and then offered to help him without accepting his kidney, it's hard to doubt that the person who donates his kidney would be handsomely rewarded afterwards. For practical purposes, there's no difference between our and his points of view except that it would gratify his vanity that he had not violated his principles. Perhaps he secretly hopes that our husbands would offer their kidneys instead of letting such a humiliating appeal be published.'

She added, 'Although, I also think it unwise to issue such an appeal, but since it would be futile to try to dissuade him, let's hope that some local man in distress who has heard of his famous meeting with the lawyer will have the gumption to get around him. As for your qualms about us having pressured our husbands and their being described as craven and selfish, there's no reason for us to feel guilty. It is in accordance with our conviction, which has been appreciated widely, that if one can afford it there's nothing wrong in paying an honest man in distress for his organ. I have no doubt that most people no less principled and affluent than Papaji will do so with a clear conscience if they can do it without injuring the donor. As for our husbands, our known opposition would serve as their defense and mitigate their criticism? The critics can't deny that they underwent the tests and were ready to donate. Between us, I don't think that either brother, considering his passion for physical fitness, was eager to part with his kidney in spite of his love for his sister. I wouldn't be surprised to know that they were scared to think that there was no honorable escape for them, and are now feeling relieved to have yielded to our pressure. They wouldn't have done so, if they were determined; apart from prolonging the suffering of Sarika, they wouldn't have been unmindful of the criticism which would follow. They now hope that something would turn up and their sister's life would be saved without their losing their organs. Perhaps another person like the lawyer would appear and Papaji would now choose to believe his profession of altruism in view of Sarika's mental suffering and grievance against him. He has no other option if he refuses to buy a kidney. At the same time I have no doubt that if he remains adamant and nobody responds to the appeal, and if, God forbid, the worst comes to the worst, neither brother will hesitate to donate his kidney despite his assurance to his wife, or his fear, if it's a fact.'

Jayanti said, 'Yes; they won't let their sister die. Meanwhile, as you think, they're shrewd enough to understand that our widely published opposition would tone down their criticism for backing out at the last moment. They realize that few men would disregard such violent opposition from their wives and make their family life unhappy for something which can be obtained honestly and without injuring anybody by people who are as affluent as we are. By the way, have you lately talked to your friend, Mrs. Chandrmukhi Narayan? What does she think now after Papaji's notorious meeting with the lawyer? She'd also be aware of what our friends and acquaintances say behind our back.'

'I talked to her only last evening. She still thinks that if the patient has brothers, an outsider's kidney shouldn't be sought except in an emergency. She didn't explain what she meant by emergency and I didn't ask. Perhaps she meant that if the brothers were reluctant to give their kidneys even if their sister's condition was serious. However, she also said that saving the life of Sarika was of the first importance. She was critical of Papaji's treatment of the lawyer. She said that if he was already skeptical of the donor's motive because of the well-known fact that the patient had two brothers, he shouldn't have agreed to the Judge uncle's request to meet him.'

'Still, she doesn't agree with our view that since we're in a position to pay, obtaining the kidney of a good and honest man like the lawyer, whose wife is gravely ill, by paying him is ethical?'

'Not unreservedly. She has learnt about our point of view from Charles, who has also told her that he fully sympathized with it. She was rather vague, but in the end she conceded, perhaps because of her high opinion of Charles's good sense and integrity, that in view of the lawyer's circumstances a contrary view was possible. She said again that Sarika's life must be saved if it can be done without causing injury to the donor. She didn't elaborate and I didn't press her, because I think that helping a voluntary donor in distress such as the lawyer can't be described as injuring him. As for what others or our common friends and acquaintances who attend her evening parties think, I didn't ask her. It would have meant that we're nervous of adverse criticism, which, frankly, I am not bothered about, because only what the critics would think in a situation similar to what we're facing would have any worth.'

'Basically, however, she doesn't sympathize with our view?'

'No. But if she were in Papaji's position and had agreed to meet the lawyer, she'd have accepted his offer. As he hadn't demanded money, Papaji had no right to doubt his motive and subject him to a humiliating interrogation.'

'We haven't gone to her evening parties for rather a long time now. Since it became known that we had prevented our husbands. Did she ask you why you had stopped attending them?'

'She merely asked me to come to the party next Sunday? She obviously knows the reason for our no longer attending them. I have no doubt that she appreciates the fact that though we are sincerely convinced of the righteousness of our stand, still as it also coincides with our private interest, we wouldn't like to get into an argument with anybody about it. And it would be no less awkward if people conspicuously avoided discussing our predicament in our presence in order not to embarrass us.'

Before ringing off, Jayanti asked, 'Anything else? I guess that lately Papaji and our husbands have perhaps stopped discussing current affairs due to their mutual embarrassment.'

Subhadra replied, 'Not at all! It's an important source of intellectual entertainment to them, especially to Papaji, besides diverting their minds from their mutual embarrassment. Yesterday, as I was passing by his office, my attention was arrested by the voices of Vishwanath and Srinath. I paused for a moment to know if they were talking about the appeal. But they were criticizing VP Singh for visiting the Golden Temple to apologize in his capacity as Prime Minister for the Operation Blue Star, obviously for the sake of Sikh votes, while he had not only not said a word against Indira Gandhi when she carried out this Operation but had continued to behave like her lackey. For the same purpose he has also declared Prophet Muhammad's birthday as a gazetted holiday, though perhaps no Muslim country has done so. Charles, who was present, also told me that he had behaved like a beggar to the Imam Bukhari of Jama Masjid by going to him and beseeching him to issue a fatwa to the Muslims to vote for his party in the coming elections. According to the Bharatiya Janata Party grapevine, he had assured the Imam that if he became PM, he would prevent the demolition of the Babri Mosque even if it resulted in the Saryu River's waters becoming red with the blood of the devotees of Lord Ram. The Imam had smiled sarcastically to remind him what he had done only a few months ago; he had tried to placate the rambhakts by issuing a midnight ordinance taking over the land around the Babri Mosque to hand it over to the karsevaks to build a temple there on the conclusion of LK Advani's rathyatra, obviously after the demolition of the mosque. But he had been so frightened by the fury of Muslims, whose votes were also needed by him for becoming Prime Minister, that he had withdrawn the ordinance within 24 hours. Unabashed by the Imam's smile, whose meaning he could not have missed, he's reported to have responded by prostrating himself at his feet and putting his head on them. Finally, he voluntarily promised the Imam that he would do everything possible to facilitate the infiltration of Bangladeshi Muslims into Assam and to enable them to acquire Indian citizenship under the porous IMDT Act, 1983. As you know, Papaji is campaigning against this Act in collaboration with some BJP—sympathetic lawyers. At last he succeeded in extracting a fatwa from the Imam in his favor. Although it is not possible to say how much of all this is true, but what can't be denied is that he who boasts of being an uncompromising secularist didn't scruple to go to the house of a miserable fanatic like Imam Bukhari to obsequiously flatter him. According to Charles, father and sons have started talking about the current affairs as before without any embarrassment. They have become used to things as they are, which is as well for the time being.'

6/2

All of a sudden, Jawaharlal said, 'The discord in our family and our meeting with the Aligarh lawyer have become known.'

The sons had learnt from Charles that a few days ago during their return from hospital after dialysis Sarika had looked at her father with such hatred that he was appalled. Afterwards, he had told him that in future for her own sake he would avoid accompanying her to the hospital.

'Such things can never remain secret,' said Srinath, wondering at his motive. He seldom said anything without some purpose.

'We shouldn't bother about what busybodies say,' said Vishwanath, looking at his brother.

Jawaharlal, who had once again been disappointed in his hope that after he had refused to accept the lawyer's kidney his sons would offer theirs, hadn't yet mentioned CP's suggestion to them. However, he would formally consult with them in accordance with the custom of the family that before taking the final decision on any serious matter the three of them should as far as possible consider it together, even if the father had the last word. If Jawaharlal hadn't followed this custom before putting all those unnecessary questions to the lawyer, it was because his sons had also, after undergoing the tests, succumbed to their wives' pressure without first talking to him. Nor, as he had expected, had they told him afterwards that their assurance to their wives was merely intended to pacify them for the time being. Had they done so, he would have waited. He recalled the day when he and the doctors had waited and waited in vain at the hospital for the brothers to turn up. At last, they had received a call from Jayanti informing him that the operation might be postponed for the time being due to "certain unavoidable circumstances"!

Today Jawaharlal's hesitation was due to his fear that his sons wouldn't go along with him, although as an occasional exception he would publish the appeal in spite of their dissent. He felt that they might object precisely to what CP considered the strong point of the appeal: The father of the sick girl is a rich and charitable person who abhors the traffic in human organs. They might think it embarrassing and ridiculous to make such a boast in view of the fact that the patient has two brothers. But then the patient's having two brothers was a fact and Sarika did not lose her right to life because of it. Jawaharlal knew that his sons were unhappy with him about his treatment of the lawyer. Later, he had also felt sorry to have put all those questions to him. He had also been shaken and humbled by his refusal to accept his offer of help. But despite wavering sometimes to the point of giving in, he remained loath to accept an outsider's kidney, whether he was an altruist or a man in straitened circumstances, when his daughter had two brothers. That he had still decided to issue the appeal was because of his fear for her life, which was made even more unbearable by her anguish and grievance against him and the dreadful possibility that she might suddenly die with hatred in her heart for him and her brothers during her last moments. She had already been on dialysis for a long time and the doctors' assurances that there was no danger to her life were always qualified by the possibility of their being proved wrong for reasons they couldn't foresee. If she were suffering from some incurable disease, Jawaharlal was strong enough to have by now become reconciled to the idea of her death.

Vishwanath looked at his watch. Then he looked at Srinath to remind him that they were late for the gym.

Seeing that they were about to leave, Jawaharlal at last decided to mention CP's suggestion.

'I was going to tell you something that CP suggested a few days ago and which seems to me to offer a way out.'

'What did he suggest?' asked Vishwanath excitedly. He had a high opinion of CP's intelligence and good sense. Although a man of principle, he was not overly squeamish like his father.

'He suggested that we might consider issuing an appeal through the press for altruistic donation. The appeal will state at the outset that the patient's father is a wealthy and charitable person who abhors the commerce in human organs. Therefore, only such persons should communicate with him as don't expect anything for their kidney except the humble and everlasting gratitude of the patient and her relatives and friends. Contrary to my opinion, he thinks that far from being immodest and self-adulatory the description of the father as a wealthy and charitable person, being a well-known fact, will serve our purpose better by impressing persons of altruistic disposition. He further thinks that in addition to upholding our principles, such an appeal will silence our critics by our seeking honestly and openly what others don't scruple to procure secretly and by dubious means. I am telling you exactly what he said.'

Jawaharlal quietly watched his sons' faces for their reaction. He hadn't lost hope that their self-respect would prevent them from assenting to such an egregious appeal. It was bound to dismay them to think of their criticism the appeal would provoke. It might enable them to disregard their wives' opposition, or overcome their fear, if they were afraid. For some time he had begun to think that perhaps there was also an element of fear in their succumbing to their wives' pressure.

'It seems an acceptable suggestion in the circumstances,' said Vishwanath after some hesitation caused by the thought that the appeal would draw widespread attention to the fact of the patient having two brothers. At present only their friends and relatives knew about Sarika's condition. And according to his information most of them hadn't expressed surprise, or had kept their thoughts to themselves, at her continuing to be on dialysis in spite of having brothers. And even fewer had openly censured them, because they were generally respected for their good nature and honesty. If any friends or relations happened to talk about her illness they said that the opposition by the wives was a problem difficult to ignore. There were still others who, imagining themselves in the brothers' position, thought that for a rich person living lavishly there was nothing wrong in obtaining a kidney by paying for it and were critical of Jawaharlal's treatment of the lawyer and his "pretensions to holiness".

Vishwanath was again surprised to recall his father's bungling with the lawyer, with whom he deeply sympathized. He felt great respect for him for spurning his charity in spite of his desperate circumstances.

'At the moment, there appears to be no alternative to it,' Srinath agreed, feeling that his father had detected his secret dissent. He knew that father had already made up his mind to issue the appeal and disagreement would be useless. After a minute's uncomfortable reflections he added, 'However, there is no need to write that the father of the patient is a wealthy and charitable person; it's a well known fact. Besides being immodest, it is liable to be misunderstood.' He thought, 'People are bound to notice that the fact that Sarika has two brothers has been conveniently omitted from the appeal! Perhaps at our request! It would make our position even more embarrassing. And hasn't it occurred to him that some people may be thinking that we enjoy his secret approval? As a matter of fact, there's no need to issue such an appeal at the moment as her condition is quite good. If he had behaved sensibly with the lawyer, Sarika would have received his kidney, his wife would have received proper treatment, there would have been no need to issue any appeal and the whole matter would be on its way to being forgotten.'

Like his brother, he also sympathized with the lawyer and admired him for his refusal to accept his father's charity.

'In fact, mention of your being wealthy and generous is liable to be misunderstood not only by our detractors but even by our well-wishers. They might think that since our meeting with the lawyer we have become desperate and it's a veiled hint that now the donor could expect secret payment for his kidney,' said Vishwanath. He added, 'Of course, we'll pay our humble tribute in an appropriate form to an altruistic donor after the transplant. I am confident that he won't refuse our prayer!' As soon as the words were out of his mouth, he grew painfully self-conscious. The next moment he grew even more embarrassed to see that his shrewd father had divined it. Desperately trying to suppress his embarrassment, he said to himself, 'It was so humiliating to doubt the word of a man in such tragic circumstances after he had said that his offer was altruistic. I wonder how he felt when he paid him back in the same coin by spurning his charity.'

'Of course, I would express my gratitude to an altruistic donor in an appropriate manner, if I'm left with no alternative to accepting such a man's kidney, but doesn't it ever occur to them that a person who has the compassion and moral strength to ignore the fact that the patient has brothers may also refuse to accept anything?' thought Jawaharlal, who had noticed his sons' embarrassment and dismissed it with scorn.

Srinath said, 'Maybe, it's also unnecessary to mention your abhorrence of the traffic in human organs; it's also a well-known fact and would sound like a boast.'

Vishwanath supported him.

Jawaharlal agreed to drop the mention of his wealth and philanthropy but insisted on retaining his abhorrence of the traffic. To him it constituted the only justification, however slight, for issuing the appeal, when the patient had not one but two brothers.

A few days later the appeal was drafted by CP, vetted by Jawaharlal and by Subhadra's doctor father, who checked that her blood group and other necessary information was correctly given, and after the last-minute mortifying scruples on the part of the brothers finally issued over the name of the patient's father. To overcome the hesitation of Vishwanath and Srinath CP impressed upon them that the criticism provoked by the circumstance that such an appeal was issued despite the patient having brothers would be more than balanced by the fact that "you refused to be guilty of secretly buying a poor man's organ, which you could have easily done".

'Far from balancing the criticism, it would make our position even more embarrassing,' thought Vishwanath, wondering whether the shrewd CP was making fun of them. He looked at Srinath, whose reflections were similar to his brothers.

Although the brothers remained uneasily conscious of their awkward position, in the end their sense of shame at their fear, the thought that they had no right to prolong the suffering of their sister, who was perhaps secretly aggrieved with them also, as well as their grim determination to take the risk of losing a kidney and probably suffering a serious injury, if an emergency arose, or if nobody responded, had prevailed.

Chapter 7

7/1

It was more than three months since the publication of the appeal for altruistic donation of a kidney by Jawaharlal. Although he had begun to regret it even before it was published, nobody had responded. The stress of waiting as well as the appeal's criticism had begun to take its toll. Now the critics included some of those who had earlier not commented on the fact because it was Jawaharlal's family affair that his daughter continued to be on dialysis in spite of having two brothers.

Besides, there were the relations and friends of Jawaharlal and his sons, persons of good will and sympathy for them in their predicament, who had begun to say openly, some of them had told so to their faces, that their problem was bogus; that if they were lucky to get the kidney of an altruist, few would believe it, and if they did believe, consider it honorable because of the brothers; indeed, they could depend upon being accused of humbug, whereas few would find fault with them if they took the organ of a genuinely needy person like that lawyer and paid him generously. Some of these critics sympathized with Vishwanath and Srinath, considering their fear not unnatural and excusable. Instead of praising Jawaharlal for his integrity, they criticized him for tarnishing the image of his sons. They said that it would have been ideal if one of the brothers had given his kidney to his sister. 'But sometimes one can't overcome one's fear, or disregard his wife's opposition. It doesn't mean that he's not a good man and should be defamed.'

Still others said that Jawaharlal had no right to expect his sons to make their family life unhappy by ignoring their wives' protests for something which could be obtained without difficulty by a rich man like him.

As regards the fact that Jawaharlal had offered to help the lawyer without accepting his kidney, while some grudgingly praised him, there were others who accused him of moral arrogance and perverseness for humiliating him by first doubting his word and then turning him away because his self-respect would not allow him to accept his charity. Sometimes the discussion of Jawaharlal's conduct extended to moralists in general or persons with pretensions to morality. There was no doubt that most of them were pests without whom the world would be a better place.

After another month had gone by without any response to the appeal, Jawaharlal was advised by his wife and sons to take a holiday and visit his brother in the USA, who had invited him twice since Sarika became ill. The reason for their advice was only partly the distress which his daughter's illness was causing him and from which they wished him to get some relief. Another reason was a disagreeable controversy inflicted upon him by Syed Murtza Ali, a rival lawyer. Syed was exasperated with Jawaharlal not only because he had recently lost a couple of important cases in which he had appeared against him but also because Jawaharlal had been actively associated with the people involved in the shilanyas (foundation laying) of a Ram Temple near the site of the Babri Mosque. The controversy had its origin in a speech Jawaharlal had delivered as the principal speaker on the legacy of Gandhi at a function organized about a month ago at a predominantly Muslim and riot-prone city of Uttar Pradesh by a local body named Ahimsa Parmo Dharma (Non-Violence Is Supreme Virtue) on January 30, the 44th anniversary of Mahatma's martyrdom.

Syed, who was also a famous intellectual and political commentator, was another important speaker at the function. He had been specially invited by the organizers because now even insincere praise of Gandhi dictated by good manners by eminent Muslims like Syed, who were known for their not very high opinion of him, was considered valuable by the Mahatma's devotees eager to ensure him universal sainthood. Since his death Gandhi like all great men had also come to need more and more defense from his critics and periodical reaffirmation of his image as a moral and spiritual giant in an increasingly materialistic and cynical world as well as due to the mercenary conduct and corruption of most of his professed followers.

As for Syed, who felt painfully inhibited by the circumstance of being a Muslim from giving full expression to his caustic evaluation of Gandhi, he was forced to content himself by describing Gandhi's devotees as fakes, with which even most Hindus who sincerely reverenced the Mahatma agreed. Jawaharlal was also included in the Syed's long list of sham Gandhians.

In fact, Jawaharlal wouldn't have accepted the invitation if he had known that Syed, who had been deeply chagrined by the loss of the cases, had also been invited.

In his speech Syed, who had been exasperated by Jawaharlal's long-winded and platitudinous eulogy of Gandhi and expatiation on his legacy of non-violence and message of Hindu-Muslim brotherhood and secularism, somewhat irrelevantly recalled the report of an unofficial fact-finding mission, which had been headed by Jawaharlal. It had been charged with uncovering the truth about allegedly one of the most infamous cases of atrocities committed against Muslims at Hashimpura, a place only a few miles from where the function was being held. The cause of this so-called Police-Muslim encounter, Syed claimed, was the politically opportunistic opening of the locks of the Babri Mosque at the instance of Prime Minister Rajiv Gandhi in 1987, which had resulted in Hindu-Muslim riots at many places, including Hashimpura, and loss of hundreds of mostly Muslim lives. Looking at the smiling faces of the bearded Muslims present in the audience, Syed recalled how the government had condoned the cold-blooded murder of 40 Muslims of Hashimpura by the police on the ground that all of them were charge-sheeted professional criminals given to breaking the law and order for personal profit or even wantonly, causing the death of innocent citizens, and hence deserved to be liquidated. Syed further claimed that the police had murdered these Muslims soon after the visit of the Union Minister of State for Home, Mr. P. Chidambaram. Despite the wide publicity of this massacre in the media, the Government had never conducted a genuine inquiry and the guilty policemen had gone virtually scot free. Syed deplored the fact that the only real or ostensible protest against this crime had been made not by a secularist but by the self-confessed Hindutvawadi, Subramanian Swamy, who had gone on a highly advertized indefinite fast at the

Boat Club, which had ended within a week, with the sole aim of politically embarrassing Prime Minister Rajiv Gandhi.

Reverting to the unofficial fact-finding mission's report headed by "an eminent Gandhian" he described it as full of rationalizations and half-truths intended to whitewash the heinous crime against Muslims.

Incensed by such boorish personal attack on him, Jawaharlal had retorted with equal vehemence, accusing "certain communalist charlatans" of posing as secularists and increasing Hindu-Muslim antagonism.

The clash between them had been enthusiastically taken up by the almost exclusively Hindu media. The resulting controversy between the two men was carried on by it for a whole week with the routine aim of assuring the skeptical Muslims, with little hope and still less concern, of the genuineness of Indian secularism by questioning the secular credentials of as many Hindu politicians and intellectual activists as possible. Jawaharlal, being a Hindu and his accuser Syed as well as the victims of the Police action being Muslims, had naturally come out the worst. It had further increased his depression due to the illness of his daughter and his regret at having issued the appeal for altruistic donation of a kidney despite having two sons.

7/2

Himanshu Mukherjee was standing in front of the massive iron gate of a palatial house in a posh colony of New Delhi. Jawaharlal, Advocate, Supreme Court, according to the brass nameplate at which he was looking with mixed feelings, was the name of its owner or tenant. The grand building, there were many such structures around, had awakened in him an inbred bias against the rich professing fastidious morality, and he was feeling ill at ease. Would he have come here, if he had known that the writer of that apparently honest and austere appeal was a wealthy man and the girl with damaged kidneys his daughter? The condition laid down in the appeal that the donor should not expect anything for his organ except the humble and everlasting gratitude of the patient and her relatives and friends constituted the heart of the matter. It had deeply touched him and after a few days' irresolution brought him here. At this moment, he was uneasily conscious of his altruistic wish to save a life being threatened by his skepticism, which had suddenly rendered that moving condition dubious. He wondered whether there was a law prohibiting the sale and purchase of human organs to dodge which the appeal had been published. Now the appeal seemed impartially capable of attracting a selfless donor or a shrewd agent or, he couldn't help thinking, even an educated unemployed person living in humiliating poverty, anticipating a price for his organ; there was no lack of such people in this country, whose corrupt rulers boasted of its being the world's largest democracy, who would gladly sell a part of their body or even welcome death instead of eking out a miserable existence.

The next moment he again recalled what had made him come here, and he forced himself to consider his options as objectively as possible. He reminded himself that though he was under no binding obligation to help the girl, her right to life and be the beneficiary of his donation was not automatically revoked by the circumstance of her being the daughter of a rich man.

'Whom do you want to meet, sir, and where have you come from?'

The question was addressed to him by a tall, middle-aged and uniformed security guard who had been talking about the corruption in all fields, especially politics, with his counterpart of the adjacent bungalow.

'Mr. Jawaharlal. And I have come from Calcutta,' answered Himanshu.

'He's gone to America,' replied the guard. His brother, who has settled in America, had invited him!'

'Is there anyone else who can meet me on his behalf?' asked Himanshu, hesitantly. He had come in a crowded second-class railway compartment filled with the suffocating stench of dried perspiration, urine and bidi smoke, to meet Jawaharlal with his extraordinary resolution. The resolution had been shaken by his magnificent surroundings, which smacked of exploitation of and callousness to the wretched of the earth like many of those with whom he had been traveling. Yet having come from so far away he felt reluctant to go back without meeting at least somebody who could speak for the issuer of the appeal. He wished to know about the circumstances of the appeal.

'His son, Vishwanath sahib, is expected any moment now. He's a professor sahib and a very learned man,' replied the garrulous guard, who never missed an opportunity to inform in as much detail as possible all newcomers about what his sahibs are and what they do.

He added, 'You can wait for him in a chair in the lawn.'

Observing the suddenly troubled expression on the face of the young man, who seemed pleasantly respectable and in some urgent need, the guard had decided not to let him go back disappointed.

'The suffering girl has a brother too!' thought Himanshu with still greater astonishment. Then it occurred to him that maybe his kidney does not suit his sister or there is some other problem.

No sooner had the guard spoken than a Mercedes Benz stopped in front of the gate.

The security guard turned from Himanshu and bent down to address a young man sitting beside the driver.

'Sir, this sahib has come from Calcutta to meet Papaji,'

The young man himself opened the door of the car and stepped out. He exuded affability and gentleness, which momentarily disconcerted Himanshu's critical reflections about the rich.

Himanshu introduced himself but didn't tell the purpose of his visit.

'Mr. Jawaharlal has gone abroad. Please come in,' said Vishwanath, with that graceful politeness with which he was accustomed to address the educated and well-dressed persons. Towards the poor, uneducated and ill-clad he had a benevolent demeanor. He politely waited a few seconds to enable the visitor to make up his mind before repeating the invitation.

All of a sudden, remembering that his father's appeal had also been published in the Calcutta Statesman, he was alarmed to think lest Himanshu should have come in response to it! Caught between their fear of surgery and the loss of a kidney, and the shame of accepting an altruist's organ he and his brother had been unable to decide how they would respond to the situation created by the possible arrival of a person in response to the appeal and the unpredictable reaction of their father. Lately they had begun to hope that the appeal had been forgotten.

Thankfully, father had gone abroad.

They walked into the bungalow together. Himanshu all of a sudden felt nervously uncertain as to whether, if this man asked him why he had come, he should state the reason. Although he had not changed his mind about donating his kidney, yet in the last few minutes he had decided to first fully acquaint himself with the circumstances of the appeal before taking a final decision. And till then not to reveal the reason for his visit. His nervousness increased as he felt that there was no time to invent a plausible answer. His mind went blank as he realized that even the slightest delay in replying to the question, which seemed imminent, might give rise to an uncharitable suspicion in the mind of this aristocrat.

The appearance of a slightly older and similarly impressive man with a busy look, who seemed to have something important to tell Vishwanath, temporarily reprieved him.

'Hello, Charles. Any news?' said Vishwanath.

'Yes. Mrs. Chandrmukhi Narayan telephoned a few minutes ago. She wanted Papaji's advice about a little problem she's facing in that case which he's handling. I told her that we would call him tonight and get back to her tomorrow.'

The three entered the drawing-room together. Requesting Himanshu to take a chair and wait, Vishwanath went out with Charles.

Charles said, 'Papaji asked about the general condition of Sarika and whether any altruist had responded to the appeal. I told him that there was no response but according to Subhadra's father her general condition was good and there was nothing to worry about. I was tempted to tell him that it seemed too late for a response; the appeal was published more than four months ago and would have been forgotten by now. You also think so. He also wanted to know about the anti-Babri Mosque Movement and whether the prospects of an amicable settlement between Hindus and Muslims had improved. I told him that on the contrary they had become worse.'

Before leaving he asked Vishwanath, 'Who's this man?'

'He has come from Calcutta to meet Papaji,' Vishwanath replied with a significant look, startling Charles.

He added, 'I have a feeling that he has come in response to the appeal. And he has probably learnt from the security guard that I am Jawaharlal's son!'

They looked at each other and understood each other's thoughts. Charles thought of going back to his office, leaving Vishwanath to deal with the visitor unhampered by his presence. He would have liked to help him in his predicament but didn't know how to. Vishwanath with his aversion to lying, especially in such a grave matter, would find it even harder in his presence to evade telling the man anything but the humiliating truth about himself, if he asked any awkward questions.

Before he left, however, it occurred to him that the man could have some legal business.

He said so to Vishwanath, who agreed. In the absence of Jawaharlal his cases were dealt with by Charles.

7/3

The luxuriousness of the drawing room momentarily distracted Himanshu's thoughts from the immediate problem before him: what should he say in reply to the inevitable question about the reason for his visit? However, the ostentatious display of wealth, which made him uncomfortable, also restored his self-confidence.

'Supposing the brother's kidney doesn't suit the sister, even then isn't it strange that people so wealthy should issue an appeal for altruistic donation? They should have had enough sense to realize that hardly anybody who like them is also in clover would respond to it!' he thought. The next moment he couldn't help vaguely reflecting that his sacrifice might not be such a big deal for these wealthy aristocrats! When he had first made up his mind to donate his kidney, his decision was untainted by vanity. But at the sight of such opulence in the midst of which his kidney seemed like a trinket, a reflection that for a moment mortified him, he had a change of heart and felt a vague longing for appreciation of his sacrifice, if he should still decide to make it. The words of the appeal that the donor would earn the humble and everlasting gratitude of the patient and his relatives and friends now seemed no more than gracefully formal and even a tribute to the issuer's own gentility!

He happened to look at the large oil painting of Gandhi. It increased his uneasiness. The association of Gandhi with rich men had always seemed to him bizarre. The greater attractiveness of the Mahatma in his loin cloth to the rich and the men in power than to the poor, whose appearance of poverty he imitated and obviously wished to make respectable in order to prevent excessive materialistic aspirations and the harboring of grudges against their exploiters, had always repelled him. Likewise, the devotion of the rich like this Supreme Court lawyer to high principles, which were too expensive and beyond the means of the poor, seemed to him an aggravation of injustice to the latter, who were forced to violate their honesty in order to survive. It was beyond Himanshu's imagination that as an idealist and a devotee of Gandhi Jawaharlal regarded his family's opulent lifestyle as immaterial and trivial because happiness depended not on high living but high thinking and devotion to moral principles.

Vishwanath returned accompanied by Charles.

'If you have some legal business, Mr. Charles Smith will deal with it. He's Mr. Jawaharlal's junior,' said Vishwanath, introducing Charles to Himanshu.

'May I know your name, sir, and where are you from?' asked Charles.

'I live in Calcutta. My business is with Mr. Jawaharlal. When is he returning from abroad?' said Himanshu with sudden presence of mind. At the same moment he also anticipated, correctly as it turned out, the next question as well as the answer he would give.

Charles looked at Vishwanath, who said, 'He might be away some time. I am his son and you can tell us your business. We're in regular contact with him and if it's urgent, he'll be informed without delay.'

With increasing self-assurance Himanshu said, 'I would rather talk only to Mr. Jawaharlal! I can come back later. I'll give you my address.' He took from his pocket book a slip of paper bearing a friend's Calcutta address and telephone number and gave it to Vishwanath.

Himanshu watched Vishwanath quietly as the latter meditatively looked at the slip, the while apparently thinking of the possible reason for the visitor's refusal to talk to anybody other than his father.

'He seems to have guessed that I have come in response to the appeal,' Himanshu thought.

Charles also watched Himanshu keenly from behind his affable expression. He seemed to him too respectable to have come to negotiate a price for his or somebody else's kidney after reading the appeal for altruistic donation between the lines. The way he had avoided answering their question he might be an altruist. If so, what might he be thinking after coming to know that Mr. Jawaharlal is a rich man and his ailing daughter has a brother? How reasonable and natural if he had become irresolute or changed his mind. He wondered how Jawaharlal would have dealt with him if instead of Vishwanath it was he who had received him.

'Do they think I have come for money?' Himanshu was thinking, watching Vishwanath and Charles. He was disconcerted to reflect how well it accounted for his insistence on talking only to Mr. Jawaharlal, the issuer of the appeal. He felt sorely vexed. He longed to leave immediately.

Vishwanath disguised his thoughts with an amiable smile: There was no question of accepting the kidney of an altruist, if the visitor was such a person. The world was not devoid of such people. He hadn't ceased to wonder at his father's motive for publishing the appeal, which had tarnished his reputation much more than his sons'. Did he regret having published it? Did he run away to America to escape the criticism? Did he expect him and Srinath to feel ashamed and instead of allowing it to be issued, offer their kidneys? Did it never occur to him that irrespective of whether we were afraid or not ignoring our wives' violent opposition would have seriously disturbed our married life? Although he and Srinath sometimes felt embarrassed before their friends and acquaintances about not giving their kidneys to their sister, they felt even more embarrassed to think of the opprobrium their father had earned. Almost everybody he knew was far more inclined to excuse them irrespective of whether they were afraid or had yielded to their wives' pressure than forgive their father for issuing such an appeal.

'I think I may go back to my office,' said Charles to Vishwanath, giving Himanshu a keen look. Months later, he would tell him that after hearing his reply he had immediately guessed that he had come in response to the appeal, which had been published in The Calcutta Statesman.

'Yes, you can go,' said Vishwanath. He had decided to treat the visitor, who had come from so far away, with the utmost courtesy instead of nervously getting rid of him to escape possible embarrassment. Besides, if he was really an altruist, he would be the first really extraordinary man he would be meeting in his life! Like Charles, he also wondered how his father would have felt on meeting such a man. Would it have reminded him of his meeting with the lawyer whose wife was gravely ill and whom he had treated like that? Would he have felt ashamed of the treatment? And what would this man think if he were to know about that meeting and its sequel, the appeal and the trouble of coming all the way from Calcutta?

Presently he was thinking, 'It's quite possible that he is a decent man in straitened circumstances, but too cultured and sensitive to confess to him why he has come. Everyone knows that a public appeal can only be addressed to altruists. Maybe, he's expecting me to broach the subject.'

'In appearance at least he seems a gentleman and perhaps isn't too sure that I have come in anticipation of a price for my kidney,' thought Himanshu as he got up to leave, endeavoring to feel at ease and wishing not to carry away an unpleasant remembrance of the visit, which had caused him so much physical and mental distress.

'Won't you have a cup of tea with us?' said Vishwanath.

Himanshu reluctantly sat down, feeling it would be impolite to refuse. The invitation also seemed to rule out the possibility, which had occurred to him a moment ago, that perhaps they had already received a kidney.

He involuntarily recalled the spiritual joy of the first moments after he had taken the decision to donate his kidney to save the life of a young girl. That decision was now tainted by his bias against the rich, his vanity and desire for recognition of his sacrifice and his and Vishwanath's mutual doubts.

They began to talk at random about irrelevant subjects with mutually polite evasiveness, afraid of the possibility of the real reason for Himanshu's visit unexpectedly cropping up. Neither of them as yet felt sure enough either of himself or of the other to comfortably deal with it. Both needed time to decide their responses. Vishwanath couldn't help thinking that he was the brother of the patient and had yielded to his wife's pressure from fear, a fact that he had hidden even from her and his father! How shameful would it be to lie to this man, if he should mention the appeal, that he had yielded to his wife's pressure from fear of the disruption of his family life! Even this explanation was humiliating to the entire family! He said that he had visited Calcutta twice. The first time he had gone there with a friend was to watch a Cricket match between India and England, which in truth was no more than an excuse, as his real object was to see an interesting city about which he had read a lot. He had met the great Satyajit Ray and visited Mother Teresa's Nirmal Hridaya. Himanshu said that it was his first visit to Delhi. They exchanged their impressions. The cordiality of Jawaharlal's son soon began to soften Himanshu's bias against the rich and his distaste for the ostentatious affluence surrounding him, which by violently contrasting with the moral courage of the appeal had upset him. As for its circumstances, Himanshu was already conscious of his waning interest in finding out about them.

Unable to resist his intense curiosity about the visitor, Charles joined them again with a teleprinter clipping, according to which the Khalistani terrorists had gunned down thirty-five Hindus at a market place in Amritsar. Vishwanath looked at the clipping and returned it to him. He was about to go back when Vishwanath, who had begun to feel awkward, asked him to stay and have tea with them.

Charles took a chair opposite Himanshu.

Presently observing that the conversation between Vishwanath and the visitor was flagging, causing embarrassment to both, he said to Vishwanath that he was reading an interesting book by Inder Malhotra.

Vishwanath looked at him gratefully, understanding the reason for his mentioning the book. Himanshu also began to feel more at ease.

'Which book?' asked Vishwanath.

'Its name is Trapped in Uncertainty. It is about the recent Indian politics.'

'It must be interesting. Malhotra is a brilliant journalist. I particularly like his style. Simple and concise. Elegant without literary frills and rich in content.'

Charles said, 'Malhotra has beautifully described the character of VP Singh. Despite being one of the wiliest politicians this country has ever produced he deluded all and sundry into thinking him Mr. Clean. During his election campaign with the sole aim of becoming Prime Minister, he used to take out his electronic pocket diary, display it to his audience, push two or three buttons and tell them that he had details of all the numbered accounts in the Swiss banks into which the ill-gotten Bofors money had been deposited. Then he would assure the audience that if he became Prime Minister he would expose the guilty persons, which meant Rajiv Gandhi and his relatives, within 15 days. The crowds would cheer him wildly. And he remained unabashed and self-righteous when after remaining in power for almost a year he failed to unearth even a shred of evidence.'

Charles added, 'In fact, his exposure as a hypocrite made him even more self-righteous. And more power hungry.'

Vishwanath agreed. 'These two qualities in him were complementary.'

The conversation again came to a stop for a minute but this time the awkwardness was dispelled by Charles asking Himanshu about the impact of the anti-Babri Mosque movement in Bengal where communists were in power. He said, 'In the Hindi-speaking states in particular, it is supposed to have its origin in the Hindus' anger at the amendment of the constitution by the Rajiv Gandhi Government to put the Muslim personal laws out of the purview of the Criminal Procedure Code. According to some jurists, the amendment violates the Article 44 of the Constitution. But maybe the Supreme Court judges, feeling snubbed by the Constitutional amendment, decided to keep quiet.'

Himanshu replied, 'Hindu—Muslim divide is as much a fact in Bengal as it is anywhere else in the country. However, isn't it surprising that Hindus should bother about the emancipation of Muslims from their medieval personal laws and social practices?

Generally speaking, the only time Hindus seriously think of Muslims as a community is when there is a communal riot or India has some trouble with Pakistan. Those who vote for the communist candidates in Bengal are also like Hindus in the rest of India. Hindus first and communists afterwards.'

Feeling relieved, Vishwanath said, 'Hindus in general are obviously not interested in the religious and social affairs of Muslims. And the anti-Babri Mosque movement was provoked not so much by the injustice and cruelty done to Shahbano, though there was genuine sympathy for her, as by the Muslims' coercive contempt for the Supreme Court judgment. Especially because it was delivered by Hindu judges. By interfering in Shariat they became kafirs or sinners in Muslims' eyes. However, that doesn't even remotely justify the anti-Babri Mosque movement.'

Continuing the conversation for its own sake as much as to relieve the embarrassment caused by the visit of the Bengali young man, irrespective of whether he was needy or an altruist, Charles said, 'What is surprising is that the Uniform Civil Code doesn't enjoy the support of the secular political parties like the Indian National Congress and the Communists. Even Nehru showed no interest in it. His secularism was for the sake of Hindus, whom he wanted to be modern and westernize. His open contempt for Muslim League and Jinnah clearly indicated his recognition of the inevitability and, I believe, also the desirability of the partition of India, irrespective of his political posturing. According to the English journalist, Ian Stephens of The Statesman, who interviewed him, he showed a special distaste for Islam similar to that shown by the British secular intelligentsia. It was hidden under his aristocratic and polished manner. After the division of India on communal lines and the Muslim representatives' violent opposition to a uniform civil code in the Constituent Assembly he didn't have much interest in the Jinnah-worshipping Muslims and left them to their own devices. He was already tired of fighting them during the freedom movement and taking advantage of the constitutional guarantee of freedom to every religious denomination to manage its own affairs astutely let them establish Shariat Courts, which he must have found abhorrent. Rajiv Gandhi, no less disdainful of the intransigence of the reactionary Muslim politicians than his grandfather, followed in his steps by passing the Muslim Women

(Protection of Rights on Divorce) Act. In doing this, he ignored the violent protest against the Bill by hundreds of progressive Muslims, who included seniormost diplomats and officials of the Government, a sitting member of the Planning Commission, a university vice chancellor and thousands of other Muslims who thought like them. '

He added with a smile, 'It would be no exaggeration to say that in this country Hindus regard Muslims as aliens who have voting rights with which they more often than not to their own detriment influence the outcome of the elections to the State Assemblies and Parliament. The position of Christians is much better, because they have little affinity with any non-Indian Christians.'

Feeling relieved that the conversation was veering away from the appeal in response to which he had come and hoping that soon he would be able to leave without it being mentioned, Himanshu said, 'It's no secret that politicians, and communists are no exception, are mainly interested in the Muslim votes. A friend of my father, who votes for the communists and whose father was a prominent member of the Communist Party, told him that the communists had no interest this way or that in the Indian Muslims' insistence on legally enjoying their archaic customs. However, this insistence is only partly because of the traditional Muslim antipathy to Hindus, whose demand for Uniform Civil Code is also not from purely charitable motives. The real reason was that Islam is innately against progress and is the worst enemy of communism. That's why during the freedom movement, the Indian Communist Party officially supported the demand for Pakistan. In a Hindu-ruled India, they had far better chances of coming to power. In a Muslim-majority undivided Bengal they would have been wiped out. They don't exist in Pakistan or Bangladesh. But the communists are rightly against the Hindu nationalists exploiting the Muslim intransigence for indoctrinating Hindus against them and disturbing communal peace. Nehru's approach was the best. Muslims should be left to their own devices.

Charles, wondering whether Himanshu could still mention the appeal and create a problem for Vishwanath, said, 'My experience is that whatever Hindu politicians might say, few of them are in favor of special dispensation for Muslims to promote their educational and economic advancement with the view of improving communal relations. Because, as a Hindu lawyer told me, educated Muslims are politically more troublesome and more critical of their treatment by the Hindus in power irrespective of the political party to which they belong than their poor and illiterate co-religionists. But it is also true that educated Hindus are more distrustful of the Muslims' loyalty to India than the poor and illiterate ones, who are content to treat their Muslim counterparts as untouchables. An illiterate Hindu Dalit would never drink water touched by a Muslim Dalit, while educated Hindu Brahmins don't mind eating and drinking with their Muslim friends.'

Vishwanath found himself wondering whether Himanshu was feeling contemptuous of his father. The next moment he said, 'The social divide and political mistrust between the two is as it was before India became free, which is proved by the Muslims' refusal to accept a uniform civil code.'

To change the subject which seemed to have been discussed too long, he added, 'I will inform you after my father's return.'

Himanshu smiled weakly, suddenly unable to repeat his assurance that he would come back on being informed. Both Vishwanath and Charles noted his reluctance, but considering that he had come to know that the patient had a brother thought it only natural. It seemed to confirm that he was an altruist, who had been surprised and become indecisive or changed his mind on coming to know that the patient had a brother.

'What do you do in Calcutta?' asked Vishwanath.

'Nothing at present. For a year, I taught Physics at a private college. I'm coming here from Agra after appearing at an interview for a lecturer's post.'

'It's rather difficult these days to be selected for such a post without a powerful recommendation.'

'I know and I'm not much hopeful of being selected, though my interview was very satisfying and I was the most qualified of the interviewees. Generally, a man is already working on the post and the interview is held only as a formality to regularize his ad hoc appointment. In fact, most of those who had come, and some of them had come from far away, thought so and were already reconciled to the almost certain prospect of being rejected. It would have been really hard for him to come otherwise, one of them said, and the others agreed with him. But, as they also said, you have got to take the chances that come your way and be prepared for the worst.'

Himanshu, who had already appeared at more than half a dozen interviews in vain, would have liked Vishwanath to know that he wouldn't have come for this one from so far away, but for his decision to donate his kidney.

Vishwanath said, 'But it isn't impossible. Even nowadays honesty and impartiality are not as rare as people are inclined to think.'

'That's true. Once in a while, a man is selected on merit.'

Looking at Vishwanath, Himanshu thought, 'It's the mark of a cultured man not to be too skeptical of the existence of virtue. At least he's worldly wise enough to know how an educated and cultured person is supposed to talk and behave to an educated and supposedly cultured stranger.'

The next moment Himanshu was again surprised to reflect that such nice people should have issued such an appeal. He tried to stop thinking and feeling bothered.

The tea arrived.

'Where're you staying?' asked Vishwanath, handing him his cup.

'At the New Delhi Railway Station. I'm feeling tired. I'll rest in the waiting room and take the night train for Calcutta.

'I'll come back on being informed about your father's return,' Himanshu forced himself to say after the tea was over. Although now he was far from being sure that he would do so, he saw no harm in showing his appreciation of what he thought a surprisingly courteous reception by this son of a wealthy aristocrat. He had been wondering as to why this man had been so graciously entertaining a stranger, who was not even prepared to tell him why he had come.

Himanshu got up and extending his hand said with a grateful smile, 'Thank you very much! I was feeling tired; the tea and the rest have restored me.'

'Please wait a minute. I'll have you sent to the railway station in my car,' said Vishwanath. It had suddenly seemed to him awful that such a civilized man who had most probably come from so far away after reading the appeal, irrespective of whether he was an altruist or was forced by humiliating poverty, should be disposed of with a cup of tea! He was deeply shocked to think that he might not be the only person to respond to the appeal!

Himanshu thanked him and declined. Vishwanath urged. Himanshu expressed his reluctance to put him to trouble. Vishwanath said it would be no trouble. Himanshu accepted. He wanted to get away as quickly as possible.

When the driver appeared, Vishwanath took the keys from him. He had impulsively decided to drive him to the railway station himself.

'Kindly get in,' said he, opening the door of the car, conscious of a vague yearning to extend his mortifying encounter with this man who had been shocked and suffered such enormous trouble not only because of his father's blunder but also due to his cravenness. Even if he was a needy person who had come in expectation of being paid for his kidney he was a gentleman who had been unable to bring himself to say so.

7/4

What should he say if Vishwanath again asked the purpose of his visit, though it was obvious that he had already guessed it? thought Himanshu anxiously, entering the car. Such a question seemed natural. Why else would he take the trouble of personally driving him to the railway station? After such a cordial reception, the repetition of the answer that he would talk only to Mr. Jawaharlal would be grossly discourteous. He had been unable to think up even a remotely plausible answer.

'I'll tell him that I came after reading the appeal and was disappointed!' he said to himself. 'I have nothing to fear!'

Soon the traffic became heavy. Presently each was not only thinking his own thoughts, which were vague and conjectural enough, but also wondering as to what the other was thinking. The silence was awkward. Each felt the other's awkwardness as much as his own.

'He may be thinking of my surprise that his father should have issued such an appeal in spite of having a son,' thought Himanshu, who had begun to feel almost sure that no health or biological problem of this brother of the patient was responsible for the appeal. 'Or, ignoring my statement that I would talk only to Mr. Jawaharlal, he would have asked me whether I had come after reading the appeal, and if I had said yes told me that the appeal had to be published because for such and such reason his kidney did not suit his sister.'

He began to look out at the traffic. Vishwanath quietly watched him and was impressed with his profile. A gentleman's profile! He escaped into agreeable reflections about the visitor. He was accustomed to do so in awkward situations, like all honest and good-natured affluent people used to the pleasure of thinking charitably without any inconvenience to themselves. He began to imagine that Himanshu was a noble man who had come to donate his kidney altruistically, though there was no question of his accepting it!

Both endeavored to think of something nice to say to break the awkward silence before they parted in a few minutes.

Himanshu had begun to feel embarrassed that in spite of having been so courteously entertained by Vishwanath and being personally driven by him to the railway station obviously in anticipation of hearing an answer to his question as to why he had come, he had kept silent. Should he now tell him without being asked again the reason for his visit? But if Vishwanath asked him as to what he thought now after meeting him, what would he say in reply? That he had changed his mind? That they shouldn't have issued the appeal? Although perfectly reasonable, the answers would be unnecessarily embarrassing and distressing to both of them after such a cordial meeting.

As for Vishwanath, as the railway station neared, if on one hand he felt nervous lest Himanshu should at last decide to ask as to why they had issued such an appeal, on the other he felt an irresistible wish to ask the reason for his visit. But the possibility, however remote, that with sudden boldness he might reply that after meeting him and knowing the facts he had read between the lines and now didn't mind telling him that he had come to offer his kidney for a price, deterred him. It occurred to him that this man was under no moral obligation to them not to demand a price for his kidney, frankly and honorably! Even more so as the patient had at least one brother and they were so rich! Their objection on ethical grounds against seeking a donor and offering him a price was their affair, not his! For the first time he realized how weak was their position, in spite of their ethical stand. The equation between them could not have been more unequal. He again realized how right Subhadra and Jayanti were, thinking from the donor's point of view, especially if he was in straitened circumstances and a sensitive and self-respecting person. He again recalled the humiliation of the Aligarh lawyer.

'I am sorry that the girl on dialysis is your sister,' all of a sudden Himanshu said and instantly regretted having done so. After all, he might never come back. He acutely felt that he had embarrassed a gracious man, who from delicacy hadn't asked him again as to why he had come. He tried to make amends: 'The appeal was extremely well drafted. After all, your father is a Supreme Court lawyer.'

But no sooner were the words "well-drafted" out of his mouth than he realized that he had committed another faux pas. As if he had said that the appeal was smartly drafted!

'The appeal ought never to have been issued at all because the patient has two brothers!' said Vishwanath to himself and he again remembered the Aligarh lawyer, whose wife was gravely ill.

'She's my younger sister. We're two brothers and a sister. She's the youngest. We all love her most tenderly. I'm grateful to you!' Vishwanath said. He felt relieved to have done what he owed to this young man—told him the truth. However, the next moment, unexpectedly recalling how father had conspired with the doctor to coerce him and Srinath into undergoing the tests, instead of frankly talking to them, he felt angrier than ever.

Concealing his surprise that the ailing girl had not one but two brothers, he said, 'I learnt about the appeal from a friend just by chance. It was published in The Statesman. I searched and found it. It was lucky. We are not particular about preserving old newspapers. Is her condition serious? I mean, does she need a kidney immediately?'

'Not immediately. One can survive on dialysis for a long time. Even for years, if one is young. According to the doctors, there are cases of people living on dialysis and enjoying good health for as long as ten years! But ultimately she has to have it,' Vishwanath replied, conscious of a longing to make Himanshu, if he was an altruist who had changed his mind, to think better of him than he did when he came to know that he was the girl's brother! However, his heart rate became uncomfortably rapid. He might ask the most natural question—whether neither brother's kidney suited her. There was no question of his telling an untruth, something which made him uneasy even in ordinary matters. But if this man was an altruist, which he now more and more appeared to be, what would he think to hear from him that his inability to help his sister was due to the violent opposition by his wife! Even this was not the whole truth, though her violent opposition, which had prevented him at a critical moment from donating his kidney, was a fact.

'So they yielded to their wives' pressure and decided to seek an altruistic donation, this man would think!' thought Vishwanath with dismay.

'Though surprised by the lack of an explanation as to why neither brother was donating his kidney, Himanshu didn't ask the question. He was equally afraid of the answer, which might not be creditable to this apparently honest man for whom he had taken a liking. As he had already ceased to think of donating his kidney, why should he go away completely disillusioned? A little scope for charitable speculation about his and his brother's inability to help their sister would be harmless. There could be compelling reasons for their inability, which couldn't be disclosed to an outsider. As it was, he had before him a long journey in squalid conditions.

However, to divert the conversation from the embarrassing subject, he said, 'What does your brother do? Is he also in the teaching line? I learnt from your guard that you are a professor in a college.'

'Yes. He teaches law in the local law college. After practicing for a couple of years, he switched over to teaching.'

The station arrived. Several security men were standing around and unobtrusively but sharply watching the occupants of every vehicle. They seemed to be waiting for the arrival of some VIP. Vishwanath couldn't remain in the station's porch a second longer than necessary. Besides the security men, there were the cars behind, impatiently waiting for him to move on. Himanshu got out and said, 'Thanks very much for the lift and everything else. Good-bye!'

7/5

Vishwanath was no less relieved than Himanshu. He was thankful that Himanshu was not a resolute altruist, or he would still have offered to donate his kidney. It would have been terribly awkward to apologize to him and refuse his offer. What would he have said if he had asked as to why then they had issued the appeal?

He could not help thinking again and more resentfully than ever of the way his father had treated the lawyer. They hadn't deviously lured him. He was a gentleman who had come of his own accord. Jayanti's uncle had honestly told him all the facts, which he had considered. Instead, he had issued such an appeal, which had made a laughing stock of them. He was again dismayed to think that another man like this Bengali might already be on his way to them with a copy of the appeal and his pathological report in his pocket!

Walking the platform in the opposite direction to a train that had just entered it, Himanshu mused about his meeting with this polished son of a wealthy man. He couldn't help feeling admiration for him. How easily he could have proposed a price for his kidney! Or was he too civilized and sensitive to muster the courage to do so himself but had been waiting all along for him to propose, and gone back disappointed? And although it was mysterious, yet how frankly he had said that his sister had two brothers and there was no hurry as one could live on dialysis for years together! In other words, it was perfectly all right if he had changed his mind after coming to know the facts about them.

The train had gone and the platform had emptied. The waiting room was overcrowded. He became conscious of a headache and felt tired. He wanted to stop thinking. But he had come from Calcutta, which now seemed a devil of a distance away, and wished to conclude his reflections on an agreeable note.

He failed to do so. Life was like that, he said to himself. It would remain a memorable adventure. When all was said and done, Vishwanath was an unusual man. He went to a paan shop, got a packet of cigarettes, a match box and two aspirins, which he washed down with a cold drink. Then remembering Inder Malhotra's book, a quotation from which by Charles had piqued his interest, he went to the railway bookstall to look for it and luckily got it. Settling down on a bench, he lighted up, opened the book at random and began to read. He would read a few pages here and a few there to first appraise the quality of writing before beginning from the beginning. He also wanted to forget what had just happened. He could not believe what he read. He read it again. The Union Home Minister had on a visit to Punjab issued armed licenses to the Pakistan-aided Sikh terrorists despite being aware that they were planning to murder at least one candidate in as many constituencies as possible, which would lead to the cancellation of elections in those constituencies. And he was doing so without any reference to the Punjab administration and supposedly with the connivance of the Prime Minister, Chandra Shekhar, on the understanding that the grateful thugs would help him get elected to Parliament in the forthcoming elections from a safe seat in that State. His wonderment at the fact of Chandra Shekhar not preventing his minister from indulging in such criminal activity was however short-lived. He recalled how only a few months ago he had allowed his thugs to soundly thrash the famous Supreme Court lawyer, Ram Jethmalani, who had gone to his house to offer Satyagraha against his conspiring to displace the then Prime Minister V P Singh.

7/6

'At last, a young Bengali came from Calcutta apparently in response to the appeal,' said Charles to Subhadra as soon as she entered his office.

'Where's he?' she asked excitedly.

'He has gone back.'

'Already gone back! When?'

'You missed him by less than ten minutes.'

'How's that? What happened? What did he want? Who talked to him? Why did nobody stop him?'

'He went back because he said he'd talk to no one but Papaji. He promised to come back after his return from abroad. Vishwanath has taken him in his car to the railway station. We may know more about him after his return.'

'What else did he say? I mean what were his terms? Did he mention them?'

'What terms? He won't even tell us why he had come. But it was apparent that he had come in response to the appeal. At present, we can only guess at what he wanted to talk about with Papaji.'

'Do you think he may have come for money? I always thought that that kind of appeal was more calculated to attract people whom Papaji would describe as venal or lacking in dignity and self-respect. I don't think anybody who gives a vital part of his body for money from dire necessity should be despised. Everybody love their body.'

'You misunderstand Papaji. He doesn't despise such people. He doesn't want to take advantage of their helplessness.'

'He considers himself morally superior to them. That's how he behaved with the Aligarh lawyer. He pities them, which is the same thing as despising them. They're equally entitled to respect. Some of them may be better persons than him! Does it ever occur to him? I wonder if he felt humbled by the lawyer's refusal to accept his help.'

Charles said, 'However, it is not impossible that the Bengali young man came for money, although he struck me as a different kind of person. So sophisticated and cultured. Maybe, he felt too embarrassed to ask payment for his kidney from a man looking as dignified as Vishwanath, even if he is in straitened circumstances and had come with that intention. He had tea with us and sat talking to us in the drawing room for over half an hour.

'What did they talk about? What's he?'

'He has applied for a college lecturer's post at Agra. He was coming directly after appearing at the interview.'

'Was he hopeful?'

'Not much.'

'So he came here not from Calcutta but Agra, where he had gone for the interview.'

'He could have gone back from Agra, instead of coming here. And he said he would come again.'

Subhadra was impressed. 'That's true; he could have gone back instead of coming here. He came with a purpose. What exactly did Vishwanath say to him?'

'He told him that he was Mr. Jawaharlal's son and he could tell him anything that he wanted to tell his father. But he said that he would talk only to Mr. Jawaharlal.'

'I wonder why he didn't talk to Vishwanath. How did he know that Papaji would be more amenable to his purposes? He was clearly being evasive. To come from so far away and go back without even hinting at what you want! It would have been understandable if he were a local man.'

Charles nodded.

She said, 'How I wish I had been present! Did you stay with them throughout?'

'I left them for only a few minutes.'

'I'm sure I'd have drawn him out. Vishwanath and Srinath are always so inhibited by peculiar notions of propriety and decorum. Do you think Vishwanath said something that caused him to change his mind? Or Vishwanath's manner discouraged him?'

'I don't think you'd have drawn him out.'

'Having come from so far away in response to the appeal, he deserved the courtesy of an honest exchange of views. If he had met me, I'd have asked him if he had come after reading the appeal. And if he had said yes I'd have explained that that's the only form in which an appeal for the donation of an organ can be published and that he need not feel embarrassed if he was needy. It's not the same thing as luring a poor helpless man by secretly paying him through an unscrupulous middleman. And if he were a resolute altruist, I'd have thanked him, expressed our inability to accept his offer and humbly apologized to him for the trouble the appeal had caused him.'

Charles said, 'If he was an altruist and had asked why neither brother was donating his kidney, what would you have answered? That you were in favor of buying a kidney because you could afford it?'

'I wouldn't have put it so crudely. I'd have said that I saw nothing wrong in getting the kidney of a man in distress and thus also relieving him of his problem.'

Charles said with an ironic smile, 'He happened to meet Vishwanath and not you. Do you think that Vishwanath could have told him without embarrassment that he preferred to pay for a kidney instead of donating his own?'

She replied, 'You're right. Vishwanath couldn't have said such a thing without embarrassment because he's in a way personally involved. That's why the appeal shouldn't have been issued. The only merit it has, if it can be called a merit, is that it might attract a needy person who'd be prepared to take the risk of being turned away by the implacable Papaji.'

She added, 'I wish I had at least seen him. I have no idea of how an educated and cultured man as you think him looks and talks who has come in response to such an appeal and suddenly finds himself being received by the patient's brother.'

'Vishwanath's embarrassment didn't prevent him from courteously entertaining him because he had come from so far away. It amounted to a brave invitation to him to open up, although I can't guess what Vishwanath would have said in reply to his questions. Vishwanath behaved like a gentleman, which he is.'

'What's he at present? What's his name?'

'His name is Himanshu Mukherjee. He's an M.Sc.'

'I hope Vishwanath draws him out and if he turns out to be a needy person they come to some sort of an agreement. That's why he has gone with him. Fortunately Papaji is away. They can't reach the railway station in less than half an hour. The traffic is heavy at this time and it may take forty to forty-five minutes. It's improbable, don't you think, that they should talk only about the weather and politics, with each uneasily conscious that the other was speculating about his thoughts?'

'I also think that maybe he has gone with him with some purpose though I can't guess it.'

'He's under great emotional stress and fortunately Papaji is away. However, it is difficult to guess exactly,' said Subhadra, hoping that her husband might try to find out whether the visitor was a needy person and had come expecting to be paid for his kidney and come to some sort of a gentleman's settlement with him. However, it would be tragic if such an educated and cultured young man as you describe him should have no alternative to selling his kidney. The Aligarh lawyer's circumstances were different and it would have been an act of charity to accept his kidney and pay him generously.'

Chapter 8

8/1

Jaiprakash was sitting in his office, checking against the revised original script the final typed script of the speech Chandrmukhi was to deliver at the seminar on Ayodhya organized by Syed Murtza Ali and Somdutt the following Sunday. He had recognized from its language that Somdutt had written it. She had made extensive changes in it, deleting or completely rewriting every reference to the "dishonest arguments" of "Hindu fundamentalists", which could be easily identified as exaggerated versions of her husband's views.

Suddenly Vishnu entered.

'What're you reading?' he asked casually.

Jaiprakash would have liked to hide from him that it was his wife's speech. He might wish to look at it out of curiosity and detect as easily as he had done from the various words and phrases that it had been written by Somdutt. Jaiprakash realized that he wouldn't be pleased to know that his wife had asked the man he disliked to write her speech. But he was unwilling to take any risk.

'It's Chandrmukhi's speech for the seminar,' he replied.

Vishnu stunned him by his behavior. It clearly pointed to his suspicion that like most of her letters to the editors, although Jaiprakash knew that he was wrong in thinking so, this speech had also been written by Somdutt. He literally snatched both the original and the final scripts from him and began to compare them. And as Jaiprakash had feared, his expression became grim and grimmer as he turned over the pages. Having finished, he handed the papers back to him and walked out without a word. His severe expression momentarily worried Jaiprakash lest, because of his wife's kindness to him, he should suspect him of being privy to her relations with Somdutt! However, his own relations with him were too good for his anxiety to last more than a few minutes.

'No wonder, he was not mollified by the fact that she had carefully deleted every offensive allusion to him,' he thought. 'How could he overlook the fact that Somdutt has the audacity and enjoys the familiarity to write in her speech anything derogatory to him?'

That day Jaiprakash had a luncheon appointment with Charles Smith. He cancelled it.

Lately, the incidence of clashes between wife and husband had again increased, mainly due to the latter's jealousy and tactlessness, though they were still quickly reconciled.

Jaiprakash was perturbed by Vishnu's reaction for another reason also and wanted to be present at lunch with them. He was anxious to see how he would behave to her. If he was really as angry as he feared, he might ask her if Somdutt had written her speech. He was afraid that if they quarreled she might think that he had shown the speech to her husband of his own accord! Jaiprakash's relations with her were not such that she could have confidentially told him that she wouldn't like her husband to know about the speech, yet there was no doubt that being a witness to the ups and downs in their relations and aware of their real cause he was supposed to have enough sense to take care! What had increased his worry was that despite the care he took to conceal his abhorrence of Somdutt for his insensitivity to his host's less than warm approval of him, which should have made him stop visiting his home long ago, she sometimes seemed to suspect it.

Contrary to his fears, however, throughout lunch Vishnu's behavior to her was not only amiable; it had an element of playfulness, which occasionally marked it when he was for some reason particularly pleased with her! Jaiprakash's surprise was short-lived. It occurred to him that Vishnu could not bear to be displeased with her for long and after having indulged his resentment had perhaps been appeased to reflect that, after all, she had deleted or modified everything critical of him! Or perhaps he had begun to feel confident of being informed by her sooner or later that her speech was ready and she had taken the help of Somdutt in drafting it. It was also possible that he had assured himself that she hadn't informed him of this fact because she thought it unimportant and not worth mention! He was capable of any such afterthought.

However, Vishnu's good-humor failed to persuade Jaiprakash that his unhappiness at his wife's friendship with Somdutt had lessened; it was no more than a symptom of his erratic behavior due to jealousy, which caused him to regard the same thing as obnoxious and, in no time, normal!

8/2

Chandrmukhi, her husband, Syed and Somdutt were sitting in her drawing room. Today Syed would have discussed with Chandrmukhi the particulars of the seminar on Ayodhya he had planned together with her and Somdutt during the next week. But now it would have to be indefinitely postponed because of the assassination of the former Prime Minister Rajiv Gandhi by a LTTE suicide bomber during his election campaign in Tamil Nadu. The assassination had saddened but also disappointed Syed because for a long time now it would be impossible to criticize Rajiv, as he had planned to do in his seminar speech. He was going to hold him directly responsible for the escalation of the Ramjanmabhoomi movement and the pernicious ideology of Hindutva by facilitating the opening of the locks of the Babri Mosque and the laying of the foundation stone (Shilanyas) of a Ram Temple near it with its clear message that in the near future the temple would replace the mosque. He had also started his election campaign from the mythological birth place of Lord Ram, which Syed regarded as pandering to the Hindu fundamentalists.

At the moment the main thought which occupied everyone's mind was whether it would bring to an end the rule of the Nehru-Gandhi dynasty with its legacy of problems and of whom the country had begun to feel tired. Despite the sympathy wave sweeping the country following his assassination, it seemed highly unlikely, if not impossible, that his wife Sonia would succeed him as PM even in the improbable event of the Congress getting a Parliamentary majority. Her eligibility was controversial and she won't take the risk of being sworn in and then forced to resign. According to some, she continued to be an Italian citizen, as per the Italian law, and was thus disqualified from becoming Prime Minister despite enjoying the Indian citizenship. She also lacked the brains to run the country with its plethora of problems. And she was considered practically illiterate not only by the neutrals but even by her sycophants who vied with each other for the honor of carrying her slippers. She would at best be a speechwritten Prime Minister. The thought that she might rule the country indirectly through the toadies of the dynasty, whose names and pictures along with their statements that she was the savior the country needed at the moment had already begun to appear in the national newspapers, was no less frightening. The alternative of a coalition of the opposition parties exercising power was considered still more disastrous because of the likelihood of the cunning and unscrupulous VP Singh or equally opportunistic and power-hungry Chandra Shekhar ruling as Prime Minister for a long time was appalling. The upshot of these reflections was that Rajiv had been the best Prime Ministerial candidate available to the country and his death was a national tragedy.

However, Syed, who hated the Nehru-Gandhi family even more than any member of the Bharatiya Janata Party, had been determined to attack Rajiv in his speech. He had also decided to mention the historical fact of Sardar Patel, Pt. G.B. Pant and many other prominent Hindu leaders before Rajiv conniving at or overlooking the act of smuggling of idols into the Babri Mosque in 1949. To appease the Muslims the mosque had been locked ostensibly to prevent the Hindu worshippers from entering it. Later Nehru's grandson, Rajiv Gandhi, had allowed these locks to be opened to let the Hindus enter it for worshipping the smuggled idols. Not only was the Muslims' demand for the restoration of the status quo ante brushed aside but the illicit act of the worshipping of these idols was legitimized by being shown on the State-owned Television!

In his determination to prove that Indian secularism was a farce Syed had ignored his brother's warning against publicly criticizing, as he had once done but had been snobbishly ignored for doing so by Hindu secularists, many prominent Hindu leaders, including Sardar Patel and Pt. G.B. Pant for watering the plant of Hindu communalism by not taking action to remove the smuggled idols. They were politically powerful enough to have done so without any risk, if they had wished to. His brother had further warned that he should realize that like them the present Hindu rulers were Hindus first and secularists afterwards and that, even if unexpressed, their grievance against Muslims for polluting and destroying their temples was as valid as the Muslims' objection to their desecrating the Babri Mosque by the smuggling of idols. His brother had further told him, 'Have you forgotten the fact that the controversial district and sessions judge, a Brahmin, who had ordered the opening of the mosque's locks to enable Hindus to worship the idols but forbidden the Muslims to enter it to offer prayers and thus pollute the idols, was later promoted as a High Court Judge with the acquiescence of the then Chief Minister, who now poses as the Muslims' lusty champion? It is a Hindu country. Don't be deluded by the so-called Hindu secularists, who enjoy the privilege of being Hindus, opposing the Mosque's demolition. They are merely glorifying their religion and showing off their magnanimity. An overwhelming majority of them who vote for any party, Congress, Socialist or Communist, would soon after the demolition, which you can take for granted, begin to expect Muslims to forget and forgive what has happened just as they would have liked to tell you Hindus had forgotten and forgiven the destruction of their temples. The Supreme Court has already dismissed the Muslims' case against the Shilanyas and the Hindus have already performed this ceremony. Even the liberals among them would deplore it less because it was shameful per se and more for tarnishing the image of their glorious religion and of the Hindu nation in America and Europe. Don't you remember how the demand of the lakhs of pious Muslims gathered from all over the country at the New Delhi Boat Club that the sacred Masjid be handed over to them was described as a threat to law and order by the Hindu politicians and the media?'

Although Rajiv's assassination had recalled to everyone the brutal killing of thousands of Sikhs all over the North India, especially in Delhi, in the wake of the murder of Indira Gandhi by her Sikh security guards as a revenge for her desecration of the Golden temple, none feared a similar reaction against the Tamils, as Rajiv, like his mother, was even more popular in the South than in the North. A sympathy wave had already begun to sweep the four Southern States in favor of Rajiv and his Congress Party, ruling out an anti-Tamil reaction in the north Indian states. The Syed, however, was not so sure.

Presently he said, 'Rajiv invited his own death by forcing his puppet Prime Minister Chandra Shekhar to dismiss the Karunanidhi Government, which enjoyed a majority in the Assembly, as well as by sending the Indian Army into Sri Lanka. Karunanidhi is a hero in Tamil Nadu and also sympathizes with LTTE. Tamils are a highly emotional people, who immolate themselves if unable to bear their grief. When their cinema idol and chief minister M. G. Ramchandran died peacefully of old age, many of his grief-stricken Tamil fans publicly immolated themselves.

Part Two

Chapter 9

9/1

When Govind Kumar Mehta's friends first saw and heard about his wife, Harimohini, they couldn't be blamed for wondering that such a good-looking sophisticated woman from Delhi's wealthy elite should have married a comparatively ordinary looking man with an ordinary standard of living. Thanks to Govind's honesty and integrity, which had never been called into question even by his rivals, since his dismissal from the Indian Police Service he had been living in relative poverty.

His friends were even more surprised when they saw her elder sister, Mrs. Chandrmukhi Narayan, and came to know about her wealth and position among Delhi's affluent elite. Chandrmukhi had at their father's request come to Bhopal with Harimohini during her second or third visit after her marriage to see for herself the conditions in which she lived with her husband, whom Harimohini couldn't praise too highly. She had concealed her astonishment at how easily Harimohini had adjusted to her husband's inferior standard of living. She herself cooked their meals and when the maid servant didn't turn up, which was quite often, she washed and ironed her and her husband's clothes and swept the house with a broom. She did all this as if she had been used to it all her life. In her wealthy father's home in Delhi she had never fetched even a glass of water, which was always brought to her by a servant. However, Chandrmukhi was consoled to think that Harimohini lived in these conditions only once in a while, less than ten to fifteen days in two or three months.

Divining the puzzled surprise of her husband's friends and their wives, Harimohini assured them that she was exceptionally lucky in marrying a man who was so devoted to the welfare of the gas victims that he had told her in so many words that he wouldn't leave Bhopal, and if she married him, it's she who would have to come to live with him; that he mightn't always be able to give her much time when she was living with him!

Her account was confirmed by the Bhopal-based correspondent of the English daily in which Harimohini worked. According to him, she had married Govind in preference to a younger and more handsome colleague of hers named Somdutt, who like her also belonged to Delhi's wealthy elite. He was the son of a Major General. He had assiduously courted her to the extent of abasing himself, but in vain. Before Harimohini's marriage Somdutt had once visited Bhopal for an exclusive story about the change in Hindu-Muslim relations as a result of the anti-Babri Mosque movement. The resident correspondent's reports that they were not much different from before had disappointed the editor, who was interested in a sensational scoop depicting heightened tension between the two communities and the likelihood of violence. Somdutt had met Bhopal's prominent persons, including senior Government officials some of whom were Govind's ex-batch mates in the Indian Police Service. Recollection of Somdutt's striking personality and intellectual brilliance had briefly renewed the surprise of these people that Harimohini should have rejected him in Govind's favor.

Her sincerity was so obvious as to make Govind seem to his friends luckier than they had thought. They were forced to dismiss their suspicion that her choice of him probably owed itself to feminine caprice or was a precipitate reaction from disappointment in love with somebody else. They congratulated him on his great good luck in having a beautiful wife, who not only belonged to a wealthy aristocratic family but was also a high-minded person, and showered him, specially on her account, with invitations to lunches, dinners and picnics.

They advised him in her presence to go and live with her in Bombay. His service to the vast number of the gas victims was a drop in the ocean. Encouraged by his friends' persuasions, she also urged him in their presence to consider returning with her to Bombay, where she was posted and where he'd have ample opportunity to fulfill his life's mission of serving the unfortunates. There were people in every big city of India living in miserable conditions.

He regretted his inability to comply with her wish. His decision not to leave Bhopal was not due to his secret dissatisfaction with Harimohini of which she was not even vaguely aware, and to which, as he deeply admired and loved her despite it, he hoped to get accustomed with time. Being a witness to the appalling condition of the thousands of people who were slowly but surely dying or had become mental derelicts from the unknown effects of the MIC gas, he had once again become emotionally involved in their welfare.

9/2

Govind sometimes recalled his meetings with Harimohini in Bombay, particularly his acute disappointments and unexpected good luck when she accepted his proposal. She had come to interview him for her newspaper and he was relating to her the principal events of his career.

Ten years ago, when he was posted as the Superintendent of Police at a district headquarters in Madhya Pradesh, the protesters against a big dam, of which the foundation stone had just been laid, went berserk. He Okayed the lathi-charge and the use of tear gas to disperse the violent mob of the largely illiterate and easily misled tribals and Dalits, but refused to order firing on the ground that it would have resulted in heavy casualties. This inaction, which he never regretted, resulted in extensive damage to the public property and injuries to a Cabinet Minister and a number of government officials, two of whom later died in hospital. It was alleged that the agitators, while engaged in destruction, shouted slogans: "Govind Mehta Zindabad! Govind Mehta garibon ka masiha (Govind Mehta is savior of the poor)!"

He was suspended from service and a departmental enquiry ordered against him. Before the enquiry had even started, however, his name was already hitting newspaper headlines, which made him out to be some sort of a hero. Although he publicly repudiated his glorification, it was obvious that it had prejudiced his case. Despairing of the chances of an honorable acquittal, he sent in his resignation and joined the Save Narmada Movement. His participation in the Satyagraha against the Narmada Dam and the resultant imprisonment led to his dismissal from service. After his release, he told the press that though he had refused to order firing out of fear of heavy casualties, it was his conviction that big dams did more harm than good. Ever since, he had been associated with some or other agitation against the government not only in his state but also in various other parts of the country. Finally, he had settled down to devote himself to the welfare of the Bhopal gas victims.

A few months before Harimohini came to interview him, Govind had been released after a six weeks' imprisonment for leading a peaceful march at Bhopal, in defiance of Section 144, as a protest against the failure of the State Government to redress the grievances of the gas victims.

During his imprisonment he had been ousted from the presidentship of the Association for Justice to MIC Gas Victims by his colleagues whom he trusted but who, it turned out, had been planted in the Association by the State Minister in charge of the welfare of the gas-affected people. The Association had been formed at Govind's initiative specially to agitate against the inefficiency and corruption of this Minister.

Finding himself in the wilderness after his release, he had come to Bombay at the invitation of a friend, a free-lance social activist working at Dharavi, Asia's largest slum.

As he had nothing to do at Bhopal for the time being, he kept working at Dharavi despite meeting with little success. The work here was much less satisfying than what he had been doing at Bhopal. The desire to work for the gas victims never left him. He felt that his life's mission was there. Sometimes he suffered from malaise for days together.

The unexpected meeting with Harimohini, who had heard of his service to the gas victims, and the interest she showed in his personal history, revived his spirits. The years following his dismissal from the Indian Police Service had been the most fulfilling period of his life, he told her. He had become associated with a number of organizations and been invited to join and sometimes lead the anti-dam movements in various parts of the country. After his return from Japan, where he visited Hiroshima and Nagasaki as a member of an Indian delegation and talked to many survivors of the nuclear holocaust, he had not only published a series of articles, but also written a play in Hindi verse, "Hiroshima". It was staged in several towns of Madhya Pradesh and a young lecturer of Bhopal, Miss Shanti Varma, was writing her Ph.D. Thesis on some selected plays in Hindi verse, which included his play.

When the interview ended he seemed to perceive on her face deep esteem for him as a person as much as interest in the subject.

In a series of articles Harimohini wrote after the interview she praised Govind so fulsomely that her editor, on a complaint by one of her colleagues whose write-ups were getting short shrift for lack of space, went through the first two articles. Suspecting that she had developed a personal interest in the interviewee, he severely edited the third one and reproved her for her over-enthusiasm and prolixity.

'You seem to be more interested in Mr. Mehta than in the victims of the gas disaster, which was the subject of your interview,' he said as he dismissed her.

To explain and apologize for the "cryptic" third installment, which contained the most important matter from Govind's point of view, she had sought another appointment, which he had gladly granted.

A few days after he had brushed aside her apology for the truncated concluding part of the interview and expressed his gratitude for giving him space in her distinguished newspaper, he invited her to lunch. During it, he matched her high praise of his social activism with his homage to her beauty, elegance and culture in astute phrases designed to flatter her without causing embarrassment. Thereafter, she phoned him often to learn more about his career and his present activities. Intrigued by her interest in him, he began to wish to meet her as often as possible to relieve the dullness of his life as an activist at Dharavi. He offered her collaboration in the writing of a book on human behavior, or the psychological changes, consequent to the exposure to the mysterious MIC gas, for which he had recently received an advance from a publisher. She accepted the proposal with alacrity and within a week they set about writing. She came to him in the evening straight from her office three to four days a week. He hoped that she would have understood that his offer was at least in part motivated by his interest in her as an attractive woman who admired him.

By the time the first chapter was finished, however, he had already begun to wonder whether her apparent lack of interest in him as a man was due to unusual modesty and self-discipline in one so provocatively lively, or to her being accustomed to a more palpable approach. After a month of the closest physical proximity during their long writing sessions she had betrayed no awareness of his attentions to her. Perhaps her apparent irresponsiveness was due to his decorous behavior, he would sometimes think. However, in spite of his ardor, he was incapable of behaving more overtly in the absence of any encouraging signs from her. He feared to lose her respect.

9/3

One day Harimohini came accompanied by a handsome young man named Somdutt, who made him uneasy with his flawless English and assiduous attentions to her. She introduced him as her colleague and friend from Delhi, who worked in her newspaper's Delhi edition and currently was on an official visit to Bombay to do a special assignment on SIMI or Students' Islamic Movement in India.

'Is her apparent modesty due to her friendship with this man which has made her immune to my interest in her? Is he her boy friend?' Govind wondered. He tried as well as he could to conceal his diffidence in the presence of Somdutt. However, during his third or fourth visit with her, he thought as if Somdutt was looking at him sullenly. He watched him closely during his next two visits. It seemed to confirm his first impression. Somdutt was anxious. He didn't like Govind. He seemed apprehensive of his having designs on his girl, who was meeting him too often for his liking.

One day when Govind was discussing with Harimohini the matter of a new chapter they were about to begin, Somdutt said with disdain that books on the Bhopal gas disaster were in fashion and too many of them with flimsy contents had already been published and rubbished. Harimohini retorted that the book they were writing was special, based as it was on the first-hand experiences of "a dedicated and distinguished environmental activist!"

Somdutt visibly paled.

This exchange bolstered Govind's spirits; Somdutt's evident jealousy couldn't be without some basis. During his next visit with Harimohini he was noticeably tense from the effort to contain his anxiety. Secretly rejoicing in his discomfiture, Govind decided to amuse himself by pretending curiosity about his special assignment. Somdutt answered his questions indifferently. During their following visits, as Govind and Harimohini animatedly discussed the matter of the book, he showed his aversion to their enthusiasm by sulkily looking at them from time to time while turning over the pages of one old magazine after another. These monthlies and weeklies had been specially bought off a footpath for him by Govind, who had begun to find his sitting with a morose and vigilant expression distracting. Harimohini paid no attention to him but Govind from time to time quietly watched him. Sometimes, ostensibly out of politeness but actually to divert himself, Govind asked him with the pretence of seriousness his opinion about some point they were discussing. He answered that he wasn't interested in the subject. It was obvious that he was feeling bored and vexed but was reluctant to leave them alone together.

One day, observing Somdutt's more than usually jealous air Govind, while wondering at the total indifference of Harimohini to the uneasy relationship between her two admirers, or was it from policy, tried to distract him. He pretended curiosity about SIMI, though he had no interest in its anti-Hindu activities. It was Government's duty to deal with them and it was doing it. To his astonishment, Somdutt instantly forgot his resentment against him and began to denounce the Governments of Maharashtra and India and the Bharatiya Janata Party and Shiv Sena and their leaders, LK Advani and Bal Thackeray. He accused them of instigating pogroms against Muslims and driving them into ghettos. Although as an agitator against the Union Carbide, Govind had dealt with a large number of Muslims at Bhopal, many of whom he respected and admired for their amiability and integrity, he was not interested in hearing Muslims' grievances, real or false, from Hindu leftists like Somdutt. He deplored their habit of incessantly attacking what they described as Hindu communalism to impress the shrewd and skeptical Muslims, which only resulted in annoying Hindus and further aggravating the relations between the two communities. In fact when he heard the views of people like Somdutt he appreciated more strongly than ever the objectivity and integrity of BR Ambedkar, who despite his denunciation of Hinduism as a deeply flawed religion had the courage to say that the distinction Islam makes between Muslims and non-Muslims is a very real, very positive and very alienating distinction. The brotherhood of Islam is not the universal brotherhood of man. It is brotherhood of Muslims for Muslims only and Islam can never allow a true Muslim to adopt India as his motherland and regard a Hindu, Christian or Buddhist as his kith and kin. And therefore, an exchange of populations between India and Pakistan at their birth would have been in the interests of the communities. But Govind also realized the futility of and the risk inherent in expressing his views, especially because the well-informed Hindu secularists in general, assured of permanent Hindu dominance, which was reinforced and further justified by Muslim fundamentalism, would describe him as a communalist.

His conviction of the impossibility of the development of a cultural synthesis of Hindus and Muslims had been further strengthened during his recent visits in the company of a local friend to a Muslim locality in Bombay where he had seen not only bearded and traditionally dressed Muslim preachers but young and English educated SIMI activists haranguing their poor and uneducated co-religionists to be "true" Muslims! The friend had told him that a change had come over the Muslim community in the wake of the Iranian revolution and their latest heroes were Pakistan's late dictator Zia ul-Haq and Ayatollah Khomeini. Govind considered the rise in Muslim militancy idiotic and suicidal. It exasperated Hindus who from their traditional prejudice against them held near absolute control over every kind of power, which they never failed to exercise against them at the slightest provocation. And the so-called Hindu secularists' support to Muslims, which was more often fashionable or simply simulated and politically expedient, was not only ineffectual but counter-productive.

Looking at Harimohini for approbation, Somdutt went on, 'I have been touring some Muslim localities in Bombay, and what do you think I have seen? There are more police stations there than in the Hindu localities in the city, as if the Muslim society produced more criminals than Hindus, which is nonsense! And all of these stations are equipped to be turned into bunkers, as if the police were in an occupied foreign land. And in the compound of every one of them there are temples devoted to Hindu gods.'

Govind like Hindus in general considered Indian secularism a farce because of the Muslims' insistence on legally enjoying their medieval personal laws basically out of spite against Hindus, who advocated Uniform Civil Code, and the Hindu secularists' secretly contemptuous acceptance of this attitude.

He said 'Government's approach to Muslims is bound to be influenced by what they see. I think it's in the interest of Muslims for the police to take special measures to prevent the violent and communal elements among them from committing mischief which would tarnish the image of the whole community. The communal or criminal activities of a few can further increase the prevailing prejudice against them.'

He looked at Harimohini to guess her reaction. Despite his excellent relations with her, whose friend Somdutt was, he did not know her political views or whether she seriously held any views at all. They had never talked politics. He wondered what she thought of his views.

Harimohini had been listening to the talk between the two men without being affected in her opinion of either of them. She had both Hindu and Muslim friends many of whom she admired as good persons irrespective of their views on politics and religion or about the current Babri Mosque controversy. Like a sophisticated Hindu she felt a mixture of revulsion against the politically motivated campaign for the demolition of the Babri Mosque and the construction of an unnecessary Ram temple at its place, and repugnance for the politicized Islam as it had been practised in India from before Independence and even more sanctimoniously and arrogantly after it. However, she had also observed the so-called Hindu and Muslim secularists' and fundamentalists' friendly relations and good will towards each other. When she was posted in Delhi, she used to visit her sister's evening parties and listen with pleasure to the discussions without being much affected in her opinion of the people who took part in them. She was aware like others that the views expressed at these parties were not always frank, good manners and personal relations being much more important. She particularly remembered one evening when Syed denounced Veer Savarkar as a murderer of Mahatma Gandhi, despite his having been honorably acquitted by the Supreme Court. The Syed's ire, as many of those present instinctively guessed from the fact of his being a Muslim, was due to the fact that not only the Bharatiya Janata Party but even many Congressmen were going to propose the installation of Savarkar's portrait in the Lok Sabha and the proposal was likely to be accepted! Syed's faux pas, as he immediately realized, had caused a near sensation because Savarkar was regarded by Hindus, even those who were critical of his political views, as one of the bravest patriots and revolutionaries India had ever produced, a man who had suffered the harshest imprisonment in inhuman conditions in the Andaman Jail for as long as twenty years. The sudden silence had embarrassed Syed. Not even his admirers, the ardent leftists Somdutt and Chandrmukhi, had supported or contested his view. If they had done either, the ensuing discussion would have ended as something ordinary and normal with the general acknowledgement that everybody had a right to their opinion. In fact, they had looked more embarrassed than those with whom his relations were merely polite and formal. For a moment Syed had felt acutely mortified by the silence. Its meaning was obvious. Savarkar was a Hindu nationalist and Syed being a Muslim deserved special consideration and extra tolerance from Hindu secularists or who pretended to be so. However, he had soon recovered to think that after all they were Hindus and therefore such attitude towards him, a Muslim, was normal and human.

A few days later when Syed came again, that day's incident had been forgotten and Syed's views on the subjects discussed were as usual supported by some and contested by others.

'So you admit that there is prejudice against Muslims?' said Somdutt.

Despite his inbred and invincible prejudice against the Muslim community, despite having Muslim friends whom he admired, in the prevailing political culture fathered by Gandhi, Nehru and others like him he considered profession of secularism, genuine or simulated, as not only more civilized but also fair in view of the undeniable fact of discrimination against Muslims. No Muslim had ever done him any harm yet he could not forget the intense disgust he had felt when as a teenager he first saw the famous Gnanwapi Mosque in Varanasi and was told by his father that this mosque was the original Vishwanath Temple which was destroyed by the Mughal Emperor Aurangzeb and converted into a mosque and where Muslims, aware of its history, regularly offered *namaz*. He had seen these *namazis* coming out of the mosque. Most of them looked poor and ill-educated as well as conscious of but accustomed to the Hindus' prejudice against them as something normal. He had also been told by his father that hundreds of temples had similarly been destroyed and converted into mosques by the Muslim rulers before the British came and put an end to their tyranny. He wondered whether any Hindu seeing this Varanasi mosque for the first time could remain immune to a similar sensation unless he considered Islam a coarse faith whose followers, generally backward and poor converts from Hinduism, not only deserved to be excused on that account but also protected against the animus of Hindus and the prejudice of the Hindu establishment. Later, thinking of some of the cultured and amiable Muslims he used to meet and admire he couldn't help feeling sorry to think that in the company of their Hindu friends they would have felt embarrassed at the sight of the mosque for which they were not responsible. He often wondered at the character of the secularism of Hindu politicians, intellectuals and media persons who regularly and over-enthusiastically condemned Hindu nationalism. Were they, or the bogus secularists among them, who he did not doubt were in a majority in every party and organization, by this posture consciously fooling the Muslims by telling them that die-hardism and isolationism were their fundamental rights and those Hindus who criticized them for it were communalists.

'Yes. But there's prejudice against Hindus also,' he replied.

Govind told him about what he had heard about and personally witnessed in Bombay. Muslims' idolization of the Iranian dictator Ayatollah and Zia ul-Haq of Pakistan and their preparedness to hail the former as a Mahdi despite his being a Shia. He added, 'Adoration of fanatics like Zia and Ayatollah could cause law-and-order problems and the authorities can't be blamed for taking precautionary measures!'

'Only illiterate Muslims are susceptible to such influence. Politically illiterate Hindus are no better; they admire fascists like Bal Thackeray and LK Advani,' Somdutt retorted. He added, 'More educated Hindus, I mean even those who pretend to be secular are biased against Muslims than appears. They vote for the Congress or other secular parties but their thoughts and feelings are not different from those of the BJP's followers. In admissions into the armed forces, police and civil services Muslims are discriminated against.'

'You're right!' said Govind. Without considering Advani and Thakre as fascists, whose attitude to Muslims on the contrary he regarded as natural and inevitable, he was unable to deny the fact of distrust and discrimination against Muslims, which too he regarded as natural and inevitable! Because, without blaming Muslims, like even unprejudiced and fair-minded Hindus, he regarded Islam as fundamentally exclusive and the Muslims' fast growing population a serious problem. And if caste-ridden Hinduism was no better, after the partition of British India on religious grounds and the greater affinity of Indian Muslims to the Muslims of not only Pakistan but of the whole world than to the non-Muslims of their own country it was only fair to regard

India that is Bharat as a Hindu country. He recalled how during America's attack on Iraq, posters and cassettes of Saddam Hussain's speeches denouncing America and George Bush were sold and bought by Indian Muslims in hundreds of thousands and how Hindus despised and made fun of them for it. However, he avoided the risk of expressing his views even before such Hindus as he suspected thought like him, lest he should be condemned as a communalist. He sometimes wondered whether while thinking like him Somdutt condemned this view lest he should be dismissed as a communalist by people who thought like him.

'As a Hindu don't you feel ashamed?' Somdutt said in an aggressive tone.

'I don't. But you're free to do so, if you think it will benefit Muslims!' he retorted unable to suppress his irritation.

The next moment he again felt uncertain about this man. Was he after all well-meaning like many allegedly progressive-secularist Hindus, who while regarding Muslims in general as religious extremists, at the same time considered secularism, sincere or simulated, as a practical philosophy? In other words, did he regard the politically opportunistic appeasement of Muslims, which injured them and not Hindus by keeping them backward, as also pragmatic and on the whole conducive to inter-communal peace and goodwill and the only possible, if not very effectual, way to lessen their sense of insecurity in a mistrustful Hindu India?

Nonplussed by his antagonist's reply and unable to control his agitation, Somdutt said, 'A few months ago, a great Muslim writer wanted to buy a house in a Hindu housing society in Bombay. Its Hindu owner was prepared to sell it to her because he planned to immigrate to America to live with his son and also because she was offering an attractive price. Do you know what happened? All its educated and so-called progressive and secular Hindu residents, many of whom were her fans, ganged up against the sale because she was a Muslim. She could still have bought it, because it was legal, but she was so shocked by their attitude that she changed her mind. It made big news for a few days, but soon everyone forgot about it because they thought the opposition was natural!'

Govind was aware of this case, which had been widely published, and also of the reason, which was an open secret, why the Hindu residents had opposed the sale. The writer had two young, educated and good-looking sons of marriageable age. Some Hindu residents who had young daughters had openly confessed to a journalist, who had headlined their confession without naming them, that among other things they had also opposed the sale because they were afraid lest their daughters should fall in love with or be seduced by the boys, marry them and convert to Islam! It was a well-known fact that educated Muslim young men generally preferred educated Hindu girls for being less inhibited by tradition and more forward-looking than the tradition-bound Muslim girls. As a rule, whenever a Hindu married a Muslim, he or she converted to Islam! A Muslim seldom embraced the religion of their spouse. The Hindu girl turned Muslim was never secure because according to the Muslim personal law her husband could always divorce her in a trice and take another wife, or have two wives. Such cases were not rare. One of her liberal opponents had even said that he wouldn't much mind if his daughter married a Christian and embraced his religion. Not only because he couldn't have more than one wife at the same time, but the divorce law governing Christians was not blatantly anti-women like the Muslim law. Besides, as there was no Christian ummah, a Christian's loyalty to India was as good as that of a Hindu. But Muslims? Unthinkable!' Her children might turn out to be more anti-Hindu than the children of non-convert Muslims. Jinnah's grandfather was a Bhatia Rajput and poet Mohammed Iqbal's ancestors were Kashmiri Pandits. The former created Pakistan and the latter gave birth to the Idea of an Islamic State within the British Empire. He also described Sufis as un-Islamic and considered Aurangzeb and not Akbar as a true Muslim. Aurangzeb who demolished Hindu temples and imposed Jaziya. Govind agreed with him but preferred to keep his own counsel lest he should quote him in support of his own views! He didn't relish the idea of being branded a Hindu communalist by the two-faced Hindu secularists-casteists who secretly thought like him and distrusted Muslims. Govind asked him if he sympathized with the RSS and voted for the Bharatiya Janata Party. He replied that like his father and grand-father he was also a Congressman and would die a Congressman! The fellow was certainly interesting and Govind, who was a lover of classical music, asked him about his musical taste. And lo! He began to sing praises of Ustads Bismillah Khan, Ali Akbar Khan, Bade Ghulam Ali Khan and many others! He worshipped them! Govind was delighted! However, enough was enough! But the fellow won't leave him and went on to describe Dilip Kumar as the greatest actor and Mohammed Rafi the greatest Bollywood singer ever. Before they parted, he said, 'I am not anti-Muslim, I am a realist!'

But there was no question of telling all this to Somdutt, because without being surprised he would bore him by expatiating on secularism.

Instead, he said, 'Why do you think she wanted to buy a house in a Hindu society as you rightly describe it? And not in a predominantly Muslim one.'

'It's you who should answer this question.'

'Because she was too modern and culturally up-to-date to be able to live comfortably even among her educated co-religionists. She might have been assaulted by a Muslim graduate from Harvard or Oxford for walking in public without a veil and displaying her still sexually attractive body! That's what the opponents of the sale told me!'

'I hope you don't believe in this nonsense! Opposition to the sale was rooted in communal antipathy!'

Despite feeling tired of arguing with this man and considering their exchanges a waste of time, Govind could not deny that Hindus' attitude towards Muslims was not the same as it was towards their co-religionists and Hindus in general thought twice before accepting Muslims in sensitive positions despite the fact that individual Muslims were regarded as neither more nor less honest and trustworthy, nor had any Muslim entrusted with a sensitive job ever been found guilty of any wrongdoing. However, irritated by the vehement and possibly fashionably insincere attitude of this man, he unexpectedly found himself saying, 'Communal antipathy is not entirely baseless. It is rooted in the vast difference between the respective Hindu and Muslim ethos. When Selman Rushdie's Satanic Verses was banned a Muslim

Professor of Jawaharlal Nehru University said that the ban on the book was not enough and Rushdie should be killed. Even an extremist Hindu in such a high position would have never said such a thing. What is even more significant is that no well-known Hindu secularist, so far as I know, criticized him for such an insane outburst though I am sure they must have despised him forever afterwards.'

He added sarcastically, 'And rightly so! Because Hindu secularists from a sense of fairness as well as prudence concede the Muslims the right to be bigoted, but rightly expect their co-religionists to be more civilized and tolerant. They don't criticize MF Husain's maliciously obscene paintings of Hindu Goddesses. This attitude of Hindus towards Muslims cannot be dignified as tolerance. To me it is expressive of hypocritical condescension and contempt.'

Suddenly feeling exasperated, he said, 'I am not interested in talking politics with you!'

'I am very sorry,' said Somdutt, rising from his chair, as if wishing to leave this odious place immediately. Then, turning to Harimohini, he said, 'Are you coming with me?'

'No,' she replied indifferently.

One day, during a tea break Harimohini asked Somdutt in an ironical tone whose full significance Govind would come to know much later: 'How is your friend Mr. Vishnu? How often do you go to Chandrmukhi's evening parties now?'

'As often as before,' he answered, growing red in the face. This was noticed by Govind, who thought: 'Who are these people? His friends of whom Harimohini doesn't approve?'

After this exchange Somdutt stopped coming. Govind wondered if there was any connection between it and the discontinuation of his visits. One day he asked Harimohini if Somdutt was still in Bombay.

'Yes, he's very much here,' she replied with a smile.

Govind felt glad and hoped he'd never see him again.

In a couple of weeks they were writing the second chapter. Harimohini continued to be apparently as oblivious of his interest in her as she was on the first day of the beginning of the book. Sometimes, she seemed to him astute enough to assume such a pose. It was hard to believe that such an intelligent woman should have failed to perceive his real interest in her, however discreet and delicate his overtures. Perhaps it was because she was used to being flattered and secretly enjoying advances so long as they didn't become obtrusive. Or waited for them to become more explicit?

At other times, observing her undiminished admiration for him, he thought: 'Maybe, in spite of her esteem for me as a social activist, she doesn't find me stylish enough in the way Somdutt is, even though she didn't mind snubbing him whenever he behaved with less than due respect to me.'

He also wondered at the fact that though uncommonly good looking and charmingly sociable, she was still unmarried; she didn't appear to be less than thirty.

9/4

However, in spite of her real or pretended ignorance of his interest in her, thanks to her vivacity and want of any hang-ups, he couldn't get her out of his thoughts.

Govind had often thought of marrying but had been unable to do so despite his forty years and having at one time or another interested marriageable women as friends; his activism had occupied him so incessantly that before he could find time to start courting the one who interested him or who had shown interest in him, she was already adrift. Or because so far he hadn't met a woman who attracted him as much as Harimohini did.

Sometimes he remembered Shanti, the college lecturer whom he had been helping with her Ph.D. Thesis before he went to Bombay. She was an eligible maiden in her late twenties with a faultless reputation and good looks, but too sedate. It was paradoxical but true that the women he desired as lovers or wives he also wished to be modest and virtuous, or the women he found modest and virtuous attracted him more than the susceptible ones. He used to long for Shanti on account of her reserve. Harimohini with her apparent inaccessibility was second such woman. Without his realizing it, this attitude had the merit of preventing excessive disappointment after a woman he had at last decided to court moved away from him. He contented himself with pleasant memories of her. Before he went to Bombay, he had desired Shanti as a lover or wife and had delicately hinted his intentions. At first her response had been encouraging and they had nearly become lovers. However, due to her orthodox upbringing and prudence, at the last moment she had checked herself. Perhaps she wanted him to be clear about what he actually desired. Would he marry her afterwards? However, before he could make up his mind and tell her that he was prepared to marry, he was sentenced to six weeks' imprisonment during which he came to know of the treachery of his associates. Too depressed to think of marriage, after the end of the imprisonment he had left for Bombay.

One day he boldly decided to propose to Harimohini, despite realizing that it was too impractical. In fact, because it was too impractical. First, he had made up his mind to return to Bhopal. After his disappointment at Dharavi, he had come to think that Bhopal was the only place for him. There he could still work independently for the gas victims. Secondly, in spite of her evident admiration for him, the idea that she would give up her brilliant career in Bombay and consent to live in a provincial town like Bhopal as his housewife was too unrealistic. Finally, for a woman belonging to the affluent elite of Delhi, a fact that he had learnt during their conversations, it was one thing to emotionally sympathize with the pathetic condition of the gas victims and admire the man who had worked for them, and quite another to work as his partner in the squalid localities and slums, which he had vividly described to her. In other words, the proposal by being turned down had the merit of curing him of her!

He decided to propose to her the same evening, when after leaving office she would come to his flat to work on the book. He reached his flat an hour before the usual time. After changing into a fresh kurta-pyjama, he made himself a cup of coffee before mentally rehearsing his proposal.

Instead, she called from her office to inform him that she wasn't coming as her mother had suddenly taken ill and she was immediately leaving for Santa Cruz to catch a flight to Delhi.

The next day she phoned from Delhi to tell him that she might have to remain there for as long as a month. He welcomed it as an opportunity to leave Bombay. He felt vaguely glad that he had been saved from proposing to her only to be turned down. Their separation would enable him to gradually forget her.

However, a few days after his arrival in Bhopal, he telephoned her newspaper office in Bombay and left his address and telephone number. He followed it with a letter in which, regretting that he hadn't her Delhi address, he wished her mother speedy recovery. Thinking his obsession with her an impediment and wishing to forget her, he expressed his inability to return to Bombay for at least a couple of months because of his involvement in the work for the gas victims. He informed her that he'd write the remaining part of the book by himself and it would be published as jointly authored by them. He decided to no longer contact her except in reply to any communication from her. He again started visiting the gas-affected areas without bothering that he no longer belonged to any group of activists. Soon, he began to feel depressed to observe the already vast and constantly widening gap between the needs of the gas victims and the maximum aid available to them from the Government and the NGOs. The victims' number continued to rise alarmingly with the appearance of the tell-tale symptoms in those who were earlier thought to have luckily escaped the effects of the MIC gas. Sometimes, after he had visited a hospital or an affected locality and seen the people who were critical and in severe pain he wished to forget and be forgotten by Harimohini so that he could again whole-heartedly devote himself to the sufferers' amelioration. Gradually, he began to feel again that the contentment he derived from working for them was greater than personal pleasure of any kind could ever be.

A week later, on December 7, 1992, only a few hours after the demolition of the Babri Mosque, which the local Muslims had watched all night over and over again on the BBC channel, Bhopal was overwhelmed with Muslim rage. As soon as it was daylight, hundreds of gullible Muslim young men in the 17-25 age group attacked government buildings and their Hindu neighbors wherever they were in a minority and accessible. The security forces retaliated mercilessly, shooting down any Muslim they could find who was mentioned in their records as an actual or suspected criminal. Quite a few of these real or alleged anti-social elements, it was alleged by Muslim leaders and denied by Government, were gas victims and innocent of any unlawful activity on that day.

Govind began to tour the gas-affected Muslim localities and at the sight of the suffering men, women and children, their utter poverty and pathetic gratitude to him for what little he was doing for them, he was sometimes momentarily overcome with remorse to remember his talk with Somdutt in Bombay.

Chapter 10

10/1

As Jaiprakash had feared, with the progress of the movement for the Babri Mosque's demolition Vishnu's defense of Hindu nationalism began to be more and more aggressive, often gratuitously and without conviction, resulting in clashes with Somdutt, most of which Jaiprakash despised as worthless. He could perceive that many other visitors shared his feelings but kept quiet because they couldn't care less. Somdutt attacked Rajiv Gandhi for secretly ordering or conniving at Shilanyas (foundation-laying) of a Ram Temple in the vicinity of the Babri Mosque at Ayodhya while at the same time assuring Muslims that the Mosque would not be harmed. Vishnu, though a critic of Rajiv, enthusiastically defended his action for its contribution to the revival of Hindu culture, which had gone into decline thanks to the illusory secularism propagated by Nehru. Somdutt criticized Rajiv for overturning the Supreme Court verdict in the Shahbano case by amending the Constitution and putting the Muslim Personal Law out of the purview of the Criminal Procedure Code. Vishnu, forgetting that he was contradicting himself, surprised him and Chandrmukhi by saying that the amendment had the eminent merit of preventing a rise in Muslim militancy which would have inevitably followed, if he had dared to touch the antediluvian Muslim Personal Laws even with a pair tongs. Vishnu attacked Prime Minister VP Singh for declaring Prophet Muhammad's birthday a gazetted holiday though no Muslim country had done so. Somdutt defended it on the ground that the birthdays of not only Hindu Gods and Goddesses but also of the prophets of Christianity, Buddhism and Sikhism were gazetted holidays. During these discussions Somdutt continued to drink, which further aggravated Vishnu though he himself poured whisky into his glass and urged him to take some more!

Remembering his family's indigence and the poverty of the people in his neighborhood in Patna to which he had been a witness Jaiprakash often found himself hating these discussions by the wealthy, who rolled in black money. It seemed to him that Vishnu deliberately provoked clashes with Somdutt because he knew that his wife would take Somdutt's part, which she did. As though unable to endure his frustration he craved the relief of exasperating himself with her and afterwards enjoying the reconciliation. The polite language of the discussions also irritated Jaiprakash; lurid vocabulary would have been more appropriate.

What aggravated Vishnu more than anything else, Jaiprakash suspected, was the irksome obligation to be polite to Somdutt and to express his regrets whenever he was provoked into using words that seemed to him strong, although they were never strong enough to relieve his feelings. Generally, before getting into his car, Somdutt shook hands with him and thanked him for his hospitality, to which he replied with matching false expressions of gratefulness for the pleasure of his company. Jaiprakash noticed that Chandrmukhi kept her eyes averted from this insincere exchange of courtesies between the two men, oblivious of the fact that she was at least in part their cause. Vishnu also avoided looking at her as they went back into the house together after seeing off Somdutt, as if he was aware of her distaste for what she had witnessed. From such behavior on their part it seemed to Jaiprakash that her consciousness of her husband's disgust at the compulsion to be hypocritically polite to his bête noire on her account was an especially painful constraint between them. Sometimes, Jaiprakash would see that even before Somdutt's car had left the porch, Vishnu's face all of a sudden became grim. Instead of accompanying his wife into the house, he let her precede him so as to be able to compose himself.

Jaiprakash would recall old times. How then the conversation between wife and husband at breakfast, lunch and dinner used to be about business matters, some new book they had both read, a play, an art exhibition or a performance by some classical musician they had attended together. It was marked by good humor and appreciation of each other's points of view. And how after dinner they would go to their bedroom and before falling asleep either read or listen to classical music, which Jaiprakash could hear in his room.

If then Vishnu with his placid temperament was more gentle and forbearing than his wife, now he had become intemperate in his criticism of the views that she had always held and which he used to listen to with a smile. Now he singled them out, sometimes utterly irrelevantly, and cruelly scoffed at them, leaving both her and Jaiprakash astounded. Now they did not always leave the table together; one of them would continue to read a book or magazine for some time before following the other.

The first few times Vishnu behaved rudely to his wife, Jaiprakash felt extremely embarrassed and quietly left their presence, but one day when he got up to leave in the midst of one such episode, Vishnu silently indicated to him to stay. He had complied, guessing that unable to prevent himself from quarrelling with her he perhaps desired his presence as a restraining influence!

In his lucid moments Vishnu appreciated the justice of his wife's unspoken objection to his wish to stop Somdutt's visits on the ground that it stemmed from his jealousy and want of faith in her, which were insulting; yet he found it hard to control himself. Indulging his resentment was the only way to be relieved of it, for a short while at least, by later thinking it unjust.

Somdutt drank uninhibitedly, often consuming up to five large pegs. And he borrowed books from Chandrmukhi which he never returned. These and some other things which were not pertinent to Vishnu's objection to him and which he would have overlooked in anybody else, never failed to anger him.

10/2

For some weeks, unable to endure Somdutt's company when no other friends had come, Vishnu had begun to politely excuse himself and leave him and his wife alone together. He would read or watch TV and eat by himself in his bedroom.

Soon, however, he began to miss the excitement of the party, where, depending upon the type of the people present, non-political subjects like the latest film, the latest best seller or singer or dancer were also talked about. In fact, these subjects were talked about more often and with greater animation than the current affairs, with Somdutt and Chandrmukhi always participating in the discussion enthusiastically. On many occasions Vishnu had discussed these subjects with Somdutt and their views had coincided, or his wife's opinion had agreed with his rather than with Somdutt's.

Presently to beguile his boredom in the bedroom, he would sometimes ask Jaiprakash to leave the party and sit with him. As Jaiprakash was a well-informed person, he began to enjoy talking with him about various subjects including the current affairs, over some of which his differences with his wife were known to Jaiprakash and about which he did not know that Jaiprakash's views happened to be closer to his than to his wife's! So far Jaiprakash had either avoided expressing them or expressed them discreetly and mildly as well as stating that a different view was also possible. To preserve his credibility, he adopted the same discreet approach with Vishnu also, more often agreeing with his wife's view, which happened to coincide with Somdutt's against his, with the proviso that an opposite view could also be sincerely held and should be respected!

Sometimes, hearing him echo Chandrmukhi's views, Vishnu found that they were more logical and reasonable than his own and his dissent from them was due to the fact that they were expressed by her in endorsement of Somdutt's views.

One day Somdutt told Chandrmukhi that in view of her husband's evident dissatisfaction with his presence he didn't think he should continue to attend her evening parties. He didn't wish to embarrass a gentleman. Although hurt by her husband's behavior, Chandrmukhi felt obliged to defend him: 'You misunderstand him! He has no objection to your presence! His absence is due to his lack of interest in many subjects we and our friends often discuss; he also feels uncomfortable at the frequent differences between our and his opinions on many important social and political issues.

I think he has a right to pass his time as agreeably as we do! He prefers reading novels and listening to music.'

Somdutt thought it as well to believe her. He said to himself that if she hadn't been confident of her husband's regard for herself, she wouldn't have defended his attitude. He also reminded himself that despite frequent differences of opinion between them whenever they were together Vishnu was scrupulously polite to him. However, he was also conscious that if he hadn't longed for her company he would have stopped coming.

One day, when Chandrmukhi, Somdutt and Jaiprakash had returned to the drawing room after dinner, Jaiprakash boldly decided to stay on past the time he usually retired, leaving the two of them alone together. In fact he had begun to think Vishnu's expression of his displeasure in this manner undignified and foolish; it was calculated to make Chandrmukhi and Somdutt more vulnerable to each other. How much more sensible would it have been for him to express his own opinions, real or sham, as spiritedly as they did, without minding the concurrence between theirs. After all, they only talked for pleasure. It was as good as playing cards for people whose main aim was to earn money and enjoy a sumptuous lifestyle of which intellectual discussions were only a part.

To his surprise, she did not seem to mind his stay, not even when he intervened in their talk as an excuse for remaining till Somdutt left. During his following two or three visits also, Jaiprakash stayed on till he left. But he realized that he couldn't always do so; he didn't feel sure that, in spite of her kindness to him, she wouldn't think his behavior intrusive. He was agreeably surprised, therefore, when during Somdutt's third or fourth visit, as he got up to leave, she asked him to stay if he wasn't feeling sleepy. He had no difficulty in understanding that she wanted him to stay for the sake of her husband's peace of mind.

Honest as Chandrmukhi's objection to giving up or at least modifying her relations with Somdutt in accordance with what she considered her husband's jealous wish was, there were also other reasons for her reluctance to do so. First, Somdutt sincerely respected her. Secondly, in addition to her admiration for his views and intellect, she had observed and was convinced that Vishnu had also perceived it, that he talked frankly, sometimes unnecessarily frankly from sheer habit, but never deliberately said or did anything to estrange her from her husband. But contrary to her husband's jealous fears, what most of all prevented her from ever thinking of becoming Somdutt's mistress was that his desire for her, which she sometimes couldn't help feeling flattered to observe in his eyes, was tinged with intellectual disdain for Vishnu, which would be gratified if she became his mistress. She feared that it might send a wrong message—that she despised her husband.

Jaiprakash knew that Vishnu had begun to take a drug, some product of opium, to alleviate his unhappiness. What he did not know was that he also took it to boost his sexual desire on which he had begun to depend more and more to mitigate their mutual objections.

Honest as Chandrmukhi's objection to giving up or at least modifying her relations with Somdutt in accordance with what she considered her husband's arbitrary and unjust wish was, there were also other reasons for her reluctance to do so. First, Somdutt sincerely respected her. Secondly, in addition to her admiration for his views and intellect, she had perceived and was convinced that Vishnu had also perceived it, that he talked frankly, sometimes unnecessarily from sheer habit, but never said or did anything with the intention of alienating her from her husband. Thirdly, though honest, yet like a well-fed and liberated member of the upper class used to all kinds of luxury she couldn't help feeling secretly flattered by his desire to become her lover, which she sometimes seemed to discern not only in his but also in her husband's eyes (she had seen it in the latter's eyes before she saw them in Somdutt's!). Gradually, she had begun to feel excited by such pictures of her relations with him as she couldn't help visualizing filled her husband's jealousy-inflamed imagination. She suffered no qualms about taking delight in these pictures, because they were evoked by her husband's jealousy and she loved him and not Somdutt. Also, her vanity had more insight than was needed to realize that although desiring her, Somdutt was not disposed to make any special effort to induce her to take him as a lover; he was content to wait for her to throw herself into his arms, and wouldn't be excessively disappointed if she didn't! Her overall attitude to him was also influenced by her knowledge that he had passionately loved only one woman, her own sister and his former colleague, Harimohini. He had chased after her in Delhi and later in Bombay till she had married his rival, sending him off into a prolonged depression. Although not jealous of Harimohini, whom she dearly liked, she couldn't bear the thought of being second to anyone. But what most of all enabled her to check herself was the awful thought of the humiliation of her husband in Somdutt's eyes.

Jaiprakash knew that Vishnu had begun to take a drug, some product of opium, to alleviate his unhappiness at her obstinate refusal to give up her friendship with Somdutt. What he did not know was that he also took it in order to boost his sexual desire on which he had begun to depend more and more to mitigate their mutual objections.

10/3

However, he had soon understood that sexual pleasure, however great, was a feeble antidote against the distress caused to both of them by his jealousy and her feeling of being wronged. Recalling their joyful days, he had realized that far from being the main cause of marital happiness such pleasure was no more than one of its results.

For some days the movement for the Mosque's demolition had begun to seem irreversibly headed for country-wide violence and anarchy. Street clashes between Hindus and Muslims, most of them riff-raff, hungry for trouble over any issue important or trivial, and devoid of any ideology or convictions, and police firings resulting in deaths, had become a frequent occurrence. So had become bitter exchanges in the legislatures and the media between the supposedly pro-Muslim Hindu leftists and allegedly anti-Muslim Hindu nationalists, with occasional interventions by astute Muslims, who mostly preferred to watch their exchanges from the side lines with amused skepticism or with a sense of being patronized and with little hope that their lot would change for the better in the foreseeable future.

The contention between Chandrmukhi and her husband across the breakfast, lunch or dinner table had gradually become more acrimonious than ever. It was invariably provoked by Vishnu under the influence of the invisible presence of Somdutt, which Jaiprakash had guessed was more provocative than his actual presence. The more they quarreled the more it seemed to Jaiprakash that their antagonistic political views were merely a pretext. And the more bogus the professed cause of their quarrel the more difficult began to seem to him the prospect of reconciliation without the intervention of something equally perverse.

One day, quietly watching Vishnu absentmindedly turning over the pages of a novel, Jaiprakash found himself thinking or divined that Vishnu was not reading but thinking, that Chandrmukhi, who had just gone to the beauty parlor, usually went there on the day Somdutt came and stayed for dinner, or he usually came and stayed for dinner on the day she went to the beauty parlor. As Somdutt was a frequent but irregular visitor, did not always inform beforehand about his visits and sometimes didn't turn up when expected, Jaiprakash began to wonder at this singular coincidence. Or was it one of the illusions that the tense and erratic relations between the husband and wife had created?

On these days, usually Fridays and Saturdays, when instead of visiting their establishments both wife and husband operated from home, Vishnu would begin to look agitated at lunch, find fault with the food or something else and start a dispute with her which would sometimes become so heated that he would rise hungry from the table and walk out. Such behavior by him soon began to remind Jaiprakash without his seeing any necessary connection between the two things that today she would be visiting the beauty parlor after the evening tea and Somdutt would be staying for dinner. As these two things did not always coincide, judging by Vishnu's unrepentant behavior, exception seemed to prove the rule.

On such days, which Jaiprakash seldom failed to correctly divine from the tense demeanor of both wife and husband, he would quickly finish his meal after or sometimes even before the quarrel started and leave the table on some pretext. But of late he had been unable to do so, as apparently afraid of being left alone together both wished him to stay till the end. Once or twice when he had got up to leave, either he or she or both had looked at him in such a way that he had felt obliged to stay. Their exchanges in his presence were bound to be somewhat restrained, especially as regards the language they used. And since quarrel was unavoidable, his presence was needed by both.

Lately, such behavior on Vishnu's part had brought out a hitherto unsuspected trait in his wife, which had further increased Jaiprakash's respect for her. Contrary to her nature, she had begun to react to his outbursts with a sad silence after he had left. One day, after Vishnu had left evidently in a state of shock at his own offensive behavior, without finishing his meal, Jaiprakash had seen tears in her eyes. Although she was strong enough to compose herself in time lest the atmosphere at the evening party should be affected by her state of mind and talked with Somdutt and others as usual, Jaiprakash could see that she was extremely unhappy.

Although they still slept together, his frequent attacks of bitterness during the day, often followed by palpable remorse, which temporarily assuaged her grief, had gradually rendered both less and less capable of desiring each other. Now he had to force himself to make love to allay his anxiety lest she should have developed aversion to him. It left both of them acutely dissatisfied. Conscious of and pitying his suffering and his fear of driving her into Somdutt's arms by his jealousy and unkind behavior, which she knew he regretted but couldn't control, she never refused. His anxiety temporarily allayed by her submission and the effect of drugs, he fell into a profound sleep, which never lasted less than eight hours.

While he slept, on many a night she lay awake beside him, sometimes until the small hours, bearing both her and his anguish silently. She was careful not to let him guess it, unsuspecting in her tender concern for him that he believed her to be on the whole happy. Assurance of her happiness was essential for him to blame her and torture himself with jealousy, or sometimes excuse his own misbehavior. And his belief seemed confirmed by the fact that despite her unhappiness, she did not neglect her appearance, regularly visited the beauty parlor, went to the Bollywood movies and social functions, read one best seller after another to beguile her melancholy, and talked on the telephone with her friends as usual to keep up the appearance of a happy family life.

Chandrmukhi and Somdutt as before went out together to various functions whose subjects Vishnu pretended did not interest him in response to his wife's or Somdutt's formal requests to him to accompany them.

As it was impossible to tolerate the things as they were, let them get worse if they won't get better, Vishnu's behavior seemed to say. And they did get worse the more irately he behaved and the more she welcomed Somdutt's visits and went out with him to escape the gloomy atmosphere at home.

Aware of her masterful temperament, which was kept under check by her amiable disposition, Jaiprakash feared that such relations between her and Vishnu couldn't continue for long and that an explosion might not be far off when he would find himself at the receiving end. He was further confirmed in his apprehension of some such incident happening any day by the fact that her lifestyle and outward behavior in society had changed little. It proved that she had a hard core and despite the anguish caused by her husband's rude behavior hadn't been demoralized by it.

It happened sooner than Jaiprakash had feared. George Bush had attacked Iraq to punish Saddam Hussain for his attack on Kuwait. Vishnu had become an enthusiastic supporter of America mainly because, as Jaiprakash rightly suspected, Somdutt and Chandrmukhi denounced it. One day Vishnu was forced to attend the evening party despite Somdutt's presence because some friends had arrived after a long time. During the discussions he and Somdutt clashed, Somdutt denounced the invasion of Iraq as imperialistic goondagiri. Vishnu retorted that Saddam was a murderous dictator who had been persecuting Shias and deserved to be punished. He also denounced the political parties, except the BJP and Shiv Sena, for supporting Saddam in order to win Muslim votes. He went on to express his surprise that a communist leader, Z.A. Ahmed, who was supposed to be secular, should have said at the Parliament's Consultative Committee on Foreign Affairs that "Jai Saddam!" Was competing with "Jai Sriram!" Somdutt said that the allegation was false and mischievous and spread by the Hindu communalist press. Vishnu retorted that it must be correct because Z. A. Ahmed was not only anti-American but like Saddam also a Muslim! He immediately retracted the latter part of the comment and apologized because it was politically incorrect! Especially incorrect and unsecular of late because America had become hated by Indian Sunni Muslims for having attacked Iraq, and secularism called for at least a formal, even if suspect, endorsement by Hindus of their profound emotion in favor of Saddam. Due to the intervention of some common friends the clash came to an end with Vishnu pouring whiskey into Somdutt's glass and he thanking him.

A few days later, during what seemed to Jaiprakash a stupid argument during lunch, stupid because of the continuing tension between husband and wife, over the permission given by Prime Minister Chandra Shekhar to the American planes to refuel in India on their way to Iraq, Chandrmukhi criticized Chandra Shekhar in her characteristic strong language. Vishnu not only supported the PM with equal vehemence but expressed the hope that the American forces would return from Iraq only after destroying the Saddam Hussain regime and thus liberating the Shia majority from the thousand-year old tyranny of Sunni minority. Momentarily taken aback by what was news to her, she brushed it aside as irrelevant even if it was a fact.

'American imperialists have no business to interfere in the internal affairs of other countries,' she cried.

'As usual, you're dutifully echoing the views of your ignoramus fan, Mr. Somdutt,' he retorted sarcastically. The very next moment he realized, as Jaiprakash could see from his face, that he had hurt her. But before he could make amends, she all of a sudden lost control of herself and after a moment's hesitation violently pulled the table cloth, sending the bowls, glasses and plates containing lunch crashing to the ground and leaving both Jaiprakash and Vishnu astounded.

After this incident, which disgusted Jaiprakash, Vishnu no longer lost his temper at her or used strong words. Mercifully, it also spared him the remorse he felt afterwards. From that day, in addition to boycotting the evening parties when Somdutt was the only visitor, Vishnu as far as possible began to avoid her also. He visited their establishments by himself and she did the same. And as far as possible, he breakfasted, lunched and dined before or after her, thus, Jaiprakash feared, dangerously increasing her vulnerability to Somdutt. Although when Somdutt was the only visitor Jaiprakash with her tacit wish continued to sit with them and participate in their conversation. But he did not think that it could prevent an affair between them if she wished to have it. On the contrary, if she should decide to take Somdutt as a lover she could easily do so away from home and his presence during their meetings would serve as a false assurance to her foolish husband.

The current affairs on which Chandrmukhi's and Somdutt's views were more or less similar soon became too dull for a pleasurable evening unless somebody else with different views also happened to be present. Therefore, If he alone stayed for dinner, most of the time she and Somdutt talked on subjects that Jaiprakash considered immaterial and passé and discussed for the pleasure of her company, so far as Somdutt was concerned, and, on her part, to beguile her unhappiness. Just the same, he participated in the discussion to justify his presence, sometimes taking her side, sometimes his. Somdutt would unfavorably compare Nehru's socialism with Mao's, describing the former as nominal, which had actually made the poor poorer and the rich richer. Chandrmukhi would defend Nehru, pointing out the Prime Minister's limitations in a democracy. He would attack Indira Gandhi for nationalizing the private sector banks not because she believed in socialism but because in the struggle for power she wanted to beat her political rivals and to ensure that her son, Sanjay Gandhi, would succeed her as Prime Minister. She would defend her, praising her for routing the Syndicate composed of rightist reactionaries like Morarji Desai, Atulya Ghosh, Nijlingappa and others like them and displaying tremendous guts in the war against Pakistan, which had resulted in the birth of Bangladesh. Both condemned the economic liberalization by Finance Minister Manmohan Singh as a surrender to the World Bank and American capitalism. They denounced the successive governments' miserable failure to provide health, educational and other basic facilities to the poor guaranteed in the constitution even half a century after the country became free. During the discussion,

Somdutt continued to sip whisky and praise its high quality, and to keep him company she, careful of her figure despite her unhappiness, drank black coffee, looking at but avoiding almonds and cashew nuts after dinner.

Sometimes, back in his room, while thinking of Chandrmukhi's unhappiness, which hadn't affected her luxurious lifestyle, Jaiprakash would absent-mindedly go back to the slum near his house in an old locality of Patna where skeletons of men, women and children in rags and in the company of dogs searched in the garbage dumps from sunrise until sunset for anything they could find to eat or sell: some grains of rice, a piece of bread, a half rotten apple or banana or a used polythene bag.

Chapter 11

11/1

After his return from Bombay, Govind Kumar Mehta had resumed his contact with Shanti for old times' sake and also because he wanted to forget Harimohini. She enquired about his efforts to establish himself as a social activist at Dharavi, about which he had told her before he left for Bombay. She told him how she had wished him to be successful in his efforts there, though it would have been a personal loss to her. She remembered how close they had come to each other and if he hadn't been as busy with his work as he always was, he might have proposed to her. She again sought his help in completing her Ph.D. Thesis whenever he was in Bhopal. He promptly agreed. He noted her anxiety about the thesis, which had made little progress since his imprisonment and, later, departure for Bombay. On the completion and approval of it depended her confirmation on her post of college lecturer. He again started meeting her in her college library twice a week. From the first day, they became friendly as before.

In spite of his inability to forget Harimohini and his busyness with his work, he couldn't fail to guess during their meetings that Shanti's interest in him had revived to the point at which they had parted when he went to Bombay. He acknowledged it with a grateful smile, but found himself unable to decide on a tangible response. Apart from his inability to forget Harimohini, he had not forgotten Shanti's inhibitions, which had prevented their becoming lovers.

From the college library he would go to the gas victims' colonies to work there. Sometimes he would think without too great disappointment that he might never meet Harimohini again. He could think of no occasion to go to Bombay, and there was no reason for her to come to Bhopal.

11/2

It was nearly two months since his return to Bhopal, when one day he was surprised to receive a call from Harimohini. After informing him that she had returned to Bombay, she further surprised him by asking him in a tone of which the warmth it was difficult to mistake as to when he was coming back. She told him that she missed him greatly. Although flattered, he couldn't help remembering that she hadn't mentioned the letter which soon after his arrival at Bhopal he had sent to her Bombay office's address. She hadn't acknowledged it! He mentioned it. She replied that she hadn't received it and would try to find out why it hadn't been redirected to her Delhi address. Perhaps it was misplaced by her Bombay office. He informed her of his decision to make her the joint author of the book, which he would finish by himself, as being busy with his work for the gas victims he couldn't say when he would be able to come to Bombay. She sounded disappointed and embarrassed and said that her own contribution to the book was negligible. She again said that she missed him more than she could express in words.

Before she rang off, however, she added, causing him even greater surprise, that she considered his work at Bhopal much more important than her feelings and her "ardent wish" to meet him! Did she mean, he wondered, that she wouldn't be particularly disappointed if he could not find time to go to Bombay?

'What does she mean?' he wondered. He recalled Somdutt. She had probably passed two months with him in Delhi. Why then did she phone him and say that she ardently wished to meet him and ask him when he was coming?

Within a week, she called again and again surprised him by offering to come to Bhopal to assist him in completing the book. Without mentioning his apparently lost letter to her, she said she could afford to live in a good hotel where they could work on the book in the evening. He would have welcomed her help because the book was far from complete and he had received a reminder from the publisher. But he was doubtful of the propriety of publicly associating with such a good-looking unmarried woman in the conservative city of Bhopal. He might be defamed by his rivals. He also recalled her apparent insensibility to his real interest in her. Thanking her, he politely declined her offer.

She continued to talk for what seemed to him a long time about things that didn't seem at all important to him. It was obvious that she was interested in him more than he had dared to think. But in what way?

He was puzzled. With a sense of relief he had dismissed as too unrealistic the idea of proposing to her with the condition that he couldn't leave Bhopal and she would have to come and live with him as his housewife. But their long conversation, which was carried on by her evidently for the pleasure of talking to him, made him wonder if such a proposal was really as unrealistic as he had thought. Then he remembered its chief merit of curing him of her, and probably her of him, by being turned down.

After a couple of weeks she called again and they had a long conversation, she recalling the "great time" they had had in Bombay together.

The next day he wrote to her without much hope but to end the uncertainty. The very first sentence informed her that he had longed for her as a partner from the day he first set eyes on her! If he had failed to reveal his heart's desire until now, it was because of the near impossibility of its being fulfilled due to certain severe drawbacks. He went on to describe them, and when he had put them down on paper, they appeared even more formidable than he had thought. One, the welfare of the gas victims being his life's mission, he couldn't leave Bhopal. Two, in the lucky event of her still accepting him as her husband on condition, which he described as perfectly reasonable, that she wouldn't give up her career, either, it's she who would have to come to Bhopal to live with him as often and for as long periods as she could. He emphasized his inability to return her visits except once in a while and seldom for more than a few days at a time! Of course, it would be all right if she was also unable to visit him often or live with him for more than a few days at a time. He further warned her that she would have to adjust to an austere lifestyle far below the standard of living to which she was accustomed. Finally, due to his heavy engagements he might not always be able to give her much time even when she was living with him!

He rewrote the letter several times and although despite the warm references to the time they had spent together in Bombay the final version remained stark, he was satisfied. It honestly described his limitations and his attitude towards her: grateful for her generous appreciation of him, yet frank; desiring her yet prepared to take her refusal without disappointment.

She replied by the return post! To his astonishment, she did not decline, as he had expected and even vaguely wished. Soon after he had proposed it had occurred to him that even if she accepted his proposal it wouldn't mean, considering the vast difference in their standards of living, of which both were aware, that marriage would definitely take place. It was quite possible that after the tranquilizing pleasure of stooping to marry below her standard from idealistic motive, she should suddenly find herself unable to forgo the more substantial pleasures she was used to and back out with graceful excuses and sincere regrets. He didn't wish to be flattered to be deceived!

However, on reading the letter again, he was somewhat reassured to note that it didn't evince any surprise, as he had expected. On the contrary, she had said that she was grateful to him for considering her worthy of being his spouse. Without committing herself, perhaps because of the difficult conditions attached, she had sincerely reaffirmed her admiration for him. He felt happy, which caused him to read it once again, now between the lines. From its tone, she seemed to be seriously considering the proposal in spite of the conditions, even if, it was prudent to think, the chances of its being accepted were slim. He wasn't disappointed; it made him realize how wholesomely he had become reconciled to the prospect of being refused. What he would never forget was that she had seriously considered the proposal, which now seemed to him unnecessarily negative in tone. He wondered whether as a gentleman he had the right to impose such conditions. The last sentence of the proposal he especially regretted: He might not always be able to give her much time even when she was living with him.

'It was ungentlemanly!' he reproached himself.

However, she seemed to be considering it!

In the evening, sipping his whisky, he would sometimes think from her point of view. By marrying him she would lose much more than she would gain. If she impulsively married him under the influence of her esteem for his dedication to the welfare of the gas victims, she might begin to regret it sooner or later and make both him and herself unhappy. But he told himself that she was an intelligent woman who understood her own interest better than he did.

On returning from his visits to the gas-affected areas, he would first look into the letterbox and then check the answering machine in case there was a recorded message from her, declining the proposal in graceful phrases and again expressing her gratitude for being considered worthy of being his wife. Whenever his telephone rang, he thought it might be she. In spite of his belief that there was not much chance of his being accepted, his curiosity was great.

11/3

One evening, Govind was stunned to hear Harimohini's voice. She had accepted his proposal with all its conditions, which to his surprise she said suited her perfectly! Later, reflecting on their conversation and the happy tone of her voice, he was puzzled. How could such conditions suit her perfectly? He recalled Somdutt, with whom probably she was having an affair but whom for some reason she could not marry. Or perhaps, he could not marry her. He didn't even know whether he was married or a bachelor. He wondered if she wished to have the best of both worlds. A famous philanthropist as a husband and a wealthy and handsome young man as a lover! However, he decided not to bother, as it was all conjecture and at the moment she owed him nothing. Moreover, it was he who had proposed marriage in full awareness of her friendship with Somdutt.

He remembered how more than once she had upheld him and snubbed Somdutt when he had got into a spat with him. Of one thing he felt certain: even if she was having an affair with him she admired him sufficiently to accept him despite his lower standard of living; unless, of course, she had interpreted his proposal to mean that she would be under no obligation to live with him in Bhopal for more than a few weeks or even a few days in a year! Eventually, even this possibility ceased to bother him. Being married to such a woman was better than being a bachelor.

The message was followed by a letter in which she suggested that the marriage take place after the book had been sent to the press. He dismissed as too mean the thought that she might back out after the book had been published. Taking a few days off from his engagements, he rushed to Bombay, visualizing as a foretaste of his future happiness a profusion of kisses, which now that they were as good as engaged would be compatible even with her singular modesty and self-restraint.

To his surprise, he found her demure, again assuring him in correct phrases of her happiness at being considered worthy of being his wife. However, he quickly got over his disappointment at the lack of any amorous suggestion in her behavior by crediting her with exceptional chastity, although at the same time he thought it surprising and a little odd that she should be having an affair with Somdutt. Was then his nagging suspicion of the affair a figment of his imagination and she had been behaving with her colleague also as virtuously as with him? He recalled Somdutt's jealousy and anxiety during his visits with her to his flat in Bombay. Was it due to her chaste behavior with him also, which he had interpreted to mean that she was having or planning an affair with him?

She further requested him that their engagement be kept secret till she herself announced it at an appropriate time in view of certain and strong opposition from her father. She described him as a snob proud of his high caste and of belonging to Delhi's wealthy elite. Quickly recovering from his surprise at her frankness in informing him about her father's contempt for the backward castes to which he belonged, he accepted her request with a smile. He had too good an opinion of himself.

During his few days' sojourn, they roamed Bombay, went to pictures, Elephanta Caves and other famous tourist spots and, in short, enjoyed themselves in every way except that. He also discovered anew that virtue in a woman was a more powerful stimulant and a greater source of joy than easy accessibility. Holding her hand he visualized in detail his first passionate encounter with a virgin on their wedding night. How he would overcome her shyness!

Before he returned to Bhopal, she again assured him that she valued his devotion to the welfare of the gas victims above anything. He immediately suspected that perhaps she meant but had discreetly left unsaid that she considered it much more important than conjugal happiness! Did she thereby mean that they would really be living together only once in a long while? However, it didn't make him feel less happy than when he had gone to Bombay anticipating kisses; on the contrary, he was gratified to think that she valued him as a dedicated social activist to the point of accepting him as a husband in preference to a more affluent and handsome and younger Somdutt. He again reminded himself that being married to a woman like her was any day better than remaining a bachelor.

However, as time passed, he sometimes couldn't help thinking that their marriage might never take place due to the opposition of her father or for some other reason. He now considered his assurance to her that she would be free to live with him or away from him entirely according to her convenience unnecessary and imprudent. While he had already begun to desire her to the point of remaining awake thinking of her, sometimes imagining her in his arms, she might end up feeling profoundly content with her admiration for him as a social activist to the complete neglect of conjugal relations!

One day, much sooner than he had expected and the book still incomplete, he was pleasantly surprised to receive a telephonic request from her father to come and meet him in Delhi about his proposed marriage to his daughter. He remembered his snobbish caste-pride but didn't feel diffident; his easygoing tolerance of such human frailties and the fact that she had prevailed over him assured him of an amicable meeting with him.

The old fellow, however, shocked him by telling him at the outset with a surly expression that he strongly disapproved of his daughter's tentative proposal to marry him!

'That's a matter between you and her,' recovering from his shock, he replied dryly. He added in a more decided tone, 'And it's not tentative but final, according to the understanding between me and her!'

'I would like to warn you,' said he, ostentatiously rolling bejeweled gold rings on his fingers, 'as much for your sake as hers that you'll regret the marriage. There's still time. Take my advice and tell her that you have changed your mind!'

Not allowing him to put in a word, he went on, 'She has declined two proposals, one of them from an officer in the Indian Foreign Service, whose father was an ICS officer and is an old family friend. The other was by a man you have met: Somdutt, son of a Major General. You'll admit that he's in every way far superior to you and far more eligible to be her husband. Frankly, I don't think you worthy of her and she'll soon repent of her choice! That's what I mean by saying that you'll regret it. She has been immaturely influenced by the combination of her aversion to what she foolishly derides as her elitist and hedonistic milieu and your contrived and inflated reputation as a selfless social activist and a brave idealist who sacrificed a high-profile career in the Indian Police Service to uphold his principles. I wouldn't have believed it even if I hadn't been better informed. It's a sure recipe for disaster for a girl as used to all sorts of comforts and luxuries as she is, and consequently for you also.'

'Did she tell you that's why she desired to marry me?' he asked, hiding his elation.

'Yes. You'll admit that it's a shaky foundation. I don't think she has seen any other virtue in you, supposing what she has seen are virtues. She's simply deluding herself.'

'If you've finished, I'd like to go. I have an appointment to keep,' he said.

'I've found out about your social antecedents as well as your present circumstances from reliable sources,' the old man went on, continuing to vulgarly roll the jeweled rings on his fingers for his benefit, 'and I am sorry to say that they're woefully mediocre. You live in a two-room shabby house in a shabby locality of Bhopal. I've no wish to detain you, but I'd like to finally warn you that if you've trapped her in the hope of getting rich at my cost, you'll be swiftly disillusioned. I am not going to give her one broken cowry, if she marries you.'

'I have never even in my dream expected anything other than her hand. I know what you mean by my social antecedents. I deplore the caste system as an evil. Please don't insult me,' he replied proudly and indignantly.

Smiling sarcastically, the old boor offered him a cup of tea and two biscuits.

'Thanks,' said he and walked out. He felt more delighted than insulted by his behavior, which showed desperation at his failure to dissuade his daughter from marrying him. All of a sudden, he remembered his lost letter to her. There was no doubt that it had been intercepted and destroyed by him, who had been alerted by Somdutt about her interest in him.

Although he was disgusted by his future father-in-law's coarseness, he decided to keep it from Harimohini. He felt glad to think that his behavior seemed to promise that after the marriage he would have little or nothing to do with his son-in-law and, consequently, his aggrieved daughter would have little or nothing to do with her father. That's how he wished his relations to be with his wife, untrammeled by an uncouth, caste-arrogant curmudgeon.

Chapter 12

12/1

As soon as the demolition of the Babri Mosque began to seem certain thanks to the Central Government's and Supreme Court's implicit recognition of its inevitability and the catastrophic consequences of trying to prevent it by force, the Hindu secularists' resistance to it became as loud as the campaign in favor of it. The Muslim spokesmen's reminders to their community of the dismissal by the Supreme Court of their community's petitions against the Shilanyas and against the High Court's delay in disposing of the Kalyan Singh Government's acquisition of the land in front of the Mosque obviously to ensure its demolition were conspicuously published along with critical comments by the professional Hindu secularists in the Hindu-dominated media as a reassurance to Muslims that India was a secular country. The Muslims were also reminded that the Prime Minister, PV Narsimha Rao had solemnly assured the country that the Mosque would not be allowed to be harmed although the number of rambhakts who had already reached or were reaching the Mosque's site was expected to be no less than half a million.

The opposition to the demolition was mostly led by the aggressive-atavistic Muslims like Syed Shahabuddin, the Shahi Imam of Delhi's Jama Masjid and their ilk with the vociferous backing of a hodgepodge of patronizing and morally snobbish as well as ritually pro-Muslim high-caste Hindu leftists and Communists together with Hindu backward class politicians like Mulayam Singh Yadav and Laloo Yadav. The latter had lately begun to pose as super secularists. Their pretense as champions of Muslims' interests was due solely to their interest in their votes, a fact of which they knew but didn't care Muslims were aware. Routine criticism of the Bharatiya Janata Party, which like the leftists and communists was also mainly led by Brahmins and other upper castes, was on the top of their agenda with manifestly impractical and unconstitutional demands for Muslims coming next. The only significant difference between the BJP and the political mix of Hindu casteists-leftists-Communists from the Muslims' point of view was that the former were less careful about concealing their mistrust of and revulsion against Muslims who would refuse to accept any reform suggested by Hindus out of spite even if they considered it good for them. Even most educated and westernized Muslims who thought that Shari'ah was out of date and detrimental to their progress insisted on retaining it because its modification was suggested by a Hindu government whose functionaries frankly distrusted them and considered discrimination against them in national interest. Nehru who insisted on modernizing Hindu society by enacting the Hindu Code Bill never showed any interest in a similar legislation for Muslims.

However, the Muslims remained skeptical that, whoever wins, their interests would be protected. They especially hated Marxists for willfully ignoring the fact that they were victims of discrimination on the ground of religion and not class. Treating the Muslim Dalits and OBCs at par with the Hindu Dalits and OBCs, who had the advantage of reservation in nearly all fields, only aggravated the former's condition. The Muslims also could not be oblivious of the fact that in the communal riots, generally it was the OBCs and not the better-off Brahmins, Thakurs, Kayasths or Banias, who indulged in anti-Muslim violence. The latter were satisfied with marketing the violence by mischievously analyzing its causes over and over again, especially in the electronic media, with lucrative commercial breaks in between.

Reports, verified or unverified, of the security forces deployed to prevent the demolition chanting "Jai Sriram!" In unison with the would-be destroyers of the now internationally famous dilapidated mosque appeared everyday on the front pages of the "secular" newspapers as a warning of the possible complicity of the Government in its imminent demolition. An ostensibly pro-Muslim leftist magazine owned by a Capitalist reported to have learnt from confidential sources that the Union Home Minister on a secret flying visit to the Mosque had exclaimed before his security officials, 'Let the bloody structure be pulled down to enable me to sleep in peace!' His predecessor, a Sikh, had reportedly told a senior journalist that he would not be a Sikh if he did not ensure the construction of a glorious Ram Temple at the disputed site.

At last, the day came when the mosque was attacked by hundreds of karsevaks, who, feeling like Ram's monkeys attacking Ravan's Lanka, swarmed to the top of its domes with iron rods, axes and hammers. Specially present on the occasion were some of the leading lights of the Bharatiya Janata Party—LK Advani, Murli Manohar Joshi, Uma Bharati, Vinaya Katiyar and the Maharani of Gwalior. They were being photographed every second to record every change of expression on their faces by the hundreds of eagerly expectant media men from all over the country and abroad, who would have felt wretchedly disappointed and let down by the karsevaks if the mosque had miraculously escaped destruction and deprived them of a great story. Many of them had already been ordered by their editors to be ready to fly at short notice to cover certain Hindu-Muslim riots in the riot-prone towns and cities where meticulously pre-planned inflammatory media coverage of the events at Ayodhya would not fail to provoke violence.

Presently these Hindutva luminaries, as was reported in some sections of the press and denied as false and calumnious, were being presented with pedas, barfis, laddoos, cold drinks and fresh fruit juice by the security forces. Some media persons, whose attention was diverted from the mosque and who tried to take the photographs of the ecstatic laddoo-eating and juice-drinking leaders and policemen were beaten and abused and their cameras snatched and broken by these security men, many of whom wielded their lathis with one hand while eating laddoos with the other, according to the bannerline in a Hindi newspaper.

The thoughts of Chandrmukhi, her husband and Jaiprakash, who were sitting together and anxiously watching the demolition on TV were as alike as their ideological convictions were unlike: They were thinking that the Muslims in general, whether intellectuals and politicians whom they regularly read or met at India International Centre and other elite places, or plebeians living in slums, thought alike: They thought that the anti-Muslim elation among the Hindus was common to the devout persons who worshipped Ram as an incarnation of God Vishnu and made daily visits to temples and those who had seldom if ever visited a temple in their life, did not believe in the divinity or historicity of Ram or even that he was an ideal man. It was obvious to all that the vociferous condemnation of the attack on the mosque by the majority of leftist-secularist Hindus, though sincere, was especially for foreign consumption and for the sake of enjoying a clear conscience in the post-demolition period. Much more than the destruction of the mosque and the hurt it would cause the Muslims, most of these Hindu opponents of Hindu fundamentalism were worried about the tarnishing of the image of a secular India and of the tolerant Hindu religion by the Hindu communalists. Even the more sensitive among the Hindus, who might be regretting the defenselessness of Muslims, would sooner rather than later feel purged of their transient feeling of shame by anticipating or even welcoming the Muslims' refusal to let bygones be bygones after the mosque had ceased to exist and had not a ghost's chance of being rebuilt. They hoped that the Muslims in general, with the possible exception of some anti-Sunni Shias, would refuse to agree to the construction of a temple to Ram on the mosque's site, if not as an act of atonement for the thousands of temples the Muslim marauders and rulers had sadistically destroyed and replaced with mosques, then at least to end a nuisance in their own interest.

Many of these Hindu pseudo-secularist and casteist politicians were already planning with an eye on the Muslim vote bank to instigate them to insist on the reconstruction of the mosque at the same spot, despite knowing that it was not only impossible but calculated to further worsen the relations between the two communities.

To the extreme vexation of Vishnu Somdutt had been telephoning Chandrmukhi every half hour from his press to express his indignation. When the third dome of the mosque was on the point of collapse, Vishnu, dreading another call from Somdutt, left without touching his belated lunch, which had just been placed before him. Jaiprakash was relieved to see him go. He had been fearful of a violent scene between husband and wife every moment but had resolutely stayed on in the hope that his presence might have some restraining influence.

And he did not leave too soon, for the moment the third dome crumbled, Chandrmukhi's face took on such a gruesome expression that Jaiprakash, despite being aware of her strong views, was astounded. As well as he knew her, he could not divine the cause of such revulsion.

Chandrmukhi had been tense since the morning. She had been agitated by thinking of her husband's grossly unjust desire to reproach her with the lofty contempt Somdutt would feel towards him as soon as the mosque fell. She had no doubt that at this moment he was eagerly waiting to visit his hatred for Somdutt upon her because she had obstinately continued her friendship with him, ignoring his grievance that Somdutt's refusal to credit his often declared opposition to the relocation of the mosque without the concurrence of Muslims was deliberately malicious. Although sympathizing with his view, she had been too incensed by his attempts to coerce her into acknowledging it as well as by his boorish jealousy. Within a minute of the collapse of the mosque, Somdutt called her again and in no time she became so immersed in conversation with him, she could talk on the telephone for any length of time on the most trivial topic, as to become oblivious of her surroundings.

Vishnu, who had gone next door to the house of a neighbor and friend, who happened to be one of those who had bought sweets beforehand to be distributed as soon as the mosque fell so as to avoid the rush at the sweetmeat shops, stayed there against his wish, fearing to return home lest he should find his wife still talking to Somdutt. The neighbor forced him to eat one laddoo after another, while his brother ignoring his protests put a garland around his neck.

Vishnu returned to his house and sitting at the window began to look outside. His next neighbor, a Chartered Accountant, was playing his transistor loudly near the gate of his bungalow to the people gathered on the street in front of it to hear the latest news, and his servants were also distributing laddoos to them out of a big basket. From his window Vishnu, his attention attracted by the distribution of laddoos, began to look at the scene. The crowd of listeners got bigger and bigger and presently they began to shout 'Jai Sriram! Jai Sri Ram! Pakistan Murdabad (Death to Pakistan)!

As if the Babri Mosque had been built by Pakistan with the collaboration of Indian Muslims after demolishing the Ram Temple! Soon there was heard a faint protesting cry by Muslims from a distance: Allah O! Akbar! Pakistan Zindabad (Long live Pakistan)! A jeep full of armed policemen stopped in front of the bungalow but only for a few seconds before driving off, obviously reluctant to take the risk of dispersing the excited mob. But not before some people rushed to it and presented laddoos to the policemen, who accepted them with smiles. The transistor man began to feel tired but stayed on, loath to disappoint the crowd.

Gradually, the uproar ceased and the people began to disperse still shouting death to Pakistan. A man was heard saying loudly, 'Sab Musallay Pakistani hain. Ram Mandir phir wahin banana bahut zaroori hai (All Indian Muslims are Pakistanis at heart and the temple to Ram has got to be built at the same spot where it stood before it was destroyed)!'

Vishnu was not surprised at what he saw and heard. On the contrary, he was convinced that his wife and Somdutt too wouldn't have been surprised, though they would have pretended to do so. It was India with its pants down. Feeling contemptuous of them he began to muse. The militant Hindu movement for the demolition of the Mosque and the construction of a Ram Temple at its site and the Muslims' violent opposition to it were a resurgence of the deep-seated Hindu-Muslim antagonism, which had resulted in the blood-soaked division of British India into the so-called secular India, a symbol of Hindu apathy and hypocrisy, and the triumphantly anti-Hindu Islamic Pakistan, which for most Indian Muslims was a symbol of victory over Hindus until the Bangladesh war. This animosity remained buried under the abysmal poverty of the masses and occasionally erupted into Hindu-Muslim riots. Not only Gandhi and Nehru, whom Hindus idolized but whose preaching of non-violence and secularism they dismissed as moonshine, but even Lord Ram was no more than the recipient of formal and perfunctory worship during religious festivals. The Hindu leftists-secularists and rightists all knew these truths and exploited them in their different ways to gather votes. The former, feeling secretly disdainful of Muslims for their fanatical adherence to the medieval religious laws, nevertheless warned them, for the sake of their votes, that if the Hindu communalists came to power their divine rights granted by Allah and his Prophet, which included the right to simultaneously have four wives and to divorce any or all of them by telephone at the drop of a hat, would be abolished the first thing. Most Muslims hated these Hindu pseudo-secularists and casteists masquerading as secularists for doing nothing for them and cheating them when in power for fear of alienating anti-Muslim high-caste Hindus, whose votes were also necessary to win elections. Nevertheless they voted for them because they could not vote for their rival, the Hindu Bharatiya Janata Party.

12/2

Vishnu began to wait to be informed that some of his friends had arrived. It was a momentous occasion and at least some were sure to come. He did not want to go into the drawing room, where his wife would be sitting with Jaiprakash. He did not wish her to feel distressed to find herself with him in the absence of any friend. Soon after the karsevaks climbed up the mosque and began to hack away at it, he had seemed to perceive on her face anguish and dread that he was longing to bitterly reproach her with her approbation of the disdain Somdutt would feel for him as soon as the mosque fell.

An hour later, he learnt from the cook that Somdutt was coming and would be staying for dinner.

'Who else is coming?' he asked.

'Nobody sir, so far as I know,' the cook replied in an unusually formal and correct tone and with an oddly formal and correct look. As if he wished his master to know that he and the other servants were aware of the tension between him and his wife due to the meddlesome Somdutt, whose entry into the house ought to have been banned long ago, and that they fully sympathized with him! Vishnu gave the impertinent fellow an angry look and was about to lose his temper, when guessing that he had riled the sahib, he slipped away.

Vishnu's jealousy flared up. He began to think whether he should boycott Somdutt today also. The reasons for doing so were compelling: Somdutt and Chandrmukhi would denounce the "vandalism of Hindu fundamentalists", implicitly accusing him to his face of being guilty of the crime through his sneaking sympathy with the anti-Babri Mosque movement; that his oft-repeated opposition to the "relocation" of the mosque (how Somdutt had scoffed at this word!) without the approval of Muslims would today be ridiculed by Somdutt, and that he would be unable to forgive his wife for not defending his reasonable and conciliatory stand.

On the other hand, would it not be cowardly to avoid a confrontation with him, as if he really felt guilty and was afraid of facing him? In his own house, too! In fact, he felt extremely unhappy at the mosque's demolition. He deplored it not only for being wanton and uncivilized in the twentieth century, but also from fear lest a demolished temple should not be found under it, which was not impossible! He was ninety-nine per cent sure that the ruins of a big temple would be found under it. He could think of no other reason for the Muslim vandals to select a Hindu holy city for building a mosque than the sadistic wish to humiliate Hindus. And if such was the wish for building the mosque, it couldn't be achieved to their complete satisfaction unless a temple was destroyed first and the mosque built over it. As a matter of fact, the destruction of a temple containing idols was infinitely more important from their religious point of view than the building of a mosque. However, he wanted to be one hundred percent sure! If no temple was found under the mosque, it would give the Muslim historians and their patronizing or masochistic Hindu supporters an excuse to say that the allegation that the Muslim rulers destroyed hundreds of temples was a Hindutva myth. But his despair of being believed if he condemned the demolition so incensed him against Somdutt that he longed to give him a piece of his mind irrespective of the consequences, if he provoked him.

Jaiprakash was surprised to learn that Vishnu would be present at drinks and dinner.

'Today he ought particularly to have stayed away,' he thought. 'Somdutt will attack Hindu fundamentalism, Chandrmukhi will be constrained to endorse what he will say, and he will regard the criticism as particularly aimed at him.'

Chandrmukhi had also been surprised to learn from the cook that today her husband would be present at the evening party, taking the risk of Somdutt being the only visitor. She could remember few occasions during the last several months when he had attended an evening party despite Somdutt's presence. And when he had done so it was because either Syed or some close friend, businessman, senior politician or bureaucrat was also visiting. Although on all these occasions he had been polite to Somdutt, today he might lose his temper. If he behaved rudely to him, who was bound to denounce Hindu fundamentalism honestly and not deliberately to annoy him, she would be obliged to support him.

12/3

At seven o'clock, tired of brooding in his study, Vishnu entered the drawing room, where Jaiprakash and Chandrmukhi were waiting for Somdutt, who as usual had not informed about the time of his arrival. Of late, she had begun to feel that it was to gratify his resentment against her that more and more often Vishnu obliquely coerced her to put an end to Somdutt's visits, because he knew that she would refuse to do so.

Looking at her husband, she was seized with fear that today he had come with deliberate intent to further aggravate their relations by forcing her to side with Somdutt, which would give him an excuse to nurse his grievance.

She quietly went to her study and telephoned Syed and Professor Zulfiqar Ali to request them to come. Vishnu listened with a friendly smile to the same views expressed by them in equally strong or even stronger language as provoked him to contest them if they were uttered by Somdutt. Like many a worldly wise educated Hindu he charitably conceded what he regarded as a fact that they were Muslims first and Indians afterwards! And without holding it against them courteously listened to their blaming not only Jinnah but also *Gandhi and Nehru for the division of India along communal lines, without realizing that in retrospect most thinking Hindus had not only become reconciled to the partition but considered that it was the best thing that could have happened from their point of view. She still remembered with what urbanity he had contested Syed's characterization as unsecular the weekly screenings of the Ramayan and Mahabharata serials by the Government TV channels for as long as two years. Vishnu did not doubt that Syed was sincerely convinced that they had made an astronomical number of Hindus more sympathetic to the fundamentalist Ramjanmabhoomi movement. After Syed's departure, while she was wondering at his courteous behavior to him, he had said to her with a smile, 'Listening to him, I was thinking whether an educated and sensible man like him really suffers from such amnesia. He feels deeply hurt by the movement for the demolition of the Babri Mosque and blames the Ramayan and Mahabharata serials for it. I don't blame him for it, but does he really not feel embarrassed before Hindus to remember that the Muslim rulers had demolished hundreds of temples, especially those in the Hindu holy places like Varanasi, Mathura and Ayodhya and built mosques over their ruins, working pieces of idols into the threshold of the newly—built mosques so that the faithful could tread them underfoot. Many such mosques have been preserved as national monuments by the Archaeological Survey of India without provoking any objection even from Hindu fundamentalists. I wonder he is so naïve that it never occurs to him that the Hindu secularists are not such saints that they never think of the vandalization of their religious places by Islamic invaders and robbers, that their profession of secularism is a source of joy and conceals a lofty sense of their moral superiority over the followers of Islam.'

It had resulted in a heated argument between husband and wife but as then there was no Somdutt it had been dissolved in kisses a few hours later.

Both Syed and Prof. Ali told her that in view of the great tension in the city they could not come. They advised her also to remain indoors till the situation returned to normal. Disappointed, she telephoned Somdutt's office and then home to ask him not to come in order to avoid an unnecessary confrontation with her husband. She had no doubt that he would appreciate her request. She was again disappointed to hear from his father that he had just left for her home.

As Somdutt entered Chandrmukhi's drawing room, his patience and caution momentarily deserted him at the presence of Vishnu. He looked at her with ill-concealed disappointment, causing her to wince because of her fear that now any gesture from him to her, however slight or innocuous, had little chance of escaping her husband's jealous vigilance. And she was right; the exchange did not escape Vishnu.

Somdutt was angry and disgusted at the mosque's demolition and sorely needed to relieve his feelings. His anger had been increased by the fact that on his way from his home to Chandrmukhi's his car had been stopped by some celebrators, who had recognized him as a violent critic of Hindu nationalism, and he had barely escaped being molested thanks to the intervention of some people who did not want to spoil their festivities by any act of violence. But he had been let go only after being roundly abused as a traitor to his religion. Despite being a Hindu, or because he was a Hindu, he believed that he had the right not only to denounce Hindu fundamentalism but even to say that Ram was a myth. As a Hindu he had also the right to say that even if it could be proved that Ram was born where the Babri Mosque stood nobody had the right to demolish it and those who advocated it were thugs! He was never more conscious of the difference between the Hindu and Muslim ethos. He couldn't help thinking despite himself that the Hindu fundamentalists were lowering the Hindu ethos to the level of that of Muslims, who had the moral right to use coercion and violence against the nonconformists.

However, he was against the demolition for yet another reason, which he could only tacitly share even with his genuinely leftist and secular colleagues and friends: He had no doubt that the Muslim politicians like Syed Shahabuddin, members of the Babri Masjid Action Committee and others like them were in a heads we win and tails Hindus lose position. They opposed the pulling down of the mosque and the building of a temple to Ram at its site for purely political reasons and not because they cared for the decrepit structure whose demolition would not be an act of sacrilege in a Muslim country. In Saudi Arabia the Bilal Masjid in Mecca where the Prophet himself had prayed had been demolished to build a road. As for those ignorant and religious Muslims who would have considered the demolition a sacrilege, it had already been defiled by the secret smuggling of the idols of Lord Ram into it nearly half a century ago when Pandit Nehru was the Prime Minister and Pt. G.B. Pant the State's Chief minister; idols which despite protests by Muslims had long been allowed to be worshipped by Hindus from outside by a court order. But the worst was yet to happen. One day, by another court order not only the mosque's locks had been opened exclusively for Hindus to enter it and worship the idols but the Muslims were forbidden to approach the building and thus defile it by their shadow falling on it.

Syed and his ilk opposed the demolition for two contradictory reasons. One, they had absolutely no doubt that to their embarrassment and Hindu nationalists' delight a destroyed temple would be found right under it. Secondly and more importantly, when the demolition had begun to look inevitable, they had stepped up their opposition to it as a delaying tactic to see the Hindus, who never tired of vaunting their secularism and religious tolerance while secretly considering Muslims pan-Islamists and pro-Pakistan, disgrace themselves in the eyes of the West by destroying the mosque. The criticism of the Ramjanmabhoomi movement in the European and American press Somdutt found especially hurtful as a Hindu and Indian, unlike the Hindu nationalists, who didn't care what was said by the white people, whom they had long ago dismissed as anti-India and pro-Pakistan or, which was the same thing, anti-Hindu and pro-Muslim!

Chapter 13

Somdutt felt frustrated at the presence of Vishnu, which would make it impossible for him to denounce the event without getting into an argument with him. Of late he had begun to restrain himself and endeavored to express his views as mildly as possible in order to keep up his friendship with Chandrmukhi. He had long ago guessed that her husband was jealous of him and didn't relish her supporting his views against his. He wished to keep coming to the evening parties because he enjoyed meeting her as well as some other people whom he could meet nowhere else.

However, it was hard for him to exercise restraint today, which caused him to feel frustrated. Vishnu was talking to somebody on the phone. Abruptly terminating the conversation and instead of losing his self-control, as Chandrmukhi had feared, he surprised her by welcoming Somdutt with his customary imitation smile. She had long ago begun to find it unbearably embarrassing and even worse than an argument between them.

Extending his hand to Somdutt, he said, 'Aaiye, swagat hai! Aapse bahut dinon se bhent nahin hui. Maze men honge! (Welcome! I haven't had the pleasure of meeting you for a long time! I hope you are hale and hearty!)'

Actually, Vishnu had instinctively fallen back on his phony style of greeting disagreeable visitors in a desperate effort to repress his ire at Somdutt's vexed glance at his wife, which he had seen. This fellow had the impudence to feel disgruntled at his presence in his own house and to express his disappointment to his wife!

Chandrmukhi frowned at her husband's effusive way of greeting a person who was aware of his feelings towards him. A civil greeting was what was especially called for today.

'Dhanyawad!' replied Somdutt with an ironic smile.

Completely at a loss as to how to behave to each other, they indulged in more such ironic exchanges, which Chandrmukhi found extremely distasteful.

All of a sudden, Somdutt's disappointment overcame his discretion and he said, 'Congratulations! It's a red-letter day for the votaries of Hindutva. The hated mosque has been demolished at last!'

Vishnu was stunned. In spite of his aversion to Somdutt he was unfailingly civil to him, who on his part never failed to politely thank him for his hospitality.

Before he could answer, Somdutt smiled at Chandrmukhi and then turning to him said, 'If you want to celebrate the great achievement, please ignore our presence!' The emphasis on "our" astounded Vishnu.

'Yes, let's celebrate!' Vishnu replied, barely able to suppress his fury. He mixed two whiskies, his hands shaking with violent tension, and extended one towards Somdutt, who was looking at Chandrmukhi and had not noticed his agitation.

Somdutt drew back. 'No sir, not today! It's a day of mourning for us,' said he, again flashing a smile at Chandrmukhi, who had become livid at her husband's pathetic exhibition of jealousy and Somdutt's reckless indiscretion, feeling agonizingly conscious of her own share of responsibility for the latter.

With tears of shame and remorse, she got up from her chair and without uttering a word or looking at either of them left the drawing-room.

Realizing his faux pas and the impossibility of remaining in the house without her even for a moment, Somdutt said sheepishly, 'Excuse me; I have to go to Syed sahib's. He's expecting me!'

He took a few steps towards the door and then turned back. 'I am sorry for any offence I may have unwittingly given,' he said shamefacedly. 'I hope you won't take it too hard and our relations will remain as cordial as ever!'

Looking at his receding figure, Vishnu wondered whether he was really so lucky; whether Somdutt's words meant that he was feeling guilty and would never again darken his door, or at least be kept from coming for a long time by the memory of his gaffe, which had mortified Chandrmukhi. Or whether they were the product of confusion and he was already thinking of resuming his visits after a suitable interval. He looked at Jaiprakash significantly, as if wishing to know what he thought of Somdutt's parting words. Jaiprakash, who had developed a silent communion with his boss and exchanged tacit thoughts with him regarding the crisis in the family, either failed to understand him or did not feel optimistic.

On the whole, however, Vishnu was pleased; at least, it would be some time, maybe a long time, before Somdutt might start coming again. As for his wife's indignation with him, he was confident that it won't last beyond a few days, a couple of weeks at the most. It was extreme vexation, not hate, even if the vexation sometimes bordered on hate.

As usual, he felt glad of his wife's anger. It again pleasantly reassured him that she was innocent, even though he knew that the reassurance had a short life. He would soon begin to worry that even if she had remained faithful to him so far, his jealousy could exasperate her any day into taking Somdutt as a lover. With a jealous husband's useless insight he knew that more wives were made unfaithful by jealousy than even by chronic sexual dissatisfaction.

As soon as Somdutt was gone, Chandrmukhi returned to the drawing room.

'I am ashamed of you!' she stormed. 'Such naked display of jealousy!'

Her rage reconfirmed his assurance that she was far from entertaining any thoughts of taking Somdutt as a lover. For a moment, he was tempted to apologize to her, which would have consummated the great relief he was feeling at the moment. But he couldn't do so in the presence of Jaiprakash and the servants. Moreover, it seemed too soon for an apology, which in the fitness of things and to carry conviction ought to appear as the result of a deep heartfelt remorse.

'It's I who ought to be ashamed of you for entertaining an impudent parasite!' he stormed back, enjoying his relief from jealousy.

As Jaiprakash looked on with shock and disbelief, their exchanges grew more and more heated. However, knowing that truth hurts more than falsehood they were careful to avoid uttering any embarrassing truths about each other. In high-pitched voices they accused each other of trifling offences or such as both were occasionally equally guilty of and which could be later dismissed as of no consequence by both the accuser and the accused. And make it possible for both to say that they had said all that in anger and were sorry. After delivering themselves, they would stop to hear what the other was saying, and delighting in the flimsiness of the accusation, retort befittingly. They especially welcomed each other's charge that they had never been so falsely and baselessly accused and insulted before!

All of a sudden, Jaiprakash felt his presence too embarrassing and instantly left. The stunned servants left, too, feeling that they should also have quitted earlier. The latter, however, noticing the petty nature of their mutual accusations, while there were grounds for far more serious ones, felt convinced that the real cause of the quarrel was cleverly being left unsaid by both; in other words, Vishnu was rightly or wrongly convinced that his wife was having a torrid affair with Somdutt, but despite his anger was too ashamed and frightened of the consequences of openly accusing her, and his wife, whether guilty or innocent, felt too embarrassed to tell him what she thought of him!

At length, exhausted and embarrassed at the hypocrisy and perverseness of each other's as well as their own behavior, they retired, confident of being reconciled soon after they had gladly confessed their fault and rendered suitable apologies.

For the time being, however, after such a high-pitched quarrel and the first open acknowledgement before Jaiprakash and the servants that Somdutt was its cause, both felt too embarrassed to sleep in the same bed or even in the same room. Their sexual life came to an end. But only temporarily, both felt, to be started afresh with pleasure as soon as they had mutually confessed the injustice of what they had said in anger and reaffirmed their warm regard for each other.

They continued to keep up appearances, behaved correctly before their friends and acquaintances and with tacit understanding and accustomed astuteness never allowed their apparent rift to prevent them from deferring to each other's opinion if it promoted their business interests. Jaiprakash especially noted this last fact with hope; it would facilitate their reconciliation.

Chapter 14

14/1

At last what seemed to Govind Mehta an inordinate wait, he and Harimohini were married. The marriage was solemnized not in Delhi, where her father lived, but at her uncle's home in Bombay. The number of guests was much smaller than it would have been, if the marriage had been celebrated in Delhi, some of her father's relations and friends told each other loudly while drinking in a room adjacent to his. He couldn't tell whether they were unaware of his presence or intended him to hear them. They added that her father didn't dare invite many of his rich and aristocratic friends and relations for fear of their scornful disapproval of permitting his daughter to marry a penniless man from a backward caste. They quoted Somdutt: He had been dismissed from the Indian Police Service for misconduct.

He heard their talk with a pitying smile, without taking offence; he had too good an opinion of himself.

Harimohini was shocked to hear her father's insulting behavior to her husband, which he was describing to some of his relatives and friends, seemingly unaware of her presence within earshot:

'Any man in his place with even an ounce of self-respect would have indignantly refused to marry her after what I told him,' he said with a sneer.

She immediately came over and apologized to her husband. He told her that he had overlooked her father's behavior because he knew how difficult it sometimes was even for people who were basically good to shed deep-rooted prejudices and appreciate merit. She was moved by his magnanimity to the point of tears.

After seeing off some of his personal guests from Bhopal, including two of his former colleagues in the Indian Police Service, at the Bombay Central, he returned to her uncle's house where preparations were being made for the wedding night, which also happened to be her thirty-first birthday. One of the things he learnt was that a basketful of rose petals had been brought by Harimohini's elder sister, Mrs. Chandrmukhi Narayan, to be strewn on the conjugal bed. Harimohini had introduced her to him as a famous socialite-intellectual of Delhi.

He was elated to recall her father's sneering references to Harimohini's admiration for his idealism and social activism and her disdain for her elitist and hedonistic culture, which explained her rejection of Somdutt in his favor. It enabled him not to feel anxious about her rather extraordinary modesty and self-restraint in the course of their writing sessions as well as later. He gathered a handful of rose petals from the bed and presented them to her with an amorous smile. She inhaled their scent as the first present from her beloved husband and smiled gratefully at him. He looked at her for a glimpse of that exquisite desire behind the bashful countenance which characterizes the bride on her wedding night. Instead, he saw on her face an utterly unembarrassed and relaxed expression. As if she was telling him that now that he was her husband, he was cordially welcome to do what husbands do on the wedding night! Her almost total lack of shyness surprised him. He couldn't help wondering again whether she was an experienced woman, although it wouldn't matter what she was before their marriage. Then he remembered her chaste behavior throughout their association.

Shaking off his momentary bemusement, he told her how he had begun to desire her soon after their first meeting. How disappointed he was at the lack of any response from her even after their long writing sessions and later during his visit to Bombay after she had accepted his proposal. Yet how happy he felt at her self-restraint and modesty! And how ardently he had been waiting for this moment!

Without change of expression, she replied that she had also begun to desire him as her husband soon after she interviewed him. How disappointed she was when he went back to Bhopal during her absence because of her mother's illness. How unhappy she felt when he told her that he could not say when he would be able to come to Bombay and later turned down her proposal to come to Bhopal to work on the book. How delighted she was when she received his proposal. What a hard time she had overcoming her father's opposition. And how keenly she had also been looking forward to this moment!

Her words made his excitement and desire to embrace her irresistible. He joyously restrained himself and after a few more exchanges expressive of their mutual adoration at last embarked upon the business of the moment with a tactical shyness and tentativeness calculated to make her excitement as intensely sweet as his own.

Instead, what he got from her in response to his strategically delicate yet warm foreplay followed by rapturous movements was a decorous submission, followed at the end by what looked like a grateful smile for his kindness mixed with a heartfelt hope that he had enjoyed himself!

Despite the sensual gratification and the assurance that she was a virtuous and complaisant wife, such as everyman desires, he was vaguely disappointed by the absence of any sign of carnal bliss on her face during the act.

He decided against rushing to conclusions.

However, when even after a week the expression of her face remained elegant and ladylike not only after but even during the act in response to his exhausting resourcefulness, he began to wonder. It reminded him of the fact that despite being so lively and good-looking she had remained unmarried for so long and most probably without having had an affair. It was improbable that she should not have been courted by attractive young men like Somdutt. However, he hopefully noted that her look before, during and after lovemaking did not betray coldness or distaste for sex. Quite the contrary.

Presently he decided to try another strategy, a bolder one. He was justly proud of his instrument, of its shape and size. It had been praised and frankly envied by not a few of his friends when in their teens they used to occasionally indulge in comparisons. She instinctively understood his wish and, looking at it with an appreciative smile, fondled it as a thing of beauty. Her expression also showed that she was proud of it for belonging to her! However, despite the genuineness of the appreciation, he failed to perceive in her expression any craving for carnal bliss.

He continued to perform as hard as he could.

Sometimes, he wondered whether she was enjoying herself as much as he, or even more, without letting it appear on her face from modesty or policy. But where was the need to do so after so many days had gone by? Or was it her upbringing or temperament? With a bachelor's insatiable curiosity about the conjugal life of married men he had heard of women who enjoyed intensely but thought it immodest and indiscreet to betray their ecstasy and participate in the act. According to a friend, during his honeymoon his wife used to express her joy and thanks by quickly falling asleep and snoring contentedly after the act was over and he had fallen on his back exhausted and panting. Later, when they had become intimate, she confessed to him that she used to behave according to the advice of her sister-in-law, who was much sought after by her newly-married women friends and relatives as a consultant about conjugal life. She had advised her to be chary of manifesting her pleasure too soon lest her husband should become doubtful of her virginity, and also to make him work harder.

After one more week had gone by, these explanations began to seem facile and unconvincing and he was beset by a gnawing suspicion that she didn't find him exciting enough, that perhaps what her father had contemptuously said was true and her repugnance to her affluent and snobbish milieu was naively romantic and she had been excessively influenced by the history of his career in deciding to marry him.

A few days later, they left for Shimla on their honeymoon. A sullen father and a happy mother, who continued to whisper tips into her ears till they checked in, saw them off at the Santa Cruz Airport.

In spite of the perplexing experiences of the wedding night and the nights following it, her undiminished liveliness during the day kept up his hopes. It maintained his faith in the ultimate effectiveness of the combination of his ardor, which had remained unfazed, and her esteem for his philanthropic character, even if it was exaggerated by her youthful romanticism. However, thinking lest her romantic disdain for her self-indulgent milieu and mundane concerns should peter out before she physically warmed up to him, he did not let up his efforts, in which he was helped by her voluptuous figure. And continued to make love energetically, inventively and with finesse. To stimulate her he assiduously sought to impart to his caresses, both physical and verbal, an ostensible tenderness that her responses didn't inspire in him. Yet he persevered.

At last, he ceased to doubt that she did not particularly care for carnal pleasure, at least not now, and had really rejected Somdutt and married him from distaste for her environment. However, she never failed to receive him with a welcoming smile and he continued to perform as hard and as hopeful of a happy conjugal life as before.

However, he couldn't help recalling her hateful father's warning that she was marrying him from naïve admiration for what he considered his worthless social activism. He hated him more than ever.

14/2

However, far from behaving as one who regretted her marriage, she was radiantly happy; in fact, off the bed she behaved like a beautiful woman who was hugely enjoying her honeymoon with her gallant. She apparently relished the admiring glances of the young and not so young men during their visits to the tourist spots of Shimla. He vicariously enjoyed her happiness at being the object of so much admiration; it a little made up for his own disappointments and enabled him to hope for better days. On the whole, her overall behavior reconfirmed his belief that she had been influenced in preferring him to Somdutt by her high-minded appreciation of the history of his career and not from immaturity.

She would enthusiastically talk to him about its high points even when they were lying together and he was caressing her.

Sometimes he wondered whether her lack of enjoyment of carnal pleasure was the result of the disgust of her sensitive nature at the excesses and vulgarity of sex to which she had been exposed from a young age in the permissive high society to which she belonged and that eventually she would be cured by his sincere adoration of her. It was a fact that the more disappointed he was by her sexual responses, the more he respected her. There was no doubt that she was an extraordinary woman.

A month after his return to Bhopal, where he had gone directly from Shimla after his honeymoon, she asked him to take a fortnight off from his work and come to Goa, where she was going on a special assignment. At first he refused, pleading busyness, but she continued to urge. A married friend of his, to whom he had been confiding both her pre-marital and post-marital behavior and her friendship with Somdutt, had told him not to lose hope and give her the benefit of the doubt because some women were late starters whose desire was belatedly awakened and then awakened fiercely. He should treat her responses as normal and not disappoint her by appearing dissatisfied. He must join her lest she should ask Somdutt to accompany her! He grew panicky and flew to Goa.

On the whole, he enjoyed the visit, yet came away finally convinced that she didn't enjoy sex as young women are supposed to do, or enjoyed it with her own brand of pleasure, which was different from the pleasure he craved for. What surprised him was that after the act she looked deeply contented. It seemed to rule out any improvement from his point of view. However, during the day she overflowed with vivacity and was assiduous in her attentions to his convenience and comfort. She ordered his favorite dishes like pilaf, dahi badas, kadhi and rasogullahs.

Every time, moved by her off-the-bed tender attentions to him he tried to draw her out, she assured him with transparent sincerity that she was incomparably happy! It gradually changed his opinion about the type of woman she was. It began to enable him to make love to her as often as he liked not only without qualms but with increasing respect for her cheerful willingness to give herself apparently without much pleasure, as he understood it. And without any hint that she was making any sacrifice to her love and admiration for him. He hoped that eventually his immersion in his work would make him indifferent to her deficiency of which he sometimes thought she might actually be unconscious, and make it possible for him to truly appreciate her fondness for him.

In addition to devoting more and more of his time to the various schemes taken up for the gas victims, he had resumed his sessions with Shanti two or three times a week in her college library to help her with her thesis. He was thankful for her not making the vaguest allusion to the fact that despite their close relations he had courted Harimohini on the quiet and married her. He could see that she was extremely worried that she might be removed from her college teacher's post for failing to get her Ph.D. Thesis approved in time. He resolved to help her till the thesis was completed.

Chapter 15

In the days following the violent quarrel Chandrmukhi was inhibited from taking the initiative for reconciliation by the thought that she would be expected to promise to him that Somdutt would no longer come and thus implicitly admit that she had been wrong in not stopping his visits before. Actually, for some time before that day's clash, she had been thinking of requesting Somdutt to stop coming. The reason was the increase in the disgruntled behavior of her husband with her following the use of more moderate language by Somdutt of late, which he obviously suspected was calculated to ensure the continuation of his visits. She was confident that Somdutt would understand her compulsion and not take it amiss. But she was loath to comply with Vishnu's authoritarian wish to do so in response to her conciliatory overture.

At the same time, she anxiously waited for him to make the first move for reconciliation and thus by indirectly admitting that he had been unjust to her, make it possible for her to admit her fault, express her regrets and request Somdutt to stop coming.

As for Vishnu, during the day he thought that if he apologized to her, she might begin to invite Somdutt to her parties again. He was also kept from expressing his regrets by the thought that, however, he wouldn't mind doing so if it should become unavoidable! At night, he thought that meanwhile it would do no harm if he waited a little longer and allowed her the pleasure of making the first move which, rendered cheerful by drugs, he felt confident she would do sooner rather than later because she knew he loved her as much as ever and regretted his jealousy, which was a helpless expression of his excessive love for her! Thinking these pleasant thoughts, he fell into a profound slumber, which never lasted less than nine hours without a break and from which he awoke feeling refreshed and optimistic that soon everything would be okay!

To prevent gossip, Vishnu and Chandrmukhi still went out together in response to unavoidable formal invitations and talked and behaved to each other as they always used to do at the evening parties. Particularly before such close friends as were aware of the tension between them and would have been embarrassed to witness it. However, days passed without any change. Somdutt seemed to have finally decided to stop coming. Both Jaiprakash and Vishnu hoped that he would not resume his visits without at least some encouragement from Chandrmukhi. He could not have missed her sullen disapproval of his behavior on that day. They also hoped that she had become wiser, although at least twice both had heard her talking to him on the phone about the Hindu-Muslim clashes in different parts of the country and the growing threat to secularism in the wake of Babri Mosque's demolition.

Chandrmukhi and Somdutt still met at the India International and other places. Watching their friendly exchanges, both Jaiprakash and Vishnu felt that such relations between them were not only nothing to worry about but a welcome replacement for their meetings at the evening parties and over drinks and dinner. They hoped that he had at last realized that the pleasure of attending the parties was not worth the embarrassments. However, while conversing politely with Somdutt, Vishnu would sometimes recall his fear, when Somdutt fulsomely praised his host's food and drink, which made him look like a parasite, that like a parasite worth his salt he wouldn't be satisfied until he had also enjoyed his wife and praised her fulsomely for her charms!

Jaiprakash continued to hope that it was a matter of time before Somdutt's absence would reconcile husband and wife. They still slept separately, but gradually had grown kinder to each other and again started taking breakfast, lunch and dinner together. If Vishnu's kindness stemmed from the fatal mix of his wife's kindness to him during the day and his overnight optimism induced by drugs, Chandrmukhi's owed itself to the gradual renewal of her anxiety. Unlike him, she had begun to fear that before he realized he might become a helpless victim of the happy illusion induced by drugs that there was no need to worry as everything would soon become all right, and that it might eventually replace their normal relations.

She also felt worried by her almost total want of desire. His prolonged sullenness before their violent quarrel on the day of the mosque's demolition and her despair over a long period during which she had forced herself to submit to him without desire had gradually filled her with revulsion for sex, which alarmed her. She sometimes feared that she had lost the capacity to enjoy it forever and that her relations with her husband would never be the same, even if they were reconciled.

She sometimes thought of laying aside her pride and slipping into his bed in his absence; she did not doubt that he would be appeased by the apologetic gesture and it would solve all the problems between them. But disgust for physical relations with him and even more with the sweet nothings he whispered into her ears during the act prevented her.

Yet she told herself that eventually she might have to do it because every passing day was critical in view of his drug habit.

Many friends had begun to talk openly about Somdutt's absence from the evening parties. Some explained it by a misunderstanding or some unsavory episode between him and her or him and her husband. Somdutt not only hadn't mentioned that day's incident to anybody but had denied that any unpleasantness with her or Vishnu was responsible for his absence. His easy and good-humored conversation with her whenever they happened to meet in her husband's presence before their common friends at the clubs or other places, and his and Vishnu's simulated politeness to each other seemed to confirm what he said. In fact, Somdutt's relations with her not only seemed but had actually become as friendly as before. Just as in spite of their mutual attraction they had never been in love, as she and her husband were from before and for years after their marriage, so they didn't feel constrained with each other because of his behavior on that day, which had then seemed foolish to both of them. In retrospect, it had begun to seem inadvertent and trivial. Its importance had been magnified by her husband's jealousy. Also, since they met quite often, neither felt the discontinuation of his visits to her home much of a loss.

However, as days passed into weeks without any symptom of change, Jaiprakash began to worry. He sometimes found her gloomy. Then she seemed to cheer up. As her melancholy spells increased in frequency and became longer Jaiprakash began to lose confidence in their good sense as a reconciling factor.

Sometimes, as Jaiprakash watched Chandrmukhi's hearty appetite and natural exuberance, which still occasionally prevailed over her despondency, he felt both admiration and pity for her and disgust for her husband.

Chapter 16

16/1

Jawaharlal had returned from the USA after three months instead of one as had been planned. Like a man of principle at the end of his tether, he had extended his visit in the hope that his sons and their wives would take advantage of his absence to procure a kidney and end his daughter's suffering without his having done anything against his principles. He would have to believe what they would tell him. Of course, some people would say that he had purposely gone away to enable them to do it. But what people were saying before was much worse! He did not rule out the likelihood that it might be a brother's kidney. However, Sarika was still on dialysis.

Vishwanath gave him a detailed but discreetly censored account of his meeting with Himanshu. Jawaharlal was surprised to hear that somebody had at last responded to the appeal. Contrary to his habit, however, he was checked just in time by his instinctive approval of Vishwanath's talk with and overall treatment of Himanshu from sharply asking him and Srinath as to why they hadn't informed him about his visit before in the course of their frequent telephonic conversations during which they had even discussed the weather. Instead of expressing his appreciation, though, he was aggravated to think that Vishwanath's conduct also amounted to a repudiation of his appeal for altruistic donation, which he had been forced to issue against his wish because both brothers had pathetically backed out after undergoing the tests.

'He said he had business with me and would talk to no one else. Did he also say that he would come back to meet me after my return, although Calcutta is so far away?' he asked.

After some hesitation, Vishwanath replied, 'Yes, he did say so.' He said to himself, 'I don't want him to come back!'

'If he came in response to the appeal he would have undergone the blood and other tests to ensure that his kidney would suit her.'

'I think so.'

Looking ambiguously at his sons, Jawaharlal said, 'Give me his address. I'll write to him!'

Vishwanath was not enthusiastic. He said, 'He may have said that for politeness' sake after I entertained him and personally drove him to the railway station to express my gratefulness. I don't think he'll come back.'

'I also don't think he'll return,' said Srinath.

Vishwanath said to himself, 'If no acceptable donor like the Aligarh lawyer appears, I'll donate my kidney.' He had once again been assured by Subhadra's doctor father that though like any operation kidney transplant was also not entirely free of risk, yet the chances of an accident were extremely rare. The doctor had also told him that the real cause of his fear, which he had confidentially confessed to him, was not so much the risk involved, which every ordinarily educated man knew was minimal, as the compulsive dwelling upon it. One had only to stop worrying for the fear to disappear. However, it was easier said than done and he need not feel ashamed as even many doctors were unnerved to think of the removal of what after all is a vital organ, or of a mishap during the operation. After hearing his father-in-law, Vishwanath had begun to feel that he would be able to overcome his fear if no acceptable donor responded to the appeal. He would never let his sister die. He didn't consider Himanshu an acceptable donor as he was almost certainly an altruist who had been surprised and repelled by what he had come to know. However, a person who had come from so far away after reading the appeal in a newspaper might impulsively come again and succumb to his father's petition made in a weak moment, and later regret it. He was shaken to think that Himanshu might afterwards be tormented by the thought that he had let himself be taken in by the shamelessly selfish brothers and their hypocritical and unscrupulous father. He would never allow it to happen. He would wait. How long would depend on the circumstances, about which there was no need to think at the moment, as according to his father-in-law, who had examined Sarika only a few days ago, her general condition was quite good.

Jawaharlal was half-thinking half-hoping, 'Maybe, he was a young man with idealistic impulses and didn't come for money, but just the same was relieved to know that I was out. Having impulsively decided to selflessly donate his organ, he gradually began to realize its consequences and came here in an agony of irresolution between self-respect and fear of mutilation. And my absence and the existence of the brothers enabled him to change his mind.'

He said, 'I also don't have much hope that he'll respond, but still I think I should write to him for politeness' sake! After all, he came from so far away,' Jawaharlal replied, feeling slightly hopeful from his sons' reluctance that they might now express their willingness to give their kidneys. The hope was instantly followed by bitterness, as he recalled reports of many honest and reasonable people condemning him for prolonging the suffering of his daughter and humiliating his sons by issuing the appeal instead of dealing sensibly with his family's circumstances and obtaining the organ of an acceptable donor by paying him. Despite Jawaharlal's conviction that he had behaved honorably, he could not help thinking that he had made a laughing stock of himself by issuing the appeal.

Srinath recalled that it was a long time since he and Vishwanath had been surprised into offering to undergo the tests. And like his brother he also couldn't help wondering often as to what his father thought about his changing his mind after undergoing the tests. He endeavored to assure himself that, in spite of his disappointment, as an intelligent and reasonable man and good father he couldn't be unmindful of the fact that ignoring the violent opposition of his wife would have made his married life unhappy. It would also have spoilt the home atmosphere. He would have told father, if he had asked him to disregard his wife's opposition and donate his kidney, which he felt sure he won't for fear of being disobliged, that he need not worry as he wouldn't let his sister die. He was keenly aware of the constraint between them, which had become more awkward after the publication of the appeal. He was sure that father knew that he disapproved of his treatment of the Aligarh lawyer. What his father thought of him was followed by what his wife thought! He knew she was too clever not to have guessed that he had submitted to her pressure from fear; she knew him better than to think that he had yielded because he was afraid that it would seriously affect their relations if he ignored her opposition! At the same time the thought of his wife's violent protest against his doing what he considered his obligation as a brother sometimes filled him with deep resentment against her: if she hadn't put up such resistance, he would have had no excuse for not donating his kidney after he had undergone the tests. At that moment he would rather have died than confess that he was afraid. And how much better off would all of them be today! He blamed her and Subhadra as much as he reproached his father for prolonging his sister's suffering.

16/2

Subhadra and Charles were sitting in the latter's office and as a prelude to talking about the real subject, discussing the sequel to the Babri Mosque's demolition. It had become a common topic of conversation in the drawing rooms, during the morning walks and in the vegetable markets, with the people in general, including astute Muslims, agreeing that the disappearance of the mosque had not signaled the end of the affair. It was a political cow which the upper-caste Hindu leftist and middle-caste Hindu casteist politicians would continue to milk with the cooperation of Muslim fundamentalists, no matter if it further alienated Hindus and Muslims from each other.

Having disposed of the Mosque, Subhadra said to him, 'What did Papaji write to Himanshu? Did you read the letter? Vishwanath merely told me that he had thanked Himanshu for responding to his appeal and informed him that he had returned from abroad.'

'He has written him not one but two letters, the second three weeks after the first. I read them before they were dispatched,' he said. He added, 'I may tell you that though he wrote the letters against his sons' wishes, he wasn't at all keen to write them, in spite of the fact that he had published the appeal after virtually extorting their acquiescence. I was present at their conversation. And I believe he forced himself to write because of the way Sarika refused to look at him and burst into tears on at least two occasions when he accompanied her during her visits to the hospital for dialysis. He was extremely upset by her behavior. On both occasions I was witness to it.'

'Do you think Himanshu will come back?'

'If he needs money, he might, though Vishwanath's behavior was far from encouraging. The letters would make him come. He might take the risk of being turned away. He might also come, if he was inspired by youthful altruism. In the latter case, however, he as well might not. After seeing how wealthy you people are and after coming to know that the patient had two brothers, it's possible he thought there was money in it somewhere. That may have caused him to change his mind, in spite of the fact that Vishwanath behaved honorably. He may have justifiably expected Vishwanath to be honest and frank about the circumstances of the appeal, after he had come from so far away. You also think so. I have no doubt that he went back disappointed.'

She nodded. Looking at her, Charles wondered whether she wanted him to confidentially show her the letters' copies and whether he should let her read them or tell her that he didn't have them.

An hour later, while Charles was studying a case, Subhadra entered his office again and said, 'Are you busy? Are you going to the Court today?'

'Yes, but after the lunch break.'

He felt that she had come so soon again because she was curious to read the letters. He said, 'Between us, the letters were not happily drafted. They contain one or two things that shouldn't have been written.'

'Do you have their copies? I'd like to read them.'

Charles took the copies from a drawer and gave them to her.

'What's in them that seems objectionable to you? Although I think that they shouldn't have been written, in the first place, but since now it's a fact, they seem to me all right,' said Subhadra after going through the letters thoughtfully twice and returning them to him.

'Papaji shouldn't have written, as he has done in both in different words, that he would owe him an everlasting debt of gratitude for his altruistic desire to save the life of a total stranger. It may have put him off,' replied Charles.

'What's wrong in saying that? It's what the appeal said to which he responded.'

'To think of his belaboring this point after Himanshu has come to know that Sarika has two brothers and how rich you people are! Vishwanath appeared quite an athlete beside him. How much value do you think he would put on the gratitude of such people?'

Subhadra said, 'You're right.'

Before she left, she again said, 'In fact, the letters should never have been written. As a matter of fact, they were written in order to put off taking a decision about buying a kidney. I don't think they have any alternative in view of Sarika's deepening gloom.'

Chapter 17

17/1

After the demolition of the Babri Mosque, Syed and Professor Zulfiqar Ali, to whose houses Somdutt had started going more often after discontinuing his visits to Chandrmukhi's home, had started coming more frequently to her evening parties where they found the atmosphere more congenial than elsewhere. They had found to their chagrin that even the nonreligious and non-communal Hindus who had reacted with outrage to the demolition had soon begun to analyze as to why it had happened and to describe the event as contrary to the Hindu ethos, thus rubbing salt into the Muslims' wounds by implicitly telling them that Islam enjoined the desecration of the places of worship of other religions. Many of these Hindus were peace loving and well-meaning and tacitly expected the influential Muslims, especially politicians and intellectuals, to be practical and not to be misled by the morally snobbish or lying and hypocritical Hindu politicians and intellectuals and further aggravate communal feelings over what had been done and could not now be undone. In other words, behave with the forbearance of Hindus who had decided to overlook the savage destruction of their religious places, even the most important and sacred ones, and forced conversions of their co-religionists by Muslim rulers for hundreds of years until the arrival of the more civilized British. While Ali regarded this approach as sensible, he also realized that it would take some time for his community to think and behave according to it, and that too if they were not relentlessly incited by the smug and self-seeking Hindu pseudo-secularists to join them in their useless protests against Hindu nationalists. Syed, on the other hand, while thinking like Ali, couldn't control his belligerent disposition and continued to attack Hindu communalism in his weekly column in a newspaper. What particularly aggravated him was that while publishing whatever he wrote and paying him handsomely, the editor as well as the staff of the paper on the sly sympathized with the fundamentalist Hindu politicians and parties he criticized. This newspaper had recently published in its magazine section an article by a famous Hindu historian and archaeologist, whom Syed hated as a communalist, to prove that a massive Temple existed under the Babri Mosque. It had followed it up by publishing a long list of the historic temples which had been destroyed by the Muslim rulers. It was obvious that the owners and editors of the magazine thought that Syed's views being characteristic of a Muslim, he had full right to exercise the freedom of expression guaranteed in the secular Constitution of the essentially Hindu India! He sometimes wondered whether they secretly despised him.

One day Syed, who criticized Gandhi, Nehru and Patel for being responsible for the Hindu-Muslim divide and the partition of India as much as or even more than Jinnah by sabotaging the Cabinet Mission Plan (He was inclined to doubt the sincerity of Hindus who agreed with him) recalled a particular statement of Gandhi about Muslims. He told Vishnu, 'Do you know what Gandhi once said about Muslims?'

'No! I am not erudite like you!' replied Vishnu, hiding his joy. He did not doubt that Syed would pour scorn on the Mahatma by selectively quoting or even misquoting his words. He had compiled a reference book of statements by Gandhi, Nehru and Patel which he quoted without reference to the context to prove how they contradicted themselves according to their convenience while Jinnah was a straightforward man who unfortunately went overboard around 1940.

'During the Khilafat Movement, a Hindu-Muslim riot notoriously known as Moplah Rebellion took place in Kerala resulting in the death and forced conversion to Islam of many Hindus. The Mahatma said that Muslims deserved praise for proving their loyalty to their religion by forcibly converting and murdering people belonging to other religions!'

Govind, who had come for a fortnight to Delhi for the third time since his marriage in response to Harimohini's wish and was staying at Chandrmukhi's home, happened to be present on the occasion. He discreetly agreed with Syed's views about Gandhi and Nehru which according to his experience he regarded as generally the Indian Muslims' views and which he did not think unreasonable from their point of view. They hated the idea of playing second fiddle to Hindus in an independent India as it was visualized by Gandhi, Nehru and other Hindu leaders and were not unreasonably afraid of being discriminated against and victimized not only from prejudice and malice but also because they were far behind Hindus in practically all fields—especially education, commerce and industry, and administration. Discreetly because he did not wish to disappoint her charming hostess and sister-in-law by expressing himself too frankly. He also considered her silly for having quarreled with her husband over her friendship with Somdutt whether genuinely or ostensibly for ideological reasons. He regarded the discussions at the evening parties as mostly humbug indulged in for pleasure by people who were addicted to the good and fashionable things of life, which included profession of secularism and the pretence that India was in reality a secular country. During all his visits Syed had happened to be present at these parties. Govind also secretly agreed with his views about the phoniness of Indian secularism. But his concurrence with Syed's views was for reasons different from his. Unlike him, he regarded even educated Muslims in general, with few exceptions, as incapable of believing in the possibility of the genuineness of secularism, except as something required by good manners, in a fundamentally Hindu India characterized by traditional view of Muslims as a separatist, backward and self-sufficient community fated to suffer from the prejudice of non-Muslims irrespective of their religion. His skepticism was as much due to what he thought the exclusivity of Islam as due to his conviction of an average educated Hindu's poor opinion of the Muslim religion and culture and the less than perfectly disguised insincerity of his views about the Muslims' emotional attachment to India, and the Muslims' perception of the Hindus' pretence and condescension. It was a common sight, which never failed to repel him, to see a Muslim in western dress and looking like a true gentleman walking nonchalantly accompanied by a completely veiled woman. And a Muslim family asserting their right to marry a minor girl on the ground of their religion which they asserted transcended the law of the land. He did not much mind Syed's criticism of Gandhi because he himself thought that Gandhi put Hindus' prejudice against Muslims in his exalted category of sins and hence practically beyond cure rather than regarding it as one of the innumerable human prejudices prevalent in the Indian society which should be left alone to cure themselves.

Incidentally, during both his visits he had also been struck with the relations between Chandrmukhi and her special assistant Jaiprakash, who had impressed him as an attractive person and something of an intellectual. He had expressed to Harimohini his misgivings about the long absences of Vishnu, which left his unhappy wife and Jaiprakash alone together. But Harimohini had assured him that his misgivings were baseless because Chandrmukhi with all her progressive views was an aristocrat and a sophisticated snob who despite her admiration for Jaiprakash's culture and intellect couldn't help thinking of him as a servant. Govind felt too embarrassed to tell her that, apart from the high intellectual and cultural standard of Jaiprakash, which was in itself a temptation and a preventive of any possible feeling of shame and humiliation for the aristocratic mistress, not only aggrieved or sex-starved aristocratic women but even those who loved and admired their husbands and were satisfied with them were not invulnerable to affairs with their servants because the latter made love more vigorously in order not only to enhance their status but also out of gratitude to them for the favor, instead of regarding lovemaking as a right as husbands did. And the aristocratic status of the mistress constituted an additional vulnerability because she could depend upon the lover to comply with her wish whenever she desired to end the affair if it should become wearisome or risky or for any other reason.

Govind himself had often imagined that if he and Shanti were living in the same house he might have become her lover in Harimohini's absence without loving and admiring the latter any the less.

17/2

Jaiprakash, who was invariably present when Syed came, never ceased to wonder at him. Syed never let go of an opportunity to criticize Gandhi and held him and not Jinnah mainly responsible for the partition of India, which he described as a tragedy. Gandhi, who in order to prevent the partition not only never spoke ill of

Muslims but even tried to explain away their and their leaders' anti-Hindu words and deeds calculated to promote separation. At the same time , Syed praised Ambedkar, who in his writings and speeches ruled out Hindu-Muslim unity, denigrated Islam as an exclusivist faith in which there was nothing but contempt and enmity for non-Muslims; who pleaded not only for the division of British India into a Muslim-majority state and a non-Muslim country but also for exchange of populations on the ground that Islam can never allow a true Muslim to adopt India as his motherland and regard a Hindu as his kith and kin. Even the fact that contrary to Gandhi Ambedkar's support for Muslims' right to a separate sovereign state, which Jaiprakash did not doubt secretly delighted the Jinnah-worshipping Syed, could not entirely explain Syed's admiration for Ambedkar and criticism of Gandhi. At last Jaiprakash understood that Syed's esteem for Ambedkar was due to the fact that he rejected Hinduism, describing it as a caste-ridden iniquitous faith, and became a Buddhist. Syed was only a little less critical of Nehru, who openly expressed his detestation of Jinnah and his description as insane the demand of Muslims, who constituted one-fourth of India's population, for equality in not only the legislature and the executive but also in the civil services, army and police, as a transitional alternative to partition till a sovereign Islamic Pakistan was achieved.

Syed's and Zulfiqar Ali's presence considerably enlivened Chandrmukhi's evening parties, especially because despite radically differing in their political views they remained intimate friends. If Syed praised the leftist and Hindu casteist political parties for their denunciation of the communalist Bharatiya Janata Party, Ali described the former's professions as false and chiefly calculated to exploit the Indian Muslims as a vote-bank. This they sought to achieve by generating fear and insecurity in Muslims and describing as fundamentalist any predominantly Hindu organization, unless it also happened to be casteist like the Laloo and Mulayam outfits. The latter were hardheaded realists and cynics who enjoyed defending and milking diehard Muslim groups for gaining and retaining power. However, he especially despised VP Singh. This blatant opportunist, according to him, had marginalized the genuinely secular Arif Muhammad Khan, regarding him as an obstacle to his ambition, and shamelessly buttered up Syed Shahabuddin of Shahbano notoriety for the sake of Muslim votes in his election from the Allahabad Lok Sabha seat. The same Shahabuddin who had openly said that for a Muslim individual religious identity was supreme, rising above race, language, geography or political jurisdiction, without thinking of the consequences if Hindus began to feel likewise. Even Jinnah never said such a thing.

Syed on the other hand praised VP Singh for helping the Bangladeshi Muslim infiltrators into Assam in getting Indian citizenship under the IMDT Act 1983 on humanitarian grounds. He also took this opportunity to criticize Jawaharlal for campaigning against this Act, despite being a Gandhian, or because he was a Gandhian! Syed let go of no opportunity to criticize Gandhi although he also quoted him in his favor when it suited him. He had in a recent article excoriated the Mahatma for preventing the "secular agreement" between the Bengali Muslim leader H. S. Suhrawardi and Sharat Bose, elder brother of Subhash Chandra Bose, on the formation of a united sovereign Bengal with the blessings of Jinnah. Jinnah had told Suhrawardi that he had no interest in having as a part of Pakistan a divided Assam and partitioned Bengal without Calcutta and without a corridor linking the country's two wings. Gandhi's pro-Hindu intervention, he said, was obviously calculated to prevent the formation of a bigger and more prosperous Muslim-majority Bengal. He also blamed Gandhi for the Kashmir problem, quoting British journalists to prove that he supported military intervention in J&K to defeat the State's Muslim freedom-fighters

'Perhaps Gandhi had long ago begun to wish for the division of India into a Muslim Pakistan and Hindu India where Raghupati Raghav Raja Ram would be sung without provoking Muslims into shouting Allah O Akbar and leading to a communal riot. But poor fellow couldn't confess it,' thought Vishnu. He had often wondered at his entertaining the illusion, if he really did so, that the Muslims who did not trust the westernized Nehru would consider him their savior in a predominantly Hindu anti-Muslim India.

He said to Syed, 'Gandhi also wanted an undivided India!'

"I don't agree with you,' Syed replied.

Vishnu personally liked Syed and welcomed his honest criticism of Hindu leaders, whether they were Vajpayee and Advani or Gandhi and Nehru, because he considered him not only a true representative of Indian Muslims, much more true than Arif Muhammad Khans, but also because Muslim politicians and intellectual activists like him would prevent Hindus from being deluded by smug leftists like Jyoti Basus and selfish sham secularists like Laloo Yadavs and Mulayam Singhs. For the same reason Vishnu did not mind Syed's violent criticism of his Gandhian uncle Jawaharlal, who had been agitating for a common civil code for all Indians.

Ali claimed to have in his possession the clipping of a letter Syed Shahabuddin had published in The Indian Express in December 1990. In it, presuming to speak on behalf of all Muslims, he had assured Hindus that Muslims would according to the Shari'ah forgo their claim to the Babri Mosque for the sake of Hindu-Muslim brotherhood. He wrote this letter, Ali claimed, because according to a report which he found no reason to doubt he had been promised a place in his cabinet by Prime Minister Chandra Shekhar as a quid pro quo. Syed smiled at his dear friend's comments, describing him as more Hindu than Hindus and advising him to join the Bharatiya Janata Party. However, he agreed with Ali in describing Shahabuddin as stupid and a fake, who had alienated the progressive and sympathetic Hindus by asking Muslims to boycott official functions, including the Republic Day.

To the delight of Vishnu, Ali and Syed agreed on one thing, though for different reasons: Most leftists, obviously Hindu leftists, especially journalists, writers and the so-called intellectual activists, Ali said, were charlatans and not friends of Muslims because their boorish criticism of Hindu nationalism aggravated rather than improving Hindu-Muslim relations. He wondered at their not protesting, or protesting feebly, against the ban on Salman Rushdie's novel, Satanic Verses, but defending Maqbool Fida Hussain who had painted the Hindu goddesses Sita, Durga and Saraswati naked. He had painted Sita masturbating on the long tail of Hanuman, Durga having intercourse with a lion and Parvati copulating with a bull and Shankar watching the act on Shivratri. The same Hussain who had painted not only Fatima but also

Mother Teresa fully clothed. Syed agreed that Hussain's paintings were inspired by malice against Hindus but it was also true that many Hindu secularists' support to him was not genuine but self-praise of a perverted kind.

Vishnu thought that if a Hindu had painted Fatima naked and publicly displayed the picture not only would he have been murdered and large scale arson and communal riots would have been sparked throughout the country by Muslim politicians with the support of Hindu secularists, resulting in hundreds of deaths, but violent protests against India would have taken place all over the Muslim world.

Vishnu, who knew that Syed hated Indira Gandhi for among other things having separated Bangladesh from Pakistan said, 'This same Hussain, who had been a prominent pro-JP activist in his campaign against Indira Gandhi, during the Emergency drew a much publicized triptych of her in oils, representing her as the Goddess Durga vanquishing all her foes.'

Syed, who was not aware of this fact, said, 'Really?'

'Yes, it's a well-known fact. And when he was questioned by some journalists, his unabashed reply was that it was his humble tribute to her, who was a secularist, while Jaya Prakash Narayan had taken the support of the fascist RSS during his campaign against her!'

Ali said that he was a cunning exhibitionist who, fearful of the consequences of walking naked in public, sought to earn notoriety by walking on naked feet with the sole aim of enhancing the price of his paintings. Further in pursuance of this design he once tried to enter an elite club known for permitting no infringement of its snobbish etiquette. And, as he had confidently expected, he was turned away. This "deplorable humiliation of a great artist" as the leftist Hindu intellectuals described it and which he played down with the pretense of humility, made big news, enabling him to bask afresh in the secular limelight, which had begun to fade.

Vishnu did not doubt that if Indira Gandhi had been politically finished, Hussain would have painted her stark naked and lolling in bed with some mythological demon like Ravana or Kansa or a villain like Duryodhana or Shakuni. And the high-caste Hindu pseudo-secularists and OBC opportunists would have hypocritically defended the work on the ground of secularism, especially because it was painted by a Muslim, whose community, they would have discreetly left unsaid, conscious of being Hindus, was fated to be a victim of distrust and discrimination not only owing to Hindus' own separatism of which they accused Muslims but also due to the Muslims' recent hostility to the idea of a united India, support for the formation of Pakistan and opposition to uniform civil code advocated by what they considered a nominally secular but in reality a Hindu India.

What Vishnu knew but thought inconsequential was that there were also enlightened Muslims who would have gladly exchanged such worthless and invidious rights and freedoms for the disabilities and discriminations to which they were subjected by the same pseudo-secular Hindus. But such Muslims were so few and so weak and moreover were constrained against their will to defend or rationalize what Hindus hated to remember—the savage atrocities committed by the Muslim rulers before the arrival of the British.

He said, 'He painted Hindu goddesses being fucked by animals as much from anti-Hindu malice as to expose the hypocrisy and masochism of his so-called secular Hindu supporters and to provoke a war of words between them and the self-respecting Hindus.

Syed agreed that most secularists, meaning Hindu secularists, were dishonest, who on the pretext of secularism did not protest against India's bloody repression of Muslim freedom-fighters in Jammu & Kashmir.

Ali said that most of them were dishonest but those who called for a plebiscite in Jammu & Kashmir were even more so! They advocated it despite being aware, in fact because they were aware, that it could no longer be held under the U.N. auspices due to Pakistan's failure to comply with the U.N. conditions before it could be held. It had not vacated the areas of the state under its illegal occupation. He mentioned as enemies of Muslims a couple of Hindu writers and columnists who had enhanced their notoriety and become rich by advocating unpopular and impossible causes, specially plebiscite in Jammu & Kashmir. The militant Kashmiri separatists were more honest than such fake secularists because their demand for secession from India was due to their frank antipathy to being a part of a Hindu-majority country.

Syed, who sometimes felt tired of attacking Hindu fundamentalism and the politicians who openly or covertly promoted it, soon began to cheer up the gathering by denouncing the Judiciary as virtually an accomplice in the mosque's demolition. He described every PIL, which he asserted would have prevented the great tragedy, besides sending to jail the contemners of the orders of the U.P. High Court and the Supreme Court, if the latter had dealt with them earnestly.

'Do you know what?' one day he fumed, after taking a sip. 'Only a few days before the Babri Mosque was brought down, the Supreme Court was reminded by one of the petitioners that the security forces were finding it tough to control the huge numbers of karsevaks gathered there. The Court was also informed that the Kalyan Singh government had in gross violation of its commitment openly provided them nourishment, transport and other facilities to reach Ayodhya. The then Attorney-General, Milon Banerjee, repeatedly urged the two-judge bench of Justices Venkatchaliah and A.N. Ray to consider appointing Central Government as the receiver of the land where karseva was to be performed to prevent the certain demolition otherwise. All this was brought to the judges' notice. And what did they do? They passed an order allowing symbolic karseva. One of the judges went further and expressed concern for the health of and sanitation facilities for the rambhakts!'

Vishnu was delighted to hear it. He wondered how he had missed such an important news and whether Syed, who did not scruple to indulge in half-truths when he wanted to make a point, was speaking accurately. And if he was correct, did it mean that the Supreme Court had wisely judged the irreversibility of the Ramjanmabhoomi movement until the mosque was destroyed and had opted for the lesser evil? Of course, he could not tell Syed out of compassion as to how violently the Supreme Court's order in the Shahbano case had been denounced by Muslims for contravening the word of God as conveyed to the Prophet and enshrined in the Holy Quran and how it was ultimately set aside by a Constitutional amendment. A Muslim Cabinet Minister had in Parliament contemptuously described the Supreme Court judges as telis (oil-pressers) and tambolis (paan sellers).

Vishnu found it easy to abide such criticism from Syed and his other Muslim friends. In fact, he did so with pleasure mixed with sympathy. First, because they were gentlemen and sincerely friendly to him in spite of being aware of his soft corner for the demand for the construction of a Ram temple at the site of the Babri Mosque. Secondly, Vishnu's attitude towards them was conditioned by the thought that they labored under the agonizing compulsion to publicly profess that India, unlike Pakistan, Saudi Arabia or Iran was a secular country, where Muslims had the same rights as the Hindus. Vishnu could not but admit that it was not a fact because of the Muslims' first loyalty being to Islam and not to the laws and constitution of the country in which they lived, or of the Hindus' deeply ingrained centuries-old rancor against Muslims, which had caused MA Jinnah to demand a separate homeland for them. Such profession was the price the Muslims had to pay for the freedom of expression, a right which they found to their chagrin the more illusory the greater the freedom with which they exercised it. For example, Vishnu could see that the Hindus' cold indifference to the Muslims' refusal to sing Vande Mataram on religious grounds, or to his and other Muslim intellectuals' criticism of Gandhi, Nehru, Patel and other Hindu greats mortified sensitive persons like Syed. He also like most intellectual but powerless Muslims often felt humiliated by the moral snobbery of the cultured Hindus in overlooking in their community what they would have condemned in their own people: Triple talaq and the right to marry four wives, which exposed their people to contempt. Whenever Syed came, Vishnu made it a special point to be present lest he should "misunderstand" his absence!

On another occasion long ago Vishnu had come even closer to giving himself away. He had barely kept from laughing scornfully when in the presence of Syed he heard Somdutt and Chandrmukhi with the conscious hypocrisy typical of most Hindu leftists describe Jammu & Kashmir as a symbol of pluralism and multiculturalism.

He did not doubt that they were as aware as Syed that so deep was the distrust of Muslims on the part the ruling Hindu elite that neither Nehru nor his successors ever intended to hold the promised plebiscite in Jammu and Kashmir. Because it would have resulted in that Muslim-majority State overwhelmingly voting either for freedom or for accession to Pakistan and then throwing out or forcibly converting its Kashmiri Pandits. And what would have further exploded the Gandhi-Nehru-fostered myth of secularism, Indian Muslims would have rejoiced in it! And was it not a fact that after the elections to the Constituent Assembly prior to Independence, in which Muslims from north to south and east to west had voted for Pakistan from deep-seated fear of their future in a Hindu-dominated undivided India, even Nehru and Gandhi had found it impossible to hug the illusion of Hindu-Muslim unity and multiculturalism and begun to secretly think like Savarkar and Ambedkar? The latter was honored with the job of finalizing free India's Constitution and the former's portrait would one day be accorded a place in Parliament with the approbation of Communists in the company of Gandhi, Nehru, Patel and other Hindu freedom-fighters. Pakistan would be a haven for Muslims where they could always go, if life in India became unbearable. And if the Mahatma and his chosen disciple still pleaded with them not to go to Pakistan it was because they thought that either unable to tolerate the inevitable discrimination against them, they would leave for there sooner or later, or those who were forced to stay back would live meekly with the Hindu majority.

17/3

The hopes of Vishnu and Jaiprakash that Somdutt's exit was permanent were soon dashed.

One day, on arriving with Charles from Jawaharlal's home Jaiprakash was dismayed to see Syed and Somdutt alighting from the latter's car. While Syed had a gift-wrapped book in his hand, Somdutt, who was used to borrowing books never to return them rather than presenting them, carried a handsome bouquet. It was Vishnu's birthday. Affecting total lack of embarrassment, he entered the drawing room and walking behind Syed presented the bouquet to Vishnu and felicitated him. Vishnu, who was personally handing drinks to the guests, was shaken to see him. However, he managed a faint smile, thanked him politely and gave him a drink.

It had so happened that Syed had come in Somdutt's car because he had sold his own a few days ago and not yet bought a new one. Somdutt had been forced against his wish to comply with Syed's request that they go to Vishnu's home in his car lest he should think that he had really fallen out with Chandrmukhi and her husband, as was alleged by some people and denied by him.

After greeting Vishnu, Somdutt with his characteristic boldness went up to Chandrmukhi and began to talk to her with a semblance of their old intimacy. Although embarrassed and conscious of her husband's vigilance, she was forced to respond politely when he said that he was particularly glad to have come after such a long time! Vishnu heard his words distinctly. He also heard his wife telling him that she was also glad. Although as far as possible Vishnu avoided talking with or even looking at Somdutt lest he should feel encouraged and continue his visits, he could not help listening to his wife's conversation with him. He noted with a modicum of reassurance that her manner was reserved.

As Syed continued to come in Somdutt's car, Vishnu sometimes felt worried, although his wife's behavior to Somdutt remained formal. Soon he began to fear that Somdutt and his wife might gradually become accustomed to his visits. He repeatedly resolved, when he was under the influence of drugs, to take the first step towards reconciliation, but invariably put it off to a more propitious moment in order to absolutely ensure success! On a few occasions he was on the point of assuring her that despite appearances to the contrary he loved her as much as ever and had never wavered in his faith that she fully reciprocated his feeling. Just then in his euphoric state it occurred to him that his fear of her taking Somdutt as a lover was silly, or, when he was sober, that his assurance to her might encourage her to begin welcoming Somdutt as before! He told himself that as instead of blaming her, he actually sympathized with her inhibitions which prevented her from making up to him in spite of herself, and she did the same, it was okay for the time being and he could safely wait a little longer.

He invariably concluded his reflections on a happy note by assuring himself that there was no need to worry as sooner or later, in fact, sooner rather than later, he was bound to make up to her, if she failed to do so, there being no point in putting off what must be done! In view of her kindness to him, he felt confident that she was waiting to respond to him positively! He invariably topped these reflections with drugs, which he had now begun to take in higher doses to enhance happiness as often as to alleviate depression.

Within a month, Syed bought a new car. But Somdutt kept coming in his car, which followed Syed's. Soon Syed began to come less often. He had started going to places where he was at home but Somdutt was not. Homes of the westernized Muslims. Somdutt had been surprised by the reaction of many of them to the mosque's demolition, its indiscriminate, irrational intensity which targeted the Hindus in general. In their anger and frustration, they made no difference between the Muslims' communal Hindu opponents and secular supporters, going so far as to accuse the latter of being useless sympathizers and no less blameworthy for the mosque's demolition! Their denunciation of Hindu fundamentalists was likened to self-praise, apart from being counterproductive. The progressive and secular Hindus, especially the Communists, were blamed by the educated Muslims for supporting even reactionary Muslims in order to flaunt their opposition to Hindu communalism. These Hindus were regarded as the worst enemies of Muslims, who wanted justice and not loud-mouthed sympathy. Some went even so far as to say that It would be better for them to seek the support and friendship of Hindu nationalists, who whether in power or out of power and to whatever party they belonged, actually they were in every party in more or less equal proportion, were the real representatives of their community. India was a Hindu country. Somdutt secretly agreed with what they said, but had hoped that they would be discreet in their own interest.

Vishnu continued to talk to Somdutt, who still came with somebody or other and never by himself, with the minimum civility in the faint hope that he might feel unwelcome and cease his visits. But Chandrmukhi had begun to find it hard to forbear talking with him with less reserve on subjects of mutual interest. Partly from her genuine interest in those subjects and partly for relief from the dreary home atmosphere.

These talks were often carried on over the phone. Occasionally, when an important political event took place, Somdutt, although he never did anything by design to vex Vishnu or strain the relations between husband and wife, couldn't forbear telephoning her; she not only didn't mind his calls but actually seemed to welcome them by talking to him with undisguised interest, without paying attention to her husband's presence.

'I'm not going to vegetate in order to placate you,' her behavior seemed to say.

Jaiprakash, who was a keen observer of this triangular drama, blamed both Vishnu for harboring unjust expectations of his wife and the latter for her stupid obstinacy in refusing to defer to his wish even if she thought it unjust.

'If I were you,' he would tell Vishnu mentally, 'I would long ago have told Somdutt to his face or on the phone that he was not welcome, daring Chandrmukhi to contradict me. Of course, she wouldn't have done it. And even if she should have, her anger wouldn't have lasted for ever, but the visits of Somdutt would have come to an end. After all, neither of you can allow your personal and social life to suffer beyond a point because of a third person. You're fools!'

It all ended up with Vishnu being galled to perceive one day that his wife's relations with Somdutt were on way to becoming as good as before.

Presently Somdutt began to come by himself, Chandrmukhi began to welcome him and talk to him as freely as before, and Vishnu began to show his displeasure by resuming his boycotts when he was the only visitor. And as soon as he reached his room he took a dose.

From that day, Jaiprakash again and with Chandrmukhi's tacit approval began to be unfailingly present from beginning to end at the evening parties and later at dinner. Soon, to end all constraint between himself and Somdutt for her sake, Jaiprakash also began to see him off with an apparently cordial handshake. As before, he did not doubt that Vishnu understood that she welcomed his presence at her conversations with Somdutt for the sake of his peace of mind which was essential for her peace of mind also.

Before long, seemingly in defiance of Vishnu's disapproval, but in reality because as the evening came on she began to find it too dismal at home with her morose husband and nobody else, she again started going out with Somdutt to various functions. However, she no longer found his company as enlivening as before. Throughout she was with him she was conscious of her husband's unhappiness and perverseness as well as the fact that Somdutt was aware of her thoughts and it dampened his spirits also.

Sitting beside Somdutt in his car on her way to some function, she now found it hard to feel or even simulate pleasure for his sake. Her lack of vivacity had also gradually indisposed him to desire her or to think that she desired him. An affair with a woman who took his fancy had always been welcome to him and he had had several, and when Chandrmukhi was happy he would have been delighted to have her as his mistress and had often pictured her in that role. Now, instead of desiring her he felt sorry for her. Sometimes, for her sake he considered discontinuing his visits to her evening parties. But was prevented by the thought that his absence, which had failed to reconcile husband and wife despite being so long, would deprive her of whatever little pleasure she still found in life from meeting him and going out with him. Now the satisfaction he felt from meeting her consisted mainly in the pleasure his company gave her. At the same time he sometimes wished her to ask him to come no longer. He recalled their meetings away from home in her husband's presence only a few months ago. How much better he felt then in Vishnu's presence, with their mutually polite behavior, even if it was forced, than he now did in his absence during his meetings with her in his own home.

Sometimes, instead of reading for a couple of hours, or thinking of the current affairs, before falling asleep, as he had always done, Jaiprakash worried about the relations between Chandrmukhi and her husband and their possible consequences for him and his family. He wondered as to how long he could bear the stress of being their personal assistant and live with them, which required normal relations between the husband and wife.

17/4

Chandrmukhi and her husband continued to drift apart. His moroseness and anger at her refusal to stop Somdutt's visits was as a matter of course followed by a feeling of injustice in expecting her to defer to his dictatorial wish. He sought refuge from this cycle by tormenting himself with his situation and afterwards enjoying relief under the influence of drugs.

As his drug addiction increased, his sense of well-being began to decline. Now he often felt too tired to do anything.

Chandrmukhi still held her evening parties, though not as regularly as before; their duration and the number of people attending them had also declined. Some had stopped coming altogether. Vishnu's jealousy and the tension in his relations with his wife due to Somdutt had never been a secret from at least some of their friends. The discussions on the current affairs and cultural events went on with markedly less animation. As before, it sometimes happened that Somdutt was the only visitor. Jaiprakash forced himself to participate in their conversation. Of late, he sometimes seemed to perceive that Somdutt not only did not find his presence as unwelcome as before but appeared to wish it. Did he think that his presence by allaying Vishnu's jealousy and fears better ensured the continuation of his visits? Jaiprakash wondered.

In apparent appreciation of Jaiprakash's diligence in preventing tête-à-têtes between his wife and Somdutt, Vishnu had become kinder to him than before. He had raised his salary, presented him with a new television set and a personal computer and refurnished his room. Chandrmukhi's open gladness at these favors to him, of which she had evidently guessed the reason, pleased Jaiprakash. Yet he sometimes felt puzzled by her wish for his presence during her conversations with Somdutt. It must interfere with her desire to take him as a lover, if she entertained such a desire. And if she did not, why didn't she stop his visits? In view of Somdutt's now disinterested friendship with her, Jaiprakash had at last been forced to recognize this fact, she could do so without hurting him. Why didn't she content herself with meeting him, as she had done for a long time before, at the clubs and other places that both frequented? Why was she tormenting both herself and her husband? It was false pride taken to absurd length.

One day, Jaiprakash, who sometimes found the atmosphere at home too oppressive, impulsively said to her when they were sitting in her office, 'I hope you'll forgive me for intruding into your private life, but since both of you are so kind as to treat me as a family member, I must tell you that I can't bear to see you unhappy. I am even more distressed at the unhappiness of Vishnu. He's too good a person not to consider himself largely to blame for the present state of affairs, even if he can't help behaving the way he does. Maybe he's depending on you to remedy the situation.'

Suddenly he stopped, shocked at his audacity. Remembering her imperious temper, he expected every moment to be snubbed and rebuked by her and perhaps even asked to pack up. This possibility awakened his pride, which, whenever he was overcome with a sense of his inferiority and the thought that after all he was a servant, he used to feel to bolster his self-esteem. He boldly continued, 'I would humbly request you to say to him just one word of regret. I have no doubt that he's waiting for such a gesture from you.'

Chandrmukhi, who had been looking down all this while, to his intense relief stood up and walked out. He seemed to perceive from her manner that far from becoming angry she had been pleased by his concern about her unhappiness, but had felt too embarrassed to say anything.

What he did not know was that only a few days ago in desperation she had at last tried to conciliate her husband, indirectly but unmistakably, and that he had conveyed to her, indirectly but unmistakably, that she must first stop Somdutt's visits and going out with him. Although she herself sometimes thought of asking Somdutt to come no longer, as a condition for his appeasement she had found it humiliating. It would have been more thoughtful of him to ask her to do so after the reconciliation.

Chapter 18

18/1

It was more than three months since Jawaharlal's second letter to Himanshu Mukherjee, but they had received no reply.

Neither father nor sons nor their wives shared their thoughts with one another, but they guessed them to be alike: They believed that he was an altruist who might have thought that they couldn't be so naïve as to suppose that such a man, however strong his unselfish impulse, would disregard the fact that the patient had not one but two brothers. It followed, he might have reasoned, that they had calculated that in case the would-be donor happened to be looking for money, he would on seeing the brothers and how affluent they were promptly become wise to the hidden meaning of the no-payment condition and start bargaining. As regards the inconvenient fact, which cast doubt on this theory, that Vishwanath had made no attempt to catch him with the offer of money during their long meeting, they explained it easily. Himanshu would have interpreted Vishwanath's silence to mean that though ready to pay for his kidney, his sensitive nature had prevented him from proposing it; instead he had been expecting Himanshu to do so. That's why he had entertained him to tea, personally driven him to the railway station and frankly informed him that Sarika had two brothers!

'Himanshu may have been surprised to learn from Papaji's letters that we are still looking for a donor,' Srinath had begun to think. A few days ago he had decided not to wait for a response from him or anybody else beyond another month and to tell his father that he was prepared to donate his kidney. Apart from the fact that he had seemed to guess from Jayanti's anxiety about the growing depression of his sister that she might no longer oppose, he had decided to ignore her opposition, if she did. He hoped that once he had declared his readiness to his father to donate his kidney, it would be impossible to go back on his word again.

He reminded himself that the chances of a mishap during the operation were insignificant; one could live a long and healthy life with only one kidney and the extent of his and his brother's passion for physical fitness, which was partly responsible for their fear, was excessive, not to say selfish. By way of further self-criticism, or assurance to himself that eventually he wouldn't fail to discharge his moral obligation, he said to himself, 'After all, I would have submitted to a more serious operation for my own sake!'

Of course, it was something else if another acceptable donor like the lawyer should present himself, which was quite possible in view of his family's reputation for generosity and integrity. Although he had not shared his thoughts with his brother, he did not doubt that he would join him in putting pressure on his father to behave reasonably and humanely with any such newcomer.

As for Vishwanath, although after his latest talk with his doctor father-in-law he felt practically convinced that the risk was insignificant he had been unable to finally make up his mind. His irresolution was fed by the unending hope that there was no lack of "legitimate and deserving" donors like the Aligarh lawyer, who would also lead a normal life with only one kidney in addition to being delivered from their pecuniary distress. He was conscious of the fact that he had begun to think like his wife. However, instead of feeling grateful to her for enabling him to overcome his scruples, he remained resentful to think that she had probably guessed his fear and exploited it to prevent him from donating his kidney.

However, he was still overcome with revulsion at the thought of accepting an altruist's offer or luring a poor helpless person by stealthily offering him money through an agent. As regards his father's attitude to a donor like the lawyer, he now felt that possibly having given up all hope from his sons he would no longer be excessively squeamish and would be satisfied if only the man didn't demand money.

Sometimes, like his brother he also thought that the surest way to overcome his nervousness was to commit himself to his father or even to his wife. He had also begun to sense that Subhadra's opposition was no longer as strong as before because her doctor father had convinced her also, he himself had told him so, that the risk was not worth bothering about. At other times, he wished her to tell him that she was no longer opposed and he could go ahead.

18/2

Subhadra and Charles were sitting in the latter's office. Today she had specially come to make to him what seemed to her an embarrassing request. For more than a week she had been in two minds whether to put him in a dilemma. At last, just when she was on the point of speaking, she received a message that her friend and Charles's erstwhile boss, Mrs. Chandrmukhi Narayan, was on the line and wanted to talk to her urgently. She welcomed this interruption as an opportunity to further consider whether to make the request or not. Charles repressed a smile. He knew that she was Chandrmukhi's confidante in the latter's problems with her husband due to her friendship with Somdutt. He admired her for the fact that though she shared her family's intimate problems with him unreservedly to the extent of criticizing her father-in-law and husband and confessing her own weaknesses, she had seldom told him what she knew about Chandrmukhi's affairs, except what was no longer secret. He had respected her discretion and seldom expressed any curiosity. She had done the same despite wishing to fill in the gaps in her knowledge by talking to him, who was perhaps better informed about the real cause of the tension between Chandrmukhi and her husband.

Charles waited for Subhadra to return. Presently she phoned to tell him that she was going to Chandrmukhi's home and would meet him tomorrow.

When they met the next day, the temptation to tell him something confidential and agreeable to both of them got the better of her discretion and she told him, 'I have some very good news for you, unless you are already aware of it. Somdutt has stopped coming to Chandrmukhi's home and she and Vishnu have become reconciled. Vishnu has no objection to her keeping up her friendship with him and meeting him at the clubs and other places.'

'It was a silly prestige issue for both,' Charles replied. 'I never thought there was anything more to it. In fact, if Chandrmukhi was having or wished to have an affair with Somdutt, she would have asked him long ago to stop visiting her home in order to lull her jealous husband's suspicions and gratify his ego. If Vishnu hadn't been my boss, I'd have told him long ago that her refusal to comply with his unreasonable wish was a proof of the baselessness of his suspicions. That's how jealous husbands drive their loving wives into taking lovers.'

During the first of her two recent impromptu visits to Vishnu's home, observing the mutual behavior of Chandrmukhi and Somdutt it had occurred to her out of the blue that she had become Somdutt's mistress and, contrary to Charles's logic, to prevent her husband from thinking so, had refused to end her friendship with him. And during the next visit she had come away even more convinced of their being lovers for a contrary reason: she had asked Somdutt to visit their home no longer in order to deceive Vishnu by assuaging his jealousy.

Subhadra said, 'Unbearable injustice of any kind often ends up by damaging its victims.'

Charles said with a smile, 'Do you ever think yourself lucky? You might have been Vishnu's wife. Your father once discussed the relationship with his father.'

'It would never have happened though I liked him. Chandrmukhi was in love with him from much before they were married. It was a fact known to everyone who knew them. She had also confided it to me. In fact, I wouldn't have risked marrying him even if for some reason marriage between them was not possible. And if Chandrmukhi hadn't been in the picture and I had married him, my relations with him would have been totally different. If he had been jealous of somebody and wished me to give up my friendship with him I would have chided him but complied, instead of foolishly making a prestige issue of it like her.'

Having overcome her hesitation about making her request to Charles by exchanging confidences about the problem of someone who was close to both of them, Subhadra said, 'Don't you think that the letters Papaji wrote to Himanshu Mukherjee have been in vain and he has decided to ignore them?'

'Yes. And Jawaharlal also thinks so,' Charles replied. 'It has been a long time. He's finding Sarika's condition more and more unbearable, although according to your father she can remain on dialysis for yet another year or even longer. Sometimes he seems to me to be even more tormented by the blunder of issuing the appeal for altruistic donation. At last, he seems to have realized the immorality of doing so while he has two sons.'

Subhadra said, 'Only God knows what he thinks. Jayanti and I want you to do us a favor. It will also be a favor to Sarika and an act of charity, even if it entails a breach of confidence by you, who're supposed not to actively interfere in what is a family affair. It is something more serious than our exchange of views about it and your keeping us informed about Papaji's thinking in the interest of the family. However, Jayanti and I think that you do it only if you unreservedly agree with our point of view, not otherwise.'

'What's it?' said Charles, looking at her curiously.

Subhadra said, 'Vishwanath thinks that the Bengali young man did not come to sell his kidney or having come from so far away he would have frankly told him so during their long meeting. And my instinct also tells me that he was an altruist who was shocked and revolted after hearing Vishwanath's frank replies to his questions. It's so natural for a brother to donate his kidney to his sister; at least, it's the general expectation. I talked to Jayanti this morning about the lack of any response from Himanshu and she also thinks that it may be the reason for his silence. In fact, we can't afford to wait much longer. Sarika must get a kidney soon.'

Charles could not contain his astonishment. 'How can you say such a thing? After all, it's you and Jayanti who prevented your husbands in the first place, or at least supplied them with an excuse for not doing what they were prepared to do when they underwent the tests.'

'I'm thinking from Himanshu's point of view,' she replied. 'In fact, it only underscores our view that we should obtain the kidney by finding a respectable donor, paying him handsomely and expressing our heartfelt gratitude to him. Suppose a patient has lots of money but no near relatives or anybody else whose kidney he can get according to the moral code of Papaji, that is, without paying him, would you expect him to die instead of trying to save his own life in addition to succoring a man in distress?

Charles said with a smile, 'Are you still afraid that your husband may donate his kidney at a pinch to save his sister's life?'

'We are not afraid at all! Neither Jayanti nor I. To tell the truth, we'll expect them to do so, as a last resort.'

'You never told me this,' said Charles, with still greater astonishment.

'I thought you had guessed it.'

'Do you think that Vishwanath and Srinath are afraid?'

'Most probably yes. There seems no other reason to prevent either of them from at least expressing his readiness to donate his kidney whenever it should become imperative. Unless they secretly agree with our view but from false shame and fear of Papaji won't admit it. Vishwanath knew, and still realizes, that we loved and respected each other too much for me not to have disapproved beyond a point, if he had ignored my protest and given his kidney. The same would be true as regards Jayanti and Srinath.'

Lately, both Subhadra and Jayanti had begun to think that their husbands should by now have brushed aside their opposition. They had felt satisfied with their assurance in the hope that they and their father would be compelled to reconsider their rejection of the only alternative left to them to save Sarika's life: To pay for a kidney. However, if that alternative was as insuperably objectionable to them as it had begun to appear, both brothers should by now have at least expressed their preparedness to do the needful to save their sister's life if an emergency arose. As Sarika could safely remain on dialysis for a long time yet, it would have enabled them, their father and their wives to wait for the appearance of an acceptable donor without too much worry or embarrassment. That they had not done so the women could explain only by their being unable to overcome their fear. The reactions to the appeal had acutely embarrassed both women much more on account of their husbands than their own. In fact, Jayanti was so afraid of the opprobrium they and their husbands would earn if Sarika suddenly died from any cause, a fear that never ceased to haunt her, that she had once proposed to Subhadra that they should tell their husbands that they were no longer opposed.

Subhadra had thought that they might wait for some more time for the appearance of another donor like the lawyer, with whom Papaji would deal more sensibly.

She had added, 'Of course, they can break their assurance to us any time. I am sure they know without being told that we won't mind. My father, who examined Sarika a few days ago, assured Papaji that her condition was nothing to worry about. Meanwhile, let them manage it the way they think best.'

She said to Charles, 'In spite of Papaji's famous munificence and his willingness to help the lawyer without accepting his kidney no needy person has contacted him so far.'

Charles said, 'Yes, nobody has contacted him.'

'It's rather surprising, isn't it?'

'Not at all!' he replied. 'People who are poor and suffering from dire necessity are not prepared to take the smallest risk, which is increased by the possibility, however remote, that they might die on the operation table. I'm sure that Papaji and his sons realize this fact, which sometimes makes me think their attitude rather strange, not to say silly. One local man who approached me some time ago was prepared to give his kidney if Papaji, or even Vishwanath or Srinath, would only assure him in my presence before the operation and name the amount. I told him that he need have no fear as there was no risk and he would get cash beyond his belief. But he wanted to be absolutely sure. In fact, most donors want half the money in advance; that's the utmost risk they're prepared to take.'

He added, 'I think that a man of Papaji's high position and mentality wouldn't accept just anybody's kidney, like that of an illiterate and uncouth fellow living in a slum, if he's forced to accept an ostensibly altruistic donation. For the sake of his self-respect, or you might say for snobbish reasons, he would like the donor to be not only healthy but also of a certain minimum quality. As you know that's one of the reasons why he rejected your father's suggestion to accept the kidney of a man killed in an accident whose poor parents were prepared to give it for a price. His kidney suited Sarika. Ultimately he was cremated. He also belonged to a low caste and looked ill-nourished.'

'Yes I know. My father told me. But Papaji's reasons for not accepting such a person's kidney may also have been that he has two sons and, secondly, as my father guessed, he was afraid of being regarded as a charlatan who had bought a kidney after issuing an appeal for altruistic donation. However, you're right that he's a snob.'

Charles said, 'Papaji probably also wants the donor to be capable of appreciating his compulsion, a man who would not secretly despise him for virtually buying his organ under pretence of morality after issuing an appeal for altruistic donation. Himanshu seems to fulfill all these qualifications, but if he's an altruist he won't accept payment, and if needy, he's unlikely to take the risk of pretending unselfishness for Papaji's benefit lest with the capriciousness of a moralist he should take him at his word and pay him nothing. All these facts and conditions are no joke! In other words, a donor acceptable to Papaji is next to impossible to find. The current price of the kidney of a respectable and healthy man, like the lawyer, is three to five lakh rupees. It's a big amount for a man in distress, which makes the fear of his eventually not getting the money correspondingly great.'

Subhadra said, 'Jayanti and I want you to do us a favor. It will also be a favor to Sarika. As I told you before, it is something more serious than our exchange of views and your keeping us informed about Papaji's thinking in the interest of the family. However, do it only if you unreservedly agree with our point of view.'

'What is it?' asked Charles doubtfully. He felt that she would ask something difficult to grant and equally difficult to refuse.

'A clever woman, though honest,' he thought.

'Jayanti and I want you to draft a letter to Himanshu Mukherjee from us. I'll tell you what we want and welcome any suggestions from you. I'll copy it in your presence and return the original to you. I need not say that it will be strictly between the three of us.'

'But it may not remain a secret. Himanshu, if he takes notice of it, may inform Papaji that he had received a letter from you, and Papaji would be very angry.'

'We're not afraid of Papaji. In fact, we wouldn't mind showing the letter's copy to him immediately after dispatching it, or even before it! But as it's not necessary, let it remain unknown to him as long as possible. What neither he nor Vishwanath or Srinath will ever know is that you wrote it for us.'

'I don't promise, but let me hear what you want me to write.'

'Papaji should have heeded his sons' evident wish against issuing the appeal and later writing the letters after Himanshu had gone back without indicating what he thought or wanted. It would have put greater pressure on them as well as on him to think of doing something more than they have been able to think so far. But since Papaji has issued the appeal and written the letters, which you moreover think he has done against his wish, thus causing wholly unnecessary embarrassment to himself and everybody else, we want to correct the mischief the appeal and the letters have done. What I mean is that if the appeal hadn't been issued and the letters hadn't been written, Papaji might have come round to the view that paying a man in straitened circumstances, like the lawyer, was preferable to making his daughter suffer. Or their self-respect and love for their sister would by now have enabled Vishwanath and Srinath to overcome their fear and stop hoping guiltily, and express their readiness to give their organs. The appeal and the letters gave them time to get used to the situation. Before that, if Jayanti and I had not protested so strongly, either brother would have given his kidney in spite of his fear. They would have been too ashamed not to do so after undergoing the tests. This is not to say that our protest was not sincere and based on conviction.'

'You think that they still feel ashamed in spite of their apparently normal behavior?'

'Yes. But, as I said, they have become used to it. To a great extent, if not entirely. Our protest delayed the transplant operation, causing their fear to grow until, instead of coming round to our view and against their father's, as we had hoped, to our surprise, when we had at last given up, they promised to us that they won't do it without our consent.'

Charles said, 'You think Papaji would have done well to heed their opposition to the appeal and the letters if he wanted them to offer their kidney?'

'Yes. Vishwanath one day told me that the appeal was not only unnecessary and useless but also extremely damaging to the family's reputation. Perhaps he was also against the appeal from fear that it would give him an excuse and further weaken him. Later, he indirectly confessed to me that the Aligarh lawyer was an acceptable donor and Papaji's treatment of him was illogical and self-contradictory. We feel it's rather unfair to the brothers for Himanshu to think them heartless cravens, as he possibly does whenever he thinks of them. Most probably that's why he has not replied to the letters. Jayanti and I also believe that they're too good human beings and love their sister too much not to do the needful even now, if her life depended on it. But what Jayanti and I fear is that one day all of us may find that we have waited too long for Himanshu's reply or for a suitable donor. Sarika may die suddenly from some other cause. It's not impossible, given her mental condition. We're also incurring a lot of odium. We can't wait much longer. We want Himanshu to know that we, the wives, have our own point of view, which we think perfectly ethical and moral. Unfortunately, our father-in-law doesn't agree with our view and our husbands are of the same view with him. Of course, we won't write that they're afraid, although he might have guessed it during his meeting with Vishwanath as one of the possible reasons for the appeal. Apart from demeaning them, it's not necessary because we are not aware of Himanshu's thinking. We want him to know that we think that saving a young life is of supreme importance and that therefore paying a needy and responsible man for his kidney is irreproachable from both the recipient's and the donor's points of view. In other words, we think that one who wants money for his organ is not necessarily less honorable a person than the one who will accept nothing.'

'It's a bold thing to say to a man who may be an altruist,' remarked Charles.

'We know, but that's what we think. Himanshu can make up his mind in light of it, if he has not already dismissed the whole thing from his thoughts. We have also considered all possible reasons why he hasn't replied to Papaji's letters. And though we think that most probably he's an altruist, who was shocked to know that Sarika had two brothers, you'll agree that it's impossible to be sure. He might as well be a needy person but was too sensitive to broach the subject to Vishwanath. If it's so, the letter would remove his hesitation and he would be exactly the kind of donor Jayanti and I wish for. We'll deal with him confidentially. If Papaji gives him nothing we'll pay him more than he would have imagined. It's cruel to inflict any more suffering on Sarika.'

'Please write frankly,' she continued, 'that we also think that if one is actuated by the compassionate desire to save a life, he should allow no circumstance to deflect him from his purpose.'

'It's an audacious statement to make, considering the fact that the patient has two brothers,' said Charles, surprised by her change of direction.

She said, 'As he came in response to the appeal, it's also possible that he won't accept anything for his kidney.'

'I don't understand you,' said Charles. 'Will you accept such a man's kidney?'

'Never! Neither we nor our husbands. What Jayanti and I think is that if the frankness of the letter arouses his compassion and he comes, and disregarding the brothers, offers to donate his kidney without accepting anything even as a humble expression of our gratitude, Vishwanath and Srinath would be too ashamed to accept his offer. Either of them would much rather donate his kidney. We'll talk to him frankly, if he comes.'

She added, 'Our sole motive for writing this letter is to make sure that Sarika gets a kidney without any more delay.'

'Are you hopeful that he'll respond?'

'Frankly speaking, not much, even if he's an altruist.'

'Because of the brothers?'

'Yes. Besides, it's quite possible that his altruistic impulse evaporated long ago and he's thinking himself lucky to have escaped. He may have thrown Papaji's letters into the waste basket!'

Charles smiled.

'Don't misunderstand. If he came inspired by the selfless desire to save a life, but has since changed his mind, even then he remains an extraordinary man. Hundreds must have read the appeal and forgotten about it in a few minutes. He came from so far away and would have donated his kidney if he hadn't been surprised and shocked by what he found.'

'And you still want to write to him?'

'We want to dispose of him and end an uncertain and embarrassing situation. The constraint between Papaji and us has gradually become tolerable, because at last he seems to have realized that he treated the Aligarh lawyer shabbily, but the mental agony of Sarika is becoming more unbearable every day. Although she agrees with our view about purchasing a kidney, yet we can't be sure that the fact that neither brother has so far offered to donate his is not one of the causes of her anguish.'

'You are averse to justifying or excusing the reluctance or fear of the brothers for any reason whatsoever. So far so good. Just the same you may have to explain it if Himanshu comes and wants to know. What would you say? That they're frightened?'

'Obviously. It would be shameful to lie to such a man. But that's not something we're bothered about. As I said, if he's an altruist and refuses to accept anything for his kidney, neither brother would accept his offer.'

She added, 'And if Himanshu doesn't reply, it would force them to stop hoping and waiting and do what they have become used to putting off. They might even come round to our point of view, if they can't overcome their fear. They won't let their sister die. And if you'll allow me to repeat myself, Himanshu may actually be a needy person but too sensitive to openly say so.'

Charles became thoughtful. At last, impressed but wishing to consider the matter further, he said, 'I might write, but I don't promise. Give me time to think until tomorrow.'

When she met him next day, he handed her the letter. It was exactly what she herself would have written if she could. The one addition Charles had made out of his own head especially pleased her: 'In such a serious matter, however, nothing that you write in reply to this letter will in any way morally bind you to anything in the future and you can always rethink and change your mind at any stage.'

'Thank you very much!' she said, returning the original to him after copying it in her hand.

She said, 'Let him come and let's see what kind of a man he is. If Papaji hadn't written to him, we and our husbands would've forgotten about him. If we receive no reply within a reasonable period, Jayanti and I will show our husbands its copy and tell them that we no longer have any objection. As I said, if what has prevented them so far from disregarding our opposition is fear they might be able to overcome it: My father told me a few days ago that he believed that after talking to him Vishwanath seemed much less afraid than before and that if he had still not offered to donate his kidney it could be because he had chosen to wait for some more time for a reply from the Bengali. We also intend to tell Sarika that she would receive a kidney soon.'

Charles said, 'And if they remain fearful, they'll come round to your point of view?'

'Yes! Even Papaji may indirectly enable us by not blocking a donation arranged by us. We have no doubt that now he's in two minds, if he was not so before. He can't sacrifice his own daughter's life for the sake of a principle to which he knows many people no less upright don't uncritically subscribe.'

Before destroying the letter, Charles read it once again. Although it was he who had written it, he found himself reading it as her letter, and it was now that he marveled at her astuteness and integrity. She seemed to him no less of an idealist and much more pragmatic than Jawaharlal, who saw everything in black and white. It made it clear that if Himanshu was needy and had come expecting to be paid but was too sensitive and shy to say it openly, he was still a gentleman! Hence he could come again, without taking seriously the letters of Jawaharlal, who had probably changed his mind due to his daughter's suffering and openly or tacitly allowed his daughters-in-law to solve the problem without involving him! And if he had come actuated by the spirit of sacrifice, he might come again, disregarding the brothers. Finally, if he doesn't reply to the letter, which was the most likely thing to happen, or expresses his inability to come without giving any reason, it would end the uncertainty and one or both brothers might offer to donate their kidneys or express their willingness to buy it with the passive acquiescence of their father. Finding a suitable donor posed no great problem, according to Subhadra's father.

Chapter 19

19/1

One day while Vishnu had gone to Bombay and Jaiprakash was having dinner with Chandrmukhi, he saw her extremely sad. A few days ago, wife and husband had had a sullen disagreement, which had replaced the heated exchanges between them. Of late, her moodiness had begun to get on Jaiprakash's nerves. Except at the now only occasional evening parties, where she forced herself to be cheerful, she had again begun to avoid her husband. She had left practically all decisions relating to their joint business to him and accepted them with melancholy resignation. Sometimes, the three of them did not speak a word to one another at dinner and retired to their rooms as soon as it was over.

Jaiprakash had more than once considered going home on leave but the thought of leaving them when they were so unhappy had made him change his mind. He was like a member of the family and did not doubt that his presence had prevented their relations from getting worse.

As soon as the dinner was over, he rose from the table to go to his room. When Vishnu was out of station, to prevent gossip he was particular about leaving for his room before the servants, while she kept sitting for some time watching TV. He had also become addicted to brooding before falling asleep. He brooded not only about the unhappy relations between Chandrmukhi and her husband, but also about the fast deteriorating political situation in the country and about his old parents and his educated but unemployed and unmarried sisters. Sometimes, to escape from reality, he would dwell upon problems which did not personally affect him. Last night he had pondered what he would have done to solve the Khalistani terrorist problem in Punjab, which had already resulted in the murder of more than ten thousand innocent people, if he were the Prime minister. Tonight, he was going to think how he would have tackled India's dispute with China, if instead of Nehru he had been Prime Minister and negotiated with Zhou-Enlai. Would he have conceded China's demands in the Aksai Chin area in return for Arunachal Pradesh? After what he had read, he was convinced that though the Chinese were cunning Nehru had not only bungled but concealed from the country for more than five years the fact that the Chinese had been increasing their occupation of the territory. And not only his blind reliance on his irresponsible defense minister, Krishna Menon, but his over-confidence in his international prestige was also responsible for the country's humiliating defeat in the 1962 war with China.

'Stay a while, if you are not sleepy,' she said. Surprised and vaguely flattered, he sat down. She remained silent and sad. Presently the last servant left after cleaning up. He remembered that Somdutt had not come for several days. He began to think of the original, if no longer the chief, source of trouble between her and her husband.

After a few minutes, he became restless and couldn't help saying, 'Forgive me, but I can't bear to see you and Vishnu so unhappy.'

'Vishnu has forsaken me,' she said in a dismal voice. Although what she said was no secret, he was moved by the grief which had actuated it and the confidence it evinced in him.

He felt deeply grieved. Such a lively woman reduced to such despair. Her husband was mainly responsible for it.

He looked at her and found her sadness unbearable. But he could do nothing about it. Time passed and his longing to go to his room grew. Divining his impatience, she said, 'If you are sleepy you can go.

'I am not sleepy at all!'

Presently she looked at him with her beautiful eyes, now so sad. Her sorrow seemed to evince a pathetic desire to be consoled and he couldn't forbear looking back at her. As their eyes met again, he for the first time saw her not as his benevolent boss but as a forlorn woman in need of solace.

All of a sudden, he had an upsurge of excitement. Within minutes he could barely keep from trembling.

Frantically trying to prevent himself from doing what he realized was bound to have dreadful consequences, he said, 'Occasionally, such ups and downs even between the happiest of couples do occur, but they pass. I've no doubt that you'll be reconciled soon because you love each other!'

'He has forsaken me!' she said again.

An unhappy woman pining for sympathy and love!

He again felt terrified at what he thought he was in imminent danger of doing and again made a desperate effort to control himself. The next moment he was caressing her hand, his heart beating violently. She did not withdraw it and continued to look down. Trembling all over, he rose and quickly went round the table. Expecting every moment for her to suddenly come to herself and realize with horror what he was going to do and with her imperious look and by violently rebuking him prevent him coming near her, he gently lifted her from her chair and embraced her. She was also trembling. She put her head on his chest. He kissed her, full of dread lest she should still realize what he was doing and repulse him. She did not do so, nor did she seem to respond; she remained passive. He was momentarily discouraged but realized that he had gone too far and now it was impossible to retract. Still incredulous of what was happening but now in the grip of uncontrollable desire mingled with guilt and fear, he kissed her passionately and long and led her into Vishnu's bedroom, not noticing that it was not her bedroom.

19/2

When Jaiprakash awoke in the early hours, the first thing he became conscious of was his perfidy against his benefactor, who trusted him implicitly! He looked at Chandrmukhi's face in the moonlight streaming through the window. There was no trace in it of the grief he had seen before he lost control of himself. It revealed nothing of her thoughts before she had fallen asleep after her delirious happiness. He could not believe how easily she had given herself when they reached the bed and when he was nervously fumbling with her even assisted him in undressing her. He quietly went to his room.

But he could not sleep. Instead of thinking what he himself had done, he began to review her behavior before and after he had impulsively started caressing her, uneasily wondering if she had cold-bloodedly set out to seduce him to revenge herself on her husband. He was unable to bear the thought of her having been actuated by such baseness, so contrary to her noble character, which he wished to cherish more than ever now that he had become her lover! At last, he succeeded in assuring himself that it was his compassion which had moved her, as it had moved him, into succumbing before she could realize the danger and control herself. Her extreme sadness and her telling him to go if he was sleepy, and the unexpected and rapturous joy he had seen on her face during lovemaking also seemed to testify against her having been motivated by premeditated revenge.

In the morning, however, when trying to control his nervous agitation he entered the dining room at the breakfast time, he expected to find her absent, or in a state of exquisite shame and embarrassment at what she had done. Or, what he thought more fitted her disposition, eating her breakfast with a composed and expressionless face, letting him finish his, and then handing him an envelope containing his six months' pay and dismissing him from service in a few dry, polite words.

What he saw instead was entirely unexpected and yet he realized no less characteristic of her. Looking as poised and graceful as ever, she was dictating a letter to her stenographer, whom she had called early, in her usual articulate and self-assured manner. In the same manner she briefly explained to him the letter's contents, asked him to check it after it had been typed and bring it to her for her signatures. Throughout the day, she behaved to him as she normally used to do in office, unaffected by his shy and acutely embarrassed demeanor, and assigned him various tasks with her usual clarity and precision. At dinner she ate quietly, without looking at him, constraining him to do the same.

Despite her having throughout the day betrayed no embarrassment, which had caused him to feel amazed at her self-possession, he was not yet sure that she was not feeling remorse and struggling with guilty desire under her calm exterior. It was possible that if he again tried to take her in his arms, she would stop him, indicating silently or by words that what had happened last night was an unfortunate accident due to her then state of mind and had changed nothing between them.

However, he realized that now it would be impossible for their relations to remain the same. Either he would live in this house as her lover or would have to go. And he wouldn't mind going. Although what had happened had happened accidentally and she had enjoyed it, he could not absolve himself because it was he who had started it. It would never have happened if he had not lost control of himself. She had only to ask him to leave.

At last, remembering the servants and the fact that yesterday he had not left for his room before them, he got up to go, half expecting her to silently indicate to him to stay. She did not. She had controlled herself, he said to himself, and perhaps it was a hint to him that now he could not live in this house. He went to his room.

But recalling how passionately she had behaved in bed last night, he couldn't sleep and time passed painfully slowly. At last, unable to bear his excitement, he went and softly knocked on her door, unable to decide how she would respond. If she did not open it, it would be a clear intimation that he should go. And he would gladly leave on some pretext before her husband returned from his business tour.

To his joyful surprise, she opened it and stepped aside to let him in. In fact, she had been waiting for this moment throughout the day without betraying by the least sign what was passing through her mind, confident that he would come. Last night's incredible adventure had rekindled her desire which she had thought had died due to her husband's jealous persecution.

When she asked Jaiprakash to stay if he was not feeling sleepy, her depression had become intolerable and sex was beyond her imagination. Not only her thoughts were the opposite of what Jaiprakash had later uneasily suspected, but her sadness was also due to her consciousness of the extinction of one of the great joys of her life. When he began to caress her hand and then took her in his arms and she passively put her head on his chest, it was still no more than an accidentally surviving spark hidden under the ash. But his long kiss due to fear lest she should still come to herself and repulse him, followed by his nervous fumbling with her when they reached the bed, had ignited the spark into a flame.

Recalling her utter submission last night and the joy on her face during lovemaking, he tried to repeat what he had done yesterday. But she did not let him. As soon as she had closed the door, to his utter delight, instead of submitting passively as she had done the night before, she put her strong arms around him and kissed him passionately. From his behavior yesterday she had guessed that he had never had a woman before. Today it was she who made love. And she did it as an expert and a guide. His astonishment increased his joy and he passed the night intoxicated by her uninhibited lovemaking. Back in his room, he thought with a pang of the happiness Vishnu's jealousy had cost him. He told himself that he had not taken it away from him; he had already lost it before he became her lover. He told himself that what he had done would save her from a possible mental derangement!

On their fifth night, reflecting on her unchanged demeanor during the day in office, he seemed to divine its meaning. She wanted to maintain their official relations as they were before he became her lover: Although she enjoyed him hugely and her caresses exuded the tenderest love and gratitude, there was no mistaking the fact that she was his boss and he her devoted servant grateful for the ultimate favor she had conferred on him for his loyalty to her!

While waiting for the appointed hour, however hard he rationalized, he found it impossible not to think that he was deceiving a man who believed in his faithfulness and had always been extraordinarily kind to him.

Sometimes he thought of not going in to her and ending the affair. But the idea of now betraying her, he did not doubt that she would feel heartlessly betrayed after having been corrupted and enjoyed by him, he found more dreadful than that of deceiving her husband. It also occurred to him that if she could carry on with him without feeling that she was doing anything wrong, she could easily become the mistress of Somdutt, who was the cause of the trouble between her and her husband. And he would have to leave.

Vishnu was returning from Bombay and Jaiprakash felt nervous of facing him. She had guessed it. She gave him a letter that she had prepared beforehand and ordered him to go to the airport to give it to him. He had seldom gone to the airport or railway station to receive him. In fact, so far he had done so only two or three times. He understood her. She wanted him to face him with confidence. He did not let her down.

Days passed as usual and the outward relations between the wife and husband and between Jaiprakash and his boss remained as before and as before Vishnu sometimes went away for a day or two in connection with his business, enabling Chandrmukhi and her lover to pass delightful nights together.

Often, looking at Vishnu, Jaiprakash would tell himself that what had happened had not only happened without premeditation but was bound to happen someday, however loving and virtuous might the wife be, if her husband was as jealous and oppressive as he had become. If it had not been him, it would have been somebody else. It would have been Somdutt. From Vishnu's point of view he was the safest man!

What further eased his conscience was that contrary to what he had feared at the beginning of the affair, she didn't embarrass him by blaming or denigrating her husband, as unfaithful wives generally do to their lovers to justify their conduct, but often only manage to lose their respect. Reading Anna Karenina, he had sometimes wondered if one of the reasons for the ultimate souring of her relations with her lover was the bad taste in which she used to talk to him about her husband, which gradually began to add to his tedium and dissatisfaction with her from other causes.

One day Somdutt came. He had returned from one of his visits abroad. Syed came with him. Vishnu was also present and he treated Somdutt with the artificial politeness that both had become so accustomed to observing others finding normal that they had also begun to find it normal. Somdutt began to relate his experiences during his visit to Germany. How he had felt ashamed as an Indian and a Hindu when at a meeting with some German journalists they made derogatory references to Hindu fundamentalism which was responsible for the demolition of Babri Mosque and the humiliation of the Muslim minority. While describing his feelings his face assumed an expression of guilt and shame for being a Hindu and an Indian.

'If I had been you, I would have thrown in their faces the murder of six million Jews in gas chambers,' said Jaiprakash impulsively, surprising not only Syed, Chandrmukhi and Vishnu but also himself. The next moment he was dismayed at his audacity in virtually questioning the moral obligation of a Hindu secularist to feel ashamed at the charge of the mosque's demolition and the consequent humiliation of Muslims, even if it was leveled by people who were guilty of infinitely worse crimes. He vaguely wondered whether he would have kept quiet, if he had not become Chandrmukhi's lover, which had removed his inhibitions. Did she also think so? And she did give him a look which seemed to assure him that what he had said was okay!

However, Somdutt's retort that others' crimes did not absolve you of yours helped him recover, enabling him to say, 'You're right!'

A week later, Vishnu left for Calcutta.

19/3

Once Jaiprakash had shelved his conscientious scruples, it seemed impossible to banish them, about deceiving a man who believed in his loyalty, the affair peaked faster than either of them could have anticipated, mainly because by resurrecting her libido, which she had begun to think she had lost forever, it had restored one of the great joys of her life. Sometimes, back in his room, uneasily reflecting on her insatiable appetite, he would remind himself that she had become his mistress not from promiscuity or amorality but from intense suffering and that she would still be suffering but for the affair.

He finally got rid of the uncomfortable thought that for the same reason she might have become Somdutt's mistress by assuring himself that he was a snob whom her vanity would never have allowed to become her lover

Chandrmukhi's happiness had gradually begun to smooth over the estrangement between her and her husband by making her less cool to him. She found it hard to see him unhappy while she was enjoying herself. At first Jaiprakash could not understand the reason for this change.

Now Jaiprakash went out of Delhi only occasionally and on shorter business trips because Vishnu wished to be away from home as often and as long as possible to escape the still far from congenial atmosphere as well as in the vague hope that separation would further improve his relations with her. Somdutt still came, though less often than before. Feeling that he was enjoying the woman that he once desired or maybe still desires in vain, Jaiprakash not only no longer felt any objection to him, but had begun to welcome him. And during the discussions he had gradually begun to express his views more frankly to the extent of sometimes supporting Somdutt's opinion against Chandrmukhi's. She was delighted to notice this new element of freedom and informality in her relations with her lover and let it be translated into their relations at night.

In its early days, the affair used to occupy Jaiprakash's thoughts to the extent of sometimes making him inattentive and negligent in his official work. It was something unusual for him and it drew admonitions from her, not only in the presence of others, but also when no third person was present. It reminded him lest he should forget that though passionately desiring and even inciting him to take liberties with her at night she wished to maintain their official relations as they were before they became lovers. It preserved the freshness and excitement of their first encounter. These little incidents surprised her husband, causing him to think it as one of the unfortunate consequences of the prolonged tension between him and her, which had also affected Jaiprakash, making him uncharacteristically remiss. And though she never reproved Jaiprakash with the intention of preventing any suspicion arising in her husband's or anybody else's mind, she reflected afterwards that it would have that effect. Formerly, Jaiprakash would have felt offended by such admonitions, but now he had difficulty repressing his excitement as soon as she had reproved him. She made up to him for her strictness during the office hours by her tender caresses when they met, sometimes with a smile whispering to him after a kiss that it was for the scolding he had received from her on that day!

Jaiprakash repeatedly assured himself that by making her happy he had prevented an affair between her and Somdutt, which could have had incalculable consequences. He also reminded himself that their affair had started unexpectedly (how spontaneously and guilelessly it had happened!) Without either of them having even remotely anticipated it. It was not like illicit wealth earned by corrupt means; it was legitimate as a windfall.

When they were together, she sometimes astonished him by fondly reminiscing about her happy days with her husband until a few months ago and expressing her confidence that those days would return. The unexpected end of her suffering and the dizzy happiness in the arms of Jaiprakash had gradually changed her attitude towards her husband. Recalling his tenderness and how he esteemed her and was proud of her intellectual reputation and glamorous presence in society before he unexpectedly became jealous, she often found herself wishing similar happiness for him and thought of making up to him by giving up her friendship with Somdutt. The question whether Jaiprakash would remain her lover after the reconciliation, she put off till that time. She said to her lover what he had said to her before she became his mistress—that she and Vishnu still loved each other as before and that though he was angry with her for continuing her friendship with Somdutt, he also realized his injustice to her. What she said delighted Jaiprakash by its evident sincerity and finally removed his uneasy doubt that her softened behavior to her husband was a calculated deception. It would have been hard for him to enjoy her as he wished, if she had been guilty of such a reprehensible motive, while he was also deceiving him. It also enabled him to think that her ingenuous amorality, which continued to surprise him, would preserve her love for her husband which guilt and the sense of sin would have polluted and destroyed. He sometimes wondered whether she had had affairs of which her husband was unaware, but eventually ruled it out in view of their mutual fondness before he became insufferably jealous. He again assured himself that though basically amoral she had become his mistress not because of it but from unending despair and desolation.

He not only expressed the hope but transparently wished, which caused her to love him all the more, for her reconciliation with her husband as soon as possible. He couldn't have as heartily enjoyed her as he wished with the apprehension that their affair, which was destined to end sooner or later, might irrevocably extinguish her desire for her husband, who was so kind to him and trusted him.

One day she said to him, 'I always liked you not only for yourself but also for your concern for Vishnu's happiness. Even more for the latter!' She added with a smile, 'It particularly pleased me that you secretly sympathized with his objection to my friendship with Somdutt, even though I thought it unjust!'

During their next meeting she asked him with a smile, 'When Vishnu began to boycott the evening parties to avoid meeting Somdutt, sometimes he had long talks with you in his study. What did you talk about?'

'He replied,' I didn't say anything to aggravate his unhappiness, and being aware of my views he was also kind enough not to ask any awkward questions.' He added, 'You'll appreciate that complete frankness is not always possible, nor is it always a virtue!'

Having never anticipated such a question from her he was delighted at the spontaneity of his answer, and he noted that she was even more pleased.

Jaiprakash was sometimes assailed by a vague fear lest she should think that instead of happening suddenly and without premeditation, his seduction of her had been motivated by his secret dislike and jealousy of Somdutt and carefully planned. He took this opportunity to relate to her how utterly unexpectedly he had become her lover: His distress when he witnessed her sorrow, his impatience to go to his room because he could do nothing about it, the excruciatingly long wait, his sudden uncontrollable desire to console her and the consequent excitement. And ultimately his great fear lest she should violently repulse him, causing him not only to lose his job but also her respect for planning to deceive Vishnu to whom he professed loyalty. Finally, her passionate response when they reached the bed, which resulted in their first divine encounter. He also confessed to her that soon after becoming her lover he had begun to feel guilty and often thought of ending the affair, but found it impossible to do so because of the joy it gave her. She replied that it would have deeply hurt her if he had done so.

Then she told him that she had also sometimes worried lest he should have thought that she had seduced him by design, when the fact was that due to her unending estrangement from her husband and her prolonged sorrow, she had begun to loathe sex. When she asked him to stay if he was not sleepy, sex was farthest from her mind. And when he began to caress her hand and then took her in his arms, though surprised, far from feeling any desire, she still felt too depressed and low to react in any way. She was aroused and began to enjoy when he continued to kiss her and then led her into the bedroom. And when they reached there and he began to fumble with her nervously and without preliminaries, which made her suspect that he had never had a woman before, she was far too gone.

He confessed that he was a virgin when he became her lover.

With the gradual end of all constraint between them, one day he said to her, 'In the society in which you and Vishnu moved, he also might have had affairs. Did you ever suspect him?'

She replied, 'Although there were women eager to throw themselves at him, I don't think he ever had an affair, considering how dreadfully jealous he became.' She added with a smile, 'Unfaithful husbands generally don't behave the way he did. Confidence in their wives' virtue is essential for them to fully enjoy their affairs. Barring exceptions, they also love and respect their wives and believe that they would remain faithful to them and with this assurance and sincere compliment to them excuse their own infidelity!'

'I mean from revenge after he began to suspect you and Somdutt.'

'Not even then. If he had a woman, it would have assuaged or at least abated his jealousy and he wouldn't have tortured himself so. I would also have been happier. But he was so obsessed with imagining me in the arms of Somdutt that he had no time to think of an affair of his own.'

One day Jaiprakash told her that he had serious objection to Somdutt not because he doubted his intentions or goodwill but because of his continuing his friendship with her despite knowing that it was the cause of her problem with her husband. She replied that it was so before and 'it's long since he has been coming despite himself, because he thinks that his friendship is now the only source of consolation to me. And that's why I haven't asked him to stop coming, which he sometimes seems to wish me to do.'

Then she told him what she had said to Somdutt ostensibly in defense of Vishnu's behavior when he started boycotting him and Somdutt proposed to stop coming to their house and going out with her. She added, 'At the time I thought that if yielding to Vishnu's coercive attitude I gave up my friendship with him, which he wouldn't have minded, it would further increase the already unbearable constraint between us. I also thought it unfair because Somdutt said only what he really thought about the social and political questions and never did anything deliberately to estrange me from my husband.'

There was yet another reason why she hesitated to ask Somdutt to stop coming to her home, but she thought it unwise to confess it to Jaiprakash: Although the relations between her and her lover had remained visibly unchanged, she feared that Somdutt could think that Jaiprakash had become her lover!

After this exchange, Jaiprakash thought it unlikely that she would let Somdutt become her lover. However, it only increased his determination to persuade her to stop his visits, which was essential for the restoration of her relations with her husband and the end of the malaise that afflicted everyone in the household, including him. He also hoped that their reconciliation might lead to the end of the affair; it was liable to be exposed any day with horrible consequences. He no longer thought as he had done immediately after the beginning of the affair—that now he could live in this house only as her lover. Chandrmukhi and he had become too intimate and could arrive at any arrangement which would be in both their interests.

One day, Jaiprakash was sitting and talking with her sister Harimohini, who had come on leave and was staying with her. She was aware of the tension between Chandrmukhi and her husband and its cause as well as of the fact that everyone in the household was affected by it. All of a sudden, during a pause, he surprised himself by expressing to her his distress at the dismal home atmosphere and pleading with her to persuade her sister to end her friendship with Somdutt. Recovering from her surprise at such a request from him, who was a personal assistant and not a family member, she appreciated the fact that the request was sincerely motivated by the despair of a person who was not only their well-wisher but also a sufferer from the gloomy atmosphere.

Although Jaiprakash had spoken impulsively and sincerely, the next moment it occurred to him that it would prevent her from suspecting him of being Chandrmukhi's lover. Unless she had already guessed it from their mutual demeanors and regarded his request as a calculated deception and an expression of his jealousy of Somdutt! He felt sick and wished he hadn't made the request which was tainted with his perfidy while Somdutt's relations with her were not only blameless but sincerely disinterested.

Harimohini had already more than once pleaded with Chandrmukhi in vain to do so for yet another reason which she could not disclose to her. Their crafty and at the same time tactless father, who was extremely unhappy at the estrangement between Chandrmukhi and her husband and judging by his unguarded remarks perhaps suspected her of being Somdutt's mistress, had more than once obliquely blamed her for being its cause. If she had married Somdutt instead of that "penniless man from a backward caste", relations between Chandrmukhi and her husband would have been normal and both sisters would have been happy.

19/4

Lately Jaiprakash sometimes seemed to perceive nervously that Vishnu looked puzzled by the change in his wife's demeanor. As if he was wondering at her no longer being melancholy, which she used often to be before the beginning of the affair. One day, he fancied as if Vishnu was quietly watching him, although when he looked up he was persuaded that it was not so.

He tried to assure himself that Vishnu trusted him too much to suspect him, but found it impossible to completely get rid of his nervousness.

One day, he mentioned the fear to her: 'It's quite possible, don't you think? After all it's something which has actually happened.'

She surprised him by confessing that she had had similar fears. 'He has seemed suspicious to me also. However, our apprehensions may be due to the fact that it's something that has actually happened. I don't think he's very sure even regarding Somdutt. It's just that due to his temperamental dislike of him, which has been further aggravated by our friendship, he has become habituated to jealousy and suspicion, which he is unable to control. If he had frankly told me at the beginning of our friendship that he didn't like the man I'd have got rid of him, but then he pretended to welcome him and praise him to his face. And when we became friendly, his dislike turned into jealousy and suspicion.'

'If he has become habituated to jealousy and suspicion from whatever cause, suspicion of one man today can lead to suspicion of another tomorrow. Why do you take any risk at all? Why don't you apologize to Somdutt and ask him to stop coming, especially as you think that he would be glad to do so and comes only for your sake. As long as he remains your friend, your relations with your husband will never become normal. Even if in his lucid moments Vishnu doesn't consider you susceptible to him, he can't get over the feeling that you're adamantly disobliging him. At least, to begin with, you can stop going out with him to the public functions where before you generally used to go with your husband. People are bound to notice that if formerly you were mostly accompanied by him now your companion is Somdutt. This fact may also have occurred to Vishnu and further added to his worry.'

Chandrmukhi was not unaware of this likelihood. Actually, she had more than once observed people looking significantly at her in the company of Somdutt instead of her husband, but she hadn't much bothered. Her public image of an intellectual with special rights and freedoms denied to wealthy philistines, her dignity and poise which had remained unimpaired in public even during the period of her extreme unhappiness and above all the fact that she was not guilty of improper relationship with Somdutt would take care of it. Moreover, in their society, which consisted of a lot of blasé idlers and busybodies such speculations were inherent and were not taken seriously for long, not even by those who indulged in them. Apart from the want of an agreeable companion, there was yet another and much more important reason why she had continued to go out with Somdutt, though she now went only to important programs where her absence would have been noticed and provoked conjectures. It was her fear, vague yet persistent, lest her jealous husband should suspect that she had dropped or nearly dropped Somdutt because she had found a lover in Jaiprakash! But she could not confess this fear to Jaiprakash even in their most intimate moments; she felt ashamed at the thought of mentioning it to him. She feared to lose his respect, which was essential for the full enjoyment of their affair, by being regarded by him as a sly woman! Despite his own fear of their relationship being discovered by her husband, he might consider it sordid to coldly scheme to delude him! She also sometimes found herself vaguely reflecting, and thinking that perhaps he did likewise, that acceptance of some fear and tension was demanded by fairness and self-respect as a penance for their conduct.

Jaiprakash said, 'As you're probably aware, he began to take drugs from unhappiness. He's now trying to give up the habit. It'll help him greatly, if Somdutt stops coming.'

'I only know that he has begun to take drugs, but not how much or how often. Has he become addicted? Are you sure? Has he confided his problem to you?' she asked, feeling a little awkward that he should know more than her about the private life of her husband.

Jaiprakash was tempted to tell her that Vishnu was consulting a psychiatrist and had confided his problem to him even before they became lovers, but he checked himself. Apart from being a breach of trust, it might shake her confidence in his discretion and trustworthiness. She might even be secretly aware of his being Vishnu's confidant in the matter and wished him to keep his confidence! Let her come to know it from him, if he chooses to tell her.

He answered, 'I won't say that he has actually confided. He has only mentioned it once or twice. I think it's not serious yet, but that's how addictions begin. He needs complete peace of mind to be able to give it up. Only your reconciliation can restore it. Why don't you start sleeping in his bed? All you have to do is to quietly enter it one day and when he comes in let him find you there. It will overwhelm him and solve all the problems between you. Remember that every day is crucial and it may be too late before you realize.'

She became thoughtful. It was the easiest way to reconciliation. She had also once considered it but had been deterred by her loathing for sex. She had even feared that it was something permanent and her conjugal life was finished. She had never imagined that her desire would revive so violently.

He went on, 'Let's consider it from Somdutt's point of view. What hardship will it cause him, if you stop his visits, which disturb your family life? Given his resources, nothing. You yourself think that now he comes only for your sake.'

'A clever boy! How long did it take you to conceive this elaborate scheme for Somdutt's elimination? And how long have you been jealous of him?' said she with a mischievous smile.

'By God, I was speaking impromptu! My only objection to him is that he keeps visiting your home despite knowing that it strains your relations with your husband. That he doesn't wish it is irrelevant. And I never felt jealous of him on your account. Because, believe it or not, even if I sometimes did fear of the consequences of Vishnu's jealousy, I never seriously worried that you'd take him as a lover.'

She said, 'Because of his intellectual disdain for Vishnu, he never had a chance. However, to be fair to him, he's not devious; as I told you, he never says or does anything purposely to disaffect me from him; he says only what he thinks and doesn't mind anybody else speaking his mind. And what neither my husband nor you realize but I know for certain, and perhaps have told you before, is that though formerly he did desire me, he no longer does so and comes to the evening parties only because he thinks I feel lonely and wish him to come.'

'But the fact remains that Vishnu is unhappy because of him, and he knows it.'

He continued, 'You must make up to your husband. Stop his visits, which will immediately end your separation. And you would be doing it as much for your own sake as for Vishnu's. You know that nobody can replace him in your life. Our affair is utterly delightful, but it isn't going to last forever, nor can it be a substitute for a happy married life.'

Having thus once again silenced his qualms about deceiving Vishnu, which still occasionally assailed him, he surprised himself by telling her, 'After your reconciliation we would enjoy even better! A contented Vishnu would be much less likely to suspect that we might be having an affair!' He added,' Do promise, my darling, that Somdutt will never cross your threshold in future and that you'll slip into your husband's bed at the first opportunity. Why not do it on the day he returns.'

How true that their affair was not going to last forever and that he could never replace Vishnu in her life! Yet wasn't it something extraordinary for a lover to speak so to his mistress? She couldn't help wondering at his total lack of jealousy. It was so unlike a lover. Was it because he felt guilty of deceiving him, or was being pragmatic?

'A clever boy, but a good boy,' said she again with a mischievous smile.

The next day he told her that for all their sakes either they should end their affair or she should give up her friendship with Somdutt, which would restore her relations with her husband, and by allaying his jealousy minimize the risk of their being found out. He added, 'Although we may still enjoy ourselves for some time, but ultimately we'll have to give up because it can't be absolutely proof against discovery.'

Two days later, Vishnu returned from Bombay after a weeklong visit. He looked unusually tired and low and replied indifferently to his wife's questions about his well-being, with which she had begun to greet him on his return from his business tours some time after Jaiprakash became her lover.

This change of behavior in him alarmed both Chandrmukhi and Jaiprakash.

That day Jaiprakash was for the first time surprised and a little disappointed to think that perhaps she was an artist; throughout the day she looked depressed and did not respond to his attempts to cheer her up and know the reason for her sadness.

'Has she entered into the character of an unhappy woman?' he thought. He felt uncomfortable and tried to discount the suspicion that her melancholy was simulated to delude Vishnu into thinking that his despondency was its cause.

She had judged him rightly. He enjoyed the affair intensely, yet couldn't bear the idea of her cunningly deluding her husband, which would have made it difficult for him to respect her. He also didn't want any complications. He wished the affair to be as simple as that when Vishnu was away they made love to their heart's content, and ceased doing so when he was present! He also feared that simulated pretence could be counter-productive and give them away and therefore she had better continue to behave not much differently from before.

One day he asked her, 'Has something happened between you?'

She did not reply. She had begun to think it unlikely that her husband's increased despondency was due to the suspicion that she was having an affair with Somdutt or Jaiprakash; the latter she still thought of as something extremely improbable, almost impossible, despite having happened. As for the former, she was instinctively aware that not only had Vishnu never been sure of it but had long ago become so accustomed to it that when they slept together it hadn't prevented him from making love to her.

Just the same, she felt worried. She had begun to find it hard to enjoy the affair if Vishnu remained unhappy for any reason whatsoever. She felt this most intensely after she and Jaiprakash had been together and she was overcome with a poignant tenderness for Vishnu. How they had loved each other before they came to know Somdutt and Jaiprakash.

More than once after a passionate encounter with Jaiprakash she had been overcome with revulsion to think of Vishnu's love and respect for her before their relations began to deteriorate due not only to his jealousy but also to her obduracy.

She recalled Jaiprakash urging her not to mind humbling herself to achieve reconciliation. Obviously, he was also finding it hard to enjoy the affair with an unhappy Vishnu present in his mind.

Presently she began to feel frightened to think that the cause of her husband's morbidity might be something deeper than mere jealousy and mistrust. She was right in thinking so. Vishnu now only occasionally thought, and that too from habit, that she might be having or longing for an affair with Somdutt or Jaiprakash; the latter possibility had only casually occurred to him once or twice and he had dismissed it as absurd. As regards his prolonged estrangement from her, which had begun to oppress him much less since Jaiprakash became her lover and their relations became better, it only partly accounted for his present state of mind. It was mainly the physical and mental strain imposed by his new business ventures, causing him for the first time to feel tired of life and the vanity of his wealth and position in society.

As he was a man of strong emotions, she began to fear that prolonged depression might seriously undermine his health. She was sensitive in a worldly-wise way. As much as her wealth, standard of living and reputation for culture and sophistication, she also wished as much as ever their being regarded as a happy couple despite the rumors and occasional mutual annoyances before others. She knew that unhappy couples derived and imparted less pleasure and enjoyed less respect in society. It was awful to visualize her life with a permanently depressed and estranged husband. And it was not only impossible but worthless to maintain the pretence of happiness before others. Jaiprakash was right. It was inconceivable that anybody could replace Vishnu in her life. She thought of Somdutt. Although she now liked him better than ever for his sympathetic behavior on finding her sad, she wouldn't mind requesting him with due apologies to come no longer. As for Jaiprakash, his concern for her reconciliation with her husband, which was never so pressing as when he was holding her in his arms, had made him as lovable as Vishnu. Yet, she would part from him also, if it should become unavoidable. And he would understand.

Before the end of the week, she had telephoned Somdutt from her bedroom in Jaiprakash's presence and expressed in more or less the same words that he had suggested her inability to receive him at her home.

'Until you hear from me. Maybe forever. You are a friend and I need say nothing more.'

'I don't mind,' he replied. 'I wish you to be happy.' He added, 'I hope it will reconcile you and Vishnu!'

As she put down the receiver, she suddenly found herself wondering whether Somdutt suspected that Jaiprakash had become her lover! She looked at him. His eyes told her that he knew what she was thinking. It had more than once occurred to him also!

'What did he say?' he asked

'He expressed the wish and hope that it would lead to reconciliation.'

'I think he sincerely said it.'

'I also think so.'

They gazed into each other's eyes.

Unexpectedly, he found himself saying, 'He was a good friend. If only he had been a little more discreet.'

She smiled withy happiness. They embraced.

Chapter 20

20/1

Vishnu could hardly believe his luck when one day in reply to his casually mentioning the fact that Somdutt had not come for a rather long time she told him that she had at last done 'what you wanted me to do. I have apologized to him and requested him to come no longer. Of course, he knows the reason, but that's neither here nor there.'

She added, 'It seemed impossible that we should be happy together otherwise. I ought to have done it long ago. I am sorry to have caused you so much unhappiness by making it a prestige issue.'

She ended his grateful embarrassment with: 'Frankly, not wishing to be unfair to him, whom I still regard as a good friend, I also considered it from his point of view. With his wide intellectual circle and practically unlimited resources of entertainment he would lose nothing. And he would be spared the painful awkwardness between you and him.'

That night they were reunited. Vishnu had become weaker. She missed the ecstasy of being caressed by a passionate Jaiprakash and the deep contentment afterwards. But such happiness was by its very nature bound to come to an end sooner or later, besides being trivial compared to the joy of living with a happy husband.

The reconciliation revived their social life dramatically. Their friends noticed it and were glad. Such ups and downs in the lives of even the happiest of couples were nothing unusual. Some people noted the fact and shared it with their friends that the change had taken place after Somdutt stopped visiting their home. They wondered whether it was because Vishnu knew that he was her lover or was merely jealous. However, all is well that ends well.

One day, quietly watching Vishnu smiling to himself over something, Jaiprakash thought with a pang that if she had ended her friendship with Somdutt or even stopped his visits to the evening parties before, they wouldn't have become lovers and this house would be a heaven for all of them compared to what it was today, a place haunted by guilt and fear.

As for her, now that she was cheerful again, she looked forward to meeting Jaiprakash joyfully but not impatiently. Her joy was enhanced by the reflection that, as he had said, like all such affairs theirs also would end. She hoped it would end soon, leaving beautiful memories behind, especially that it had led to the reconciliation. Assuring herself that she wouldn't mind if the affair ended tomorrow, she looked forward to enjoying it till it came to an end in the normal course! A month later Vishnu left for Calcutta. They embraced before he left and she sincerely asked him to return soon and to go on tours less often. She hoped it would enable her to taper off and eventually end the affair, though while he still held her in his arms she couldn't help looking forward to meeting Jaiprakash the same night.

20/2

That night she and Jaiprakash tacitly hoped that now the end of their affair being certain, their fear of being found out would also end! It was accompanied by the thought in Jaiprakash's mind that it would put an end to his deceit against Vishnu which he had been excusing with the end of her sorrow after they became lovers, her sexual amorality and lack of remorse for her infidelity, and her concern for her husband's well-being, which the affair had revived.

With the end of Somdutt's visits, Vishnu was restored to his former good humor, geniality and kindliness, causing Jaiprakash's nervousness that he suspected him to ease. But it did not vanish entirely and every time he and Chandrmukhi met in his absence it revived. He had begun to think like his mistress. Did Vishnu sometimes suspect, however vaguely and briefly, that she had banished Somdutt because she had found a lover in him? It revived his fear mingled with a feeling of guilt: How probable that the affair should be accidentally betrayed some day before it ended! And, therefore, how awful that he should be sinning with the wife of the man to whom he owed so much! This thought would occur to him especially after he and Chandrmukhi had made love, which, both realizing the inevitability of their happiness coming to an end soon, they now indulged in with greater abandon than ever. To assuage his fear that the unlikeliest things happen when they are least expected and Vishnu might find them out before the affair ended, he would tell himself that he would be absolutely careful and never take the slightest risk. He did not dare share his fear with her lest he should aggravate her similar fears.

Sometimes, while impatiently waiting for her lover, she would think how free of worry and tension both of them would be if for some reason he was forced to leave them, and how much happier would she be despite the loss of pleasure, anticipation of which had lately begun to make her uneasily wonder whether after her reconciliation with her husband, Jaiprakash's increased passion was owing to the thought that she was an adulteress and would also have enjoyed fucking by Somdutt, who despised Vishnu as a philistine, and that he had saved her from such ignominy. Once she had been so deeply affected by this reflection, which she could not confide to him, that his tenderest caresses had failed to arouse her and he had returned to his room without making love.

As for Jaiprakash, after every encounter he would tremble to think of the unforeseeable future. He could not now say when their affair would come to an end, and however careful they might be, it was impossible to be sure that their mutual behavior, even the slightest gesture, would not give them away some day.

In spite of her increasing despair, her passion for her lover increased. And it increased not because of the difference between the two men, which was no longer material, but because it was illicit and she had become a different woman, controlled by the power and logic of sin, which even her grateful tenderness for Vishnu could not cure. In fact, his happiness had produced the opposite effect by assuaging the remorse she used often to feel to see him sad before their reconciliation. Like her lover she was also sometimes seized with great dread. She could not now trust herself not to take dangerous risks even when Vishnu was in town. It was not so before the reconciliation, when she used to be instinctively careful even in her body language. Given Jaiprakash's passion for her and lack of self-control, which invariably followed in the wake of his renewed resolution that the affair must end before disaster overtook them, she could not trust him to check her. A couple of times they had kissed in office and at home when they had found themselves alone even for a short while. Even more often she had only just been able to restrain herself from doing so or escaped provoking him into doing it by looking at him with desire in her eyes. On any of these occasions they might have been surprised by a servant or anybody else arriving unexpectedly.

As if desperately wishing to confirm her worst fears and in her frantic quest for a decisive episode to ensure Jaiprakash's final exit, which alone could end their affair, but the thought of which inflamed her passion the more since she had begun to regard it as unpardonable and sinful, one day she behaved with shocking recklessness. It for the first time made Jaiprakash seriously consider quitting. Soon after lunch, while Vishnu had gone out for a couple of hours and the servants were eating their midday meal in their quarters, finding herself alone with him in the office, she became wildly excited, and ignoring the possibility that Vishnu might return sooner, proposed that they make love on the office sofa. And ignoring his dismayed protests she closed the door. The very next moment, looking at his white face and realizing the dreadful fate to which she was exposing both her husband and lover, she reopened the door and burst into tears. Moved by her condition, he was about to console her, when suddenly feeling terrified lest they should be surprised by somebody coming unexpectedly, he left her. Coming out of the house and in his agitation not knowing where to go he continued to walk till he remembered his uncle Dr. Awasthi. He stopped a passing taxi but was too agitated to remember his address. The taxi driver waited a few seconds and then drove off. Avoiding the areas where he could be recognized by somebody, he continued to walk, which gradually allayed his agitation.

Presently he found himself in a poor and predominantly Muslim locality through which he had passed only two or three times before and always in a vehicle because of its revolting congestion and squalor. Looking around he had an awkward feeling, which distracted his thoughts from what he had just escaped from.

He remembered that it was a Friday. Bearded men, young and old, were streaming out of a mosque. Most of them were ill-clad, physically weak and uneducated and, he unexpectedly found himself thinking, conscious of being discriminated against and distrusted and despised by the better-off Hindus and beaten and killed by the police during the communal riots. They instinctively reminded him of Somdutt and Chandrmukhi, who used to quarrel with Vishnu on their account. Their luxurious lifestyle and these people's abject poverty and vulnerability, and once during a heated exchange with Somdutt Vishnu's accusation, which he had immediately retracted for being politically incorrect, that for most Indian Muslims Pakistan, Iran, Saudi Arabia and other Muslim countries were more important than India. As he looked at them, he was struck by the cruelty and inhumanity of the accusation, whether it was true or false.

He again recalled what had just happened. And what might have happened if somebody had unexpectedly arrived. To distract his thoughts from the sinfulness of his own conduct, he again tried to focus his mind on the inhabitants of the locality. Presently they didn't seem as depressed as his contempt for their self-complacent affluent champions like Somdutt had made them seem. They were devoid of that bleak air which hit you in a comparably backward Hindu quarter. They didn't need the useless sympathy of the affluent and corrupt Hindus who rolled in black money and politically exploited the poor belonging to all religions and castes. The pride of being a Muslim and devotion to Islam and Allah not only enabled them to bear their hardships from the day they were born till the day they died; it went a long way in allaying any sense of inferiority. The knowledge of some verses of the Holy Quran made up by a long way for the lack of modern education, which was beyond their dream anyway. On these bearded and skull-capped faces he seemed to perceive a desire for sacrifice and suffering in the cause of the faith, a thing of which he reflected Hindus were incapable, even to the extent of inviting certain destruction of their life and property.

Vaguely conscious that despite expressing a shocking reality these reflections were casual and due to what had just happened in Chandrmukhi's office, and would soon be forgotten, he recalled his visit to Bombay in search of a job when the bus in which he was traveling suddenly began to be pelted with stones by a violent Muslim mob. He later came to know in a hotel where he had taken shelter, and after many of these agitators, almost all of them innocent of English, had been killed by the enraged police firing into the crowd, that they were protesting against Salman Rushdie's Satanic Verses. The book had already been banned by the Government of Rajiv Gandhi even before any Islamic country had done it.

A few yards ahead, he saw painted on the wall of a mosque a likeness of Ayatollah Khomeini, the anti-American Iranian hero of a few years ago. He was trampling on a craven-faced Uncle Sam begging for mercy with folded hands and tears big as ping-pong balls. Below the picture against the wall was sitting on a mat a shabbily clad old man selling roasted gram to two ragged children. Beside them stood a woman in burqa, begging impassive passersby: "Ek paisa de do. Do din se bhukhi hun (Kindly give a paisa. I have eaten nothing for two days)".

Again remembering what he had just escaped from, he looked at the woman and recalled the huge procession of Muslims he had seen in Patna a few years ago during the Shari'ah Protection Week organized by the All India Muslim Personal Law Board. He heard the cries denouncing the Supreme Court's audacity in awarding, in violation of the Quranic law, a piddling maintenance allowance to a 74-year old destitute old Muslim wife named Shahbano, divorced by her husband, a lawyer, after forty-three years of marriage. Prime Minister Rajiv Gandhi had amended the constitution to establish the supremacy of the Quranic law. Since then Shahbano had become a symbol of Muslim atavism which he did not doubt even the backward Muslims privately deplored. A Muslim lawyer, a friend of his father's, had told him that Rajiv Gandhi had rejected the demand made with ulterior motives by the Bharatiya Janata Party for a uniform civil code and used his majority to pass the Muslim Women (Protection of Rights on Divorce) Act not only because it was politically expedient to do so but also because like most educated and even genuinely progressive Hindus he also thought it a waste of time to try to cure the Muslims of their ghetto mentality. The lawyer did not doubt that Nehru was of the same view.

'Like Shahbano, this woman could also be a victim of triple talaq and she may end up a prostitute, if she has not already become one!' he thought.

Suddenly the thought that she might be suffering from tuberculosis or some other fatal disease or starving for God knows how long and might give herself for a few rupees to appease her hunger pangs, reminded him of Chandrmukhi, her pampered sumptuous body, her surfeited appetites and her ideological convictions. The next moment he realized the irrelevance of the comparison and felt ashamed of his thoughts about his mistress. Despite anything and everything she was a good human being who had also suffered and was still suffering. How she had reopened the door in panic and burst into tears. He began to walk faster, looking straight in front of him, endeavoring to think nothing.

When two hours later, having forgotten what he had been thinking, he returned from his uncle Dr Awasthi's home he found the husband and wife discussing the latest share market and what they should sell and purchase, which, as he was deeply shocked to learn from her later, had caused Vishnu to return only a few minutes after he had left!

In despair, the next day she urged Vishnu that for some months he should stop going on tours and send Jaiprakash instead. She also proposed to him to consider appointing Jaiprakash as the head of the branch office of the company they were going to open at Lucknow. He agreed that he needed rest and assured her that after his next visit to Bombay, which was unavoidable, he would start sending Jaiprakash on business tours. As for Jaiprakash's transfer to Lucknow, he said, 'It would now be difficult to manage here without him. Don't you think he's become indispensable?'

'Nobody is indispensable!' she said. 'We did perfectly well before he came. Moreover, we need an absolutely trustworthy and loyal person who also knows our mind.' She added with deep conviction: 'Jaiprakash is such a person! The local man you have in view has a professional degree and experience and a good record in his previous company. But he's virtually a stranger to us. We may also have to accommodate Charles. He's thinking of leaving Jawaharlal and isn't much hopeful of joining the solicitors' firm he told you about. He wouldn't like to leave Delhi, or he could have taken charge at Lucknow.

Vishnu promised to consider. He thought of Somdutt and from old habit couldn't refrain from briefly indulging and assuaging his jealousy, like once in a while relaxing by smoking a cigarette which he had given up as bad for his health. It was followed by his assuring himself that it was absurd to think that she wanted Jaiprakash out of the way in order to pursue her affair with Somdutt. She might be anything but was not calculating. In fact, she was the opposite of it, which was one of the reasons for his mental problem or his problem with her. He had always feared her taking Somdutt as a lover impulsively and from exasperation rather than planning an affair and conducting it clandestinely. It had forced him to conceive a preventive against such a possibility. With the ingenuity of a jealous husband periodically needing relief from anxiety he had conceived it without much difficulty: Being a proud and dignified woman and jealous of the respect she enjoyed in society, she wouldn't take such a dreadful risk, however aggrieved she might be with him! And his jealousy and fear were baseless. He had swung between these opposite poles.

Within a week of the sofa episode, as they would later describe it, Jaiprakash received a letter from his father in response to his phone from a public call office that he urgently wanted to come home for some time but couldn't do so without a letter from him. An hour before he was to leave for Patna, she asked him anxiously when he was returning and whether he was going away forever! The question expressed both her irrepressible desire that he should come back as well as her fear and despair lest he should really do so. Sometimes, she wondered at the fact as well as hated him for not having repulsed her advances after her reconciliation with Vishnu which she owed almost entirely to him.

'What do you mean? Of course, I'm coming back. But it can't go on like this.'

'It was madness. It'll never happen again.'

Jaiprakash returned after fifteen days. A week later, Vishnu left for Bombay.

That evening, determined that her relations with her lover must end, looking at him calmly she told him not to come to her that night. They had dinner in complete silence and immediately after it she went to her bedroom and bolted the door. But her eye falling on the bed, as she had feared, she became excited; every minute she grew more frightened that she might do what she had never done before: go and knock on his door if he should comply with her wish not to come to her.

She remembered once asking him, 'Swear that you'll never forsake me!'

'I swear!'

'Even if I asked you?'

'Not even then.'

She quietly unbolted the door and waited impatiently to see whether he would keep his promise. She felt he desired her too ardently to be able to do so. At least he might come to check whether she was still determined not to receive him and had bolted the door. As the minutes ticked away she grew more and more desperate.

A few minutes later, Jaiprakash gently pushed the door and entered.

'I have kept my promise never to forsake you, even if you asked!' said he. She embraced him with tears of joy.

Afterwards, he had a resurgence of fear; such passion was bound to give them away. Any day! The consequences of the discovery, which seemed inevitable, were too horrible to imagine. He told himself that his days in this house were numbered. He must return to Patna.

He wondered what should be done to prevent the "almost inevitable catastrophe".

'What are you thinking?' she asked.

He told her.

She listened to him in silence. After the end of Somdutt's visits, the fear, which she had not the heart to share with him, had again begun to assail her: Vishnu could think that the reason for her suddenly banning Somdutt was that she had started an affair with Jaiprakash. Today, she could not resist confiding it to him.

'What do you think?'

'It has occurred to me also, but I didn't want to worry you. In fact, he may be thinking so in Bombay at this very moment and be unable to sleep. I should go away,' he replied.

'He's right. He must go away,' she thought. Then occurred to her what seemed the ultimate reason for ending the affair, which was possible only if Jaiprakash went away for ever: If Vishnu were to discover her in the arms of Somdutt, their conjugal and social life wouldn't be irretrievably lost. His wish to maintain his position in society together with her grief and remorse and his realization of his own guilt would eventually force him to reconcile himself to what had happened. But if he discovered her affair with a "servant" whom he trusted he would never forgive her and his sense of being betrayed and dishonored would destroy their relations for ever.

Her social life flashed before her. It had slowed down, but not as much as it might have. And since the reconciliation it had revived. She remembered her front-rank status among the elite. Her sitting on the dais or in the first row at seminars, music conferences, award presentation ceremonies, etc., which were attended by Cabinet Ministers, sometimes even the Prime Minister and the President, screen idols, writers, artists, intellectuals. She recalled her group photographs at various functions with Rajiv Gandhi, Pandit Ravi Shankar, Satyajit Ray, M F Hussain, Lata Mangeshkar, Amitabh Bachchan and numerous other national and international celebrities in various fields, which were published on the front pages of newspapers. Quite a few of them had honored her by visiting her home. Some of these photographs adorned the walls of her drawing room while hundreds of them contained in albums lay on the shelves from where they were sometimes taken down to verify a remembrance.

She said to him, 'Would you like to go as the head of our office at Lucknow?'

He concealed his joy lest it should hurt her! Nothing was half as important to him in the world as the welfare of his family at Patna. Contrary to what he used to think at the beginning of the affair, in his gloomy moments he now sometimes thought that since coming to Delhi, he had degenerated beyond redemption; no extenuating circumstance, not even the fact that the affair had helped prevent the destruction of the conjugal and social life of the woman he was now holding in his arms and her husband, could atone for his sinning with the wife of a man who once trusted him to guard his honor. It was infinitely worse than the sin of adultery into which he had fallen. The only way he could repent was to leave them forever. Her question made him wonder if he was really so lucky. His posting at Lucknow would eliminate all risk and ensure security for his family. He remembered his days in Patna. His strong frame belied the fact that he and his sisters had grown up mostly on roti and daal, cheap seasonal vegetables and a glass of milk. How his sisters loved their Dada. How they used to press him to take one more roti and some more daal so that he would be healthier and more contented. How they washed and ironed his clothes so as to make him more presentable and prayed in temples for a lucrative and respectable career for him and a beautiful and loving wife and children whom they would adore. They were in their late twenties and well educated but had yet to know love of which he was having a surfeit. His parents were too poor to find husbands for them. Their welfare meant much more to him than even the joy with this aristocratic and passionate woman, remembrance of whose generosity before they became lovers and she began to adore him, he cherished as fondly as his present relations with her.

He said, 'Have you talked to Vishnu?'

'Yes, and he has promised to consider. I'm sure I'll be able to persuade him. Charles is likely to take your place. As you know, he has decided to quit as Jawaharlal's junior.'

The next day, he asked her anxiously, 'Are you sure that Vishnu would appoint me as the head of the Lucknow office?'

'I think he would.'

He became thoughtful.

She asked, 'Have you any doubts?'

'I am not aware of his thinking.'

'Are you really keen to go there?'

'I am absolutely keen.'

'And if he appoints somebody else? He has been talking to a highly qualified local man.'

'I'll go back to Patna.'

He was dismayed at the thought of leaving their service. What would happen to his poor family?

She wanted him to leave, yet she felt unhappy. Did he no longer love her?

'Are you serious? You really want to go away!'

'Oh no!' he said, divining her thoughts.

'But your going to Lucknow will be in both our interest. And in Vishnu's interest too.'

'That's true!'

'It seems unavoidable.'

'You know why I want to leave here as soon as possible,' he said.

'I do.'

'We'll still meet occasionally when you are visiting here and Vishnu is away,' she said, kissing him and desperately hoping that he would soon leave here and they would never meet in the absence of Vishnu.

'But I want to end our relations for ever in order to be absolutely free of risk,' he said to himself, too preoccupied to return the kiss. He couldn't help again recalling his family's problems at Patna.

All of a sudden, he was shocked to think of what would have happened to his old parents and sisters, and to Vishnu if he had found out about his treachery. Vishnu wouldn't have been wrong in thinking him a villain who had basely corrupted his wife by taking advantage of her unhappiness.

Part Three

Chapter 21

21/1

In his wife's absence Govind Mehta had continued to help Shanti with her thesis whenever he could find time. During these meetings, he would often remember that despite their close friendship in the course of which they had at least once nearly become lovers, he had courted Harimohini on the quiet and married her. It must have shocked Shanti. She often expressed her gratitude to him for his disinterested help, but the old feeling between them was not there. Although he no longer desired her, he missed that feeling.

Another possible reason for her lack of interest in him, he would sometimes think, wrongly, as he would come to know later, was the discouraging effect on her of Harimohini's reputation for good looks, her aristocratic background and famous attachment to him. These had been spread by word of mouth by some of his friends and their wives.

Although she had been deeply mortified when one day she unexpectedly came to know of his marriage, his disinterested help to her with her thesis, when with such a brilliant wife he had no reason to desire her, had not only enabled her to forgive him and forget her humiliation, but made her feel grateful to him and wish him the joy of his good luck.

21/2

Harimohini had again come after a long interval of three months, although she had been writing him beautiful letters at least once a week, which he kissed both before and after reading them. He had long ago ceased to think that she might be having a lover over there; she was incapable of doing anything dishonorable or that which she would be forced to hide if challenged. It was her career. And he was also responsible. In his desire to marry her, he had assured her that so far as he was concerned marriage would not interfere with her career. Neither had he ever doubted her devotion to him. As for her lack of animal lust, though she always gladly responded to his desire, it had made her even more lovable than she would have been otherwise.

One day when Govind was going around an art exhibition with Harimohini, they ran into the art gallery's Director. He introduced her to him as his wife. An outstanding artist of national repute, the Director looked grand in his crumpled khadi kurta-pyjama and old rubber slippers. He was smoking a bidi. Between his lips it enjoyed the dignity of a Havana and the ashes from it were caught by his long bushy Tagorean beard, which doubled as an ash tray. Just then Shanti happened to walk in. Seeing Harimohini and guessing who she was from the way she was holding Govind's hand, she decided to slip away. The memory of her humiliation at having been deluded by the man who was now unselfishly helping her had made her feel uncomfortable and she had no wish to be introduced to his wife who was innocently its cause. In fact, she now sincerely wished them happiness. Just then the Director, who was famous for his pranks, descried her. In a loud voice he asked her to come over, making it impossible for her to escape. As soon as she joined them, the Director, who was her neighbor and enjoyed fancying her and Govind as lovers and sometimes thought of them as models for a painting in the nude, introduced the two women to each other. Between reckless puffs of acrid bidi smoke, which he blew into his admirers' faces, stinging their eyes and making them cough and choke, by way of acknowledging their tribute to his genius, he told Harimohini that Shanti was "working devotedly" on her thesis on Govind's play "Hiroshima". Joyously exercising a famous artist's sovereign right to offend anybody's feelings, he concluded the introduction by informing Harimohini with an ironical smile of Shanti's "special relations" with her husband.

'I have been assisting her with her thesis off and on for a long time,' said Govind, assuming a casual air to try to explain away the "special relations".

Instead of appearing surprised and looking questioningly and suspiciously at her husband and Shanti, as the director had hoped and Govind feared, Harimohini bestowed on her a gracious smile and thanked her for her favor to her husband.

'I am grateful to you!' said she. 'And I hope you'll do full justice to the play. Although I haven't read it, I've no doubt of its high quality.' Then turning to her husband, she said, 'You should continue to assist her with the thesis till it is completed!'

Before moving on, she invited Shanti to tea at her home.

The Director was so surprised that he couldn't help shaking his head, causing the ashes resting on his beard to drop on to the carpet.

Both Govind and Shanti had been acutely embarrassed by the Director's roguish act, but they had been even more astonished at Harimohini's spontaneous reaction. They wondered if it was expressive of her trust in her husband's character or signified something else.

Judging from Harimohini's behavior during her week-long stay she did not seem to Govind to have been at all affected by what she had heard. As if it hadn't happened at all! He wondered whether her behavior was assumed to spare him embarrassment while she considered the implications of what she had heard; she was capable of such self-control. Or whether with her benign disposition and great fondness for him, their living together so infrequently and above all the possibility that the insinuation could be false and mischievous, she had decided to ignore what she had heard. Her instantaneous response to it seemed to confirm this supposition.

What she said to him the day before she left further reassured him that either she hadn't believed the artist's insinuation or indirectly told him that she didn't mind either way. On his asking her whether the relations between her sister, Chandrmukhi, and her husband, had improved and whether Somdutt still attended her evening parties, she had replied that they hadn't improved mainly because his jealousy had its origin not so much in his lack of trust in her as in his fear of the rumors spread by their friends about her relations with Somdutt, causing him to expect her to give up the friendship to quell the reports. She rightly refused to do so! An important reason for the refusal, Chandrmukhi had told her, was that the sudden termination of friendship would have strengthened the rumors instead of ending them.

'You have no right to distrust your spouse simply because of what others think or maliciously insinuate,' she had said.

Govind without being sure thought somewhat differently on the basis of what he had heard from her and personally observed, especially the fact that Chandrmukhi had begun to sleep separately from her husband. During his visits to Delhi, he used to stay at her home, where Harimohini used to come to live with him. He had attended several evening parties and had talked with her sister's friends, including Somdutt. He had also talked with Jaiprakash and been impressed with him. He had secretly deplored Chandrmukhi's obstinacy in keeping up her friendship with Somdutt in defiance of her husband's reasonable or unreasonable wish. According to his guess, she was most probably innocent so far as her relations with Somdutt were concerned, but it did not excuse her foolishness. He had told so to Harimohini, who thought differently. He had also wondered at Vishnu's long absences, which left his reasonably or unreasonably displeased wife and Jaipraksh, an attractive bachelor, together. How likely that he should have become her lover as he himself might have become if he had been in his place, or become in the future! But he hadn't given the matter much thought. In fact, he had thought about it only casually. Instead, his thoughts were much more seriously occupied with the luxurious character of Chandrmukhi's and Vishnu's private and social life, especially the highfalutin subjects discussed at the evening parties, which he enjoyed but also thought of as no more than pure entertainment indulged in by the complacent rich. He was intimate with several such families at Bhopal, whose praise of his activism he considered sincere but devoid of significance.

As for Shanti, she thought it not improbable that without dismissing such a serious insinuation by the Art Director out of hand Harimohini had acted tactfully to save her husband's face. Or had she thought that if what the director had hinted at was true, she should overlook it because she lived with him so rarely? This explanation didn't seem unlikely in view of Harimohini's extraordinary admiration for her husband, whom she had married for a no less improbable, not to say quixotic, reason: His social activism and wholehearted dedication to the welfare of the gas victims.

When he met Shanti after Harimohini's departure, Govind criticized the Director for his mischievousness and assured her that it had created no misunderstanding in his wife's mind. Shanti replied by praising her for her graciousness and tact, especially her inviting her to tea at her home!

During her following meetings with Govind, Shanti wondered whether it really had not occurred to Harimohini that her infrequent visits and short stays might actually have driven her husband to induce her, an unmarried woman and old friend, into becoming his mistress. Or, could her apparently magnanimous response to the director's insinuation mean that she had welcomed it, if it was true, because she also had a lover? Shanti, particularly dwelt upon Harimohini's inviting her to tea; although it was only fair in the absence of any evidence of her husband's guilt, yet it could be sheer astuteness. Did she wish to assure both her and her husband that she didn't mind and they could carry on?

At their subsequent meetings they continued to tacitly exchange reflections. They had again begun to think that but for Harimohini's unexpected entry into Govind's life they might have been wife and husband, or lovers.

Shanti had heard of happy-go-lucky women who dismissed the allegations or suspicion of their husband's unfaithfulness as a nuisance, which, apart from possibly being false, might become a greater nuisance with unpredictable consequences if they questioned them, and which it was therefore silly to allow to disturb their peace and tranquility. A famous socialite she knew, despite her husband's reputation for philandering, talked to him good-humouredly before their friends, who knew about his affairs, went shopping and to pictures with her friends, ate delicious snacks at her favorite restaurants, returned home in the evening pleasantly tired and ended the day with two or three fast pegs, of which she made no secret. Lying with her back to him, she enjoyed sound sleep, making him wonder. Some of their intimate friends had caught her sometimes looking ironically at her husband, surprising and disconcerting him. Harimohini, who was the daughter of a rich man in Delhi, might be such a woman. She also enjoyed picnics and parties at the homes of their friends. She loved life and allowed no problem to interfere with her happiness. Her invitation to her to tea at her home after the director's insinuation and Govind's assurance to her that she hadn't at all been affected by it could mean that she wished her husband happiness!

As for Govind, he knew that Harimohini had no lover other than him. With her natural generosity and lack of jealousy she might have thought, he reflected, that even if Shanti was his mistress there was no point in being upset and it was better to put a graceful face upon it. The affair, if it was a fact, would like such affairs eventually come to an end. Many wives who like Harimohini loved their husbands adopted this benevolent and shrewd attitude. Eventually, the mistress made her exit, often a humiliating one due to failure to estrange the lover from his wife, and their married life went on as pleasantly as ever.

It gradually removed their mutual inhibitions and enabled them to see in each other's eyes Harimohini's tacit sanction if they wished to have an affair!

One day, after Shanti's thesis had been submitted and approved to her great relief and profound sense of gratitude to Govind for his unselfish help, to which Harimohini's invaluable contribution had also to be acknowledged, these exchanges of thought resulted in their becoming lovers.

21/3

Govind began to pass delightful nights with Shanti. However, sometimes they seemed to sense each other's pangs of conscience for deceiving a woman who, whatever her motive, had reacted so magnanimously to the artist's dirty-mindedness. Govind tried to silence his pangs by feeling full of gratitude towards Harimohini for her generosity, and after making love to his mistress by telling himself that he was unworthy of such a wife! And should end the affair as soon as possible. But without appearing capricious and mortifying Shanti. This presented a problem. Watching the joy on her face during lovemaking, the joy of a woman who had due to her circumstances and orthodox upbringing remained a virgin till the age of thirty, he thought it would be cruel to suddenly end the affair without first talking to her. He concluded his reflections by assuring himself that she would agree and they would find a way to end their relations with expressions of mutual gratitude for the pleasure they had given each other. Another important reason for ending the affair, Govind thought, was that like all such affairs it was also liable to become known and be talked about and some people might even think and tell their friends that most probably Harimohini was not only aware of it but had allowed him to carry on. This possibility especially disturbed him as it involved loss of prestige for Harimohini whom he wished people to esteem highly for her character.

Shanti sought to ease her embarrassment by mentioning her magnanimity and refusal to believe the director's mischievous insinuation and by unfavorably comparing her own plainness to her "extra-ordinary good looks"! Concealing his joy to hear the praise of his beloved wife, he assured her that far from being plain she was adorable! He thought of those unlucky lovers, about one of whom he had heard, whose envious mistresses, unable to bear the thought of being hated and despised by their paramours' virtuous wives, who were aware of the affair but generously or prudently ignored it, and unable to endure the thought of their lovers enjoying them also, not only routinely ridiculed them and declared them fully deserving of their husbands' deceitfulness, but also forced the lovers to endorse their derision of them before allowing the first kiss. Shanti loved Govind all the more, a fact which Govind had divined from their occasional references to Harimohini, for his praise and high opinion of her. One day she delighted him by mentioning this fact to him. She told him how one of her friends was admired despite having had an illicit affair with a married man. This woman had broken with her paramour, as she had told her friends, because she was repelled by the bad taste in which he used to talk about his wife, a good woman and loving wife according to all who knew her, in order to please her. No decent woman can respect a lover beyond a point who despite his own unfaithfulness disparages his faithful and loving wife in order to please his mistress. Well-bred lovers are never guilty of such meanness.

He believed, rightly, that Shanti had understood that their affair would not adversely affect his marriage in any way. Yet, to prevent any hopes, he gave her to understand that he was living apart from his wife, or she was living apart from him for such long periods, not only due to his work for the gas victims but also because of his opposition to her giving up her intellectual activism and her brilliant career in order to live with him as a mere housewife. She was a powerful critic of Government's policies which she considered detrimental to the common man. Sometimes Harimohini actually expressed the wish to settle in Bhopal, he fibbed, and then he had a really hard time dissuading her. He was satisfied that what he had told her was essentially true. Although living with him only once in a while, Harimohini was more caring and unselfishly devoted to him than any wife he had heard of. He had heard of wives who with a highly gratifying sexual life, which produced a child every year, made their husbands' life hell by cantankerously grumbling over trifles during the day. They endlessly complained of their domestic problems to their friends on the phone, purchased whatever took their fancy on credit, and shocked their husbands by presenting them with exorbitant bills.

Sometimes, as he watched Harimohini moving about the house as its happy mistress and thinking of ways and means to minister to his comfort, he felt grateful to Shanti. Without the affair, he said to himself, as if he was paying a compliment to his wife by enjoying Shanti, he wouldn't have been able to so fully appreciate the golden side of his life with Harimohini. Loving him without lust.

Chapter 22

22/1

It was more than a month since Subhadra had written to Himanshu Mukherjee.

Charles said to her, 'I don't think he'll come or even reply to you.'

'I have also begun to think so. His failure to reply is understandable. If he was an altruist he quite sensibly changed his mind after meeting Vishwanath! And if he was a good man in pecuniary distress, he was either embarrassed by Vishwanath's apparent shyness about mentioning money or outraged to think that perhaps they really expected an altruistic donation. It is cruel that Sarika should die for want of a kidney. And if she must have it, she had better have it as soon as possible.'

Charles said, 'You may ask Jayanti to request her judge uncle to try and persuade Papaji to once again meet the Aligarh lawyer.'

Subhadra became thoughtful; the suggestion was so unexpected.

'Judge uncle was extremely unhappy at Papaji's treatment of him. However, he loves Jayanti and has an obliging nature. But do you think the lawyer will now agree to meet Papaji?'

'Let's hope he does. I've heard that he's more desperate than ever. After his meeting with Papaji became known he was approached by some agents; he found their proposals too disgusting and humiliating. But he may not be averse to dealing with decent people. I hope that what I have heard is correct.'

'I have also heard more or less the same thing. That's why I think he may not like to meet Papaji again. Papaji is unlikely to behave differently from the way he did then. However, there's no harm in trying.'

'Papaji can't be unmindful of the fact that he who refused his charity doesn't deserve to be equated with men who bargain for their organs. Let us hope they meet again and the pitiless moralist behaves more humanely. In his own interest too.'

'I think the lawyer is still the best donor from all points of view. I hope uncle won't mind trying to persuade both Papaji and the lawyer.'

'Uncle will have to disclose to the lawyer in confidence that he'll definitely get a large sum of money after the kidney has been grafted. This absolute certainty may help counteract any reluctance on his part to meet him.'

He added, 'The lawyer may also have to convince a more skeptical Papaji that he had been misunderstood last time and would not accept anything.'

Subhadra said contemptuously, 'I don't think he would again abase himself by pretending unselfishness to a man like Mr. Jawaharlal. He has had enough of it! Now, if his kidney is still acceptable to him, he will have to take it without embarrassing him and with humility.'

Getting up, Subhadra said, 'I'll talk to Jayanti. Let's hope for the best. If nothing happens, the brothers are there. If they are unable to overcome their fear, we'll ignore Papaji and arrange a kidney. We'll take the donor into confidence. It may take some time but it's not too difficult, and it's not explicitly illegal at present. We've talked to Sarika and now she can wait without fear of death or tension. Thankfully, her general condition is still quite good.'

'I am going to Court. We'll meet in the evening. By then you may possibly have come to know Papaji's response to judge sahib's request.'

'Papaji has agreed to the judge sahib's request to meet the lawyer. I was present during their telephonic talk a few minutes ago. He has just left to argue a case,' a couple of hours later Charles told Subhadra, who had called to inform him that the Judge uncle had agreed to speak to Papaji.

Subhadra said, 'Judge uncle has also talked to one of the lawyer's friends, who has promised to ensure that he meets Papaji. Uncle thinks that the lawyer, who had been bitterly chagrined by Papaji's attitude, may still say what he expects to hear.'

22/2

Although Jawaharlal had ceased to believe that Himanshu Mukherjee would reply to his letters, he did not feel disappointed. In fact, he felt lucky! He did not have the vaguest idea how he would respond if the Bengali young man, misunderstanding the letters, should come and demand money. Or if he were an altruist, would it be just and fair to denigrate his sons and daughters-in-law by telling him that he was forced to issue the appeal because his sons were cravens and under the influence of their wives, who were in favor of buying the kidney? Although these were facts, he had gradually become doubtful of the fairness of criticizing his sons, especially to an outsider. On the contrary, he had begun to feel more and more inclined to acquit them on the ground that they were masters of their lives and he had no right to expect them to make their family life unhappy by conforming to his ethics or blame them for their inability to overcome their fear. Wouldn't it be better for him to be satisfied with their buying a kidney without questioning his ethics in principle, or not telling him what they had done? He sometimes wondered that they had not quietly found a donor and paid him and told him, if he had asked, though he would never have asked, that he was an altruist who to their acute chagrin had refused to accept anything as a token of their gratitude. He had also begun to feel more acutely than ever the hurt he had caused the Aligarh lawyer whose wife was probably dying. Sometimes, recalling his daughter's emotional condition he thought that paying would be a lesser evil than letting her die or accepting Himanshu's kidney if he should be a resolute altruist.

Sometimes, in quest of relief from his depressing thoughts he would go to Vishnu's home and if he happened to meet Chandrmukhi, plead with her to behave sensibly and give up her friendship with Somdutt. He did not believe that her differences with her husband ever had anything to do with the fate of the Babri Mosque, which in any case had already been finally decided and become an issue between hypocritical and belligerent politicians. It reminded her of her affair with Jaiprakahsh and she felt too embarrassed to tell him that her friendship with Somdutt had already ended.

Sometimes involuntarily or for diversion's sake he found himself suspecting that Somdutt had become Chandrmukhi's lover. Or, alternatively, that she was a virtuous woman and her husband's suspicions were unfounded. And if he happened to meet Vishnu, in order to say something he would try to persuade him to think fairly and reasonably. Vishnu would respectfully listen to him and before they parted, guessing the real reason for his coming and wishing to please him, tell him that he didn't think that buying a kidney was morally wrong in all circumstances. He did not doubt that Jawaharlal was glad to hear his opinion, which was the opinion of almost everybody both he and Jawaharlal knew, and that eventually it would overcome his scruples. It was also possible that Jawaharlal had already changed his mind and was waiting for a little more pressure from his friends and relations before agreeing to buy it with a show of regret and reluctance.

Jawaharlal invariably ended by ascribing Vishnu's problem with his wife, or her problem with him, to his possessiveness and her obstinacy. More often, before he reached home he would forget that he had been to their house only a few minutes ago. Sometimes, wishing not to think of his problem, he would begin to study a case only to ask Charles a few minutes later to prepare a note for him about it. His legal practice had declined and he no longer took any new cases. He also knew that his colleagues and friends had become used to his problem and talked about it only when they had nothing else to talk about. He felt sure that few of them believed that he would let his daughter die. Meanwhile he was unnecessarily making her suffer. Most of them said that for a lawyer who with a clear conscience solemnly declared before the judge that his client, whom both he and the judge knew to be a criminal, was innocent, it was ridiculous to let his daughter suffer. All he needed to do was to buy a kidney and not bother about what people would think or say. Nobody would ask him how he had got it. He had also begun to think that though what he had done with regard to his daughter's suffering was beyond reproach his friends and well-wishers were not unreasonable in thinking that in his peculiar family circumstances buying a kidney or, if he considered it immoral, treating his daughter's illness as incurable and letting her die would have been better than issuing the appeal for an altruistic donation. This acknowledgment and his criticism by even his sincere friends had changed his views about many things which had nothing to do with Sarika's illness. It had had a relieving and liberating effect on him. It had gradually liberated him from many principles and ideas which used to uneasily inhibit him from appreciating others' points of view or appreciating but feeling constrained not to express his view. He had again started taking active interest in the social and political issues and expressing himself more freely and frankly than he had ever done. He had begun to accept invitations to speak at conferences and seminars. In leisure hours he had again begun to discuss the current affairs with his colleagues and friends. Despite worshipping Gandhi and sincerely endorsing his passion for Hindu-Muslim brotherhood, he no longer minded reading or listening to the criticism of the Mahatma's principles and private life and his faulty approach to the brotherhood question which had lately become an industry. He had recently read a book on him by Ved Mehta. Although to protect his image of a Gandhian he had been obliged to criticize the writer's derogation of the Mahatma in a solicited magazine article, he had enjoyed the book. In fact, he had read it a second time with even greater pleasure. He sometimes wondered whether Gandhi, if he were alive, would have gone on fast unto death for the rebuilding of the Babri Mosque and what would have been the reaction of Hindus and Muslims to it. Unable to conceive it, he had thought that if Gandhi were alive the Ramjanmabhoomi movement would have been nipped in the bud by his threatening to go on fast unto death.

A few days ago he had against the advice of his son Srinath, who as a lecturer in a law college with Muslim colleagues and students was aware of the general attitude of the educated Muslims towards the country's Constitution, accepted an invitation to speak at a symposium. The subject was the setback to the Indian secularism caused by the demolition of the Babri Mosque and Jawaharlal intended to plead for uniform civil code as the first step towards the equalization of the different religious groups. Srinath had told him that although in general educated Muslims, especially lawyers, were as liberal and forward-looking as Hindus the traditional Hindu-Muslim antagonism and the Hindu politicians' exploitation of their community as a vote bank had so deleteriously influenced the attitude of many, if not all, of them to their own modernization that it would be not only imprudent but a disservice to them for any Hindu to try to advocate any change in their religious laws and customs. Even Nehru never dreamt of doing it; that is why he not only rejected the demand for uniform civil code, but incorporated the outdated Shariat Act 1937 into the constitution. Their religious leaders, whose influence on the masses was supreme, regarded any reform suggested by a Hindu government or social activist or politician as Hinduization. What Pandit Nehru had not dared to do nobody else should think of doing. Srinath had added, 'We should wait hopefully for the change to come from within. And it is coming, though slowly. Particularly, don't speak against the essentially political agenda of The All India Muslim Personal Law Board whose main aim is to defend the Sharia laws from any constitutional amendments or judicial interpretations by the Hindu law-makers or Judges which according to them violate them. Don't speak against their custom of child marriage or any change in the divorce laws for Muslim women. Also don't plead for right of Muslim children for free and compulsory education, which in their opinion will cause infringement of the madarsa system of education.'

'Unless you want to get into a controversy as a relief from your private problems,' he had said to himself.

Jawaharlal had considered his son's views and advice but despite agreeing with him decided not to back out of his commitment, which he could have easily done. The organizers of the symposium would have invited someone else of equal intellectual prestige. Going through his notes for the speech he felt satisfied with them for their honesty and frankness, despite being aware that it would lead to controversy and questioning of his credentials as a true follower of the Mahatma, who shrewdly never suggested to Muslims to change with the times. However, like any follower of the Mahatma, despite his reservations about many of his acts and statements, he was always prepared to be accused of being a false one.

Before beginning his speech, he loudly cleared his throat several times, though there was nothing wrong with it, causing one of the organizers' helpers to rush to him with a glass of water. It gave him time to reconsider what he was going to say and about which he had suddenly developed misgivings. However, after a few sips, realizing that reconsideration might actually lead to confusion, he decided to go ahead according to the notes.

Describing the Mosque's demolition as contrary to the Gandhian ethos, he regretted the practice of "professional Hindu secularists" in politics and the media to hypocritically describe anything in praise of Hinduism as smacking of Hindu fundamentalism. He described this mind-set as veiled self-praise, which did not deceive intelligent Muslims. They could easily perceive that while the same political and social views as were denounced as fundamentalist and deplorable if expressed by Hindu politicians and intellectuals were not only tolerated but described as legitimate and unexceptionable if expressed by the Muslim spokesmen. As if the latter being less civilized deserved special consideration. In fact, intelligent Muslims saw in this smug self-praise by the Hindu secularists no real prospects of the advancement of their community. He regretted that almost the only thing done by Hindu secularists in power, many of whom were in reality opportunists and sectarians, for the amelioration of Muslims was to condemn Hindu communalism! Hands were raised in protest, but only by Hindus. Muslims on the other hand looked at each other with grateful smiles, a fact which did not escape notice by the secularists. Affecting to ignore both types of reaction and clearing his throat, Jawaharlal further surprised his audience with the remark that he had begun to find the views expressed in many Urdu newspapers, which were unfortunately edited by religiously narcissistic or paranoid Muslims, and were the principal source of information or brainwashing (he laid emphasis on the word brainwashing) of the poor and ill-educated Muslims, as a great threat to secularism, especially as these journalists enjoyed the dubious endorsement of the sectarian and opportunistic

Hindu politicians posing as secularists. Clearing his throat again, he went on to say that the description of the Babri Mosque in a book written by a senior Muslim journalist as a martyr to Hindu communalism was not only overly sentimental and indiscreet but also provocative, as it unnecessarily recalled to Hindus what was a bygone, the destruction of thousands of Hindu temples by the Muslim invaders and kings. There were more protests by Hindu secularists, which too he ignored. Alluding to an ex-Union Minister, belonging to an upper caste, who had been removed from the Cabinet because of his notorious habit of harping on Hindu communalism in season and out of season, which alienated many traditional Hindu supporters of the party, he said that Muslims should be wary of such Hindu politicians, who habitually describe any praise of Hinduism as Hindu communalism merely to prove that they are secular even though when in power they do nothing for the progress of Muslims. There were more cheers. While he could appreciate the leftist Hindu historians' whitewashing and even blatant denial of the forcible conversion of millions of Hindus and the destruction of Hindu temples by Muslim rulers as an act of magnanimity and charity towards Muslims worthy of Hindu culture and tradition, he said, he couldn't help thinking that hardly any important Muslim historians or politicians had ever publicly regretted this cruelty and vandalism. He wondered whether the reason for this silence was their embarrassment in lucid moments over this savagery combined with the realization that Hindus, contrary to what their secular spokesmen professed, hated these Muslim rulers as tyrants and actually celebrated the establishment of British imperialism. He was convinced, he further said, that the equally uncritical defense or even praise of these malevolent Muslim iconoclasts by the leftist Hindu historians was regarded by honest and cultured Muslims as not only disingenuous but calculated to disgust Hindus and remind them afresh of the nearly forgotten brutalities.

Suddenly looking at the few Islamically bearded and dressed people in the audience, like a true follower of the sex-obsessed Gandhi he found himself thinking that with the special freedoms accorded to them under the country's secular constitution some of them might be having more than one wife and even enjoying them one after another during the same night with legal sanction as well as physical, moral and spiritual fulfillment. It reminded him of the fact that Gandhi was overcome with remorse even if he had an involuntary orgasm, for which quite unnecessarily and to the acute embarrassment of his devotees, he publicly criticized himself as a sinner. No wonder if these hedonistic Muslims despised him as a demented fellow or a hypocrite whose political views didn't deserve to be taken seriously.

Fully conscious that he would be attacked for what he was going to say by not only Muslims but also by the Hindu secularists, especially those who secretly agreed with him, he pleaded with the modern-minded intellectuals in the Muslim community to campaign for a uniform civil code, lack of which was retarding their progress and tarnishing their image. He went on to say that Turkey and Tunisia had abolished polygamy and Syria, Egypt, Morocco and even Pakistan had restricted or banned it. Remembering the Indian Muslims' special affinity to their Pakistani brethren, he said that in Pakistan a man could take a second wife only after getting the necessary clearance from a court of law. Besides, Muslims who live in the Western countries gladly accept their uniform civil code.

Next he proceeded to quote from a newspaper column of a great lawyer, who he said with emphasis was neither a Hindu nor a Muslim:

'Divorce petitions take a long time. Consequently, couples are in suspense about their matrimonial status and future matrimonial prospects. In this connection Sunni Islamic seminary Dar-ul-Uloom Deoband has made a unique breakthrough. A husband had angrily said talaq three times to his wife on the phone. The wife claimed that she had not heard it even once and that nobody was around either of them to bear witness. The husband inquired whether talaq had taken place. In its reply, Dar-ul-Ifta said, "if you have given three talaqs to your wife, all the three took place and she became haram (forbidden) for you". The seminary clarified that it was not necessary for talaq to take place that the wife hears it or the witnesses are present. '

There followed a stunned silence. Taking advantage of it, he quoted another example even more incredible and shocking. A Muslim father-in-law had raped his daughter-in-law in the absence of his son. When she appealed against the sexual crime to the religious leaders, instead of punishing the offender they pronounced that henceforth she should treat her husband as her son and his rapist father as her husband. And when a Hindu Chief Minister of an important State with a large percentage of Muslims most of whom had no alternative to swallowing his false promises and voting for his party, was asked his opinion about this preposterous fatwa by the Muslim clerics, he said that India was a secular country where the religious laws of every community deserved equal respect!

'If there had been a uniform civil code the old criminal would have been tried and punished,' he concluded.

The speech had visibly embarrassed the educated and enlightened Muslims among the audience many of whom he knew wanted radical amendment of the Muslim personal laws, but were in a helpless minority. However, some Hindu secularists, who in order to assuage the Muslims' sentiments for the sake of Hindu-Muslim unity, no matter if it remained elusive, as well as being impelled by their compulsive hypocrisy, felt obliged to accuse him of speaking irrelevantly and being an unworthy follower of the Mahatma who never hurt anybody's sentiments, not even of those with whom he totally disagreed. Suddenly a bearded Muslim in the audience, unable to hear praise of the Mahatma from Hindu secularists whom he suspected to be anti-Muslim liars, stood up and retorted that even in old age Gandhi slept naked with naked young girls under the same sheet on the dubious pretext of increasing his power of sexual continence. If he regarded sexual desire as a sin and went so far as to publicly deplore his failures to control it, why was he so particular about eating highly nourishing foods like goat's milk and dates, which he could not but have been aware increased it and caused nocturnal emissions. There appeared spontaneous smiles on the faces of Muslims. Jawaharlal was not surprised by the bearded Muslim's reaction or the smiles. As a follower of Gandhi, he was more keenly aware than the Hindu secularists-leftists, who had reservations with him about political rather than sexual matters, that Muslims had always been suspicious of him because of his being revered also by the anti-Muslim Hindus. His opposition to the creation of Pakistan was also like these Hindus' rooted in their sense of overlordship of the whole of India, even over the Muslim-majority provinces of India. These Hindus felt assured that despite his harping on Hindu-Muslim brotherhood and chanting that Allah and Ishwar meant the same thing, like them the Mahatma also regarded the beef-eating Indian Muslims as physically, sexually and morally unclean inferior beings, a mixture of foreign predators and forcible Hindu converts mostly belonging to the scheduled castes, who deserved unqualified generosity, love and forgiveness, but had no right to a separate sovereign state or any part of Mother India. And although Jawaharlal criticized these Hindu nationalists his private views were similar to theirs and like devotees of Gandhi in general he was doubtful of the genuineness of the Mahatma's views about Islam and Muslims, with this exception that as a great soul, he loved them all the more on that account.

Realizing his indiscretion, Jawaharlal had tried to make amends by begging not to be misunderstood and to be heard to the end. Then with the dexterity of a brilliant lawyer, expert at gaining time to extricate himself from an awkward situation of his own making by puzzling the judges with extraneous quotations and observations, he had said that the ban on Salman Rushdie's Satanic Verses was justified! Although during his visit to America he had read this novel and been revolted by it, he had forgotten about it until this moment. He succeeded. Momentarily puzzled, the audience became curious to know how this novel was relevant to the subject of the symposium as well as what were its objectionable contents.

Jawaharlal went on to describe them. 'Rushdie's claim that the book is a work of fiction is the lie of a coward. Its character Mahound is actually the Prophet, whom he has vilified in nearly every chapter. He has described his wives as lacking in character. He has also attacked Islam as an evil faith. He committed these blasphemies in order to become famous among Europeans, who have a poor opinion of Islam, and to boost the sale of his books, which he knew were devoid of any literary merit. '

Finally, Jawaharlal sat down, smiling with satisfaction at his apparent success in appeasing the Muslims in the audience, who he felt sure were especially pleased because it was the first time that the satanic novel had been criticized by a Hindu, whose co-religionists despite its poor quality enjoyed reading it or defended it without reading it because they did not doubt it insulted and humiliated the religiously arrogant Muslims.

However, Syed had seized this opportunity to express in a long magazine article his dislike for Gandhi by defending Jawaharlal by misquoting him and describing him as a true follower of the Mahatma and his critics as ignoramuses. Jawaharlal did not react to the article because like most Gandhians and secularists he thought but couldn't openly say that neither Gandhi nor the Indian Muslims in general, whose hero was M.A. Jinnah, had ever politically trusted each other.

Jawaharlal's criticism in the media had served as a welcome diversion of his thoughts from his daughter's illness.

22/3

Charles was sitting in his office when he received two letters by the morning post. Both were from Himanshu Mukherjee and were addressed to Subhadra and Jawaharlal, respectively. After a moment's hesitation, he opened the former. After all, it was in reply to the letter he had written, he told himself. Himanshu had written that he had been selected for the post of lecturer at the Agra College and was going there to join. He hoped to come to Delhi to meet Mr. Jawaharlal and Ms Subhadra, especially the latter, in a few weeks. Though the letter did not say why he was coming, it expressed admiration for Subhadra's candor. It was also full of praise for Vishwanath. Charles read it a second and a third time but could not decide whether Himanshu was an altruist and influenced by Subhadra's sincerity had decided to disregard the brothers and donate his kidney; or whether he was a person in need who had been relieved of his embarrassment by the letter. He called Subhadra and informed her. Within minutes she appeared.

'Sarika's suffering may come to an end soon. That's what Jayanti and I wanted. If he's an altruist, Vishwanath and Srinath won't accept his kidney. And if they can't overcome their fear they would let us buy one. They won't let her die, which would amount to murder,' she said after reading the letter.

Charles would also have liked to know the contents of the letter to Jawaharlal, but he could not open it. He wondered whether Himanshu had mentioned in it what Subhadra had written to him and what would be his reaction. He had ceased to doubt that Jawaharlal had guessed that Subhadra, who met him often, and he discussed their family's problem. But with his usual discretion he had never asked him what she told him and what he thought of her views.

When Charles went to him with Himanshu's letter he was reading about a dozen letters he had received that day. While only one person had condemned him as a Hindu communalist, who had at last come out in his true colors, the rest had praised him for speaking frankly and truthfully. The latter assured him that so far as the Muslims were concerned the overwhelming majority of Hindus were of the same views with him.

'He hasn't written that he's coming to donate his kidney. His motive is not clear,' Jawaharlal said to Charles after going through the letter. He didn't look particularly pleased. Looking at him again, Charles thought that he would much rather not have received it.

He gave the letter to Charles. Charles was relieved to find that Himanshu had made no reference to Subhadra's letter. He wondered whether the omission was deliberate or unintentional and signified nothing. Apart from writing about his meeting with Vishwanath, whom he praised highly for his courtesy and kindness, he had merely informed Jawaharlal that he had received both his letters and would be coming to meet him in a few weeks after joining his post.

'To me it seems all right,' said Charles, returning the letter. 'I feel his coming means that he's an altruist and your condition is acceptable to him! What with his high opinion of Vishwanath and Vishwanath's impression that he's an honest good man, I think it should be enough for the present. Let him come and then we'll see.'

'If he turns out to be an altruist would you accept his kidney despite having two sons?' thought Charles, looking at him.

Jawaharlal said, 'The lawyer is coming again. It's difficult to imagine what he's going to say now that he didn't say before. Then he indirectly conveyed that being in great distress he expected to be paid for his kidney. Now perhaps he's hoping, whatever he might swear to, that if we accept his kidney, we'll pay him afterwards. There seems no difference between then and now. Anyway, let him come and let's see if he has anything new to say. I have the greatest sympathy for him. I am still prepared to help him without taking his kidney.'

Charles thought, 'If you have sympathy for him, why don't you accept his kidney and pay him? Why do you expect him to behave like a beggar?'

He said, 'He's a proud man. He refused your offer to help him without accepting his kidney.'

As soon as Charles had spoken, it seemed to him that Jawaharlal was feeling perplexed, as if he was having an inner struggle. Charles knew he was prone to such struggles, whose contents he seldom disclosed to anybody.

'Never having felt the pinch of poverty, he places rectitude, as he defines it, above suffering, however terrible it might be,' thought Charles with contempt.

Jawaharlal again found himself in the same dilemma that had confronted him when he first met the lawyer. He couldn't bear the thought of a poor man debasing himself by lying in the secret hope of gain. At the same time, he had acute scruples about accepting anything, let alone a part of his body, from one who was already poor, if his offer was really altruistic and he was a man of character who would refuse to accept anything even as an expression of the recipient's gratitude. No ethics could justify the exploitation of a poor man's unselfishness. He again realized that hardly any wealthy person living in luxury, however kind and compassionate he might be, would allow serious diminution of the quality of his life, let alone suffering the loss of a vital organ, for a stranger or even a relative. Like his sons, whom he still considered good men, he would rather it was some needy person whom he would generously recompense. He knew that his sons were annoyed with him for his refusal to accept the lawyer's kidney because he had behaved correctly and with dignity and demanded no money, even if he expected it. If he had accepted his kidney and paid him afterwards, they would have considered it an act of kindness. Sarika's suffering would have been over and they would be feeling fine! He had more than once glimpsed on their faces resentment mixed with compassion and guilt.

What was especially worrying Jawaharlal was that in spite of his great distress the lawyer might now refuse to accept anything after donating his kidney in order to avenge his humiliation! It was not an unlikely obstacle, which threatened to make it even harder than before for him to decide whether or not to accept his kidney.

Jawaharlal was again beset by fear lest he should be unable to bear his daughter's suffering and succumb. On such occasions, like a moralist faced with an insoluble dilemma, he thought he had no right to doubt the lawyer's word, who had not demanded money in spite of needing it for the treatment of his wife. He was shocked to think that such a man had refused his help. More than once he had also found himself wishing that his sons and their wives had arranged a kidney and if he had asked any questions told him to mind his own business and not interfere! He could have done nothing about it and his daughter's life would have been saved. The only reason he could think of for his sons not having done such a thing was that they were ashamed of their fear. If they hadn't been afraid, they might have thought like their wives, who honestly believed, he no longer doubted their sincerity, that paying a man in need for his organ was not unethical.

The next day, Subhadra informed Charles that the lawyer was down with typhoid and couldn't come for at least a couple of weeks or even a month.

Chapter 23

23/1

A few months after Govind had settled down to a joyful relationship with his mistress, one day Harimohini told him with her characteristic fond smile that soon she would become senior enough to get the post of her newspaper's Bureau Chief at Bhopal. The circumstances also favored her as the present head of the bureau had fallen out with the Chief Minister, who was trying to get him shifted from here. And if she did not succeed in getting the appointment, she would apply for longer leaves more frequently and if that too was not possible she would seriously consider giving up her job in order to live with him permanently. She had enough private means for both of them to live comfortably at Bhopal without her earning anything.

This unexpected development disturbed Govind, who, having remained unmarried for forty years, had at last been blessed with an adorable wife who never said no and a passionate mistress. He wondered if Harimohini had secretly believed what the art Director had said, or from some other source heard of the affair, which he had lately begun to suspect had become known to some of his friends, and was thinking of living with him in order to put an end to it. He had been afraid for some time that sooner or later the affair would like all such affairs become known and some busybody would tell her, but hadn't dared to think of the consequences. If Harimohini began to live with him permanently, his relations with Shanti, whom he could visit only at night, would come to an end.

On the other hand, it was possible that either she hadn't heard of it, or heard but disbelieved it, or with her generous nature chose to disregard it as something that had started before their marriage, continued because of her living with him only once in a while and would end when she started living with him. And her decision to come and live with him hadn't much to do with it.

266

Still the question remained as to what he should tell her if she had heard of it or should do so in the future and choose to mention it in the hope that what she had been told was untrue. After long consideration he decided to be truthful. Not only was it not possible to hide the truth but it would be base to lie to one who was so unselfishly devoted to him. But could they live together after he had confessed his unfaithfulness and lost her respect?

After worrying for some time, he decided to leave the problem alone until it should arise. However, no sooner had he done so, than he found himself thinking again that either she hadn't heard of the affair, or heard but decided not to mention it out of fear lest he should confess that it was true. She might remain silent in future also. Her dilemma might be as difficult as his.

It was also possible that if she asked him and he confessed she might leave him. However, no sooner had he thought that she might leave him than arose the opposite possibility in his mind that actually she might never mention what she had already heard or might hear in the future, and even if convinced of the veracity of the reports secretly overlook the liaison in consideration of the fact that like many a husband he loved his wife despite having affairs!

However, at night before falling asleep he couldn't forebear thinking again of various possibilities and alternatives, including those that he had already considered, found perplexing and self-contradictory and shelved. Presently he was reminded of another problem, which had occurred to him before and about which also he had stopped thinking after a while. It was that if she began to live with him permanently or even for long periods and he was forced to let her accompany him to the places where he worked for the gas victims, she couldn't sit at home all day long, her sensitive nature might not be able to stand the filthy environment and the human suffering. And eventually leave him.

One day, it occurred to him that although Shanti waited for him with such longing and made love with such passion, marriage was something else. So far, she had not even vaguely hinted that in the long run if possible she would like to change their present relationship for marriage. Hence there was no harm in at least finding out whether she would be willing to marry him, in case

Harimohini left him for any reason, which was not impossible. Or he was forced by unbearable mutual embarrassment to leave her on her coming to know about the affair.

But this question gave rise to another question. What would an undoubtedly astonished Shanti think after hearing his proposal? Mightn't she think that perhaps Harimohini was unfaithful to him with someone in Delhi and was thinking of leaving him for that person, a fact he was ashamed to confess to her. Perhaps he had long been aware of her unfaithfulness and that's why she lived away from him for such long periods and that's why he had started the affair with her. She might not be above sharing his proposal and her own interpretation of it with her intimate friends, who would share it with others. It might end up messing up both his and Harimohini's reputations, besides his losing her respect for being a deceived husband who had been hypocritically lavishing praise on his unfaithful wife!

He again decided to do nothing and wait and see.

One day Harimohini informed him that she had finally decided to come and live permanently with him. She had told her sister, Mrs. Chandrmukhi Narayan, who had powerful connections, that she would accept any post at Bhopal if that of the bureau chief was not available. She hoped Chandrmukhi would be able to persuade the newspaper's new managing director, with whom she had considerable influence. And if she did not succeed, she would resign. Govind tried to dissuade her from making an unnecessary sacrifice for his sake. He assured her that he was happy with the things as they were. Giving up her job and living as a mere housewife would greatly diminish the quality of her life. He reminded her that her present prestige was also due to her being a senior journalist in an All-India English paper. But she was not to be moved. She didn't care for false prestige!

He said, 'I leave for my place of work after breakfast and return in the evening, sometimes quite late. What would you do all day long? Pass your time at the officers' club or at Kala Bhawan? So far, I have managed to reschedule or skip my engagements because of your short stays.'

She replied, 'I'll work with you for the gas victims. I'm sure I'll be able to help you. As I have told you before, I wish to work for them! I did not insist because your love for me would not allow you to let me dwell in what you call a filthy environment. Now I have finally made up my mind, because I do not doubt that the happiness of living and working with you would more than make up for the discomfort of working in those surroundings.'

'Your romantic illusions will expire at the first sight of the conditions in which I work,' he thought. He said, 'You'll cause me to feel guilty by injuring yourself for my sake.'

'Oh, no!' she said. 'I'll do it entirely for my own sake.'

He knew that she was telling the truth. She was incapable of thinking that she did anything exclusively for him; in fact, when she did anything for him, she felt that she had done it for herself. She was also a determined person. He recalled how she had defied her father and married him. He was perturbed. He had passed two delightful nights in succession with Shanti. The affair would come to an end if Harimohini began to live with him. It was inconceivable that he should continue it with her secret knowledge and helpless acquiescence. As much as she adored him, she might close her eyes to it. But it might grieve her no end to think that he was capable of deceit. He couldn't conceive of greater cruelty than wounding a woman who thought nothing of sacrificing the comforts to which she had been accustomed all her life in order to live with him.

Sometimes his reflections took a different turn and he thought it not impossible that if he confessed and humbly apologized she might not only excuse his past conduct but tacitly allow the affair in view of her solicitude for his happiness! She was capable of it. But what would their friends think who had either come to know of the affair or should hear of it later? So far, they may have excused or nearly excused it because she was living with him only once in a long while and it appeared to have made no difference to their mutual love and respect. But would they still think nothing of his unfaithfulness once she had sacrificed her career and the life among Delhi's elite in order to live with him in comparative poverty? And wouldn't she also lose their respect for winking at his infidelity?

In short, it would be impossible for him to continue the affair once Harimohini had begun to live with him. On the other hand, Shanti might herself end the affair, finding it disagreeable to have relations with a man whose wife was living with him and often waiting for him while he was with another woman; it was not the same thing as having an affair with a man who was practically a bachelor and came to her to assuage his loneliness when his wife was away.

At last he seemed to see a way out; at least, it would afford mental relief from a problem which continued to obsess him despite his wish to avoid thinking of it. He would propose to Shanti, not with definiteness but conditionally, describing the proposal as his wish whose fulfillment depended on circumstances he could not at present foresee. At any rate, if he was to propose at all, he must do so without any more delay and know Shanti's mind before Harimohini resigned and started living with him. The likelihood that having warned him of her decision, she might suddenly wind up there and come made him uneasy.

However, before talking to her he should be clear in his mind as to what he would do or would not do, irrespective of the consequences. He found it much easier than he had thought.

First, he would never voluntarily leave Harimohini and would gladly give up the affair if she continued to live with him after or without coming to know about it; the fear that she might leave him had made him realize that there was no pleasure equal to the companionship of a woman like her. He felt convinced that the affair wouldn't have started but for her too frequent and long absences. Secondly, he would not lie to her, nor find fault with her, if she asked him whether the reports were true. In other words, despite extenuating circumstances, he wouldn't plead anything in defense of his conduct, because it would amount to blaming her. However, she might leave him, for which there were reasons, or it might prove too embarrassing for them to live together.

Finally, there was no question of his telling his mistress anything in the least disparaging to Harimohini.

He decided to tell Shanti that although he was abundantly satisfied with their present relations, yet he wished to marry her. He hadn't thought of all the hurdles, but if she was agreeable, he would take the necessary steps. The proposal would be so framed as to express his desire to marry her and to elicit her response without any time-bound or irrevocable commitment on his part, which he hoped she would appreciate it was not possible to make at this stage. It occurred to him that the proposal would flatter her self-esteem, even if eventually nothing came of it! Of course, she would always be free to change her mind, he would tell her. He recalled that he had proposed marriage to Harimohini in a more or less similar frame of mind: wishing to marry her but prepared to take the refusal without disappointment.

But what if a surprised Shanti were to ask, in fact, she would almost certainly ask, the reason for his sudden wish to break with his wife, whom so far he had been praising? He would tell her that he wouldn't like to go into the reasons, which he would assure her were not at all important for her to know. She must consider his proposal exclusively on his eligibility as her husband without reference to his past or present relations with his wife. He hoped she would understand that for some reason, which he was not in a position to disclose, at least not now or until they were married, his relations with his wife had taken an unfavorable turn, something to which the happiest of marriages were liable.

23/2

He decided to talk to Shanti at their very next meeting. If she refused because of the indefiniteness of the proposal or for any other reason, he would be disappointed but also relieved! The rejection would have the merit of saving him the trouble of doing something which began to weigh heavily on his mind and seem much more difficult than he had thought as soon as he had decided to do it!

As he started for Shanti's house, he was uneasily conscious that he had been changing his mind too often, thinking one thing one moment and quite another next and confounding himself to no purpose and that today also he might fail to dispose of the no less vexatious problem of whether to propose or not!

Sipping his coffee, which she made him on his arrival, and armed with the indefiniteness of the proposal and the absence of any firm commitment, he said to her with a solemn face to forestall incredulity, 'Will you marry me, if it should be possible? I haven't thought of the hurdles. I am merely expressing my wish. I want to know your mind before I act further.'

He was pleased with the impact of his words. She looked surprised, though he couldn't say that she was flattered. She seemed to rate herself better than he had thought, which was as well. Her reaction seemed to promise that if she accepted his tentative proposal and he was later forced to withdraw it with due apologies, she wouldn't feel mortified and find it easier to appreciate his inability and forgive him.

Before she could reply, he said, 'I am serious, though I wouldn't like to go into the reasons for wishing to leave Harimohini. They are not important for you to know, anyway.'

He added, 'Think it over. Take your own time. Meanwhile, I am perfectly satisfied with our present relations!'

Shanti was thinking how one day more than a year ago she had opened her letter-box and found in it an invitation card formally inviting her to his marriage in Bombay to a woman named Harimohini, which according to the date given in the card had already taken place! Although he had proposed to her nothing, still, in view of their growing friendship, which had given her a definite impression that he was interested in her, the invitation had shocked her. He had been secretly carrying on with this woman simultaneously with displaying interest in her. She had felt bitter. The least he ought to have done for decency's sake when he had started courting Harimohini was to give her a hint, or start distancing himself from her.

However, over the last one year and a half, after his return from Bombay, he had not only made ample amends for having humiliated her in the past by disinterestedly helping her with her thesis, but in course of time become her lover. And she was satisfied with him. However, it was something else whether she would be happy with him as his wife. It required the most careful consideration. It also occurred to her that the proposal lacked definiteness. It only expressed his wish, or was due to his present unsatisfactory relations with his wife. If they improved to his liking, he might withdraw it.

Although conscious that he was watching her, she said nothing. Not even that she would consider the proposal.

He left a little after midnight, but she remained awake till the early hours. Why did he wish to divorce Harimohini, a far superior woman in every respect and with whom according to what she had heard on the grapevine he was so much in love that even his dedication to the welfare of the gas victims just outweighed it? What was no less important to consider was that, according to the reports from the same unimpeachable sources, Harimohini ardently reciprocated his love. She had more than once requested his friends to persuade him to go and live with her. Besides, unlike her, who was a temporary lecturer in a Government college and liable to be transferred to any backward town in a backward state, again depriving him of the company of a woman, Harimohini was in a superior profession, lived in a great city and worked in one of the best English newspapers in the country. Finally, what was no less important a reason for his sticking by her, she was, as he had once told her, one of only two heirs to her father's large fortune, the other being her sister, who was already wealthy.

Instead, he wanted to divorce her! It was mysterious. What was even more important to consider was whether while at present she had the pleasure of treating him as an equal, after marriage he wouldn't sooner or later begin to behave to her condescendingly for being the successor to a superior woman; if and when she failed to satisfy him for any reason, which happened in the most successful of marriages, he might mention his ex-wife's riches, beauty and other virtues with regret! Yet another important point to consider was whether he would be faithful to her. It seemed highly unlikely, judging by his conduct so far. It was not the same thing to be the mistress of a married man as to be a deceived wife. In spite of professing a high regard for Harimohini, which she now for the first time seriously doubted, he had never evinced the least compunction about deceiving her. In fact, once to a question by her whether he ever felt guilty, he had surprised her with the reply that his deep love and respect for his wife, which had remained undiminished by their utterly delightful affair, ruled out remorse! She had pondered the answer and eventually recalling the apparent spontaneity with which he had given it accepted it as possibly true, though strange. Now the answer seemed false and cleverly premeditated. She had also sometimes thought that perhaps Harimohini had come to know about the affair but decided to overlook it because they lived together so rarely. Now it seemed that she had come to know of it for the first time. And though for both her and her husband's sake behaving before the world as if she were unaware of it or didn't believe it, she had either decided to divorce him or for the time being warned him, keeping her options open, which explained the indefiniteness of the proposal. He didn't wish to recklessly throw away the advantages of being the husband of such a superior woman; the proposal might be no more than an expedient to keep her in reserve, if eventually his wife refused to forgive him and left him.

23/3

While waiting for Govind to repeat his proposal, Shanti had kept thinking. Presently she had begun to look at the other side of the coin. Whatever his reasons for proposing, he was a good man. Despite his detractors, he enjoyed considerable prestige. There was no other person half as good who was interested in her. Although about ten years older than her, he promised to last as a satisfactory husband long enough. And if she couldn't be called unattractive, it was mainly due to her youth and shapely figure, which wouldn't last forever. In fact, in a few years her marriage prospects might disappear altogether.

Despite its indefiniteness, the proposal upset the contented tenor of her life, which until then was blessed with a delightful lover without involving any obligation or her freedom being abridged in any way.

Although she had never expected or even vaguely wished for such an offer, but having received it, she found it difficult not to give it careful thought. She wished to be fully satisfied that he would be less than a good husband lest she should later regret that she had thoughtlessly thrown away a reasonable chance of a happy married life. She loved her freedom, but did not exactly look forward to the life of an old spinster. She personally knew and had also heard of several such women whose last years had been sad despite their being well off and having caring relations. They had no companion or even the memories of a husband and children to comfort them in the evening of their lives. She had personally heard one of them, an unmarried professor in her late forties, who had missed several chances of marriage, saying openly that life with even an uncongenial husband and selfish children, which incidentally was the fate of her own sister, was better than living alone and brooding as an old spinster. Another senior colleague had told her friends that even an unfaithful husband, which was what her own uncle was, but on whom her aunt still doted, was better than no husband. She looked forward with something like terror to her post-retirement loneliness.

Shanti decided to accept her lover's proposal if and when he should remind her. Because of its indefiniteness she considered a reminder necessary in order to be sure that in the meantime circumstances had not altered, causing him to change his mind. Meanwhile, she would go all out to make him happy. And if he did not remind her, without taking offence she would forget about it.

Chapter 24

24/1

A month after her last conversation with Jaiprakash about his appointment at Lucknow, Chandrmukhi for the first time missed her period. She waited anxiously. Another week, two weeks, a month. She was pregnant.

They had always been careful, but not as much as they ought, she realized. It was natural for people as passionately in love as they were and for a woman who had not conceived even after ten years of a happy married life.

She did not panic.

She had also been with her husband when she conceived, but there was little doubt that it was the lover's child. She instinctively decided not to mention it to him, nor to Vishnu. She considered abortion. She considered her dilemma between foisting another man's child on her husband and, if he came to know about the abortion, which was not easy to conceal, destroying his happiness forever by planting in his mind a suspicion that she had been deceiving him all along. She instinctively shrank from the former. Would she be able to live at peace if he should believe the child to be his and feel grateful to her for it? But the consequences of his coming to know that she had concealed her pregnancy from him and secretly aborted were fearsome.

She thought of Dr Mrs. Rege, who was a good friend. However, she was bound to be surprised and become suspicious of her secret and confidential request. Five years after their marriage and before the introduction of Somdutt to them she and her husband had once expressed their wish to her to have a child. She had assured them that it didn't mean that she couldn't become pregnant still, for it was not unusual for a woman to conceive after an even longer period. At the same time, she had suggested certain tests for both of them to find out why she had not conceived. They had considered her suggestion for a long time and in the end tacitly agreed to reject it. They had guessed each other's reasons, which were more or less alike and protective of each other. In the first place, as according to the doctor she could still conceive, both had preferred to hope; they were still young, less than thirty. Secondly, according to her guess, he had probably thought, partly no doubt out of a sense of fairness to her, that in the elite society where people mixed freely, knowing that she was incapable of conceiving, in a weak moment she might accidentally succumb to some friend. Secondly, she might still slip up and become pregnant despite knowing that her husband was incapable of fathering a child, and put both herself and him in a fine pickle. As such, it was better for him not to know who was responsible for her not having conceived so far and to hope that she might do so in future.

As for her reasons for not undergoing the tests, according to his guess, which was correct, she had more than once seemed to perceive him to be transiently suspecting one of their close friends of desiring her or being desired by her as a lover.

Thus, it would be prudent for them not to know whether she was incapable of conceiving or he was incapable of reproducing. And if one day she did conceive, he would consider it normal and not entertain any doubts. Then Somdutt had been introduced to them and Vishnu had become obsessed with jealousy. Later, Jaiprakash had come and further complicated their relations.

She considered the worst that could happen if she did not go in for abortion, which she had everyday become more fearful would be difficult to conceal. Supposing Vishnu suspected, as almost certainly he would from sheer habit, that she, who had not conceived for more than a decade after their marriage, might have become pregnant by his enemy. Could she still depend on him to overcome his suspicion by thinking "reasonably and justly" in the absence of any evidence of her guilt and for the sake of his own peace of mind? After long consideration she thought she fairly reasonably could. First of all, he would think whether he really was the father. In order to be fair to her as well as to himself he would try to find reasons to think that it was so, the alternative being the possibility of condemnation of his own child as illegitimate. Further, it wouldn't fail to occur to him that, as Dr Mrs. Rege had told them, many a wife has conceived after an even longer time. To further assure himself, he would also think that many a husband has either never doubted, or if like him he is by nature jealous and suspicious, without believing in his suspicions for long, has eventually persuaded himself from a sense of justice and fairness mixed with a little pragmatism to give his wife as well as himself the benefit of the doubt. After this more important question has been disposed of and he has decided to consider himself the father, or that it is unwarranted and unjust to her to think that he is not, would arise the less important but still significant question of what others would think on coming to know that she was pregnant. It wouldn't fail to occur to him that even if he was absolutely sure that Somdutt had never been her lover, or if it was established beyond doubt that he and not Somdutt was the father, though Somdutt may have been her lover, at least some would still think, or say to their friends without necessarily believing it themselves, that most probably Somdutt was the father. In other words, what people thought and said couldn't be helped. On the other hand, there were people who would think that in the absence of any credible evidence to the contrary, rumors and suspicion being no proof, it would be unjust to think that he wasn't the father. Furthermore, as everybody knows, sometimes even legitimate children are suspected of being offspring of illicit unions, and vice versa, and after some time neither they nor their parents care what people think. People stop thinking after a while anyway. Finally, who knows but that the child might be Vishnu's. It was conceived after the reconciliation.

At last, she decided to take the lesser risk of becoming mother. Ultimately, all suspicions and rumors die or become stale and boring and are superseded by fresh rumors and suspicions.

But there was yet another worry. Should Jaiprakash know? He would almost certainly think it was his child and she would have to acknowledge that most probably it was so. What would be his reaction? What would he think of her if she told him of her decision to palm off his child on her husband? She might lose his respect, if she hadn't already lost it! For the first time, the horrible thought occurred to her that for all she knew, despite his own conduct, he might be secretly despising her for deceiving her husband even more voluptuously after they had become reconciled and he had begun to respect and trust her as before. And it was a fact. The happiness of her husband since their reconciliation had by freeing her of her remorse increased the intensity of her passion for her lover as well as her vanity. This unexpected thought worried her for a whole day and night and she could free herself of it only by recalling his conduct throughout their affair. He had not only pleaded with her but sometimes literally prayed that she make up to her husband. He would also appreciate the fact that she was as helpless about her passion for him as he himself was in desiring her, and that letting her husband think that she was with his child was a lesser evil than causing him to suffer to think that it was not so and that is why she had secretly opted for abortion.

However, the knowledge of her pregnancy could worry him to think that jealous Vishnu, tired of suspecting only Somdutt, for a change might suspect him also! He had never been completely free of this doubt. He had more than once said to her, especially after Somdutt stopped coming, that at least sometimes Vishnu might have suspected him to be her lover. It might affect his behavior towards Vishnu, which mightn't remain unperceived by him. Would it be possible for him to live at ease in this house or even at Lucknow with the fear that perhaps Vishnu suspected him present in his mind? Although all these possibilities were far-fetched, it was not prudent to rule then out.

She also felt nervous to think of the uncertain element the fact or belief of his paternity, which would confer a special status on him, would inject into their idyllic relationship in which she was the boss and he was especially happy to think that she still adored him. And what about her relations with her husband which had become as good as ever? They might not remain unaffected by Jaiprakash's presence and his anxious demeanor towards Vishnu. Once he's out of sight, any suspicion that he might have been her lover would fade.

The more she considered, the more she became persuaded of the necessity of concealing her pregnancy from Jaiprakash and of ensuring his departure as soon as possible. There was no time to be lost. In fact, it was already quite late. She was supposed to inform Vishnu at the most within a month after missing her period. Jaiprakash must be made to go away immediately.

But how? Vishnu had not only accepted her suggestion to appoint him as the head of their Lucknow office but begun to express his confidence to him that he would be a competent manager. How could she now tell him to leave their service without giving a convincing reason? She again considered whether to take him into confidence and again decided against it because she could think of no other explanation than that from certain signs Vishnu seemed suspicious of their affair. And her pregnancy, which had occurred after the end of her association with Somdutt and about which she had not yet told him, would strengthen his suspicion and create a serious problem for both of them. Hence he should leave them on some pretext before she informed him. Although she instinctively shrank from falsely accusing her husband and lying to her lover, in addition to making the latter feel guilty, she didn't rule it out as a last resort.

His appointment as the head of their Lucknow office was still at least two months away. By then her pregnancy would become conspicuous with all its complications. In fact, much before that he would learn it from Vishnu, who must be informed without delay. And what would he think on learning it from him instead of directly from her?

Vishnu was to leave for Lucknow in a few days. Her behavior to Jaiprakash underwent a complete change. She grimly determined to shun him as a lover to begin with. Then she would consider the next step. She felt no doubt that he would appreciate that she had done so because she was frightened of her longing for him which exposed both of them to great risk. And she felt that it was a fact. Although she would not tell him that she was most probably pregnant with his child she might still lose control of herself in Vishnu's absence, she thought fearfully, if he knocked on her door!

Grimly, she began to treat him as a friend and well-wisher valued for his ability and loyalty. Nothing more. She didn't feel anxious because he was by nature discreet and sensitive. When they were alone, she began to behave as she used to in Vishnu's presence—without a semblance of the fact that they were lovers.

Noticing her altered demeanor when they were alone, Jaiprakash had no difficulty in understanding that she was again desperately trying to end the affair, but that as before she might lose control of herself when Vishnu was away.

'It would be infinitely fortunate for everyone if she succeeds in her effort and it's the end,' he told himself.

The day Vishnu left for Lucknow, Jaiprakash wasn't surprised when at dinner he found her eating silently. It was not the first time he had found her looking pensive and a couple of hours later receiving him joyfully. It was good policy to leave her to her moods. After dinner he as usual left for his room while the cook was still in the kitchen cleaning up.

At ten o' clock, he gently pushed her door, wishing and hoping that today he would find it closed and afraid lest it should be open. To his surprise he did find it closed. He turned back but instantly changed his mind. The closed door inflamed his passion. His hope that he would find it closed evaporated and he began to long for one last kiss, a last embrace, a last conversation. He looked at his watch. It was a little earlier than usual. Yet what did it matter? He knocked softly and waited. After a minute, he knocked a little more loudly. Then more loudly still. He was going to meet her after what seemed to him a long and must seem to her an even longer time. There was no answer. His excitement and impatience became unbearable. He looked at his watch. Ten minutes had gone by. It was improbable that she should have gone to sleep. She was a late sleeper and, besides, should be too excited to be able to sleep. He knocked a couple of times more and waited another ten excessively long minutes. Either she had suddenly fallen asleep or decided not to receive him. He returned to his room, but did not bolt the door, which he scrupulously used to do by way of extra precaution after the sofa episode, lest overcome with desire she should come to his room even when Vishnu was at home.

He could not sleep, hoping in spite of himself that she might yet come to his room although she had never done so, his precautions notwithstanding. On two occasions, when Vishnu was away and he did not feel up to it, he hadn't gone to her. Next day, on his explaining and apologizing, she had confessed that she had been unable to sleep for desire. She hadn't told him as to why, then, she hadn't come to his room. He knew why: She was an aristocrat and his boss and it did not behoove her to go to her servant's room driven by lust to be violently and uninhibitedly made love to by him on his bed! As if she were his wife and instead of enjoying a favor he was exercising his right as a husband! The idea would have made her wince although she had not only allowed him every liberty that he wished on her own bed but incited him to take more.

He did not know when sleep overcame him. Throughout the next day she did not tell him why she had not received him last night, although for long periods in the office there was no third person present. And he didn't ask. Recalling her incontinence, he could not help marveling at her self-control. He had become a prisoner not only of his passion but even more of hers. He recalled her proposal that they make love on the office sofa with even greater amazement than he had felt then, despite the fact that she had burst into tears and opened the door immediately afterwards. Sometimes he could not help imagining with horror the perfidy and wickedness of which he would have felt guilty if Vishnu, who had unexpectedly come only a few minutes after he left, had surprised them. As an expiation of his crime of corrupting her he would have liked to be killed by him on the spot.

24/2

A week had gone by. She had neither received him nor even alluded to the fact, of which she could not but be aware, that he had knocked on her door on four consecutive nights. However, the fact that she had not told him not to come to her any more caused him to hope that she still longed for him and was controlling herself with the greatest difficulty. The hope was followed by fear lest her resolution should break down.

He was glad to think that during the day when they were alone together he had done nothing either by word or by gesture to weaken her self-control. Although unable to sleep for desire hour after hour, he had thought both her and himself blessedly lucky on the four nights when he had returned to his room after knocking on her door in vain.

Yet he feared that he would be unable to resist her if her resolution broke down, and that it was sure to end in a tragedy. He felt frightened lest any more trouble should touch her life after the agony she had gone through and the gulf into which it had thrown her. He began to lock his door and throw the key under the sofa from where it was difficult to retrieve, lest seized with desire she should break the taboo and come to his room. He also began to take Valium in order to fall asleep quickly. The more he longed for her the more he prayed for her self-control not to give way. Sometimes he found himself wishing her to find the strength to end the affair out of love for her husband whom she had begun to love and respect as much as ever. At such moments he would again recall that she had become his mistress accidentally and from prolonged suffering. It was a matter of only a few weeks before he would leave for Lucknow.

What she thought he did not know and the memory of which caused her to tremble was how one night she had actually gone to his room and knocked on his door. And how finding it closed she had turned back feeling infinitely relieved but also seized with great dread lest he should have heard the knock, open the door before she had escaped and follow her to her room. Actually, he had heard the knock but not opened the door.

Vishnu had returned. In his presence she continued to behave to him like she used to do before as well as after they became lovers: with the affability and kindness of a boss, which barely concealed her despair: What should she do to make him go away without knowing the truth and without feeling hurt?

One day when there was no third person in the office, suddenly wishing to be reassured that at least he enjoyed the status of an ex-lover, he said to her, 'I am very happy and grateful to my darling. I shall never forget our blissful nights together, but in future our relations should remain as they have been during the last some days.'

She looked at him as if she had not heard him. She said, 'At six-thirty and seven you have appointments with Mr. Charles and Mr. Jawaharlal, respectively. You'll get the papers after Vishnu's arrival. He's returning by the afternoon flight.'

Her demeanor during the following week remained unchanged. In Vishnu's presence, she continued to treat him as good-humouredly as she used to do before as well as after she became his mistress, but when no third person was present, which was often, and when he wished her to be tender and reminiscent of their joyful days, her manner became remote. It was so uncharacteristic of her, so contrary to her amiable nature, that at first he found it unbelievable. Then he understood her great fear and the desperate effort she was making to control herself. He realized that even a little perseverance and tenderness on his part would finish her.

At last, he understood what she wanted. She didn't want to take any risk and wanted him to go away. So far as she was concerned his appointment as the head of their Lucknow office, to expedite which Vishnu was working overtime, seemed a thing of the past; she no longer even indirectly mentioned it. He realized that it was impossible for him to go to Lucknow or remain in her service against her wish. One day when they were alone he made bold to ask her whether she still wanted him to head their Lucknow office or go away.

'You should go away,' she said, looking at him with a grave face.

'Although Vishnu is as nice as ever, but maybe he is suspicious?'

Unable to lie all of a sudden, she said, 'He suspects nothing at present, but he would, if you remain here any longer. You must go away. The sooner the better!'

He wondered about the reasons but decided not to ask if she didn't want to tell. She looked away as if she didn't want any more questions and answers.

Even if her reply was unconvincing, her intention was clear. She wanted him to leave. Suddenly he felt no less desperate. What would happen to his old and ill parents and sisters? The money he had saved would at the most last a few months. He had been hoping to at least see his sisters married off before his income ceased, if it was destined to cease. At present they were working as teachers in a private school for a pittance. He had no foreseeable prospects in Patna.

He could not help saying, 'I assure you it will never happen again.'

'I am sorry, but you must go.'

It seemed as if she was about to break down. The next moment she had pulled herself together.

'Has Vishnu somehow come to know of the affair and in desperation asked her to ensure that without suspecting it he leaves?' he wondered. 'And like a repentant and loving wife she has decided to keep his confidence in return for his forgiveness?'

He recalled Vishnu's cordial behavior to him? Was it calculated to prevent suspicion? The idea that Vishnu had come to know of his perfidy was horrifying and he tried to dismiss it. It was more probable, he tried to assure himself, that Vishnu knew nothing and she was ashamed of confessing her susceptibility to him? She also did not trust him to control himself. He had knocked on her door four nights running instead of helping her to control herself.

'All right!' he said. He must go away, whatever the real reason for her asking him. Most probably, it was fear of their mutual susceptibility? The rest was his imagination. He would never know. He didn't want to know. He owed them so much and this was the least he could do in return for their goodness to him.

The same day he called his father to tell him that all of a sudden his service conditions had become impossible and he wanted to return home immediately, but could not do so without a credible reason. He asked him to send him an urgent telegram.

It cost him a great effort, especially the doubt that Vishnu had probably come to know of the affair, yet his demeanor remained as free and easy as ever. Once or twice he fancied to see on her face a semblance of sorrow. Did she wish him to regret her?

Two days later, he and his uncle, Dr Awasthi, received telegrams, informing that his father had been diagnosed with a heart problem and his presence was immediately required. The doctor, who received the wire an hour before it reached Jaiprakash, telephoned Vishnu, who was sitting with his wife and Jaiprakash in his office.

They condoled with him and expressed the hope that his father would soon get well. Looking at her, Jaiprakash wondered if she had really believed the telegraphic message, such coincidences not being unusual. They asked him to immediately call his home. His father's illness was a fact but it was not serious. Vishnu also expressed the hope that his father would soon get well and he would be able to take charge at Lucknow!

Looking at him, Jaiprakash again found himself wondering whether they were acting in concert to get rid of him without letting him suspect that Vishnu had come to know of the affair. He would never know. Neither of them was devious and it was so uncharacteristic, but if it was a fact, there couldn't be a better and kinder way of getting rid of him.

24/3

Jaiprakash had finished packing and was resting on his bed, staring at the ceiling. Unlike other days, he was not awaiting sleep. He would have time enough to sleep in Patna. He was leaving on the morrow, never to return. If Vishnu was unaware of the affair, his old age and ill health would be sufficient reasons for his inability to come back. Since the hardship his family would face was a circumstance that could only be remedied by his doing something there, and his father's illness was not serious, nothing had happened to lessen his inexpressible relief at his departure. Its full intensity he had begun to feel only after the severance of his connection with this house became final and irrevocable: How he had escaped committing the crime of destroying Vishnu's life. He had also got over her coldness. It was the only way she could control herself. She was a good and wise woman. She had rightly refused to accept his assurance that their affair had ended. She would treasure their happy moments together. He felt happy to think that the affair had saved her sanity and love for her husband which unrelieved grief and depression would have destroyed. He wished she would remember his efforts to reconcile them and begin her life anew, forgetting what had happened as a brief episode.

All of a sudden, he was startled to hear a knock on the door. He momentarily froze to think that it might be Vishnu, who had been suspicious for God knows how long! He realized with a pang that despite Vishnu's appearances to the contrary he had never got rid of the fear that at least sometimes he thought that he had become his wife's lover. This fear had begun to assail him particularly after Chandrmukhi stopped Somdutt's visits. And once or twice, like his mistress, to whose unexpressed thoughts his were often similar, he had also thought that perhaps that's why Vishnu had agreed to send him to Lucknow! Thinking that he was going back never to return and tormented by the desire to be rid of his suspicion he might have momentarily become oblivious of the ignominy and absurdity of obtaining a declaration of his wife's innocence from the suspected lover himself! Did he still trust in his loyalty so much that he was confident of being assured by him of what he desperately wished to hear: His suspicions were insulting and humiliating to both him and his wife!

He was hit by the absurdity of these thoughts, a product of momentary mental derangement caused by deep-seated fear, before he reached the door. It would be she!

After the sofa episode, when Vishnu might have surprised them, he had been so extremely particular about bolting the door before retiring, when Vishnu was at home, that he always rechecked whether he had done so soon afterwards as well as whenever he happened to awake in the middle of the night. Today he had thought it unnecessary, as he no longer saw any danger of her acting rashly. Suddenly realizing that he had wasted precious moments, he rushed to close the door, but before he could reach it, she had quietly entered. There was sufficient light for him to see her face. She was sad. She advanced to put her arms around him, but he drew back.

An hour ago she had risked making Vishnu suspicious by avoiding his caresses. It could provoke his chronic jealousy that she was longing for Somdutt. She had guessed that he still occasionally indulged it in order to later dismiss it as baseless. After their reconciliation, he had once by way of an apology confessed how he sometimes used to imagine Somdutt as her lover without ever seriously believing it possible and later reproaching himself. She had been tempted to tell him that he still sometimes imagined it and perhaps had done so just now! Instead, she had said, 'I admire Somdutt as much as ever for his intellect and convictions, but believe it or not, I never felt any love for him. He's an honest good man but is incapable of feeling or inspiring love in any woman. That's why Harimohini rejected him in favor of a less attractive man.'

She could bear permanent separation from Jaiprakash without any feeling of loss, if it was unavoidable in both their and especially in her husband's interest. She also wished to enjoy her conjugal and social life as she used to do before Vishnu became insanely jealous. But she could enjoy it wholeheartedly only if, as she had realized as soon as Jaiprakash's departure became final, it was replaced by an unalloyed remembrance of their happiness on both sides. It had begun to seem indispensable because the child would always remind her of him. She owed the restoration of her married life, which had once seemed lost forever, entirely to him. The idea was intolerable that he should think her ungrateful. The equanimity with which he appeared to have taken his dismissal, never betraying by the least sign that he thought he had been coldly removed as a hindrance, had made her suspicious that he had been deeply hurt but was concealing it. Soon after his departure became a certainty, she had begun to regret that instead of conveying her meaning to him by behaving coldly in order to ward off temptation, she had not told him to go away because Vishnu was suspicious, which was not at all improbable. Instead she had foolishly said no when he had asked whether it was so. She wondered that as well as she knew Vishnu she should have denied what had once occurred to her also—that he might have agreed to her request to send Jaiprakash to Lucknow not only because of his confidence in his ability but also to secure complete peace of mind by removing another present or future lover! It would have achieved the purpose without hurting Jaiprakash. His departure in a few hours had revived her suspicion that he was going away with a wounded heart. It had rendered her unable to respond to Vishnu's caresses. Watching Vishnu sound asleep, and remembering that she would never see Jaiprakash again, she had quietly left the bed.

Jaiprakash had a frightful vision of Vishnu awaking and finding her not in the room, suddenly becoming suspicious that she had gone to him and following her!

'How can you? My God!' he said, looking at her with disbelief and amazement.

'He's sleeping soundly. Nothing short of an explosion can wake him,' she replied.

'How can you be so sure? One can awake at any moment. Have you no care for your and his happiness? Go away this instant!' he whispered. 'For God's sake!'

'Forgive me. I have hurt you,' she said and tried to put her arms around him. He violently repulsed her.

'Do you want him to commit suicide or kill you?' he said with a furious grimace. 'Go away!'

She remained standing.

'Do you want me to hate myself forever? Get out! I don't want to see your face!' he whispered fiercely.

She stared at him in deep shock and began to sob.

He grew contrite, but she had turned back and gone.

She went into the bathroom, washed and dried her face and eyes and quietly returned to bed. She recalled her fear that Jaiprakash's calmness and composure after she told him to go away concealed his hurt. She could not sleep, brooding over his behavior. Did he hate her or was his anger due to the fear of their being discovered by Vishnu?

Chapter 25

A week after Jaiprakash's departure, as Vishnu held her in his arms, despairing of her ability to simulate a joyful smile, she at last decided to confide to him without it that she suspected she was pregnant.

'It's more than two months since I had my period,' she said.

'Are you sure?' he asked, barely able to prevent his surprise and suspicion appearing on his face.

She replied placidly, 'It's only a suspicion. I may be wrong because it's so unlikely. After twelve years!'

Quickly recovering, he embraced her and said with a forced smile, 'It's very much possible! Let's see Dr Mrs. Rege tomorrow.'

Afterwards, having made sure that she was sleeping soundly, looking at her he began to relieve himself of the tension of uncertainty by indulging his doubts which he would later dismiss for lack of evidence: 'Is it Somdutt's? That's why she stopped his visits? To prevent suspicion? And does he know?' The latter possibility bothered him only a little less than that Somdutt might be the father. He began to calculate. It was more than four months since the end of his visits. But she could have been meeting him away from home.

'And why didn't she tell me earlier? Because it's not mine? Or because of fear that though it's mine yet I would suspect it to be Somdutt's, she was anxiously waiting for the symptoms to prove false? My jealousy has made her afraid of becoming mother.'

Deciding to stop harassing himself with suspicions he quietly left the bed and took a Mandrax, which he used to keep concealed in his purse.

Dr Rege confirmed that she was pregnant and congratulated her and Vishnu, especially as it had happened after so many years when most couples give up hope.

'But it happens,' she said. 'Many a woman has conceived for the first time fifteen or even twenty years after marriage. And many a child is born fifteen or twenty years after its sibling without the parents having planned it. It's quite normal.'

'It's of course quite normal, and he knows it,' Chandrmukhi thought. 'But it may make him more suspicious. How logical that the more normal a thing is the greater the scope for deception it affords. But eventually he'll get over his doubts for the same reason. We love each other and need each other as we never did before.'

Vishnu remained uncertain. Of course, he could do nothing about it. Besides, as Dr Rege had said, it was something quite normal. Not only he but almost everybody had heard of such late and unexpected pregnancies and births either in their own or in one or another of their relation's or friend's or neighbor's family.

People would talk. But how long? Moreover, sober and responsible people didn't have time to indulge in such tattle. What was important was that he must appear happy and take at least some of his friends into confidence. And she should do the same. They shouldn't delay the announcement.

The next day he told her so with a joyful smile that he had pictured on his face while breaking the news to his friends and which he now unconsciously assumed before her also. She was relieved: He really believed or had wisely decided to believe that he was the father!

'Yes we should do it without delay!' she replied, repressing the sudden painful thought with a smile that she was deceiving him. Presently she excused herself for a few minutes and went to her study to get rid of the feeling that she was vile, that she should have confessed that it was not his child and taken the consequences. In a few minutes she returned with a smile.

Sure enough the tattlers, who had stopped exchanging notes about the cessation of Somdutt's visits to the evening parties as something outdated, had a new subject to divert themselves with. And sure enough they began to be snubbed both by those who did not share their suspicion as well as those who did, but with others and not with them. Soon almost everybody was confidentially sharing his suspicion with some and denying the possibility with others. The opportunity was also availed of to recall the name of many a famous person, without detracting from the luster of his or her achievements, who was suspected to be the child of someone other than their mother's husband.

Sometimes she regretted that she had not been more careful. If she hadn't become pregnant, the affair would have been a passing episode in her life. Many happily married women had such experiences. In addition, it had restored her relations with her husband. But the child would remind her of him forever and it would take the limelight from her life with her husband, whom she had begun to love again like she did before Somdutt and Jaiprakash entered into her life. She wished she had no secrets from him.

'It's also possible that Vishnu is the father, after all,' she would sometimes think. But the possibility was so remote. She would become sad.

Dr. and Mrs. Awasthi came with sweets to congratulate them. Mrs. Awasthi told her that she had her first child three years after her marriage when her husband's mother had already begun to worry.

Soon Chandrmukhi began to have headaches. One day on her way from office to home, she dropped in at Dr Awasthi's to get her blood pressure checked.

They talked about how happy Vishnu was. Dr and Mrs. Awasthi had also heard rumors of his wife's affair with Somdutt.

But they had also heard rumors of many other affairs not all of which could be true. Moreover, from his behavior they didn't doubt that he was genuinely happy, either due to the fact that he really believed himself to be the father or, which was the same thing, had decided to think so because there was no evident reason to think otherwise. He would also be aware of rumors about her close friendship with Somdutt. But gentlemen didn't pay attention to rumors.

'How is Jaiprakash's father?' Chandrmukhi asked. 'He telephoned Vishnu a few days after he left and told him that he was better.'

'Yes, he's better,' the doctor replied. 'It was a mild heart attack.'

Mrs. Awasthi said, 'Jaiprakash will be very happy to know that you are pregnant. I forgot to tell him.'

'Yes. He was very devoted to Vishnu,' she replied without a trace of self-consciousness. She knew that Somdutt was the only person generally suspect as her lover, and he had been suspect from much before she became pregnant without either of them being guilty of anything but friendship. For some he would remain suspect even if she were with her husband's child. The falseness of the suspicion enabled her to remain composed when once in a while she fancied suspicion on people's faces. She did sometimes wonder whether Somdutt suspected Jaiprakash to be her lover. But it would also be no more than a suspicion. And Somdutt was a true friend. He would never indulge in loose talk against her even if he disliked Jaiprakash.

Chapter 26

26/1

'Himanshu Mukherjee has come!' said Vishwanath to his father as soon as he returned from the court.

'I never gave up hope that eventually he would come,' said Srinath.

'Where's he?' asked Jawaharlal, looking at his sons and wondering anew at their apparent lack of embarrassment while informing him about Himanshu's arrival. In fact, they looked surprisingly relaxed, as if they had at last found a solution to the problem.

'Have they secretly promised him payment for his kidney? Have they already paid him? He didn't write to me that he was coming to donate it,' he thought.

He said to himself, 'If they have done it, they won't tell me and it'll be humiliating to ask them and be told a lie. It's a matter between them and their sister. It's a matter of their conscience and I've no right to interfere. I've done nothing wrong!'

'He has gone with Charles to see the Qutub Minar. They're expected to return about seven o' clock.'

Vishwanath could not tell his father that he had sent Himanshu away immediately after lunch for sight-seeing because he had come in response not only to his letters but also to the letter written by Subhadra secretly from all of them, and which had influenced him much more than his letters! And that it was the main reason he had sent Charles with him, instead of going himself or asking Srinath. Further, after Himanshu had praised Subhadra for her candor he didn't feel at all confident of handling him if he asked him any questions arising from her letter. Vishwanath, who had taken her aside to find out what she had written, had been shocked by her reply that she had frankly written what was no secret from him or his father and brother: that in her and Jayanti's opinion neither the suffering recipient who paid for an organ without any prejudice to the donor nor the man in straitened circumstances who accepted money for it and thus saved a life was a less good human being on that account than an altruist. Although in answer to his angry questions she had told him that she was not so tactless and crude as to have written that they wished to buy his kidney if he was prepared to sell it, he hadn't felt confident of facing Himanshu. He had recalled his meeting with him several months ago. On his asking her if she had written anything else, she had replied that she had also written in different words what was contained in Papaji's appeal, namely, that for an altruist every consideration other than saving a life was irrelevant. In other words, she had written, Vishwanath was mortified to reflect, that the fact that her husband and his brother were selfish cowards was unimportant! Grasping its implication, Vishwanath didn't know whether to be angrier or ashamed. So, if she was telling the truth, she had related both her own and his father's views and it was impossible to tell which had influenced Himanshu. Finally, he didn't feel sure that she had told him everything. He couldn't have confessed to Himanshu without embarrassment, what might have seemed incredible to him, that until they heard from him no member of the family knew that she had written to him. Above all, he would have liked him to know that far from approving of any secret letter to him both he and his brother wished him to forget about it!

Vishwanath cast a glance at Srinath, who had heard from him what his wife had told him and whose thoughts were similar to his.

'He would have undergone the blood and other tests before coming?' asked Jawaharlal, remembering again that Himanshu had made no commitment in his letter. He had visited Sarika in the hospital in the morning and had been so deeply affected by her emotional condition which bordered on hate that he had begun to waver in his determination neither to buy a kidney nor to accept an altruist's who would almost certainly be poor. In fact, he had been thoroughly confused for a long time. Meanwhile, being as practical as he was a man of principle, the first thing he wanted to be sure of, irrespective of Himanshu's motive for coming, was that his blood group and other things were compatible with Sarika's and his kidney would be acceptable to her. The questions whether he was an altruist or had come expecting to be paid and whether or not to accept his kidney could be dealt with later.

'Yes, he has brought the reports. How could he have come without first finding out whether his kidney would be acceptable to Sarika? Her blood group as well as other necessary information was all given in the appeal. In fact, he told us that he had undergone the tests and brought the reports before also, when you were in the USA.'

Jawaharlal lapsed into his usual meditative silence, making his sons wait patiently, without trying in vain to guess what he was thinking. He emerged from it with a look of extreme dissatisfaction. He had been thinking whether his sons had sent Charles with Himanshu instead of one of them going because they were afraid of being asked by him, if he was an altruist but not naive, whether there was any insurmountable problem about their saving the life of their sister. He thought that it was their duty to talk to him frankly instead of sending Charles and behaving like shameful cowards. It would have been more honorable to frankly confess their fear and offer him money (cowards had no right to accept or even expect altruistic donation!) for his organ. Vaguely hoping that his daughter's life would be saved, all he now wished was that they would not tell him about what sort of an arrangement they had come to with him.

He said to Vishwanath, 'Instead of sending Himanshu, either you or Srinath should have gone with him!'

'Charles will handle him better than we would have done. I had quite a long meeting with him when he came before and he gave no indication of what he thought or wanted. There's nothing new that we could say to each other. He might be more frank and forthcoming with Charles than he would have been with me or Srinath,' Vishwanath replied. He added, 'I have told him that Charles is like a member of the family. We also informed him that you would be back by five o' clock, and he would have understood that we wanted him to talk to you first. He himself had said so when he came before because you had issued the appeal and later you wrote those letters! Still we have asked Charles not only to frankly and truthfully answer all his questions but to discreetly encourage him to ask any and thus fully satisfy himself about us! Besides, we're also meeting the Aligarh lawyer, whom you have given time! His train is about to arrive. I have sent my car to fetch him. Hopefully, our meeting with him will be over before Himanshu and Charles return.

He thought, 'Now only God knows what chance there is of our accepting his kidney though he is still the best possible donor. Because of your warped behavior with him before, your humiliating offer to give him money for nothing. And your foolish appeal and letters to Himanshu, which have influenced him into coming again and of whose intentions we're not sure.' '

Srinath said, 'Himanshu's visits in response to your appeal and letters most probably mean that he's an altruist and his motive is to save a life. In other words, he may be the kind of donor you insist upon. We have asked Charles to find it out for certain.'

Jawaharlal could again only just manage to prevent his astonishment at his sons' bold statements from appearing on his face. He wondered at their motive for such frankness. Was it unbearable tension of which they wanted to be relieved by knowing the real intention of the Bengali boy? If so, what would they do after knowing it?

Jawaharlal was again puzzled to think as to why Himanshu hadn't clearly written in his letter that he was coming to donate his kidney. What exactly did he want?

'Where have you put him up?' he asked

'In the guest room on the second floor, which I got ready for him while we were having lunch,' replied Srinath.

'What are his parents? Has he brothers and sisters?'

'His father was in the trade union movement, but now does nothing. His mother is a housewife. He has two brothers, one of whom is a temporary lecturer in a private college somewhere and the other is still a student.'

Jawaharlal was about to leave to rest for a while and think about his forthcoming meeting with the Aligarh lawyer, whom he wouldn't have given time if he knew that Himanshu was also coming, when Vishwanath stunned him with: 'Papa, one thing you must not do, whether you like it or not. You must not start questioning Himanshu the way you questioned the lawyer about his circumstances for your personal satisfaction, simply because he hasn't written in his reply to your letters that he's coming to donate his kidney. You've no right to do it! Your principles are your affair and nobody else's! Whatever you think of me and Srinath, having come in response to your letters, Himanshu owes you nothing and you've got to behave courteously with him and believe whatever he says! Whether you accept his kidney or not for whatever reasons.'

Srinath added, 'You had no right to behave the way you did with the lawyer! You insulted and humiliated a proud and honest man! We're meeting him again in less than an hour before Himanshu and Charles return from sight-seeing. Unfortunately, we didn't know that Himanshu was also coming or we shouldn't be meeting him today.'

He looked at Vishwanath, who nodded.

Jawaharlal stared speechlessly at his sons, who had always behaved with him with the greatest respect, and though angered, he was too confounded to think of a reply. He realized that he was no longer the same Jawaharlal; his daughter's suffering and his own waverings, the lawyer's proud behavior and his appeal and letters to Himanshu against his own wish and in order to indirectly pressurize his sons instead of frankly talking to them had changed him and he had lost his authority. Silently he retired to his room.

26/2

Charles was thinking of the Aligarh lawyer, whom Jawaharlal had given an appointment in the evening. He wouldn't have agreed to meet him today if he had known that Himanshu was also coming. But since he had given him time he would certainly receive him. In fact, he might already have met him. But he didn't have much hope that the meeting would have been fruitful. If Himanshu hadn't arrived today, something might have come of it, though he couldn't say what.

Looking up at the Qutub Minar, Charles said, 'It's a tremendous structure, isn't it, considering the period when it was built.'

'Yes. And hundreds must have perished to satisfy the builder's ruthless ambition,' Himanshu replied. He had been wondering as to why Vishwanath, or if he was busy, his brother or his wife Subhadra hadn't come with him. Instead they had sent Charles, although they had described him as a member of the family and their confidant. Did it signify something? He remembered his last visit several months ago, his tea and the drive with Vishwanath to the railway station and his dignified behavior and truthful answers to his questions as well as his puzzling reticence about his and his brother's inability to donate their kidneys to their sister. He recalled Subhadra's letter, which contradicted the appeal and Mr. Jawaharlal's letters. He wondered whether Mr. Jawaharlal knew what she had written to him. He couldn't help recalling her candidly expressed view, with which he agreed, that if a man in desperate circumstances wanted to be paid for his organ, he was not a less honorable person than an altruist. However, he would have told her equally frankly, if she had come, that though he agreed with her, yet he hadn't come for money. And even though he might disregard the brothers and donate his kidney, he would still like to know why neither of them was doing it. He felt that he owed it to himself to know the reason. That's why he had not written to her or to Jawaharlal that he was coming to donate his kidney.

He would also have liked to hear from her as to how the brothers could like their father have scruples about paying the donor, as Subhadra had written, if for any reason other than a serious health risk neither of them had so far given his kidney to his sister. Most of these questions had arisen in his mind and made him doubtful after his first reading of her letter. Reflecting on the appeal in the context of Jawaharlal's and his sons' circumstances and Vishwanath's behavior and what he had told him during their first meeting he had wondered at their motives and even at their sanity. The whole thing was so baffling. And if he had at last decided to write to her that he would be coming it was because of the same feeling of compassion to end the poor girl's suffering as had moved him after he read the appeal. It had possessed him more than once after he set out for Delhi for the second time. In fact, he wouldn't have come but for it despite her letter, which had merely excited it by its sincerity and straightforwardness.

26/3

An hour ago, Jawaharlal and his sons had again met the Aligarh lawyer in a different part of the house to prevent any accidental encounter between him and Himanshu. The meeting had upset the father and sons alike. If they had not exchanged their thoughts with one another after his departure, it was because they wished to avoid unnecessary perplexities before their unpredictable meeting with Himanshu in a short while. The lawyer had told them that he had come to atone for his earlier "sinful expectation" of being paid. The expression of his face when he uttered those words had perturbed Jawaharlal. It had revived his doubts, which he had not shared with his sons, that he might have come purposely to spurn their grateful present afterwards! Jawaharlal thought it awful that such a desperately needy man whose wife was gravely ill should donate his kidney and accept nothing in order to avenge his humiliation. Jawaharlal had again offered to help him without accepting his kidney. And he had again refused his offer. The pathetic condition and the obstinately proud behavior of the lawyer was the cause of their malaise.

Charles at last said to Himanshu, 'From your behavior the members of Mr. Jawaharlal's family are inclined to think that most probably you're an altruist and your sole motive is to save the poor girl's life. Yet they may be excused for wondering that you didn't write in your letters to Mr. Jawaharlal and Ms Subhadra that you were coming to donate your kidney.'

'They have guessed rightly that I don't want anything,' replied Himanshu. 'However, I may also be excused for wondering as to what is preventing the brothers from saving the life of their sister, unless as a rare case their kidneys don't suit her. I didn't commit myself because I wanted to know the reason for the brothers' inability. And even though eventually I may disregard them and do the needful, yet I would like to know the reason.'

'The reason is excessive fear of the consequences of losing a vital organ and possibly sustaining a serious injury or even death during the operation, which is not impossible. They're too ashamed to confess it, but it is obvious to every member of the family, including their wives,' replied Charles.

Recovering from his surprise at the bluntness of Charles, whom Vishwanath and his brother had described as like a member of the family and their confidant, Himanshu said, 'I had guessed it as one of the possible reasons during my first meeting with Mr. Vishwanath.'

Charles said, 'Many good people suffer from such fears. I'd like to assure you that despite their physical fear the brothers are gentlemen in the true sense of the word and would never take undue advantage of a donor's unselfishness.'

Himanshu found himself at a loss to know as to what Charles was trying to convey.

Charles said, 'In spite of their fear, the brothers find it painfully hard, in fact they find it humiliating, to lure an impoverished person with the offer of money through an agent. However, as I said, a good man is not necessarily exempt from fear. I know them and can appreciate their painful dilemma. On the other hand, their wives think that it's perfectly honorable to pay a responsible man in distress for his organ. In fact, they are dead against accepting an altruist's kidney because the patient has brothers!'

Himanshu was puzzled. He said,' Frankly, I don't understand it. She wrote to me in the same letter in which she said that a person in serious trouble who wants to sell his kidney doesn't cease to be a gentleman that an altruist should not allow any circumstance to deflect him from his purpose of saving a life.'

'The purpose of her letter to you was to find out whether you're an honest man in trouble who wants to give his kidney for a price, but is shy of admitting it, or an uncompromising altruist. If you'll excuse me, none of us have felt absolutely sure that you're an altruist. Without doubting your integrity, she and her husband as well as her husband's brother and his wife aren't as sure as they'd like to be even now. You didn't exactly disclose your intention during your first meeting with Mr. Vishwanath, though you impressed him as a gentleman and most probably an altruist. Nor did you write in your replies to her and Mr. Jawaharlal's letters your reason for coming.'

Before Himanshu could speak, Charles said, 'I would like to tell you something which I consider important for you to know before you decide one way or another. It happened before they published the appeal.'

'It's a moving story,' said Himanshu after Charles had finished. 'Ms Subhadra and her husband are right in thinking that Mr. Jawaharlal should have been satisfied with the lawyer's assurance that his motive was altruistic and paid him generously afterwards, instead of pestering him with his conscience and causing needless suffering to his daughter. And if I had been the lawyer, I would also have refused Mr. Jawaharlal's charity!'

Looking with admiration at Himanshu for possessing such good sense despite being an altruist, Charles went on, 'I would like to tell you that after meeting you today Mr. Jawaharlal's sons have developed serious misgivings. They have begun to think it dreadful to accept a young idealist's kidney for nothing while they were keeping theirs from fear. In fact, they're not interested in your kidney, unless you happen to be needy and will accept their grateful present for your donation. That's why they have sent me. They have asked me to talk to you frankly and find out the truth. They felt too embarrassed to do so themselves.'

'Whatever their view, I can't even for a moment think of accepting money,' replied Himanshu. 'And if they had such invincible scruples about accepting the organ of a man who would not accept what they choose to call their grateful present, they shouldn't have issued the appeal for altruistic donation, nor written me those letters. Instead, they should have tried to find another man like the lawyer and told him how to behave and talk to Mr. Jawaharlal.'

Charles thought it unnecessary to tell him that the brothers and their wives were against issuing the appeal and writing those letters to him.

He said, 'You have a point in that they should have considered all this before issuing the appeal and afterwards writing to you and putting you to so much trouble. But it's not always possible to foresee the consequences of one's actions taken under such great stress.'

He added, 'Their wives would once more try to persuade their father-in-law, who has been much weakened by his daughter's suffering. They also hope to find an acceptable donor.'

'I wish all success to Ms Subhadra and her sister-in-law!'

Charles said, 'If Mr. Jawaharlal remains unbending, or they fail to find a suitable donor soon, neither brother would hesitate to part with his kidney. However strong their fear, they would not let their sister die. I have told you all this with their authority!'

Himanshu said, 'Thank God it's only I! The father and sons between them might have put many more persons to trouble!' He added with a smile, 'I was joking! Tell them from me that I respect them as true gentlemen.'

26/4

After hearing from Charles his talk with Himanshu, Srinath went to his father and told him that he had decided to donate his kidney.

He added, 'Himanshu Mukherjee is an uncompromising altruist and neither I nor Vishwanath can accept his offer. He'll return to Agra by the Taj Express tomorrow morning.'

Jawaharlal became speechless with astonishment and joy.

Srinath said, 'Thanking him for his great humanity and apologizing to him for the trouble we put him to, I have told him that his kidney is no longer needed. I have decided to donate mine.'

'Have you talked to your wife?'

'She's agreeable.'

When Vishwanath came to know of his brother's decision, with his wife's surprisingly prompt approval he went to his father and told him that he was also prepared to make the donation. After examining the brothers, the doctor said that they were both perfectly fit as donors, though Vishwanath's overall condition was better.

Charles surprised a still incredulous Jawaharlal that instead of the brothers it should be the Aligarh lawyer. At first Jawaharlal refused point blank. He insisted on it being a brother's duty to save the life of his sister. And he confessed to Charles what he had already guessed, that he was against issuing the appeal and later writing to Himanshu but had been compelled to do so because of Sarika's suffering and his fear that his sons' and their wives' attitude might not change.

Charles had never expected an intensely private and self-sufficient man like him to express himself so frankly. He resisted the temptation to ask him whether instead of accepting the kidney of an honest man in distress and paying him he would have let his daughter die if his sons were unable to overcome their fear or were selfish and callous; or whether in desperation he'd have accepted an altruist's kidney as a last resort despite having two sons and exposed him to a possible post-donation trauma caused by the realization afterwards that he had been swindled by charlatans. Instead, he continued to urge him to accept the lawyer's kidney. He reminded him of his refusal to accept his charity in spite of his desperate circumstances. He said that it was preposterous to reject such a man's offer on ethical grounds.

In the end, his happiness at finding that neither his sons were shameful cowards nor his daughters-in-law selfish and callous, as he had often thought with secret anguish, induced him to accept the lawyer's kidney. And he confessed as much to Charles, who was shocked to hear that such a thing should have mattered more to this man of principle than helping a man whose wife was gravely ill.

Before expressing his consent, he said to Charles, 'But you must first make absolutely sure that he would accept the money we have decided to present to a voluntary donor.'

The next moment, he again astonished Charles with the confession that during his second meeting with the lawyer, when Himanshu had already arrived, he would have accepted his kidney and rewarded him handsomely afterwards rather than accepting the latter's donation. And if he hadn't done so it was because of his fear that the lawyer might not accept his present in order to avenge his humiliation.

'Why didn't you frankly tell him that you'd accept his kidney only if he would accept your money?' thought Charles with disgust.

Charles offered to go to Aligarh to talk to the lawyer, if the judge sahib was now reluctant to do so. The judge was as willing as ever to approach him again.

The next day Charles and Subhadra were sitting in his office when she telephoned Jayanti to ask her to find out from her uncle whether he had talked to the lawyer and what was the result. The next moment, she turned pale. The judge had just told Jayanti that he had learnt from one of the lawyer's friends that his wife had died and he had committed suicide.

'Is everything all right?' asked Charles, struck by her suddenly grave expression.

'His wife has died and he has committed suicide.'

The day after Vishwanath's kidney was grafted into his sister, Subhadra said to Charles, 'I'm glad that he has done it at last and Sarika's suffering has ended. Thousands die for want of a kidney in spite of having near relatives, who suffer from unconquerable fear and console themselves with the thought that it's God's will. Think of the lifelong shame and grief of a man who from fear has allowed a beloved brother or sister or wife to die. Think of the lawyer. Both he and his wife might be alive today.'

Chapter 27

27/1

'Let's begin. Harimohini is not joining us. She's going out with some friends,' said Vishnu. He asked Jaiprakash. 'How's your father now?'

They were three, including Charles, who had last evening told Jaiprakash that the general guess was, and he also thought so, that Chandrmukhi was with Somdutt's child when she killed herself. They had been waiting for Chandrmukhi's sister Harimohini to join them at breakfast. She had excused herself at the last moment.

Harimohini was aware of every fact and circumstance about her sister's suicide. She had directly learnt it from her only a few days before she killed herself. Her feelings towards Jaiprakash were ambivalent. Without disbelieving Chandrmukhi that he had accidentally become her lover, she found it hard to forgive him for continuing his perfidy against his benefactor, even if, as she thought, Chandrmukhi had become infatuated with him, after wife and husband had become reconciled. She recalled with loathing his request to her to persuade Chandrmukhi to end her friendship with Somdutt! She could think of no other reason for the request than his jealousy of Somdutt! She found it hard to believe that he had appealed to her out of a sincere wish for the reconciliation of husband and wife and hopefully for the end of his affair with her, as Chandrmukhi had told her.

'His heart trouble is not serious, but his general health is poor. And my sisters are unemployed and still unmarried. They're well qualified and I am trying to get them appointed as teachers in some good institution,' replied Jaiprakash, wondering whether these circumstances convincingly accounted for his sudden loss of interest in returning to Delhi. He thought, 'He doesn't seem to be interested in talking to me at all about his wife, and only God knows if he suspects me also of having been her lover. However, he might still have suspected me even if it was not a fact!'

Jaiprakash had had great difficulty getting over the thought, which had kept him awake practically all last night, that before committing suicide Chandrmukhi might have confessed to him that he had been her lover and she was carrying his child and not his antagonist's. At last he had been able to dispel it. It couldn't have failed to occur to her that it would cause her husband far greater shock and anguish than if Somdutt had been her lover that the man he trusted had so vilely deceived him and his own wife had taken advantage of his trust in his loyalty. He also found it hard to believe that to protect him she would have falsely ascribed her pregnancy to Somdutt. She had no alternative but to assert that she was carrying her husband's child.

He recalled how yesterday Somdutt had told him to take the greatest care of his health and how Vishnu had thanked him for his kindness! It seemed to explain Vishnu's grief: Her suicide had made him indifferent to whether she was innocent or guilty and who had been her lover, and made him realize that it was his jealousy which had murdered her.

Recalling his conversation with Charles yesterday and his guess that Somdutt was her lover he again found himself wondering as to why, if the child's legitimacy was so deeply suspect in Vishnu's eyes for any reason, a sensible woman like her had with his tacit or explicit consent or even without his knowledge, not opted for abortion, a commonsense way out of the trouble. It would have relieved her husband of the torturing doubt whether it was his child or his enemy's or his servant's. The need to preserve their good name and the memory of his oppression of her would have eventually enabled him to get over the past. On the other hand, according to the testimony of so many of their friends, as reported in the press, both wife and husband had openly rejoiced.

Another troubling question was why she had kept her pregnancy from him. Before he fell asleep towards morning, however, it had occurred to him that she might have come to his room on that night to inform him of this fact. Soon he had felt sure. He regretted that he had been harsh with her. But he consoled himself with the thought that she would have understood its reason: Vishnu might suddenly wake up and follow her into his room.

'My advice to you, sir, is not to take it too hard. It's fate,' said Charles to Vishnu, who had lapsed into gloomy silence.

After a while, Vishnu said to Jaiprakash, 'I have decided to convert my property into a trust.'

Jaiprakash expressed his gladness at his decision. He had already learnt it last evening from Charles, who was to be one of the trustees. That Vishnu had not selected him, whom he used to respect and trust for his caliber, integrity and loyalty, as a trustee was what had provoked the suspicion that she might have confessed to him that he had been her lover.

'All this is mere speculation,' he thought, as an hour later he entered Dr Awasthi's home.

27/2

'Some days before Chandrmukhi committed suicide I told her that your father's illness was not serious, yet you might not return because you wanted to settle your sisters and complete your law course and Ph.D., which had been interrupted by your coming to Delhi. That's what you had told me before you left.'

Mrs. Awasthi was relating to Jaiprakash Chandrmukhi's last visit to her house before her death.

Dr Awasthi said, 'She had a headache and had dropped in to get her blood pressure checked. She was glad that the Bharatiya Janata Party had badly lost in the Assembly Elections in the states where its governments had been dismissed following the demolition of the Babri Mosque. I told her that the general impression was that during the movement people were more interested in the mosque's demolition to avenge their humiliation by the Muslim aliens than in the construction of one more temple, and with the disappearance of the eyesore it was the end of the affair. She seemed to agree with me but said that she was proud of being a Hindu and considered it a shameful act. We talked about various things. I told her how grateful you were to both her and her husband for their kindness and generosity to you. I told her that I had advised your father to persuade you to return to Delhi as soon as he was well enough, instead of wasting time in acquiring those degrees. I know of many law graduates and Ph.D.s who are unable to get the job of a lower division clerk.'

'What did she say?' asked Jaiprakash, concealing his intense curiosity to know her answer. If she had changed her mind and no longer had any objection to his coming back, though, of course, he wouldn't have returned, it would further confirm that she had not confessed to her husband that he had been her lover.

'She said that Vishnu liked you very much and wished you to return as soon as possible and work here as before. Their business had begun to suffer after your departure. Your successor Charles was a changed man and no longer liked the same work that he used to do as your predecessor. He was thinking of joining a solicitors' firm as soon as Vishnu found someone to replace him, in case you were unable to return.'

'She didn't say that she also wanted me to return,' he thought. It was true to his wish when he left her that she should forget about him and begin her life anew, as he himself had decided to do. Two years did not constitute a whole life.

'Why did she commit suicide?' he found himself thinking again. The fact that both she and her husband had openly rejoiced had rendered every possible reason for her doing so unconvincing in the end. Unless he came upon some fool-proof evidence. But what could it be? He had left behind nothing that could incriminate her. They had never written a word to each other.

Was it Somdutt? Did he suspect him of being her lover and from jealousy conveyed his "knowledge" to Vishnu by an anonymous letter, with which Vishnu confronted her after they returned home and which so surprised and disconcerted her that unable to deny it she broke down? And it ended in her suicide. However, despite blaming Somdutt for being no less responsible than her for the beginning of the trouble between her and her husband, he could not persuade himself that he could be guilty of such wickedness. It must be something else.

Mrs. Awasthi said, 'I mentioned your family's straitened circumstances, which were then uppermost in my mind. I told her that's why you had given up your studies and come to Delhi. I said that for the time being you had no prospects in Patna except some ill-paid job in a charitable institution run by some Hindu organization. She was surprised. She said that you had never even indirectly mentioned your family's problems. In view of your intellectual standard and self-assured manner both she and her husband thought that your father's family would be well off.'

Jaiprakash asked, 'Was she surprised to hear the words "Hindu organization"? She was an extremist and like Somdutt prejudiced against Hindu nationalism. It was unfortunate because though strong-minded she had a generous nature. It ended up with her husband becoming or talking like a Hindu fundamentalist as a reaction from his insane jealousy of Somdutt, whom she admired for his convictions. It was an unnecessary tragedy.'

Mrs. Awasthi replied, 'She asked whether your father was connected with some Hindu organization. And she was visibly startled when I told her that you had been a BJP activist and but for your family's hardship, you would never have left Patna.'

Dr. Awasthi said, 'She committed a mistake by disclosing to Chandrmukhi your family's straitened circumstances. I had kept it from them. You'll remember that while introducing you I had told them that you were intellectually ambitious and wanted to move out of a backward State. They're very good people yet I feared that their attitude to you would be influenced by the knowledge of your family's indigence. You also didn't wish it to be known. Chandrmukhi and she were talking within my earshot, but I was examining an elderly family friend who had just then dropped in. The words "Hindu organization" also surprised her. I had never mentioned to her or her husband your BJP connection, thinking it unnecessary. I had left it to you to decide what they should know about your political background. But she had already told

Chandrmukhi all that in a few minutes while I was examining my patient.'

'I did it inadvertently and realized my mistake when I saw her reaction,' Mrs. Awasthi said.

'What was her reaction?'

'She said that everyone thought you were a progressive, who naturally detested the communalist Bharatiya Janata Party. For a few minutes she appeared quite upset.'

'However, she soon recovered,' said the doctor. 'I told her that in spite of having been a BJP activist you were not narrow-minded. I assured her that you were basically honest and if you did not frankly express your thoughts on every subject she discussed with you during your first meeting it must have been from discretion and out of personal regard for her and not from any intent to deceive. You urgently needed a job. I told her that what had influenced you most was the impression she had made on you at your very first meeting with her. The first thing you said to me after coming from her, I told her, was that she seemed a wonderfully nice person for whom it would be a pleasure to work. I emphasized that you said that it was the main thing. It was even more important than the urgency to get a job because you were highly sensitive. She was visibly impressed when I told her that I didn't tell her or her husband about your family's circumstances because you didn't want her or anybody to think that you needed a job that badly; you were proud and hated to be regarded as a suppliant.'

'I am sorry that she came to know about my political background. It must have surprised her. At our very first meeting, I was lucky to see both sides of her nature. While waiting in her study and hearing her telephonic conversation with somebody I fortuitously witnessed her aggressive assertion of her views on some political issues. Afterwards, when she interviewed me I was impressed by her affability. I told you about it the first thing after coming from her. As I urgently needed an income to support my family, I decided to hold back my views on those issues. I decided to consider the difference between what I thought and what I told her irrelevant to the job I would be doing. I said to myself that I was not joining a political party whose ideology was different from mine. Later, it became more and more evident that although she was satisfied with my work and personally liked me, she would be surprised and hurt, if she came to know that I had not been completely frank with her about my background. I sometimes felt uncomfortable but consoled myself that as everybody was happy with the things as they were, it would be unwise to do anything that would upset them.'

While they talked Jaiprakash had continued to wonder that neither the doctor nor his wife had expressed their own conjectures about the probable cause of her suicide, which they should have done the first thing. They weren't supposed to be so correct with him. Did they by any chance suspect him? At last, he couldn't help saying: 'After all that I have heard since I came I have not been able to think of a single credible reason for her suicide. According to their friends, she and her husband were seen together at India International Centre only a few hours before her death and both were jolly as usual. You'll also have heard something about the probable cause of the tragedy. What's your guess?'

Anxiously, he waited to hear their answer.

Mrs. Awasthi said, 'Probably, Vishnu suspected Somdutt to be her lover and the father of the child she was carrying. His display of joy may have been for the sake of the world. Although we don't know much about their mutual relations, you must know more, we think the suspicion was baseless, which hurt her deeply and ultimately drove her to kill herself.'

The doctor nodded. 'It's the most probable explanation.' He added, 'Now she's dead and any speculation whether she was guilty or innocent will be unfair to her as well as a waste of time.'

Jaiprakash said, 'His jealousy of Somdutt had its beginning in his dislike of him for being a parasite who was notorious for drinking and dining at other's tables and instead of behaving urbanely with his host, unnecessarily getting into arguments with him. He also borrowed books from her which he never returned. It gradually began to anger Vishnu. Also, her honest but indiscreet endorsement of his views against her husband's before others unfortunately resulted in his becoming jealous of him and fighting with her. Being a strong-minded woman, she felt insulted and refused to yield. This was the main reason of their quarrels and the tragedy, though I believe she remained pure and innocent of any wrong-doing!'

Neither the doctor nor his wife appeared interested in this detailed explanation designed to prove not only Chandrmukhi and Vishnu but also himself blameless. It made him uncomfortably self-conscious. Did they suspect him? In a few minutes he left.

27/3

On his way back, Jaiprakash felt sad. Knowing her as he did, he thought it unlikely that her unexpectedly coming to know his political background and the thought that he had not been completely frank with her could be even a minor contributory factor in her suicide. Yet remembering their intimacy he could not but feel that it would have aggravated her grief from other causes. Did she think during her last moments that such a man had been her lover and by making her pregnant the cause of her death? He tried to assure himself that it couldn't have failed to occur to her that they had become lovers by sheer accident. She enjoyed good things of life and neither of them had ever doubted that her position in society of which her family life was an essential part transcended the affair and that he could never replace Vishnu in her heart. It was what had enabled them to enjoy the affair with only occasional qualms. And she was too sensible a person not to have appreciated the fact that it was his family's poverty that had compelled him to talk the way he did when he first met her and didn't know the kind of person she was. And once he had become committed he could not tell her his political background without needlessly upsetting her. Her final opinion of him would also have been influenced by the realization that not only before he unexpectedly became her lover but afterwards also he wished her family life to be happy and expected nothing so much of her and her husband as their good will.

Yet it was impossible for him to get rid of the saddening thought that during her last moments when the smallest thing would have afflicted her deeply, her belief in him may have been shaken by an extraneous circumstance. How much less unhappy she would have been, if her faith in his honesty with her had remained unimpaired till the end.

27/4

When Chandrmukhi returned from Dr Awasthi's home she was inconsolably upset. She recalled her first meeting with Jaiprakash when she was talking on the phone to Bhula Bhai Saraf, one of her business partners and a leader of the Vishwa Hindu Parishad. How promptly he had decided to dissemble! What astounded her was the absence of any sign that he had ever felt remorse. And the perfection with which he had sustained the character for so long! For her peace of mind, she tried to find an alibi for his conduct: his family's poverty had forced him to behave the way he did, and as a lover his conduct had been unusually considerate of her family happiness to the extent of sometimes making her wonder. He had never tried to take any worldly advantage of her passion for him. But she found it hard to excuse him for not being perfectly honest with her, and she cried: She loved him.

Chapter 28

28/1

It was more than two months since Govind had proposed to Shanti. One of the reasons why she had not been able to make up her mind was that he had not repeated the proposal, although during this period he had passed several nights with her. He ought to have done so at least once, she thought. During his last visit she had been particularly anxious for him to remind her in order to enable her to make up her mind. In fact, as he had only expressed his wish instead of making a firm offer, she wouldn't have minded if he had been forced to withdraw for some reason that he could not disclose. It would have clarified the situation.

One day, as she was waiting for him, she decided to question him about his relations with his wife. It had occurred to her while trying to figure out his silence that if his relations with her were really so disappointing that he wanted to leave her, how come that she hadn't stopped visiting him. During the last three-four months she had come to Bhopal thrice and they had visited their friends together and appeared to be quite happy. He had also paid her a week-long visit.

As he sat drinking his customary cup of coffee, she said, 'I have been wondering whether your relations with your wife are really so bad that reconciliation is not possible. Maybe, your decision to leave her is due to some misunderstanding, which may eventually be cleared up. I like you and am not against marriage in principle, but I am completely satisfied with our present relations.'

'I won't say that our relations are unpleasant, but they're unsatisfactory from my point of view,' he replied, in spite of himself, lest she should think it scandalously irresponsible of him to have made such a serious proposal lightly.

Although he intensely enjoyed the affair, which had progressed from being largely physical to the point where without becoming less enjoyable physical pleasure becomes secondary , he had gradually begun to feel that scarcity or even absence of sex between him and Harimohini would be no hardship. Living with her was joy enough.

Sometime after proposing to Shanti he had begun to feel doubtful of the desirability of marrying her even if Harimohini left him on coming to know of his unfaithfulness or for any other reason. It would arouse all sorts of speculation. Secondly, Shanti would never trust a husband who had been unfaithful to his first wife. Yet another reason was the certain loss of prestige for both him and Harimohini, who might be suspected of some grave blemish known only to him, perhaps even unfaithfulness, by their friends who at present admired her for being a devoted wife. He found this possibility much more painful than the loss of prestige for himself. The loss to Shanti would be the heaviest; she would be accused of wickedness for having broken up a happy marriage. It would give a false start to their marriage.

While considering the undesirability of marrying Shanti, he had begun to find reasons that despite being delightful as long as it lasted and he considered how to end it without abruptly letting her down, it was not justifiable for a man who had a devoted wife! It had occurred to him that there were husbands who never regretted living with their wives even if they were chronically ill. Many vigorous husbands not only patiently bore sex deprivation and remained faithful throughout life but lovingly did all they could to lessen their wives' suffering. They remained virtually unmarried. There were husbands who took their wives whenever they desired without bothering whether they were in the mood for it and would enjoy it or not, and the wives, though irked for a few minutes, didn't hold it against them for the sake of a happy family life. And how many wives bluntly refused if they didn't wish it without their husbands minding it, except for a few hours or even a few minutes. Conjugal happiness ultimately consisted in willingness on the part of both partners to forgo their rights and overlook their partner's obligations.

As for Harimohini, she never refused. Her happiness consisted in his happiness. Furthermore, because of her voluntary advances lately for whatever reason, the lack of sex had ceased to be a hardship. It was always open to him to avail himself of her eager wish to give him joy, which was a pleasure in itself for her. He had begun to think it arbitrary and inconsiderate of him to wish her also to enjoy as uninhibitedly as he did.

In short, he had begun to hope that Shanti had not considered his proposal seriously because of its indefiniteness and the affair would soon come to an end.

Before he could add that he was also satisfied with their present relations, Shanti asked, 'Are your relations with her unsatisfactory from her point of view also?'

'She appears perfectly satisfied and wishes our marriage to continue! I have tried my utmost to make our relations at least tolerable, and to be fair to her she has also tried her best to make me happy! But in vain. It's sheer bad luck!'

'You told me something else before,' said she with an ironic smile.

'Marriage is a serious matter and the happiest of couples have ups and downs which it is not proper to lightly discuss with the best of friends. One doesn't decide to break without ample justification. I tried my best for adjustment and proposed to you only after realizing that it was not possible. Before it, I thought it only right to profess that we were happily married.'

'But, according to your friends, who have observed your relations, you're an exceedingly happy couple.'

That's very true!' he said to himself. He said to her, 'I have to keep up appearances to prevent gossip, and she by her behavior, which seems unaffected and natural, has strengthened the impression of our being happily married.'

'Her behavior seems unaffected and natural to others. How does it appear to you?'

'Frankly, it appears unaffected and natural to me also! As I told you, she wishes our marriage to continue.'

He had vaguely anticipated some such questions from her and tried to think up plausible answers, but had failed because he was loath to denigrate Harimohini. He felt satisfied with his answers, although he realized that they could not satisfy Shanti, or for that matter any third person.

'You mean she wishes the marriage to continue because she's contented and happy, but doesn't care for your happiness. She's selfish.'

He restrained himself from saying that she was utterly unselfish and did everything possible for her to make him happy, lest Shanti should blame him for their unsatisfactory relations and consider him a bad husband whose proposal didn't deserve to be considered. Although he no longer wanted her to consider his offer, he wished her to think that he would have made her a delightful husband!

He tried to end the talk with, 'Maybe our unsatisfactory relations are due to my own shortcomings!'

Dissatisfied with his answers, she said, 'Has she come to know about our affair and decided to divorce you? It seems to me you're making a virtue of necessity.'

He replied, 'I am sure she's as yet unsuspicious, though some of the people she meets may be aware of it. Had she heard about it, she would have mentioned it to me.

'You are sure?'

'I think so.'

'And you respect her, in spite of your dissatisfaction with her?'

'Yes. I respect her in spite of that!'

Although she was not convinced by his vague and evasive answers, she felt increased respect for him: He was dissatisfied with his wife to the extent of thinking of leaving her, yet he was reluctant to speak ill of her in order to please her. It showed his character. He also did not seem as unhappy with his wife as she had thought, which she considered an essential condition for accepting his proposal. She felt relieved of the burden of deciding what to do. Perhaps, he had proposed in a weak moment and later changed his mind or become doubtful. His respect for his wife as a person also constituted a risk. It was not prudent to marry such a man, who might later regret the woman he had left. Even the most passionate lovers didn't have more than a fifty-fifty chance of being happy as husband and wife. As a matter of fact, love marriages were notorious for breaking up for insufficient reasons while arranged marriages went on with all their ups and downs. She was happy enough with her present relations with him and there was no need to accept or turn down his proposal. It was best to let the matter remain vague. Govind was even happier as he took her in his arms.

28/2

A month later, Harimohini came on indefinite leave and stayed six months, which completely changed their relationship for a reason that had seemed to him extremely improbable. In fact, what happened was the opposite of what he had feared when she telephoned him one morning to inform him that she was leaving for the airport in a few minutes and would be staying for a longer period than she used to.

'You need not come to receive me. I'll take a taxi and reach home in half an hour,' she said, as usual thoughtful of his convenience.

There was no question of his not going to the airport to receive her. The first thing he did was to inform Shanti that in a few hours his wife was coming by flight.

He for the first time felt seriously disturbed to think that if she carried out her intention, which had at last begun to seem certain, of coming with bag and baggage, she would sooner rather than later return to Delhi never to come back! This likelihood had worried him off and on and he had once talked to her about it when she told him of her decision to live with him permanently. It had been obscured by what now seemed the much less serious problem, or no problem, of the end of his affair with Shanti. It was how long he could shield a refined and sensitive woman like her from the untold human suffering and the repellent environment in which he worked. As so far her visits had been short and infrequent, he used to take her to his friends, who were always glad to entertain her. Having been a witness to her lifestyle at her sister Chandrmukhi's home where she used to come to stay with him during his visits to Delhi, he had been skeptical of her ability to endure the physical and moral conditions to which he had become inured over the years. He again feared that she would be horrified at the sight of human suffering and degradation and her wish to help him with his work would eventually vanish and she would leave him, however remorseful she might feel afterwards. This possibility distressed him. He couldn't bear the thought of life without her.

As it happened, during the following week he was unavoidably busy and could not spare a single day for lunches, dinners and picnics with their friends. However, realizing that it was impossible to shield her for ever from the reality of his life, he at last decided to expose her to it today itself. That day he was to visit some of the most polluted areas inhabited by the poorest of the poor, yet where most of the gas victims, or non-victims whose near and dear ones had perished in the gas disaster, had stoically recovered from the horror of the black December 2. In their struggle for survival they couldn't afford to brood over their losses and sufferings. How many men and women he knew who had immediately after cremating or burying a loved one gone to work lest their children should sleep hungry at night.

Two hours later, he was on his way to the airport in a ramshackle autorickshaw, which behaved like a jaded and recalcitrant horse and stopped after every half kilometer, and which its driver, a former tongawallah was forced to restart angrily. He lavished on the vehicle the picturesque oaths with which he used to paternally reprimand his horse before the autorickshaws ousted the tongas, or horse carts. Looking at the emaciated body of the driver as well as to calm his impatience at the slowness of the progress, Govind asked him if he was a gas victim. The driver replied that it was indeed so, that his wife and father had actually died from the effect of the jahrili gas, and that even after so many years he had received neither any treatment worth the name nor a paisa as compensation despite having filled in the required forms. Govind began to curse the government and sympathize with him. It was not necessary to believe him because he was frailer than many gas victims. Govind had long ago discovered that many a poor non-gas-victim of Bhopal, accustomed over generations to chronic poverty, malnutrition, disease and exploitation, had added one more calamity, a dramatic one, to his misfortune, by declaring himself a victim. To allay his passenger's impatience at the vehicle's slow progress, the driver recited in chaste Urdu the glorious days of the Nawabi rule. More in verse than in prose! Govind had heard that soon after the end of the Nawabi rule many versifiers and even some genuine poets had been forced by the loss of Nawabi patronage and lack of modern education, especially ignorance of English, to work as barbers, tongawallahs, tailors, cooks, waiters, peons, etc without any sense of inferiority due to their profession. A poet, even if he was a tongawallah, barber or cook, did not for a moment doubt his superiority to a person with lots of money but devoid of aesthetic sensibility, and without breach of politeness was always prepared to put him in his place by reciting a double entendre in verse! However, such was the aristocratic culture of Bhopal that even the proudest noble stood up to welcome a poet irrespective of his profession. The English educated, on the other hand, neglected their cultural heritage and prided themselves on their knowledge of the foreign manners and customs and were more eager to go to Europe and America than to Mecca.

'When the Nawab sahib failed to persuade the Laat sahib (Lord Mountbatten) to grant azadi to Bhopal for which its residents were prepared to shed the last drop of their blood, but which martyrdom was denied them by cruel fate,' said the driver in verse between spells of coughing up phlegm of a dubious color and cursing the vehicle, 'the contents of the royal treasury and the royal palace in the form of gold, diamonds, rubies and other precious stones worth thousands of crores of rupees were buried overnight in the Bhopal lake, which, as huzoor knows, is the world's greatest lake. On that day ended the dream of the Nawab sahib, who had drawn up plans to develop Bhopal into the most glorious city in the world and gift one thousand rupees to every citizen irrespective of his caste or religion after the departure of the Angrej.'

Concluding his narration, he stopped his vehicle a mile from the airport and said apologetically in prose, 'Huzoor, it cannot go any further; it hasn't a drop of petrol left! When I went to sleep last night, the tank was full. Some opium addict stole the petrol during the hours of darkness and by now he would have sold it to buy the stuff! A brilliant Urdu poet of Bhopal, whom the Nawab sahib graciously patronized, has described such addicts in exquisite verse. If the huzoor will kindly give me only a few minutes, I'll recite it!'

Repressing his shock and rage at being stranded so far away from the airport and even more at the weird proposal to recite an opium addict's verse, Govind paid the driver in consideration of his poverty and after waiting for a few minutes in the faint hope of getting a lift in the passing vehicle of some friend or acquaintance decided to walk. All of a sudden, the driver, exhausted from pushing and cursing the vehicle, began to cough violently, which in a few seconds turned into choking, forcing Govind to stop and look at him. The coughing and choking continued and before Govind, who was already late, could decide to leave with the hope that some Good Samaritan would help him, he brought up a huge amount of bright red phlegm. On closer examination, it turned out to be blood. However, though shocked at this symptom of approaching death in a person as emaciated as he was, Govind thought he couldn't stop any longer. He advised the driver to sit in his vehicle and wait for help. The driver thanked him and said, 'Huzoor, it's because of the jahrili gas and the jahrila paani I'm forced to drink like thousands of others. That I'm still alive is due to the all merciful Allah.'

'Where do you live?' Govind couldn't help asking.

The locality the driver named, Quazi Camp, was near the Union Carbide plant around which tens of thousands of metric tons of toxic waste and chemicals had been buried over decades and had polluted the soil and the underground water over a large area, guaranteeing fatal poisoning of those living there as well as the generations yet unborn.

'So he was not lying and is really a gas victim,' thought Govind. He felt ashamed of his thoughts and decided to wait some minutes in the hope that the driver or fare of some passing vehicle would be kind enough to take the man to hospital. Luckily, in a few minutes the driver of a passing taxi he stopped proved as helpful as he had hoped.

28/3

On his way home with Harimohini in a taxi he saw the autorickshaw standing by the roadside. Maybe, the driver was dead. He began to think of him: bearing his wretched existence with the tales of glory of the Nawabi rule and poetry and calmly awaiting death.

To ward off his intrusive image, Govind began to ask her about her sister and whether she had lately attended her evening parties and what she and her friends had chiefly discussed. She replied that the demolition of the Babri Mosque had gradually become stale and was discussed and deplored only if any Muslim friends like Syed were present. Nor did any Hindu seem to feel really guilty except if he wished to show off Hindus' moral superiority. She had noted another fact. The Hindu secularists, though strongly condemning the demolition, didn't seem to relish the Muslims having the best of both worlds by talking like secularists and at the same time insisting on legally enjoying their decadent and disgusting private and personal morality. Govind, who like any Hindu was also aware of this fact, couldn't help thinking that even progressive and secular Hindus like Chandrmukhi and Somdutt thought of ultra-conservatism of Muslims without any hope or wish for their reformation because of their obduracy. Uniform Civil Code was an old hat. The subject most talked about at the evening parties was the increasing corruption in the country in every sphere, especially in the judiciary, which was a new feature of our democracy. What was described as the weakest feature of our Constitution was the virtual impotence of the law to punish even the transparently corrupt judges who were shielded by the laws of impeachment and contempt. Although the number of corrupt judges was as yet very small, but everybody agreed that it was destined to increase as a result of the judges now behaving like politicians and in appointing their friends to the higher judiciary. And of course the increasing number of people suffering from discrimination and exploitation, though it had also gradually become less interesting because the victims themselves regarded it as natural and had adjusted themselves to it. Govind also felt no interest in the mosque's demolition or the Hindu-Muslim antagonism. The latter he regarded as too deep rooted and not worth bothering about. His experience as a social activist had gradually convinced him that as human beings Hindus and Muslims were not at all different. He had even begun to think Indian Muslims' attachment to Pakistan or Muslim ummah as only human! As regards the corruption in the judiciary, he regarded it as insignificant. However, all these facts he regarded as trivial compared to the number of people living at the starvation level and the misery of the gas victims.

Presently he stopped talking to look at the picture, which all of a sudden had arisen before his mind's eye, of the driver lying dead covered with a cloth, his orphaned children and relatives crying and their neighbors condoling with them. The scene had a fascinating quality for him. It was a long time since, instead of avoiding scenes of suffering and death, as he used to do in the beginning, he seldom missed them. His compassion and the sorrow he felt at the sight of them had become an addiction. He laid aside whatever he was doing and rushed to the place where the death of a victim he knew had taken place or he was in its throes, as soon as he heard about it, and remained there till the end. And he was sadly disappointed if he reached the place too late.

'What are you thinking?' she asked.

He was no longer listening. More neighbors of the driver, most of them gas victims, had gathered before his house. He was listening to their conversation which he knew by heart, having gone to innumerable houses where a person had died or was about to die. How many people he knew whom he had talked to or heard joyfully humming a popular film tune in the evening had died in sleep when he visited the slums the next day. He had heard from the doctors who had treated the gas victims that the more badly exposed among them with severely damaged lungs, who were daily wage earners and manual workers and forced to continue to work to the limits of exhaustion despite knowing that they might collapse and die any time, did collapse and die in a few minutes. And how many of the mentally damaged continued to work, even if they didn't have to, awaiting sweet death.

'God was merciful to him and he did not know that he had so little time left; he was cheerful when he went to bed last night,' the neighbors said about the dead.

She stopped; he was thinking of something serious and she shouldn't disturb him.

He was thinking of those people who wished to die because they knew they were not only suffering themselves without hope but also adding to the suffering of their wives or husbands or sons and daughters. And of those who had committed suicide, relieving themselves and their relatives, and were quietly buried or cremated.

They arrived. Instead of taking her in his arms and giving her a ritual kiss, as he used to do on her arrival from Delhi as soon as they entered the house and she had closed the door, he went to his room, leaving her wondering at his unusual behavior.

The image of the dead driver had possessed him. He lay down on his bed and gave himself up to it. He was conscious that soon he would cease to think of him as he had ceased to think of hundreds of others and become absorbed in a new case. He began to think of those surviving gas victims he personally knew who had become reconciled to their personal tragedies and begun to celebrate the Eid and Diwali and other festive occasions with old enthusiasm while awaiting death. He longed to meet them and talk about good old times. It was profoundly soothing. Man had infinite capacity for suffering and could surmount any calamity.

Having put the house in order to her satisfaction, her face shining with perspiration, she entered his room and gave him a joyous smile. If any visitor had seen her at that moment, he would have ascribed her happiness to a different cause.

She went into the bathroom, where she passed nearly half an hour. She couldn't help thinking that today he hadn't as usual welcomed her with a kiss. Of late she had begun to worry that he rarely made love; she knew that now when he saw that she wished him to do it he thought that she didn't enjoy it and only wished it for his sake; it made him look away or give her a perfunctory kiss before going to his room. This misunderstanding distressed her, because she enjoyed love in her own way as he did in his.

After lunch he informed her how busy he was during the whole of the following week. He told her either to stay at home, or visit their friends without him. Or if she had the stomach for it, accompany him to the localities and slums inhabited by the gas victims. She accepted the last option with enthusiasm in spite of his warning her in some detail about what she would have to endure.

It was a locally religious occasion and many inhabitants of the shanties on the banks of a foul-smelling drain with the filthiest objects floating on it were enjoying a holiday. Some were playing cards while some others were singing romantic and hilarious folk songs to the accompaniment of dholak and manjiras. Some had become so excited that they were dancing.

He introduced her to them as his wife. They were astonished at her good looks and air of prosperity, but only momentarily, and to express their gratitude for coming to their humble place invited her and her husband to tea inside their huts. Govind looked apprehensively at her. To his surprise, she eagerly accepted the invitations and entered the low huts with him. She sat on the dirty sheets spread reverently on the floor for them by shy and grateful men and women, without wincing ate and drank what they offered her, lifted and kissed dirty, unwashed children without flinching, joyfully talked and played with them till her unaffected pleasure overcame their shyness, and promised to bring them toys and sweets.

She passed the whole day with him enthusiastically and assisted him in whatever he did. It was a hectic day, but neither of them felt tired when they returned home. They were too excited. She had found it unbelievable that he had been working in these conditions for years! And Govind was excited at her reaction to what she had seen. She must have been shocked and distressed, but how quickly had she recovered!

She was animated by a unique experience. What had struck her was that in spite of the appalling poverty and the devastating effect of the MIC gas on them and their living or dead relatives and friends, the survivors appeared as briskly busy with the business of living and enjoying life as people she had seen anywhere else. People living in the shanties on the banks of the drain were not the only ones singing and dancing and amusing themselves in various ways. The gas victims had long ago taken in their stride the horror they had gone through. It was the most startling revelation of the human spirit in her experience. What had also profoundly impressed her was that these people's shy expressions of their inability to entertain her and her husband in a better manner seemed really like genuine regret rather than expressive of any feeling of abasement. Their poverty and contentment with what they had had helped them preserve their self-respect. Their behavior seemed to say that those who could be happy with no more than two meager meals a day and sometimes went to sleep hungry and in pain did not need anybody's pity or sympathy! Yet they were grateful for what anybody did for them.

Watching the pleasure she took in mixing with people and helping them with their work had made it difficult for him to say whether like him she was working with a sense of mission, or enjoying herself. Soon he realized that she was doing both; there was no difference between the two things for her. Did her relationship with him was of the same kind, enjoying life with him, of which sex was only a part, in her own way?

For him it was a different Harimohini when she returned home with him in the evening. The first day turned out to be an example of what was to follow during the rest of her stay. After dinner, when she had watched her favorite TV program, he would take her in his arms and make love.

As the days passed, the more passionately he craved and enjoyed her the more it seemed to him that it didn't matter whether she derived as much physical pleasure as he did. What he no longer doubted was that she was enjoying it; he no longer even felt sure that in her own way she didn't enjoy it better than he did! It was a part of their life together. That's how, unlike him, this wise woman had always regarded it.

Harimohini's work was presently noticed in the local press. It was greeted with surprise, complacent admiration and pride in the upper-class drawing rooms. After all, she belonged to their class. Occasionally, she and her husband gave themselves a holiday and attended lunches and dinners at their friends' homes or went on picnics with them. The friends no longer remembered their surprise at her decision to marry Govind; it had been superseded by unceasing wonder at the ease with which she had taken to her new life. The unwonted strenuous work and the exposure to the polluted and diseased environment seemed to make no difference to her, and on reaching home at the end of the day, after she had bathed and drank a cup of tea, she looked as fresh, beautiful and gay as ever. Her upper-class friends eagerly listened to her experiences. As they praised her between sips of whisky, they contentedly discussed the nature of happiness and the vanity of riches, and exchanged philosophical reflections! The better they drank and ate the more they became convinced that it was a delusion to think that they were luckier and happier than the poor living in slums and the more philosophically they dwelt on the vanity of their luxurious lifestyle the more they enjoyed it! Those who habitually took a drop too much felt grateful to her for the "revelation" that one living in foul surroundings and sleeping on an empty stomach could be as happy as or even happier than they were in their posh flats or bungalows, eating three or four sumptuous meals a day!

She couldn't help comparing the life of the slum-dwellers and the gas victims with that of the people attending the evening parties at her sister Chandrmukhi's home where occasionally she used to go when she was in Delhi. During her unexpectedly long stay in Bhopal she had frequently received phone calls while an evening party was in progress and questioned about her experiences by the journalists attending it. Some of them had visited Bhopal for a more detailed coverage. Many an evening party which would have been dull had been enlivened by the discussion of the sub-human conditions in which the gas victims were living and indignation at the Government's apathy and criminal negligence, which had resulted in thousands of avoidable deaths and untold agony.

At the end of six months, being no longer interested in her career and considering it in her own interest as well as fair to allow her husband to say goodbye to his mistress, when she was thinking of going to Delhi for a few days, she received a call from Chandrmukhi, who wished to see her urgently. She was again going through a domestic crisis. She was surprised. During their last meeting she had been delighted to be told by her that she had stopped meeting Somdutt and she and her husband had become reconciled and were happier than they had ever been. She had never seen her brother-in-law more cheerful. She had also talked to them on the phone many times and had always been assured by them of their perfect felicity.

'It's a normal domestic trouble and will be resolved like all such troubles,' she told her curious husband.

She left the same evening.

28/4

Shanti's lover was coming tonight. During Harimohini's unexpectedly long stay she had also heard and read in the papers about her work for the gas victims. After initial skepticism she had been forced to believe it and like her friends and acquaintances feel a deep respect for her; the reports about her work and character seemed to explain Govind's reluctance to say a word against her. Now the most likely reason for his desire to leave such a woman for her seemed to be that she had a lover in Delhi. However, the thought that she had eschewed the embraces of the lover in order to work in the dirty slums for as long as six months seemed unlikely. Most probably, she had no lover.

That night, after drinking his customary cup of coffee, he tried to take her in his arms. She gently disengaged herself. She had decided to end the affair. 'Good bye and Good luck!' said she with a significant smile.

Chapter 29

29/1

Although publicly rejoicing, Vishnu had begun to desire his wife less often and less ardently. It sometimes worried her. But she explained it by the prolonged use of drugs, which he had assured her he had given up, and by his still lingering doubts about her pregnancy because it had occurred after such a long time. She thought that it was a matter of time before his pragmatism and zest for life and their mutual love would enable him not to trouble himself about the past and to long for her again. She recalled how he had been unable to resist her even when he was angry and suspected her. And even if now he desired her less it wouldn't matter, provided he continued to take interest in business, enjoy the company of his friends and attend stage, musical and other entertainments of which he was so fond. Now her sole wish was that he should enjoy his social life.

At the same time, especially when Vishnu was on business tours, which to her gladness he had resumed, during the lonely nights she couldn't help thinking of Jaiprakash. Even if she was a bad woman, as she couldn't help thinking whenever she saw Vishnu depressed, she couldn't bear to think Jaiprakash a bad man; the thought that she had been sleeping with such a man would have been horrifying. She told herself that it was impossible for her to be so completely deceived or for a bad man to be as good as he still seemed to her.

She began to recall in minute detail his behavior, his gestures and expressions and their conversation whether in bed or in office. Gradually her opinion of him underwent a change again. She reminded herself that in spite of occasionally being guilty of dissimulation, if it could be called that, into which he had been forced by his family's poverty, he not only loved her but constantly worried about her and her husband's unhappiness and their strained relations. With what dignity and self-respect he used to behave from the very beginning in spite of his family's poverty and his utter dependence on them. Yet how he never tried to take any worldly advantage of her passion for him. How sincerely he admired her as a person when he did not think of her as his mistress even in dream. How earnestly he used to think ways of persuading her to give up her friendship with Somdutt because it made her family life unhappy. How when they were passing delightful nights together, he never betrayed the least jealousy of Vishnu or tried to disaffect her from him. On the contrary, he never lost an opportunity to remind her that he could never replace her husband in her life. He could enjoy their affair only if it didn't disturb her family life. How desperate he often was to end it lest it should be discovered by Vishnu and mortally hurt him. And despite his family's poverty he was prepared to return to Patna if he didn't get the Lucknow appointment. How horrified he had been to see her entering his room on his last day in her house and how indignantly he had repulsed her.

29/2

As time passed, however, contrary to her hopes, Vishnu's desire for her seemed to have vanished completely. And when he was at home even the pretence of joy that he was going to have a child at last had begun to wear thin. A few days ago she had been greatly upset to learn from his psychiatrist that he had relapsed. Although he had told her that such relapses were not unusual and he was still hopeful that he would be cured, she had felt desperate.

Gradually, she began to find it dishearteningly hard to sham happiness before friends and simultaneously bear her husband's painful efforts to do the same for the sake of not only others but also her! Sometimes he seemed to behave as if he was afraid lest she should think that he still suspected her. Whatever he knew or suspected, he wished her to be happy.

In desperation she again considered abortion. She thought that if despite his suspicion that she was not carrying his child he was not unkind to her from a sense of his own guilt, abortion might gradually enable him to forget or disregard the past and not think her a bad woman. It would also enable him not to brood over what he had done to her. It was impossible for them to live happily together otherwise. And if they could not live happily they could not live together at all.

But now it would have to be in his knowledge and with his consent, because she didn't know how to induce it safely, and confiding her problem to Dr Awasthi or Dr Mrs. Rege and entreating them to confidentially salvage her family life was too embarrassing. They might say that they couldn't do it secretly because it was too late and risky. She would have to confess to him that it was not his child. Although shocked by her confession that she had sinned (his desolation never ceased to remind her that she was a sinner), he would eventually appreciate her motive, she hoped. She felt that he would prefer abortion to seeing another man's child growing up before him, constantly reminding him of his own jealousy and her awful reaction to it. The removal of the fetus would relieve him and eventually restore their relations. Above all, it would save her from the everlasting guilt of having imposed another man's child on him.

Having at last made up her mind to confess and propose abortion without any more delay and irrespective of the consequences, which couldn't be worse than her present situation, she suddenly found herself up against an unexpected problem, which seemed so obvious that she wondered it hadn't occurred to her before. The more she thought of it the more terrible it began to appear. What if he asked whether it was Somdutt's child? Although, if there was going to be no child, there was no need to ask the question, yet he might do so by the way, or to get rid of a lurking suspicion that she had been having an affair with Jaiprakash. She had told him that Somdutt was incapable of loving or inspiring love in a woman. And he was aware of her admiration for Jaiprakash. However, confessing that she was carrying his child was unthinkable. The child of a servant! What if he should think that it was she who had seduced him, it being extremely unlikely for a good and loyal man like him to do so? She had no alternative but to lie that it was Somdutt's, which was even more awful. Apart from it being contemptible to falsely ascribe it to Somdutt, he would naturally think that she had cold-bloodedly lied to him that he was incapable of inspiring love in a woman!

Days and then weeks passed without her being able to make up her mind whether she should ascribe her pregnancy to Somdutt, if he asked the name of the lover. All of a sudden, there occurred to her yet another problem. She had conceived after their reconciliation! He was bound to think that the reconciliation was consciously deceitful, intended to cover continuation of the affair during his absence. She could never convince him that she had made up to him because she couldn't bear his anguish; and that she had accidentally conceived before she could succeed in ending the affair.

At last it began to seem too late and hopeless. She was already over five months pregnant. There was nothing to do but trust to fate.

He had not kissed her for more than two weeks and seemed to be pretending to be asleep as they lay together. In desperation she determined to take the initiative. She began to caress him.

He gently repulsed her.

'Are you unhappy with me?' she asked, unable to conceal her anxiety.

He did not answer.

She again tried to caress him and he again gently but firmly repulsed her

'Do you suspect me?' she said with sudden uncontrollable fear.

He remained silent.

'Please answer me!'

He still remained silent.

She began to cry.

'It's not my child, according to the doctor who tested me,' said he sadly. 'I committed the greatest blunder of my life by undergoing the test! What had happened couldn't be undone. But you should have taken precautions!'

Looking at her horrified countenance, he grew contrite: 'My jealousy is to blame. I hope he's a gentleman and will not betray you.'

She began to sob. He felt sorry and tried to kiss her. She drew back. He left her alone.

Presently he was sleeping under a heavy dose.

She could not believe that a sensible man like him should have wished to confirm that it was his child. How many husbands, even if they are by nature suspicious, do so? Perhaps his desire, which had remained unfulfilled due to jealousy, to feel sure that she loved him too much and was much too good a woman to defile herself from revenge, had proved too strong to resist. The fact that he hadn't told her before today that he was incapable of fathering a child, nor asked her to abort the fetus and started taking drugs again could mean only one thing: He no longer cared for anything and had lost interest in life itself. She stifled a sob!

29/3

His remorse over having undergone the test was more terrible than her despair. Driving his own car, he had gone to a doctor who was an acquaintance but at the last moment changed his mind and walked out. But the next day, remembering Dr Rege's opinion that such late pregnancies were quite normal, the temptation to make sure beyond doubt that he was the father and be rid once and for all of the torture of uncertainty had proved too strong to resist.

He had set out on his second visit to the clinic. And almost at the same moment that he entered it, he had changed his mind again. The doctor, who was sitting alone, seeing him for the second time, had looked at him questioningly. Confused and unable to think of a plausible explanation for coming again, he had involuntarily told him the reason. Just then he had been disconcerted to think that even if the test showed that he was capable of fathering a child, it would not necessarily mean that the child was his and therefore it was needlessly risky to undergo the test! However, he had lacked the will to retract.

If only he had been a little less sure that he was the father than what Dr Rege said had made him, or really sure, which he never was, that his wife was capable of deceiving him, he wouldn't have taken the risk! Time would have done the rest. The child would have grown into a man knowing him as his father and he would have loved him as his own child in the absence of any proof that he wasn't. But to his horror the blunder couldn't be undone.

His grief was greater on her account than his own. Even in his violently jealous moments, when he suspected her of being Somdutt's mistress and when perhaps she was still innocent until his relentless persecution drove her to seek solace in another man's arms, he had never doubted her love for him, which had roots in their adolescence and a happy married life.

29/4

As days went by, she began to see her own end in his decline. It increased her grief at the same time that it consoled her, containing the promise of liberation. One day, watching him asleep under a heavy dose, a shadow of his former self, she was appalled to think of the nightmare their life would be with his increasing addiction to drugs as he watched the child of her shame growing up before him. It was now impossible for her to live with him.

The next day, she called her sister Harimohini from Bhopal and told her everything, including the circumstances of the beginning, the progress and the end of the affair, especially emphasizing Jaiprakash's role in her reconciliation with her husband and the restoration of her family life. She blamed herself for the tragedy and acquitted him. Harimohini, who thought herself her confidante, was astounded to hear the story. She was aware of the full intensity of her crisis with her husband and had met her on several occasions in the presence of Jaiprakash after their affair had started, but never even vaguely suspected it.

She consoled her as best as she could and offered to take her to Bombay and arrange a safe abortion.

'Actually, you should have told me much before. Believe me, once the child is not to be, he'll become reconciled. That's what he was implying when he said that though his jealousy was to blame you should have taken precautions. The way he has been keeping up appearances to the extent of avoiding appearing under the influence of drugs before others, he's not as far gone as you think. Your love for each other and your elite status and wealth will do the rest. It's not so easy to sacrifice these advantages. Only the pregnancy must be terminated. Above all, irrespective of what he thinks, or what people would think if the abortion becomes known, you owe it to him not to inflict on him another man's child. I am sure he won't mind being presented with a fait accompli. He may actually be expecting you to terminate the pregnancy without delay.'

'Much of what you're saying I considered before I called you,' Chandrmukhi thought.

Harimohini said, 'All you need to do is to make a new beginning. Both of you are so young. As for his drug addiction, once the child is not to be, I've no doubt that he won't mind being admitted to a de-addiction centre if necessary.'

Chandrmukhi was not consoled. 'I have mortally wounded him,' she replied. 'After all, Jaiprakash was a servant, whom he trusted. I can't falsely blame Somdutt, if he asks. Besides, the child was conceived after the reconciliation, which would thus appear a shameful trick to enable me to carry on the affair. He'll never forgive me for it. That's why he didn't tell me the result of the test, nor asked me to abort. It can mean only one thing: He's no longer interested in me and so far as he is concerned we are dead for each other.'

'I agree that it will be immoral to blame Somdutt and that you should have ended the affair after the reconciliation, but I still think that with the termination of the pregnancy he'll be too relieved to take the risk of knowing your lover's name. He may actually be more afraid of knowing it than you are frightened of his asking it.

That's why he didn't ask it when he said that though his jealousy was to blame you should have taken precautions. As for your worry that the affair continued and you conceived after the reconciliation, he would appreciate the fact that you didn't make up to him in order to cover up an illicit conception and that it takes time to end such affairs. First of all end the pregnancy. We can fly to Bombay today itself. He need not know where we're going for what purpose. Let him come to know after it has been done. And if he still remains unreconciled, start living separately and don't bother about what people say. After all, the affair started accidentally when you were under great stress for which he was largely responsible. He has confessed as much.'

Harimohini confided to her how her husband, without loving and respecting her any the less, had started an affair with a woman because for the sake of her career she had been living away from him too often. The affair ended after she started living permanently with him.

'I didn't reveal to him my knowledge to prevent mutual embarrassment with its unpredictable consequences. And perhaps he's still not sure that I am aware of it. And if he sometimes suspects that I know, he loves me all the more for never having even vaguely alluded to it. It is in the past. We were never happier and you also have a reasonable chance of being happy again.'

Harimohini related to her true stories of how thousands of gas-affected people had recovered from frightful calamities. People who had lost their whole families had made a new beginning.

She added, 'After the abortion, you can also make a new beginning. As a last resort, you can come to Bhopal and work with me for the gas victims. I have no doubt that the joy of relieving the suffering of people who are in great pain and destined to die will relieve you of your anguish.'

However, Chandrmukhi couldn't get rid of the thought that as she had conceived after the reconciliation he had dismissed it as dishonest and designed to lull his suspicions.

Chandrmukhi had read and discussed at her evening parties the sufferings of the gas-victims and talked to Harimohini about them on the phone. She sympathized with them as deeply as Harimohini and condemned even more violently the people responsible for the tragedy, the criminal negligence of their rehabilitation and the piddling compensation paid them. However, it hadn't occurred to her even in dream to go and work in those squalid surroundings. She had frankly told Harimohini that considering their colossal number, her working in that sordid environment did not make an iota of difference to their misery though her suffering physical discomfort afforded her moral and spiritual gratification. Instead she should have devoted her energies to organizing seminars and campaigning in the press for a better deal for them. Harimohini had replied equally frankly that she enjoyed working among the victims and was not conscious of any kind of physical discomfort; nor were the victims miserable in the way she thought or in need of the kind of sympathy intellectual activists like her felt for them. It was the intellectuals' affair not the victims'. During her stay, Chandrmukhi and her husband had as usual eaten sumptuous breakfasts, lunches and dinners with her in their immaculately kept and air-conditioned dining room.

Harimohini couldn't appreciate Chandrmukhi's attitude, which seemed to betray a craving for pain and suffering. Was it her atonement for her passionate enjoyment of the affair while her husband was in agony? Harimohini considered such atonement useless because it was only prolonging his torment, while her first duty was to end it or at least try to do so by getting rid of her pregnancy. She thought her attitude sadly misguided and her remorse self-centered. At last, she came back disappointed and fearful of her sister's intentions.

After the confession, Chandrmukhi felt relieved. She had unburdened herself and could now die peacefully.

Although she hadn't planned the affair, she meticulously planned her end. She had not only enjoyed life but also suffered pain and remorse like a person accustomed to a superior lifestyle and now planned to quit in the same style. On the fateful day, after the departure of Harimohini, she visited India International Centre with her husband, attended a program and chatted with her friends about the political situation in the country. She returned in the evening, ate her dinner with him and after watching the latest news on TV went to bed and lay down beside him. Soon he was asleep.

Before bidding him goodbye, she nostalgically recalled their adolescence, when they were too shy to steal a kiss, their marriage, honeymoon and happy love life. How her love and concern for his well-being had grown deeper and more poignant when the affair with Jaiprakash was at its peak.

She looked at her watch. It was two o' clock in the morning and he was in oblivion. She wrote her suicide note and put it under her pillow. She knew nobody would believe it, but it must be written for his sake. She could not hold back her tears as she kissed him for the last time and went into the room where she had passed many forlorn and no less joyful nights and bolted the door. It was here that Jaiprakash had pleaded with her to end her friendship with Somdutt and save her husband from becoming a drug addict. She couldn't help thinking about him. He would learn about her suicide from Dr Awasthi. Would he come to condole with Vishnu? Most probably he would to prevent Vishnu thinking that she might have been carrying on with him also? What would he think on coming to know that she had kept her pregnancy from him? That he could have helped her in secretly terminating it? Would he feel guilty for being at least partly responsible for her death and for having betrayed Vishnu, who trusted him? This thought disturbed her peace of mind, which she had never needed as much as at this moment. She acquitted him again. She was the real betrayer.

While putting his neck tie around her neck, she recalled his significant words: 'I committed the greatest mistake of my life by undergoing the test. My jealousy is to blame but you should have taken precautions.'

Her last thought before she kicked the chair was: If it had been Somdutt and not Jaiprakash, she would have voluntarily confessed the lover's name and proposed abortion and despite his anguish he would have agreed to be rid of his jealousy's child and eventually they would have become reconciled.

A year has passed since Chandrmukhi's death. Harimohini still mourns her. She has visited Delhi several times since then to console her brother-in-law. He has more or less recovered and resumed his social life. Sometimes she wonders that such a sensible woman should have failed to realize that the error into which she had fallen would remain a fact whether she lived or died. And by killing herself she would only inflict on her husband an everlasting feeling of guilt, which the prevention of the birth of the child and their mutual love would have enabled him to get over. Charles, who looks after Vishnu's affairs, agrees with her. He hasn't asked her who the lover was.

END

India And The Clash of Civilizations

Rajendra Kumar Mishra

Somdutt and her suspected mistress Chandrmukhi are Hindus belonging to India's affluent bourgeoisie. Like most Hindu secularists-leftists, they are astute moral snobs who attack Hindu fundamentalism not only because it will impede the modernization of their co-religionists but also to deceptively appease Muslims whose resistance to the reformation of their archaic traditions and personal laws mainly out of spiteful antipathy to Hindus, who advocate it, they secretly despise as asinine! Their cold apathy to the Muslims' economic and educational backwardness and the general discrimination against them are further expressions of their contempt for their suicidal fundamentalism. Chandrmukhi holds sumptuous evening parties where her upper-class friends and admirers shed crocodile tears for the poor. Her husband, Vishnu, without having any political convictions to begin with, gradually becomes a champion of Hindutva from jealousy and hatred of Somdutt, whom with excruciating lack of certainty he suspects to be his wife's lover. Unbearably distressed by her husband's jealousy the loving and virtuous wife accidentally succumbs to and becomes pregnant by an admirer, of whose identity the circumstances prevent Vishnu from becoming certain, and commits suicide from remorse.

Vishnu's uncle Jawaharlal, a wealthy lawyer, is a typical devotee of Gandhi who preaches Hindu-Muslim brotherhood as basically virtuous despite being conscious of the fact that most Indian Muslims, who voted for Pakistan but stayed behind in India, despise his idol as a sanctimonious and wily Hindu politician who desperately tried but failed to prevent the formation of a sovereign Muslim State.

About the Author

Rajendra Kumar Mishra is a short story writer, book reviewer and freelance journalist. He has published three collections of short stories. It is his first novel. He lives at Indore, India.

Cover Design by Vimalendu Sharma